CHASING *the* WILD

ELLIOTT ROSE

CRIMSON RIDGE SERIES
• BOOK ONE •

Published by: Cosmic Imprint Publishing
Cover Design: Maldo Designs
Copy Editor: CreedReads Author Services
June 2024

Paperback: 978-1-991281-13-5
Epub: 978-1-991281-12-8
Kindle: 978-1-991281-11-1

FOR THE READERS READY TO WEAR THE HAT, AND GET RAILED IN THE
BACK SEAT UNTIL YOU FORGET YOUR OWN NAME...

DADDY COLT HAS A SPOT IN HIS TRUCK JUST FOR YOU.

CONTENTS

Introduction

Hello dear reader,

Welcome to Grimson Ridge...
For those of you who wish to go in to this book blind, please keep in mind this taboo romance is a work of fiction.
This is an interconnected-standalone, ex-boyfriend's dad, cowboy romance, with a happily ever after.

Please be aware that if you have triggers or content you prefer to avoid, this story may contain topics or subject matter that you might want to consider before proceeding.

Content Notes

This book includes the following, but not limited to:

Death of parents/grandfather (off page, historical); suicide (off page, historical); blood; hunting; guns; injured cattle; animal harm; mental health discussions, including a panic attack (on page); negligent parent (off page); dementia (off page); unwanted pregnancy (off page, historical); drug addiction (off page); discussion of drugging/sexual assault (off page and alluded to briefly on page); and explicit sex (including breeding kink without pregnancy and cum play)

Please note, you can email COSMICIMPRINT.PUBLISHING@GMAIL.COM for more information or clarification on CW's.

D•P•R

The Playlist

Home . Good Neighbours
LEVII'S JEANS . Beyoncé, Post Malone
Thinkin' Bout Me . Morgan Wallen
older . Isabel LaRosa
Just Breathe . Pearl Jam
My Hero . Foo Fighters
Too Sweet . Hozier
If She Wants a Cowboy . Zach Bryan
Daytime Friends Nightime Lovers . The Nashville Sound
The Kind of Love We Make . Luke Combs
I'm On Fire . Bruce Springsteen
Sundown . Gordon Lightfoot
Run On . Jamie Bower, King Sugar
Wild as Her . Corey Kent
Too Good to be True . Kacey Musgraves
Daylight Savings . Kidd G
Fearless – The Echo . Jackson Dean
Tennessee Whiskey . Chris Stapleton
Throw Your Arms Around Me . Eddie Vedder, Neil Finn
Black Dog . Led Zeppelin
Everlong (Acoustic) . Foo Fighters
Empty Heart Shaped Box . Bensen Boone
Girl from the North Country . Bob Dylan, Johnny Cash
NFWMB . Hozier
Like a Stone . Audioslave
Wildest Dreams (Taylor's Version) . Taylor Swift
Beautiful Girl . INXS

CHAPTER I

Layla

S traight to voicemail. *Again.*

I huff out a frustrated breath and drop my forehead against the steering wheel.

For fuck's sake, let my douchebag ex-boyfriend answer his phone for once in his goddamn charmed life.

Keeping my head rested against the baking hot plastic, I put the phone to my ear, trying his number for the fifth time. My eyes squeeze tight, already knowing the outcome, but for whatever reason I persist anyway. It doesn't even ring, just goes straight to his non-personalized voicemail service.

He's either lost his phone, lost his charger, or is lost at the bottom of a bottle somewhere.

Maybe all of the above.

Kayce Wilder was all blue eyes, dimples, and cowboy charm... until he wasn't.

I'm just thankful to every fucking star in the sky that it was a six-month fling. By the time we might have even considered ourselves to be dating, our relationship—if you could even call our situationship that—was already over.

While I never did find him face-first in some other pair of tits, I had my suspicions. Kayce wasn't intentionally mean, or hurtful, or

1

abusive. In fact, he's the type of happy drunk liable to pass out in the corner anywhere, but that is his problem. He's a waster and a drinker who is coasting through life on his good looks while busy getting black-out drunk at three in the afternoon on a Tuesday.

Making all his rodeo talent and big dreams that he dazzled me with that night we first met seem laughable in comparison to the *reality* that is Kayce. Underneath that facade, when I finally met the scared little boy, I realized just how much of a waste of time he allowed himself to be.

Chalk that life experience up to being one of the greatest blessings of my life. I'm relieved it only took me six months of giving parts of my life to him, rather than six years.

Or worse.

I shudder, despite the sweat dripping down my spine in the stifling heat.

Imagine if I'd accidentally gotten myself pregnant by a guy like that.

The horror.

And if anything, that was the foundation of our relationship. Sex. Not that it was anything to write home about, mind you. He was ok, and I was ok, and that seemed to be enough for me to tolerate some mediocre fucking. Now that I think about it, we didn't exactly talk much at all.

Between my hours working at the bar and picking up as many overtime shifts as I could around my studies, there wasn't a lot of time for dating or hanging out. But when we did find the time, it was easy to fall into bed with him. Kayce was a good time. He made me laugh. And for someone like me, who desperately wanted to forget the difficulties in my life that stifle my laughter, all he had to do was hit me with that cheeky blue-eyed expression, and I'd fold. Promising myself that I'd tell him to sort his shit out, or clean out the trash, or do his own fucking dishes in the morning.

God, I'm so glad I don't have to come home to a sink stacked full of dirty dishes anymore.

But guess who's the sucker sitting in a sweltering car with a backseat full of boxes that contain his crap he left behind at my house?

Kayce had been 'in-between' places to live, so I foolishly said it would be fine for him to store a few things until he had a new address. His stuff has been in a closet for the past couple of months while I've been finishing my latest vet apprentice placement, but now I'm on my way to the next job, a new town, and I really need to cut cords with this guy once and for all.

My first instinct was to chuck them all in the dumpster behind my apartment when he didn't return my calls, or emails, or messages on Instagram. Fucking useless little shit. But when I rifled through them, I found his childhood photo albums, and school awards, and cute ribbons from junior horse events. All things from his time living in the Midwest with his mom.

From what I know, she's a pretty shitty parent, and I know all about those. But something tells me there might be a time in his life when he'll want to have these memories. The greatest love of Kayce's life right now comes in a bottle, but perhaps in the future, he'll regret not taking care of these things.

Even if he can't appreciate them right now.

I bang the phone against my forehead. *Think.* Goddammit.

All I have is his address scribbled down on a Post-it note from when he gave it to me ages ago, sometime around when we decided to go our separate ways. I don't even know if that's his exact address anymore in this tiny little middle-of-nowhere-Montana town. He's even more transient than I am, and that's saying something. What I do know for certain is that he's here *somewhere* in this quaint little mountain village and it's the only reason I'm sitting parked on the side of the road.

Crimson Ridge is on my way to my next job, and surprise-surprise, I'm once again being Layla Birch, eternal good girl and pushover, by calling in here to do my ex a favor because it is *kind of* on my way.

He knows money is tight for me—story of my goddamn life—until I get to this next job for my placement, but I have to pay for

3

this tank of gas anyway. I'll need it to get me over to the next town where I'm due to start work on Monday.

So, while I sit here sweating like a pig, with my copper curls turned to frizz around my face, I can't help but notice the lazy summer afternoon unfolding all around me. Like I'm somehow not part of the world that belongs to young women my age. I watch as girls with their tiny shorts and bikini tops lounge in the park across the road. They're lying propped on their elbows in the cool grass, laughing and giggling behind their hands. Each of them eye-fucking the parade of cowboys hopping out of their big trucks as they pull up and park in the wide main street.

Days like today, I feel a thousand years old, not twenty-five.

I flip through the same sequence on my phone, refreshing notifications to see if, just on the off chance, Kayce has replied within the last two minutes to either my emails or my texts. Just a simple reply is all I'm after, to let me know that he'll be here in town to meet me, like I'd asked.

For fuck's sake. Still nothing.

Chewing the inside of my cheek, I dig around in my purse for the address. Hoping to god it hasn't got rubbed off, or torn somehow. The yellow Post-it is a bit faded, covered in crumbs I have to brush off, and more crumpled than the last time I looked at it. Fortunately, it's legible.

Kayce's pigeon scratch handwriting scrawls over the page in blue ballpoint.

3488 Devil's Peak Road, Crimson Ridge.

It sounds like something out of a slasher movie. One where the girl gets chased through the woods by a guy in overalls and a hockey mask wielding a chainsaw.

Looks like I'm going to have to take a drive out into hillbilly territory. Because there is no way in hell I am leaving here with these boxes still in my possession. I don't care if I have to dump them on the front porch for him to find whenever he gets back from his latest bender.

"Fuck this shit." Cursing out loud, I throw the car into drive.

There's minimal traffic and I pull out, searching for the gas station I know I passed earlier on my way in. This tiny, one-horse town vibe is cute enough, though, and I kind of wish I could eventually find a job in a place like this when I'm qualified and graduated. Tall trees line the middle of the long, straight road, with quaint Victorian-era wooden storefronts along each side of the wide boulevard.

This place has a *Stars Hollow* feel about it, where they probably have regular community gatherings. Annual pumpkin growing contests, cider festivals in the autumn, summer hoedowns under the twinkling night sky complete with couples slow dancing to a live band beneath strings of fairy lights.

The big red and white 'Crimson Ridge Fuels' logo looms up ahead, and as I turn in, bumping over the rough curb, my little car looks like an ant compared to the cowboy-sized wagons and Chevy's rolling around this place.

I pull up next to the pump and unstick my thighs from my seat one by one as I climb out the driver's side. *Ew.* The cotton of my tee clings to my lower back, and I have to discreetly readjust where my denim shorts dig into my inner thighs.

This is one of those rare blink-and-you'll-miss-it towns where they still allow customers to fill up prior to paying at the checkout. Cute.

Punching the *Fill* option, I start pumping the gas and take the chance to sort my hair out. Tugging on the tie, I shake the mess of pale copper curls around my shoulders before I pile it back up in a loose top knot again. It is way too fucking hot today to be bothered with wearing my hair down. Sure, my white tee and faded denim cut-offs would look great with my hair all nice and hanging over one shoulder—but today is about being a practical bitch and getting shit done, which means I'm not out here dressing to impress anybody. Especially not Kayce, if I ever do track the bastard down.

Behind me, an impressive black truck pulls in. One of those really big Dodge's. Racehorse sleek, practical as an ox, absolutely enormous. As it pulls up on the other side of the pumps, it dwarfs me and my Honda runabout. Immediately, my stomach does a little swoon over how guys with trucks like that are just effort-lessly hot.

I'm subtly trying to check just how wild my hair is in the reflec-tion of my car windows, which is ridiculous when my only agenda here is to fill up with gas, offload these damn boxes, then carry on my way out of this town. But even so, I sneak a peek at the vehicle pulled up alongside mine. All I see when the door opens on the far side is the brim of a black cowboy hat and some messy dark curls.

The pump clunks to a sudden halt, jolting me back to earth before I can catch a proper glimpse, and I quickly hang the nozzle up.

Christ, Layla, get it together.

Before darting off inside, I glance at the dial to double check the total. The numbers are broken—of course they are, fucking typical—but I know what it costs on average to fill my car's tank up, and the eighty-nine dollars left in my bank account will easily cover that, plus some Ramen for dinner until my next payday.

I push through the heavy metal door and hear the metallic chime go off. A fan hits me with a momentary breeze, but it's just hot air being blown as an unwelcome greeting straight into my face. The floor is in desperate need of a mop, and the place gives off a funky smell of gasoline and grease.

There's a bulldog-looking man in a stained undershirt behind the counter, who rings up the register as I walk towards him.

"Just the fuel today?" He's scowling, with slicked-back gray hair and a faded tattoo wrapping his bicep—something military. This guy looks like he eats Jack for breakfast and Jim for lunch.

"Yes, please," I chirp. Trying my best to plaster on a smile in the face of his dour customer service, and wave my debit card. He points a stubby finger at the grimy card reader and the screen lights up.

I hold my card over it until it beeps, and am already walking away when he clears his throat with a little more aggression than is really necessary.

"Says declined." When I turn around, his glare is unnerving.

Jesus. What would he do if I actually tried to steal something? Probably hurdle the counter and kneecap me with a baseball bat. So much for the friendly, small-town vibe. Why does this asshole allow customers to pump first if this is his response when something like this happens?

"Oh." My cheeks heat, and I let out a little flustered laugh. I know there's enough money in my account. But in scenarios like these, I can't help but feel a tinge of shame. There's nothing worse than feeling like I've been called out or have failed in some way.

Which is stupid, I know, but it is what it is.

"Let me try again." Smiling through a grimace, I hold the card out again.

Ogre-man grunts something and jabs at some buttons on his register, before the terminal lights up. The way he's studying me makes my neck prickle, my hand is now far less steady than it was a moment ago, as I carefully hold the card flat against the screen this time. Trying to make sure it wasn't a contact error or something stupid like that.

Again, it beeps. Lifting the card, words I absolutely do not want to see are stamped in bold black capitals across the screen.

DECLINED.

"You got another way to pay?" His tone is accusatory, and as he exhales sharply the guy slaps the counter.

What a grade-A asshole.

"Um. Just give me a second."

A tightness forms in my throat as I grab my purse and start making a show of rummaging through it for the alternative payment method that I know fully well doesn't exist. I'm so certain there was enough money in my account, having checked only this morning to make sure before I drove out here. But now I'm panicking and doubting myself all because this asshole is being such an over-the-top wanker about it.

As I'm searching, I hear him make a dismissive noise. "You people are all the same. Turn up here from out of town and think you can rip off businesses like mine. If you can't pay, lady, you're going to have to siphon that fuel out of your tank."

I'm stammering in the face of his brash rudeness and feeling clammy from head to toe. If I can't fuel up today, and get to my placement in time to start work tomorrow I'll undoubtedly risk losing this job. My next three months of bills and expenses and Evaline's payments start going up in smoke in my mind's eye.

"Please... if you can just give me a moment."

Over my shoulder, I hear the door bang open and the screech of the chime. Oh, god, now there's a queue forming behind me to enjoy my humiliation first-hand.

"Just... could I try the card one more time, please?" I try forming a smile while a sting pricks behind my eyes. "I know there's enough money there to cover the gas."

Although, now I'm actually sweating. Doubt has crept in. Maybe there was an unexpected bill I forgot to take into account?

But the man is shaking his head and growling something at me about siphoning and the nerve of fucking him around and my cheeks are flaming hot.

"Silly air-headed girls like you have no idea how to be responsible. Always coming in here running up bills you can't pay for. That's you parked at pump three? The Honda?" He sneers at me and looks me up and down, before jabbing a finger in my direction. "Stand right there and don't fucking move. I'll deal with you in a second."

I'm stunned. My hands are shaking. This prick has no idea about me, or my life, and thinks he can talk to me like a chauvinistic, condescending asshole. I feel like he's slapped me, the tirade is so unexpected.

My step falters backward as I step aside, making way for the next person in line. What the fuck am I going to do?

As I'm spiraling in the middle of this shitty gas station in the middle of nowhere, a low, smooth voice cuts in.

"Christ, Kurt. Take your heart pills already. I'll cover it."

CHAPTER 2

Layla

I'm rendered speechless.

The man beside me reaches across and taps his card on the screen. Green lights all perk up, indicating a successful payment, and the asshole behind the counter mutters something resembling a *thank you*.

But that's not exactly the reason I'm left without the ability to form words.

A stranger just paid for my fuel, and he is absolutely someone who I had no idea could exist in real life.

He's a wall of rugged man, and I have to tilt my head a little in order to take all of him in. With a faded black t-shirt revealing a tanned neck, scruffy dark curls, and a short beard with a bit of salt and pepper gray in it.

When he turns around to face me, I'm immediately caught in the snare of his bright hazel eyes. There's something wild about him, and I am nothing but a fawn stunned in high-beam headlights.

"After you, ma'am." His voice washes over me like rain after a long, hot day as he gestures politely toward the door with something in his hand. When my eyes drop down, they catch on the jet-black cowboy hat in his big paw.

Oh, god... and then his tightly fitted wranglers.

This is the real danger out here in small towns like this. Cowboys with impeccable manners who look like they can sweep you off your feet one minute and rail you until you forget your own name in the back seat of their truck the next.

I stammer something incoherent and move toward the door. I'm still not sure what just happened back there, but am more than relieved to escape the silent glare of the prick who will never get my business again in this lifetime.

Ever the country gentleman, this cowboy holds the door open for me. Behavior that is entirely foreign—especially coming from a stranger. In my world, I'm used to fending off men with wandering hands trying to cop a feel at two a.m.

Once back on the forecourt, it's like the world rushes in again. Birds chirp, the drone of a truck rattles past, and the sweet fragrance of jasmine climbing a trellis drifts from the cafe next door.

"Thank you." I blurt out. Regaining use of my tongue. "You didn't have to do that." I twist my purse in my hands.

Gorgeous-cowboy drags a hand through his unruly hair, before putting his hat back on. As he does so, I catch a little glimpse of the lines around his eyes that don't exactly tell me his age, but they place him somewhere in the *older* category.

This man certainly isn't in his twenties, that's for certain. Possibly his late thirties.

Jesus. My thighs clench as I take him in properly now. He leans a shoulder against the tailgate of his enormous vehicle.

"No sense arguing with Kurt over a tank of gas. He'll take any opportunity to make up for having a small dick."

Something between a cough and a laugh bursts out of me. I was not expecting that the third thing to come out of this man's mouth would include the word dick.

But I'm certainly not mad about it.

"It was very small dick energy, wasn't it." I roll my lips together. Immediately my slutty brain makes a comment about how this man is the complete opposite of that. Big dick energy radiates off him like the sun.

Something about my response seems to please him. I don't hate the way that makes me feel, like I would enjoy finding ways to please this rugged man.

"Even so, thank you, that was very gallant what you did in there."

He narrows his eyes on me. "Gallant?"

"Uhh, you know..." I'm stuttering under his intensity. "Like, chivalrous."

"Sounds like you're calling me old. Or old fashioned."

My mouth opens and closes a couple of times, thinking I've offended him somehow, but then I spot the crinkles at the corners of his eyes.

He's teasing me.

Dear sweet Jesus. This man is hiding a sense of humor underneath that gruff exterior.

This isn't fair.

"Let's just say that girls like me don't happen to come across men like you very often. I mean, especially not men offering to pay for a whole tank of gas out of the blue." I gesture between the two of us.

He fixes me with a hard look. One that leaves me swallowing down a lump in my throat.

"You're hanging around the wrong men in that case."

Somehow, I feel like he just told me off and turned me on in the same breath.

"Don't I know it." I offer a small smile. My mind wanders briefly to the boxes in my back seat and Kayce while I shudder a little on the inside, considering the current mess I've found myself in. All because of his useless ass. The exact type of *wrong man*.

I want to ask what his name is, but something tells me that's not wise. What do I need to go asking this man's name for? It's not like I'm ever going to see him again. *Unless...* unless what? I could always offer to pay him back for the fuel. But even then, to what end would that be. I've still got nearly a year's worth of study and placements ahead in my future.

I'm in no position to even be *thinking* about dating, or doing anything but putting my head down and working for at least the next twelve months.

This feels like one of those sliding doors moments. In another time, if we were different people, maybe then I would ask his name, and he'd ask for mine. A world where I have the job of my dreams, running stables and taking care of horses all day, and I can buy a whole cart of groceries without checking my bank balance.

Instead, I'm standing here in the beating sun, as sweat trickles down my back and my thighs stick together. I've got nothing more than a declined card and a tank full of fuel thanks to the charity of a stranger.

All the while, God's favorite cowboy watches me from where he leans casually against his truck. A vehicle that's probably worth more than my entire annual take home pay.

"I hope it didn't ruin your visit to Crimson Ridge." His hazel eyes are still fixed on me with a keen expression. Even though his gaze might be glued to my face, I can feel him taking in every inch of my appearance.

My body heats under his perceptive stare.

"How do you know I'm just visiting?" I tilt my head to one side. For some reason he's still standing here talking to me in this grimy gas station, and I'm making no effort to move toward my car. Not only that, but I can't help but feel like he's definitely, absolutely flirting with me a little.

His attention feels warm and not too forward. This stranger isn't being overly direct, but there's something sparking between us, and I'm sure it isn't just my imagination.

One of his dark eyebrows lifts a little and he nods towards my license plate. The one that says OLEANDER TOWN AUTO, from the dealer where I bought it years ago. "We don't have those kinds of plates here."

"I could be borrowing a friend's car." I tease.

This time, his eyes most definitely drop down my body, and every inch of me comes alive.

"A friend, hmm?" He mulls the word over. "Is that the kind of friend that comes with a dick, or without one?"

Well, fuck. Is he asking if I have a boyfriend?

"Uhh. No friend." I chew my cheek a little. "Boys my age aren't worth my time, I find."

That makes his eyes snap up to mine. Oh, holy hell, I might as well just wave a big sign that says *please fuck me, I'm single*, with that kind of statement.

He rubs a thumb along his jaw, still leaning against the truck, and he looks so damn good I want to melt. As he shifts his arm, it drags up the hem of his t-shirt a little, revealing a sliver of tanned skin above his belted jeans. Am I having heart palpitations? My pulse thuds relentlessly in my ears.

This man is stunning, a little rough around the edges, with a lump at the bridge of his nose hinting at stories from his past. This cowboy is just my type, only I've never actually met someone like him in the flesh before. He's compelling, attractive, enticing in a way that makes my skin prickle with excitement.

"So, if you're staying here in town... what are you doing on Friday night?" His voice is all rumbly, and I feel it right in my chest.

But then I realize what he's asking. Or maybe, is about to ask.

And I fall back to earth with a jolt.

"Oh, no." I shake my head, and his expression hardens. "I'm sorry, I don't know what I was saying... I really am just passing through." Jesus, I'm such a fucking idiot. It took me all of two seconds to lead this guy on, and now I feel like the world's biggest cock-tease.

In another time, or life, I could maybe be Layla Birch: carefree woman who says yes to handsome strangers asking her out on a Friday night.

I could be the woman who gets to enjoy an easy conversation with a gorgeous man such as this one. Indulging in drinks and stolen glances and the giddy moment of wondering whether the night might end with being treated to more intimate pleasures.

Wondering whether there might be the type of *goodnight* that involves a brush of lips and sensual glide of hot, seeking tongues.

Instead of all that, I'm stuck on a hamster wheel of bills to pay, a qualification to finish, and forever feeling older than my years.

When, by all rights, I should be dating and kissing handsome men with enthralling eyes and unruly hair.

"Well." He pushes away from the truck, and suddenly ice solidifies in the air between us. Those shoulders of his are now tense beneath the thin cotton of his tee. "Travel safe, then." And as quick as a flash, he's fishing his keys out of his back pocket and is on the move, opening the cab of his truck without so much as another look in my direction.

I make a start toward him. "Wait, I need to pay you back for the gas." God, I've fucked this all up.

"Don't worry about it." He swings up into the driver's side and slams the door.

The giant black truck roars to life as he revs the accelerator, taking off out of the gas station. Leaving me standing there coated in sweat and shame and feeling my heart sink into the oil-stained concrete.

MY FOUL MOOD only worsens when I plug the stupid hillbilly address into the map on my phone, and all I can see is a long-ass road finishing in a dead end. The red pin glares back at me like a big middle finger.

Surely, it can't be right.

I pinch the screen to zoom out, and this address isn't even hillbilly territory. It's on Mars.

The location is so far out of town I want to cry. It'll use up a large chunk of the gas that the handsome stranger just paid for in order for me to drive out there and back again.

Kayce Wilder can go fuck himself, I bet he wrote the address down wrong—it would be typical of him—so I decide to get resourceful and go in search of some local knowledge. Crimson Ridge is small enough, surely someone will know something, but I certainly won't be setting foot back inside the gas station.

So I park my car under the shade of the trees lining the median and make my way into the cute little cafe next door. The outside is surrounded by jasmine blossoms winding along the porch, shading the footpath from the beating sun. The place is quiet, with the lunch rush long gone, and when I cross the threshold, cool air welcomes me inside. Thank fuck for that. My shoulders sag with relief.

A girl around my age is behind the counter washing some glasses, so I make my way over. She's got long, poker-straight black hair, with bleached ends. Her tank top is way too tight, but hey, if that's what gets her tips then so be it.

Sometimes, a girl's gotta do what a girl's gotta do.

I can hardly judge, considering the places I've had to work over the years just to take care of myself.

"Excuse me." I plaster on my best friendly smile. "Would you be able to help me with some directions?"

"Sure." She eyes me and tosses the hand towel over her shoulder.

Loudly chewing gum, she looks me up and down as I approach, which immediately sets my teeth on edge. Whatever, I don't need to be her friend. I just need some fucking confirmation that my trek to the middle of nowhere isn't going to be a colossal waste of time.

"This address here, can you tell me if it's real?" I show her the screen of my phone, the one with the pin located way off in the middle of nowhere. "Like, is it legit? I'm trying to find a friend, but I think the address might have been written down wrong."

The girl taps at the screen and then gives me an odd look. The kind of sidelong glance that seems weirdly knowing and curious at the same time. It makes me feel uncomfortable within an instant, like I'm missing something and she's in on a joke that I don't get.

Her lips curl into more of a sneer than a smile. "You wouldn't be the first girl trying to find your way up to his place." She hands me back my phone and leans on the counter. Putting her tits right in my face. Like she's pissing all over her territory or something.

Fucking hell.

Kayce Wilder. Certified man whore.

"I'm taking it *you* certainly know how to get there, then?" I'm about done with all of this and have half a mind to just toss this girl the boxes right here in the middle of the cafe and let him come and get them from his fuck buddy.

She just gives me a coy smile and smacks her gum loudly.

"Might have been there before. But you're a bit young for him, ain't you?"

What? I can't even with this level of weirdness going on. It's hot as hell and I'm dying for a cold glass of water and feeling just about done with being the *good girl*.

"Look, it isn't like that. Can you just tell me if the address is correct? That's all I need to know." I shove my phone in my pocket and give her a pleading look. Yep, that's right. I'm at the lowest ebb yet, groveling to some slut who my ex has obviously been fucking. Or maybe is currently fucking. Or, I don't know... I just want to get this dealt with so I can get on the road.

"That's the one. Right at the top of the mountain. It's a dead end, so you can't miss it." She picks up a dirty glass and runs it under the tap. "Hope you don't get lost... if the beasts up there don't eat you, the wildlife might." And with that, she saunters out through the back with a flick of her hair.

For fuck's sake.

I shove my sunglasses on and stomp back to my car. Cursing Kayce and his unique brand of uselessness the whole way as I start to follow the directions on my phone.

The drive takes me away from town, and pretty quickly, I start climbing what must be Crimson Ridge. I keep glancing at the screen perched on my thigh, and there's no other place to go but to follow this one road as it snakes up into the trees.

If I wasn't in such a shitty mood, I'm sure this place would be gorgeous. There's lush forest rolling across the hillsides, without any signs of houses or people. Just endless shades of green, punctuated by sheer outcrops of reddish rock extending in frighteningly sharp drops into the valleys below.

The ridgeline itself forms a long sharp cut into the sky, like a knife lying on its side, and in the golden light of summer, the exposed rock looks a bronze kind of color. I can only imagine in autumn when the leaves turn red and brown and orange out here, it must look spectacular.

As I keep making my way higher and higher, I realize I must be approaching Devil's Peak. I start to catch glimpses of the jagged top of an imposing black outline against the sky. It cuts across the pine trees and protrudes up into a cloud formation, even on a sweltering day like today when there is only blue sky as far as the eye can see.

I've been driving for about twenty minutes already, and I look down at my phone and see there's no service. Just fucking great. Even if I did decide to bail now and wanted to leave Kayce a scathing voicemail about how I've burned his stack of photo albums, or god-forbid broke down, I'm stuck out here with no choice but to either carry on or brave a chainsaw-toting hillbilly and hike the ridiculous distance back to town.

The voice in the back of my head reminds me that I'm too nice and that he doesn't deserve my kindness, but even though I'm deeply regretting my choice to try and help him out with this last favor, I'm also never going to change.

This is the type of person I am, for right or wrong.

Just as I think this insanity will never end, with the gravel becoming chunkier beneath my tires and the road growing narrower, I crest the final bend and emerge into a clearing amongst the trees.

It's a small plateau, looking directly out at the view of Devil's Peak.

My foot almost slams on the brakes as I take it all in with my mouth hanging open.

But the gravel veers left along a winding driveway, guiding me beneath a wooden arch with a steer skull hanging from the middle. It snakes a path leading me toward a yard and large, plain wood barn which looks like it must be the stables. Sweeping down below the property is a meadow of wildflowers and long grass, and I can see the elegant, bowed necks of horses grazing off in the distance. My eyes are darting, bouncing, flitting everywhere at once as I pull up in front of what can only be described as a mountain-property wet dream.

It's wood and stone and has wide-span glass windows overlooking the view. A porch wraps around the entire length of the building, which sits low and elongated against a backdrop of pine trees rising steeply behind the roofline.

This is no rundown old shack hidden away in the hills.

What I'm seeing is a thing of beauty, designed to blend in with the landscape and not only that but it looks modern as all hell.

As I get out of the car, the scent of hay and wild herbs tickles my nose. Lazy, chirping crickets in the baking sun greet me. Sweet fucking relief, it's a little cooler up here than down in town, with a crisp wind blowing from the direction of the forested ridge.

How the fuck has Kayce Wilder landed on his feet in a place like this? I was expecting him to be shacked up in someone's drafty old farmhouse, with a stained couch and mice in the walls.

Not a five-star luxury lodge.

Lettering made of iron hangs above the double doors to the barn, spelling out the letters: D.P.R in bold black set against cedarwood planks.

Devil's Peak Ranch.

Wide stone steps lead me up to the front door framed by rough pieces of stacked slate in charcoal and gray, and the woody smell mixed with cut grass is divine. Someone has taken a lot of care to create this place and I'm in open-mouthed awe as I reach the imposing front doorstep.

There's no knocker or doorbell—I'm guessing you don't need those way out here—so I raise my fist and bang on the wood.

Before I can even drop my hand, the door is yanked open so hard I almost fall into the entranceway.

What greets me on the other side is a wild tangle of curly dark hair, wetted locks that sit against tanned, damp skin, and fearsome hazel eyes.

And the man before me is naked, except for a towel.

CHAPTER 3

Layla

I don't know how long I stare. But the gorgeous cowboy from town, the very person who paid for my tank of gas, clutches a towel low on his hips, pinning me with a murderous expression.

Nothing makes sense in my mind.

Why is he here?

What the fuck is going on?

He's got the door gripped so tight in one hand that I can see white ridges on his knuckles, and he looks about one second from slamming it in my face.

We both seem to be caught in some kind of limbo, staring at each other while our minds try to make sense of this situation. His forehead is creased in a way that tells me this is not a pleasant surprise. In fact, there's so much *fuck off* energy rolling off his muscled torso that I'm surprised I haven't been bowled backward down the steps.

This must be his house.

Holy fuck. Is this his ranch?

From the hostile reception I'm guessing he lives out here for a reason. No visitors.

Especially not the unexpected kind.

My mouth is full of sand, and I'm shrinking beneath his glare. Meanwhile, he's all bronzed skin and a thick chest, with a v extending down below his towel that I definitely should not be tracing with my eyes.

"Layla fucking Birch?!" A slurred shout cuts through the potent tension hanging between us.

My ex-boyfriend, Kayce, barges past the man in the towel like he owns the place. Suddenly, I'm being lifted off the ground in a bear hug and twirled in the air like I'm five years old. "What are you doing here, princess?"

All I want to do is demand to know the same thing. Oh, and this asshole has definitely been day-drinking. Kayce only ever called me that when he'd had a few. Probably me and every other girl riding his dick. I stiffen at the thought of the bitch from the cafe in town.

"Kayce, put me down." I'm so flustered by what is happening right now I feel like I can't think straight.

"Oh, shit, sorry. My bad." He drops me and then slings an arm around my neck, pinning me to his side. My skin crawls with a weird sensation. I know we dated, and we've had sex, for god's sake, but right now, I want his hands off my body.

I don't want him to touch me so openly.

Especially not in front of this other man.

Kayce beams down at me with that blue-eyed charm turned up to megawatt status. Giving me a look that, for a brief moment in time, used to make me go all gooey inside, thinking that he was looking at me as if I was someone special. Only now, it does absolutely nothing for me.

"Dad, this is my girlfriend, Layla."

My brain and body separate into different dimensions for a moment.

Dad?

I'm staring slack-jawed, taking in the bare-chested, muscled dream before me, who is glaring right back with darkness in his eyes and a tic in his jaw. My eyes keep drifting to the point where he's still gripping his towel, and it's like I've stumbled into some kind of cowboy Bermuda Triangle. *Mayday. Mayday.* All the dials are spinning, alarms are blaring, and a crash is imminent. When this wreckage is found, there will be no survivors.

Wait. *No.* "Not girlfriend. *Ex.*" I correct Kayce, strongly emphasizing the word *ex* a little louder than necessary. Unwinding myself from beneath his arm, I take a step to the side and put some breathing room between me and the younger Wilder man.

His father—holy shit, his father—stares at me with cold indifference. Gone is the charming cowboy from our brief interaction earlier. It's like he murdered that version of the man I swooned over so easily, and dumped his corpse in the ravine I just drove past.

"We dated briefly." I offer as a totally unnecessary added explanation. Words feel clumsy and acidic on my tongue.

"Come in. Man, this is so cool. I can't believe you're here. I'll grab us a drink." Kayce moves toward the kitchen and I feel his father's eyes lasered on me. I can't look at him. This is all too much. This day can go fuck itself. I'd like the ground to swallow me up whole, thank you very much.

"Horses need packing. There's a group arriving in an hour." The stony-faced man barks after his son, still glaring at me. He seems angry at Kayce, and isn't moving from the doorway either, effectively barring me from entering his house.

I'm trapped right in the middle of something I don't want to understand.

"Yeah, yeah. I'll get to it later." Kayce shrugs him off and I cringe. He's a dick to his father too, how predictable.

"Later won't cut it. They should have been sorted out by now. Tonight's group booked a twilight ride."

"I got busy." Kayce wanders back over and attempts to press a beer into my hands, but I shake my head and turn it down. All I want to do is leave his boxes out here on the porch, and get the hell off this mountain.

"Jesus, Kayce." His father shakes his head and looks like he wants to chew him out but stops himself. I don't blame the guy, I know the exact feeling.

Without another glance my way, he stalks off to the depths of the house, and I'm left alone with Kayce Wilder, who is double-fisting beers, looking like the cat who got the cream.

"You couldn't have at least replied to me? I've had to drive up a fucking mountain to track your ass down and bring your shit here, you know." I growl, following behind his long strides across the wooden decking.

He shrugs and doesn't offer an explanation, or an apology. But that's Kayce for you. All effervescence and crooked smiles that have enabled him to coast through life without any consequences for any goddamn thing.

"So, now you've officially met my dad." Kayce changes the subject and dumps himself into a chair on the front porch. He readjusts the trucker cap he's wearing with one hand, resting one of the beers on his knee.

It's inviting out here, the wooden porch is wide with a railing along the edge and there's a handful of comfortable outdoor armchairs. From the look of the floor to ceiling ranch sliders further down the far end, the bedrooms must have access out here too. I'm sure the mornings and evenings must be stunning, with the south-facing vantage point getting sun all day long.

But I will not be sitting down.

"He seems nice." I offer. Shuffling on my feet.

Kayce snorts. "Colton Wilder? Nice? That man is the most miserable old bastard you'll ever meet. He never leaves this shit-hole mountain, and it's nothing but fucking work up here from dawn 'til dusk." He tips his beer back.

Ok, so maybe I am smarting more than a little at the way his father completely blanked me back there. He didn't say a single word to me. Not even a polite acknowledgment that we'd only just met down in town? Maybe the guy is the exact kind of asshole Kayce says he is. It was kind of rude.

It would be typical, that someone so cold could have a place this stunning to call home.

"I dunno, it seems pretty up here, though." I shade my eyes to look out over the late sun caressing the tall grass in a golden hue, and from here, not only does Devil's Peak command the horizon, but I see the infamous Crimson Ridge that gives the town its name towering like a shard of reddish-colored rock beyond the dense pine trees.

"Don't be sucked in. Summer is all soft and warm and flirty right now, but winter is an icy-hearted bitch who wants nothing more than to steal your soul." Kayce rubs his hand over the back of his neck. "It's months and months up here with no cell reception, Wi-Fi that drops out every five fucking minutes, and nothing to do but feel like you're going to go insane in the dark before they reopen the roads in between storms."

No cell reception, even up here in the clearing? I dig my phone out and see there are still no bars. Well, that at least explains why Kayce was even more useless than normal in replying to my messages.

"Yeah, and Dad's piece of shit Wi-Fi hardly works. He doesn't use technology because he's such a grumpy dickhead, and can't see the benefit in joining the real world. This place is like a fucking jail or some shit."

I wrap my arms around myself. "Then why are you here, Kayce?" Why stay if he hates it so much? I want to kick him in the balls for being such a spoiled bitch about it. What I would give to land a job in a place as incredible as this...

"Because I fucked up, princess. I didn't get a sponsor this season. While I figure out my next move, Dad is cool with me staying here for the rest of summer. If I'm really desperate for money, I figure I'll stick around and work the winter for him, too."

"Sounds awesome. Good for you."

He snorts.

"What isn't so awesome is how he rides my ass all the time, trying to make up for being a shitty father when I was a kid. We've never gotten along. So it's real fucking peachy, let me tell you."

Now it makes sense why I didn't hear him talk about his dad while we were together. Two and two are now adding up as to why the albums in the back seat of my car don't have a single photo featuring him and his father.

"Well, you could stay with your mom?" I don't even know why I'm getting into this with him. Kayce Wilder is not my problem. Not my circus to tangle with anymore.

Those blue eyes are hazed with sadness when they land on me.

"Nah. I'm not going back there." He says it with such finality that I know things really can't be good if he'd tolerate being here rather than stay with his own mom.

That right there is a feeling I know intimately well.

Swigging back his beer, he kicks his long legs out. My ex looks like he's settling in for the afternoon, and I don't have time for this self-indulgent pity party he's got going on.

I spin on my heel and set off for the steps, calling over my shoulder as I go.

"Put the beer down, Kayce. I need you to come grab some boxes."

I'm also about done with his shit... and this whole confusing, *gorgeous-father-I'm-still-flustered-over* situation. I need to get moving, and when I haul-ass out of here in a cloud of dust, I'll never have to see either of the Wilder men, ever again.

CHAPTER 4

FIVE MONTHS LATER

Layla

"Your resume looks great, Layla. It would be a pleasure to have you join us at Shipton Stables for the rest of the winter."

I close my eyes and mouth a silent *thank you* toward the roof of my car while clutching the phone against my ear.

"Are you sure starting at this time of year isn't a problem for you? Many people your age are still on holiday this side of the new year, and we really can't hold the position if there are any delays. We need to fill it urgently." The lady on the other end of the phone is firm, but kind.

I get it, I really do.

They have a business to run, and finding apprentice veterinary students to work the winter season must get frustrating at the best of times, with part-time contracts starting and ending every few months. Not to mention, we've just emerged from the usual fuckery of Christmas and New Year and all the crap that comes with people picking up casual shifts over the holiday season. There are plenty of assholes out there who love to call in sick or never show up for their rostered hours—I know all about having to cover late notice for *those* kinds of dickheads.

She's very, very politely asking me not to fuck her around.

"No, I'm absolutely sure. You can count on me to be there." Nothing says eager and broke like already being packed before I even got confirmation this job would accept me. The few belongings I've been carting around since last summer are neatly crammed in the trunk of my car, ready to roll out of this shitty little motel parking lot.

Basically, I was waiting on this call. What she doesn't need to know is that the job I had been promised fell through right before Christmas, leaving me well and truly in the lurch over the holidays.

I've had to chew into my meager savings just to scrape through the past few weeks until I could secure a job—any vet placement would do—on extremely late notice and at the height of the festive season, no less. So when Shipton Stables put out an urgent 'help-wanted' request online, I couldn't care less about the three hour drive to get there. I just needed them to give me the green light that they'd be happy to take me on.

"Great. Well, in that case, we'll have paperwork ready for you to fill out when you arrive, and the first shift we'll roster you for starts at eight a.m. the day after tomorrow."

We chat a little more, going over some basics about my orientation before hanging up. Tucking my phone against my chest, I flop back in the driver's seat with relief.

Thank you Shipton Stables and the kind receptionist lady whose name I have already forgotten.

I. Have. A. Job.

While I've been sitting out here taking the call, icy crystals have already started to form on my windshield. I quickly turn the ignition and wait for the warmth to start pouring in. Wiggling my fingers in front of the air vent, the chill bites more than a little painfully.

New gloves are going to be one of my first purchases.

First, I have one more week to get through before my paycheck from Shipton arrives, and that should tide over the payments for Evaline. I swipe open my emails on my phone and hit reply to the conversation I've been having over the past few weeks with the administration office. They'd been kind enough to give me an extension on December's payments, but that means January is going to need to be repaid at double the usual amount.

I tap out a quick one-liner explaining that my new job is confirmed and that I'll be able to cover the overdue fees within the coming week. Then, I email my course supervisor to let him know that I've secured my next veterinary placement, along with forwarding him their business details, website, and other administrative information they need to register in my file.

One step closer to being graduated come August, fully qualified, and securing a permanent position somewhere.

While there's no requirement for me to complete my work placements within a set period of time, there is a minimum of twelve months of on-the-job apprenticeship training required before I can become fully certified. As of this winter, I'm in a race against my own life to become a graduated, qualified veterinarian. And with that comes the security of being able to finally land a job with a full-time salary, guaranteed hours, insurance, and medical. I simply don't have the luxury of taking my time while surviving on part-time wages and picking up as many bar shifts to supplement my income as possible, like other students my age.

The financial weight of supporting not only myself, but taking care of the woman who was a better mother to me than my own, is drowning me slowly day by day. The home Evaline is in has been the only place able to meet her needs, but it comes with a price.

I need this job, and just need to survive these next seven months until the earliest possible moment I can graduate.

As I sit here waiting for my fingertips to thaw, my phone buzzes in my lap. Without looking at the screen, I answer the call —expecting it to be Shipton Stables ringing back about some other detail for my impending arrival.

"Hello."

"Am I speaking with Miss Birch?" A clipped voice appears on the other end of the line.

My stomach sinks. This isn't the woman I was speaking to moments before.

"Yes, I'm Layla Birch." As I reply, I angle the phone so I can see the number on the screen.

Restricted caller ID.

Fucking brilliant. I mentally chide myself for picking up. Calls like this terrify me, and I usually send them straight to my voice-mail graveyard. These people only ever call for one reason, and it's almost always to do with owing money.

"This is Bonnie Wilton from Gratitude Finance." My nose wrinkles like I've just stepped in pig shit. Even the name of the company sounds slimy. Gratitude for what? Being scammed out of money by promises of instant loans and insanely high interest rates. Ugh, these people are vultures.

Good news is, I've never heard of them before, and certainly would never take out finance with a company like that, so they must have the wrong person.

"I'm sorry. I think you must have the wrong number." I can't be fucked being polite. I'm freezing and want to get on the road to my new job, ASAP.

"Is your last known address 3488 Devil's Peak Road, Miss Birch?"

Why does that sound familiar?

"In the town of Crimson Ridge?" The woman persists.

My stomach hits the floor.

"Uhh. No." My insides flop like a fish on dry land as I picture Kayce and the ranch and him sitting on the porch with a beer when I last saw him over the summer.

"Well, the information I have on file here says you have an outstanding amount of two thousand, five hundred and eighty with us. And you've missed your last three repayments." She thinks I'm lying. I can hear it in her tone.

"That's not me. I haven't taken out any finance, I promise."

"Can you provide me with proof of your permanent address?" She taps at a keyboard in the background.

Shit. Shit. Shit.

"Unfortunately, I can't, you see I've been—"

"We would need copies of utility bills covering the past six months, or something to indicate where you have been residing to prove that isn't your address." The woman on the other end of the phone sounds bored. Like she's heard it all before and doesn't give me a chance to even finish speaking.

My hands are trembling. Did she say two thousand dollars?

"Without being able to provide us with that proof, we need to settle the amount in full, otherwise our team will have to move to the next stage of enforcement action."

I think I'm going to be sick.

Kayce Wilder is a dead man.

"Can I ask how long ago this finance was taken out?" I mumble. There's no way I can pay that, and I shouldn't have to, but these assholes don't care about who or what or where. They'll come for me and every dollar I've worked so hard for and take everything plus the sky-high interest they believe they're owed.

The woman is silent, but I can hear the clack of her keyboard as she looks up the information.

"You've been a client of ours since May last year."

I quickly do the math. That was about a month before Kayce and I officially ended things. He'd been sponging off me, staying in my apartment for almost six weeks by that point, if I remember rightly.

What a piece of shit.

"And how long do I have to make the full payment?" I think I've gone numb. At this point, I'm just going through the motions.

"Because you are already three weeks behind in your repayments, you have passed our leniency period when we might consider extensions or requests for other alternative payment structures." She drones into the speaker. "We tried to contact you at your primary listed number multiple times, Miss Birch, but you have been unresponsive."

Hot tears prick the back of my throat.

"Fine. Just tell me the due date, please."

Another round of clacking, and I'm pretty sure I hear a heavy sigh on the other end of the line. To this woman, I'm just another number in a computer system. One who they now get to come after like a bully in the locker room with threats of enforcement and legal action.

I swallow down the tears.

None of this is my fault, nor should this loan even have been allowed to be registered in my name. What would something like this do for my future? I'm twenty-five and work every goddamn hour of my life just to make ends meet, for fuck's sake. I don't have a life, I don't go out, and this is the shit that gets tossed my way?

Bitterness starts to churn somewhere deep in my gut.

"You must repay the amount in full by January tenth at the latest. We accept bank transfers and deposits, no credit."

Barely one week to come up with over two thousand five hundred dollars? "Fine."

"I've sent a text to this number I'm speaking to you on with my details and you can contact me on my extension if you need to discuss your case further." True to her word, I feel the vibration of her incoming message.

"Ok."

My mind is reeling.

"Happy holidays, Miss Birch." The woman deadpans into the phone, then the line goes dead.

Meanwhile, I'm left sitting in an icy parking lot, feeling like an elephant is sitting on my chest.

My FINGERS WRAP around the steering wheel like a vise as I imagine it being Kayce's pretty boy neck.

"I want to punch him in his smug fucking face and knee him in the balls. Actually, scratch that, I want to string him up by his balls and castrate him like a bull."

I yell into the unhinged voicemail I'm leaving my best friend, Sage. Letting her know where I'm going, so at least one person in this world knows where to look for me.

"That douchebag took out a loan in my name without asking, and then forgot to meet his payments. And, fucking typical, his number is going straight to nowhere. He is the worst. THE WORST."

Of course, the line was dead when I tried calling him earlier. Because he's living up a mountain in the middle of nowhere, avoiding life and every goddamn adult responsibility that comes with it.

"No wonder he couldn't find himself a sponsor and had to drop off the rodeo circuit. Useless dick." I thump the steering wheel with my palm.

"So in case you have to look for my body, instead of being on my way to my new job, I gotta detour back to Crimson Ridge... it's a fucking tiny place, in the depths of goddamn winter, because hell will freeze over before I let him get away with this shit. You will be pleased to know I'm channeling my inner Sage Maloney and will absolutely claw his eyes out of his motherfucking skull."

My best friend is feisty, loud, and would shred Kayce to pieces on my behalf given half the chance. She's my ride-or-die, and we grew up as close as sisters, with her family living next door to Evaline. For as long as I've known that girl, she's called her *Aunt Evie,* and we spent our childhood and teenage years roaming between the two houses like wild creatures. I was welcomed with open arms, living with utter freedom while we giggled our way through endless sleepovers and homework dates, bouncing between her family home and my aunt's place.

My only option is to march onto that ranch and demand every dollar is paid while I watch him do it.

Thank god I was more or less having to drive in this direction to reach Shipton Stables. It's not exactly enroute, but close enough that a minor detour into the mountains won't set me back too much.

Get in, get this shit sorted, and get out.

Maybe after I pluck his eyeballs, I'll leave my handprint across Kayce's jaw while I'm there for good measure. Or run him over.

"Ok. Bye. I'll text you when I'm done, but I'll probably be out of service when you pick this message up. Wish me luck, Sergeant. Love you. If I get taken in for grievous bodily harm please front my bail for me, we both know I just can't pull off orange with my hair color." I stab the red button to end the call and let out a frustrated exhale.

As I drive through the wide boulevard of the town I last visited in the height of late summer, I can see that the winter season has certainly taken a firm hold. Lights are on in all the storefronts open at this time of year, and even though it is currently midday, the sky feels somber and dark, like someone forgot to remind the sun to get out of bed.

The trees that hung lush with green leaves five months ago are now bare. Thousands of spindly fingers form twisted patterns against the ominous-looking sky. Hardly any vehicles line the streets, and there are certainly no cute girls lounging in the park working on their tans. Only piles of grit lie mounded up on either side of the road, and an eerie quiet hangs over the place.

My phone has the address pulled up on screen, but I remember the drive towards Devil's Peak like it was yesterday.

I also remember the last time I was here as if it were yesterday, too.

Colton Wilder.

Over the course of the past five months, I've replayed our conversation at the gas station a hundred times. In quiet moments, especially while lying in bed, always oh-so-fucking-alone, my mind can't help but keep returning to that day and raking over every detail with a fine-tooth comb. Did I completely misread his signals?

Maybe. Possibly. *Ugh.*

Why is it so hard to get that man out of my mind? Usually, by the time I'm done overthinking everything, I've convinced myself that I threw myself at the poor guy, demanded his money, and then came onto him so strong that he took off speeding down the main street to escape my assault.

Oh, and I then proceeded to follow him to his home, like a stalker.

Yup. That would absolutely account for his ice-king demeanor and death glare when I knocked on the door.

I should count myself lucky he didn't march me off his property with a shotgun between my shoulder blades.

But then again, when I'm not being so hard on myself, I remember the warmth of his hazel eyes as they held mine. I can still hear the rumble in his voice when we joked together. Can clearly picture the veins on his hands as he raked his fingers through his hair, right before putting his sexy-as-hell cowboy hat back on.

My heart does a little flutter when I recall the way he told me not to hang around the wrong type of men, and asked if I was free for an evening.

Quickly followed by the cold indifference he showed me as he blocked me from entering his house.

My nose wrinkles at the memory of how uncomfortable that felt.

Prick.

As the road winds its way like a snake up the incline, I can see thick drifts of snow coating the embankments, and the temperature outside plummets the higher I climb. The drive up the mountain is vastly more treacherous this time around.

My little car isn't made for these conditions, nor are the tires I currently have, but I am a woman possessed.

When I finally make it to the entrance to Devil's Peak Ranch, I feel like I can exhale again. Thick purple clouds billow on the horizon and the peak is painted in a solid lacquer of white. Most of the trees up this high are covered in a sugary dusting of snow, but the house and yard are clear. For now, at least. Judging by the clouds, it looks like there's more snow heading this way.

Hurling myself out of the vehicle, I slam the door, feeling fired up and ready to serve both barrels to my asshole ex. Those last few miles were filled with giving myself a pep talk about all the creative techniques I intend on using while skinning Kayce alive.

Only, I'm crossing the yard, and it feels a lot emptier than before. Last time I was here, there were a couple of vehicles, and now there is only the sight of the big stallion of a truck that presumably belongs to Colton Wilder.

What if Kayce isn't even here? My shoulders deflate a little and I immediately start debating whether to turn around with my tail between my legs.

"You lost or something?" A gruff voice shouts from over by the entrance to the barn, and I'm halfway toward the steps leading up to the front door when a familiar figure strides in my direction.

My ex-boyfriend's father is kitted out in a rugged weatherproof jacket, with a faded ball cap on backward. His hands and side of his face are smeared in blood, and those hazel eyes of his are burning. But that's not what makes my heart stop in my throat. It's the sight of the bloodied carcass slung across his shoulders.

A headless deer is slit open right along where the creature's stomach should have been, and the smell of copper burns straight up my nose.

Behind him, a bloody trail carves through the snow where it drips onto the ground.

In my line of work, I'm no stranger to the reality of ranch life. Death is an ever-present part of vet work and managing livestock and rural living. But the gruesome sight of him carrying a freshly killed animal feels more confronting than I was prepared for.

The man before me heaves the body onto the flatbed of his truck and turns to look at me. He's coated in crimson, and the smell is even more overwhelming up close. There's hot, thick, pooling blood collecting on the ground from where the head has been severed.

His sharp gaze flicks between me and my shitty little car, and recognition colors his features.

"Is Kayce here?" My stomach churns.

"Thought you two were broken up." He tosses a giant knife down beside the gutted animal. The blade glistens, slick with red as it clatters against the metal. I find myself unable to look away from the slaughtered beast laid out right before me.

"We are." I can't get into this with him right now. My skin feels prickly as all hell. I just need this money disaster sorted and can't wait to get out of here before that ominous-looking weather rolls in. You don't need to live on a mountain to know things are always more extreme, more likely to flip on a dime, at altitude. "I just... I need to talk to him is all."

"He knock you up?"

Jesus. What the fuck?

Speechless doesn't even begin to describe how I'm feeling right now. Who the hell does this asshole think he is?

I don't know if this man thinks my silence is agreement or what, but he strides right up to me and crosses his arms. Giving me the all too familiar ice-glare from months ago as he looms large and macabre-looking with the evidence of his kill coating his skin.

"Kayce isn't here. Try one of the bars in town." With that, he stomps past me up the steps and kicks off his boots at the door.

Unbelievable. Un-fucking-believable.

A snowflake lands on the back of my hand, and that cold kiss against my skin seems to galvanize me into action.

"Whatever," I mutter and turn back for my car. My teeth are gritted so tight there's every chance I'm going to crack a molar, and I yank the door open with far more force than necessary.

The giant dickhead watches me from just outside his front door, as if he's standing guard to make sure I leave his property.

Gladly. *Asshole.*

I shove the key in the ignition and chuck the car in reverse, not bothering to look behind me before I tear out of the yard. Blinding rage sweeps right down the back of my neck beneath my sweater.

Rounding the first bend, I see the clumps of snow start to drift faster and harder in my rearview mirror as the ominous outline of Devil's Peak disappears behind a cluster of pine trees.

Good fucking riddance. Now, I've just got to get back into town and ransack every inch of Crimson Ridge until I chase down my good-for-nothing ex.

I'm still smarting from the way that man just spoke to me. The scathing tone of his voice and immediate assumption about my circumstances has my hands shaking.

God, I wish that I could have come back with something smart in response. Instead of standing there gaping at him with nothing to say.

The gravel road curves up ahead, as I make my way deeper into the forest. Except, when I continue following the path back down the mountain the car starts to shudder beneath me. My heart is in my throat as it fishtails a little and I'm suddenly seeing just how steep the drop off on the side of the road is, plummeting into the darkness of the ravine below.

The jolting gets worse, and my car gives a groan as I apply the brake and pull over to the side. With an awful demonic sound, it lurches to a halt with a relentless knocking. Steam proceeds to billow from under the hood. There's a grinding of metal against metal and a heavy clank that absolutely doesn't sound good, before everything dies. All the lights on my dash pop on at the same time.

"No. No. No. Come on, come onnnn." Praying to whatever patron saint of motor vehicles exists out there, I try the key in the ignition, but it doesn't even turn over. Nothing flickers. I'm greeted by stubborn silence and the stench of burnt oil. My Honda sits there as lifeless as the corpse I just witnessed being dumped in the back of Colton Wilder's truck.

All the while, thick clumps of snow settle on my windshield so fast, that within seconds I can't see the hood of my car any longer.

I'm so fucked.

CHAPTER 5

Colton

There's a girl nearly half my age standing in my kitchen with puffy red eyes. It looks like she's either going to try and swing at me, or crumple like a tissue.

"I just need to arrange a tow truck. *Please.*" She won't fucking sit down, even though I've offered her a stool at the kitchen island several times.

Letting out a heavy sigh, I rest both hands on the countertop. Trying to keep my eyes on her face. Trying *not* to think about the fact the girl from the gas station is here.

She's *here* and standing in my kitchen.

"No chance of that. Not with this snow coming down." I grunt.

The girl checks her phone again for what must be the tenth time since I brought her inside out of the cold. Out of the corner of my eye I can see a layer of white growing thicker by the second on the porch railing beyond the window.

Of course, her piece of shit car broke down. I'm not at all surprised, more amazed it actually made it up here in the first place.

I'd barely had a chance to hang the deer, shower off the blood, and get dressed when she reappeared. Banging on the front door, frozen to the bone from having to walk from wherever she abandoned her car in the snow. After I was sure that would be the last time I ever saw her.

"Look. I can't get stuck here. I've got to be somewhere tomorrow, and I need to find Kayce before I leave town." She's got a look in her eyes like the horses do when something has spooked them.

If I didn't know better, I'd say she's running from something.

But none of this shit is my problem. Kayce has fucked up again? Big surprise. That kid never knows when to quit, or how to keep his dick in his pants. If he isn't too drunk for either of those things, of course.

The way this girl has shown up twice in the space of several months has my teeth on edge.

There's only one reason girls like her come visiting out of the blue, needing to *talk*.

"If you could just tow me yourself—"

"Sorry. Even if I could get your vehicle down to the shop, the snow would be settled by then. Can't risk getting stuck in town."

"But... it wouldn't take long..."

She's looking at me with those fucking mossy green, pleading eyes, and bitterness lines my throat. This isn't my problem.

"Listen, sweetheart. I don't know what shit you've got yourself into with my son, but I've got a business up here and livestock to take care of. If I take you down the mountain, I won't be getting back myself until the roads get cleared, and that could take weeks."

Her face pales, and I see the way her nostrils flare.

Tough shit. The truth is a bitter pill to swallow sometimes.

"Oh my god. This can't be happening." She's mumbling and her fists are clenching and unclenching. It's said more to herself than me. The next moment, she's headed off toward the front door. I'm not exactly sure what the fuck this girl intends on doing, but it's turned into a blizzard already out there in the time it took her to walk back up to the house.

"*Hey,*" I call after her. She's either not listening, or is ignoring me.

Pinching my brow, I hesitate in the kitchen rather than follow after a girl I don't even know. My son's fuck buddy? Girlfriend? Jesus Christ. She could be a buckle bunny from his time on the rodeo circuit, for all I know.

Maybe she just needs a moment. Life out here is testing at the best of times, and right now, I've got to figure out what the fuck to do about having an unexpected house guest stuck under my roof until I can ship her off this mountain.

Jesus. Kayce really couldn't have picked a worse time to disappear off with his buddies in town, could he? In my mind, I've already torn the useless little shit a new one.

I run my fingers through my hair and quickly turn over the mental checklist of what I've got in the house. Supplies are well stocked from my last run to town, the freezer is full, and I'm pretty sure at least one of the spare bedrooms has clean sheets. If not, it doesn't really matter, she can sleep in the room Kayce has been using, since they're obviously still a thing.

The thought quickly tightens my chest. That girl has haunted me since the day outside the gas station over summer.

Turns out she's Kayce's woman.

I'd shoved aside everything about our interaction months ago, but seeing her again, unexpectedly, has brought all sorts of memories flooding back.

The kind that need to stay buried the fuck away.

There's a sharp howling noise, followed by a crash of the front door closing. What the fuck? I jog through to the foyer and see the outline of her shoulders disappearing down the steps into the thick flurries of white whipping around the yard.

She's barely got more than a thin sweater and jeans on. Christ, does she have a death wish or something? Of course, Kayce would go for the crazy ones.

I grab my jacket plus a spare one from the hooks just inside the door and hurl myself outside, following after her. "What the hell do you think you're doing?" I yell into the wind as I shrug into my coat and boots. But she keeps heading down the steps like she's got somewhere to be, and I have to lengthen my stride to grab her before she does something fucking stupid.

Catching up to her in the yard, my fingers wrap around her arm, but when I yank the girl around to look at me, the stricken expression contorting her features is instantly recognizable. There's a mask frozen on her face I know all too well.

Shit.

Hands clamped into fists. Mouth hanging open like she can't taste oxygen. There's a glazed look to her green eyes and even though I'm standing right here in front of her, she's not seeing me right now.

That much I know from personal experience.

"Come here," I mutter and bundle the coat around her shoulders, but she's as rigid as a plank, and it's not due to the cold.

Panic attacks aren't pretty at the best of times, but in the middle of a below-freezing snowstorm, having her locked up like this could be deadly.

I'm cursing my son with every unholy thought I can muster as we get safely back inside, setting her down on the armchair closest to the fire. Gently pushing her head to drop between her knees, I leave the room for a moment, going to rifle through the pantry and cupboards. Jesus, this is the last goddamn thing I need to be doing.

When I return, she hasn't moved, and her tiny fingers are still cramped into the shape of claws. She's making a desperate, gurgling sort of noise and as much as I've got the horses to look in on, and wood to stock, and storm warnings to check, I can't leave her hyperventilating like this.

I do my best to soothe her, encouraging her to sit up now and pressing the paper bag I've just grabbed from the kitchen over her nose and mouth and slowly rub circles on her back.

It's not a perfect solution by any means, but right now, it's the best I can do to triage a crappy situation.

"You gotta breathe nice and slow for me. You're ok."

I see the bag inflate just a fraction, then hollow out.

"Slow. Deep breath. Again."

We sit like that for a long moment. Me talking this stranger through a panic attack while planning multiple ways to murder my own son.

Her shaky, shallow breaths fill the bag a few more times, deepening one by one, until I see her fists begin to uncurl just a fraction. That's enough for me to toss the bag aside and with my free hand, I take one of hers and then the other. Massaging the tense muscles, I help her fingers to straighten out.

As I do so, I feel her stiff frame ease slightly beneath my palm. Guiding her by the shoulder, I press a little, encouraging her to shift her body more upright.

"Count to four while you breathe in." Her eyes won't meet mine, and I'm not surprised.

It was the same for me. *Afterward* was always somehow worse.

Confident that she's somewhat out the other side of it, I get up and head over to grab a glass of water from the kitchen. While there, I swipe a bag of gummy worms from the back of the pantry.

Returning to the lounge, I crouch down on my haunches, holding out the water. "Can you take a sip of that for me?" Nodding, she clutches it in two hands, bringing it to her mouth, grip more than a little unsteady.

"Good. Now eat these..." Removing the water, I offer an exchange and hand over two worms, setting the glass down on the coffee table beside her. "And don't think about moving."

A GOOD FIFTEEN minutes pass while trying to get a message through to Kayce. For now, the Wi-Fi appears to still be working. However, the asshole probably hasn't charged his phone, so he won't be checking his email. Of course, he hasn't picked up or returned the call I put out to the radio fitted in his truck. I'd been nagging him about the forecast and the risk of getting stuck down in town, but of course, he still disappeared earlier today.

Now, I've got an even bigger problem, and she's sitting in my lounge.

Whatever is going on with this girl, it's bad enough to send her spiraling into a panic attack, and I've got a really bad fucking feeling about the trouble she's got herself into.

There are too many old, familiar sensations buzzing through my veins right now. Memories of fluorescent lighting and the smell of disinfectant. Shoes squeaking along hospital corridors and the beep of machinery at all hours of day and night.

Wanting to crawl out of my own skin all because of a stupid fucking mistake I'd made at seventeen years old when I thought nothing could ever touch me.

How wrong I was nine months later when the consequences of one foolish decision arrived.

Inside my fist the radio crackles, and a familiar, deep voice distorted by static fills my postage-stamp-sized office just across from the kitchen. The place where I keep a computer, business shit, paperwork, all the parts of being a rancher that aren't my forte, but that I have to deal with all the same. While the device in my hand might be considered old-fashioned technology to some, up here in the mountains it's about the most reliable thing we've got.

It can be the difference between life and death.

"All good up there, old man?"

"Stôrmand," I grunt in reply.

"Piss off with that *Stôrmand* bullshit, Wilder."

A wry smile crosses my face hearing his growl. I've got young bucks I call in to help when I need it up here. Storm is about the only person on this mountain who I'd willingly sit down and crack open a beer with, though. He's got a fucked up past like me and doesn't talk much, and that suits us both just fine. He's not a rancher, but he's the only half-decent farrier who I trust with my horses, and the guy used to willingly climb on an angry bull for money back while he still had a pro career. Crazy son of a bitch.

When the roads are clear he comes and shoes the horses for me, keeps them in good shape with the busy summer season, and in return I help him out around his property if he ever needs anything.

He's been up here a long time on his own, too.

However, after the shit he's been through, I can't blame him for being even more reclusive than I am.

"Snow's already stuck good down here. Must be packed in solid already at the ranch?"

Storm confirms what I'd feared. If the weather has hit hard for him, then it's a bitch of a front that has closed in... fast. He's at a slightly lower elevation, but lives across the valley. We're not exactly *neighbors,* but round these parts, our properties are close enough to one another to count.

"Mountain roads are closed. Spoke with Hayes a couple of minutes ago." Storm continues on.

Sheriff Cameron Hayes is a good bastard. Another man I'd consider a friend and someone who I will happily grab a drink with and give the time of day to. Man works his ass off over winter to make sure the mountain is cleared as fast as possible, on top of everything required of him on the Hayes family ranch, and I can always rely on him to keep in touch to let me know how conditions are looking out there. Especially when we become cut off from the rest of the world here on Devil's Peak.

I know he worries about the gruff old assholes like Storm and myself who live out in these parts on our own. Fucking mother hen that he is.

"Weather should fuck off quick enough, it's only likely to keep snowing until tomorrow."

"You're all good for supplies over there?" I mean, the man might have spent a career hanging onto the back of a bull like a goddamn lunatic, but he's particularly shit at taking care of himself.

Storm lives hard and fast, and more than once, I've wondered if he gives a damn about anything other than horses and finding his next one-night stand.

"Aw. Offering to saddle up, ride over here and tuck me in are you, sunshine?"

"Fuck you very much."

He chuckles. "Still need a hand with the next cattle round-up?"

"Assuming you can get your ugly ass up here by then... you know I won't say no."

Having the likes of him as an extra pair of hands when I need them around this place is a godsend, even though the majority of the time I can manage by myself, some jobs just need a team working the stock. Storm can handle a horse and knows cattle like it's in his blood. Plus, the other guys who help on the days I need it are young. Too fucking young. They might be good in the saddle, but Jesus, each year they make me feel older, and each year, they seem to get more baby-faced.

After exchanging a few more words with Storm—neither of us are exactly *talkers*, and that's fine by me—he's passed on the relevant updates I need to know from Hayes.

Despite the front bringing this heavy snowfall, it'll pass quickly, which means the crews should be able to get a clear run to re-open the mountain. That should mean a long enough window of time to do a trip into town for restocking supplies, and also get this girl's busted vehicle towed to a mechanic.

Considering where we are, at the very top of the mountain access road, that could be two weeks away, at best.

I can get her down on horseback tomorrow if she wants to go find accommodation in Crimson Ridge. That might be the best place for her while she waits until we can get her car off the mountain, but she won't be driving for a while.

As for tonight... well, no one is going anywhere in this whiteout. Unless they've got a death wish.

I tuck the radio handset back in its cradle and return to the lounge. The girl hasn't moved, like I instructed. Just stares at the flames dancing in the fire and looks completely wiped out. But at least she's had some water and some sugar and seems warm enough.

"You ok?" I grab a couple more logs from the stack against the wall and start loading up the fire.

"Maybe. I don't know." A bit of a raspy edge colors her voice, sounding sexy as fuck, and the very, very wrong response my body has is to feel a rush of blood heading to my dick.

This girl is pale and shaky and has hardly pulled herself together, and I'm thinking about what that voice would sound like gasping my name in the dark?

Of course, that's where my mind goes. Of course it does. Because I've thought about her way too many times over the past few months, and now I'm having all my fucked up daydreams, unexpected desires I've never felt compelled by before now, thrown back in my face.

Willing my self-control to at least put in an appearance—to make some sort of effort not to outright stare at her—I sit on the concrete mantle that spans either side of the fire, leaning on my knees. Focus locked on my hands, I study the creases of my knuckles.

"Want to tell me what that was all about?" My voice is hard. But then, I don't know any other way to be, especially not with someone soft and pretty and so fucking young. She's got to be close in age to Kayce, and that puts her in her mid-twenties at the most.

That puts her firmly in the *too-young* category.

Inwardly, I cringe. What the hell was I thinking that first day I saw her at the gas station? She seemed so much older and easy to talk to, and I must have had fucking heat stroke or something for even considering asking this girl out.

Out of my periphery, I see how she twists her lips and shakes her head gently. "It's nothing. Just my whole life exploding in front of my eyes."

The fire cracks and pops to fill the silence.

"Why the rush to get out of town?" I'm still not entirely convinced it hasn't got anything to do with the fact she's dating, or has dated, my son.

"My new job starts tomorrow." She takes another small sip of water. "I've got bills and things owing, and without sounding like the useless idiot you probably think I am... I promise I work really hard. Just seem to have shitty luck."

"Like when your card declines at a gas station." My eyes sweep over her and she's got her gaze fixed on a spot on the floor. It's a quick look. One I allow myself under the guise of checking that she's ok. Nothing more.

I'm allowed to look at a person in need of my help, aren't I? This is me being dutiful and caring.

She lets out a resigned sigh. "Exactly like that."

"Still doesn't explain why you're out here hunting for Kayce." I can't help but glance at her stomach again. She doesn't look pregnant, but if it looks like a duck and quacks like a duck...

"He and I—" The girl stumbles over her words before trying again. "We had a joint account, and I needed to withdraw my savings to cover some unexpected bills, until my next paycheck. But if he's not here and I can't get hold of him, I don't know what to do."

My jaw works. I don't buy it, but that's none of my concern. There's no telling what shit Kayce has got himself into, but I'm certainly not letting him screw this girl out of her hard-earned money. At least she's got a job and a plan for her future, which is more than I can say for my own kid.

"How much do you need?"

Those green eyes of hers glimmer with tears. Fuck. It's that bad.

"You don't have to fix this for him."

"Let me handle Kayce, and I'll front you the amount until he's able to get his ass back up here and make this right."

"It's over two thousand dollars." She blurts out.

"Will a bank transfer do?"

"You can't be serious?" This girl is looking at me like I'm a lion, and she's just been asked to stick her hand inside my cage.

"Deadly serious. Consider it done, and if you want some free advice, don't open a joint account with a useless prick like my son."

Her eyes nearly hang out of her head.

"Noted." She dips her chin while still gaping at me.

Cracking my knuckles, I figure it's best to keep her talking. "What do you do for work?" What I'm expecting her to say is: admin, or office shit, or marketing, or something that townie girls like her seem to do. But her answer surprises me a little.

"I'm a vet. But I'm only in training." The second part is tacked on hastily. Like she's quick to point out a perceived flaw.

A vet student on her work placements.

While hearing that puts some parts of this story into context, it still doesn't explain the panic attack. From what I understand, their apprenticeship programs can span a few years of part-time work, nothing to warrant a dive off the deep end about.

"It's Layla, isn't it?"

She nods.

"Help me out here, Layla. You gotta give me more than that. From where I'm sitting, there seems to be a lot of rushing and stress for something that shouldn't be as serious as all that."

She looks defeated. Slumping a little against the back of the armchair. "I need to graduate in August, so in order to do that I gotta complete my apprenticeship hours as fast as possible. If I don't get to my new job with Shipton Stables by tomorrow, they'll give my position away, which means not only kissing goodbye to the hours I need to complete, but a paycheck I can't afford to miss."

There are layers to what she's saying, but I can sense how carefully guarded her walls are.

"Well, I hate to be the bearer of rather obvious news, but you won't be in Shipton by tomorrow." My chin jerks towards the huge window overlooking the ranch. The vista is solid white beyond the triple-glazed glass pane.

Her brief moment of composure starts to crumble.

This job is clearly important to her. Or maybe the money is

important, who knows, but I can't deal with her losing her shit again tonight.

Fuck.

My mouth is moving before I can stop myself.

"What do you need to satisfy the requirements of your apprenticeship?" I scrub a hand over my jaw.

Her big green eyes, brimming with a sheen of tears, bounce up to meet mine. "Um, I need a placement where my hours are logged professionally. Working with a registered business for a minimum of eight weeks. I've already done all my bookwork by distance learning, so it's anything that involves hands-on experience with stock, horses, farm animals..."

Eight weeks.

I turn over that piece of information.

There's a part of my brain screaming at me, but I ignore it. Because I can't for the life of me let this girl be fucked over by crappy circumstances and whatever else it is that she's not willing to tell me, yet.

I'm trying to make amends with my shit-head of a son, and make up for the years when I should have been there for him, but couldn't be, thanks to my own crap and his idiot of a mother. But if I can't make any headway with him, the least I can do is try to help his *maybe* girlfriend out.

So, I do the worst thing imaginable, considering the way my cock is more than interested in the young woman sitting across from me.

I offer her a job.

CHAPTER 6

Layla

It's pitch black outside and deathly quiet.

The house feels like it resents my presence just as much as its owner does.

Somehow, I fell into a fitful sleep last night surrounded by eerie howls of wind and floorboards creaking like the hull of a ship. Eventually waking up to nothing but silence and my phone screen proclaiming the time.

Four thirty a.m.

Rather than engage in any more futile attempts at sleep, I figured it was better to find some coffee and get my head around the day to come. Quietly getting myself dressed in yesterday's jeans and sweater, before I splashed some cold water on my face, and made my way to the kitchen with only the hallway sensor lights casting a dim glow to see by.

Right now, I'm waiting in the dark for coffee to brew after trying to rummage around a stranger's kitchen in order to find things without making a peep. I've found a spot to stand in where the Wi-Fi seems to be strongest, sending Sage a quick explanation of the chaos my life has become over the course of the past twenty-four hours. Bless her heart because she had replied to my voicemail last night, letting me know that she was going to see Aunt Evie today to check on her for me.

She's also insisting on sending me every cowboy-related meme she can find.

At least one of us finds this situation humorous.

Meanwhile, I find it impossible to explain *anything* about the man who has so kindly taken me in and offered me work. So... I just... don't.

For about the fiftieth time, I reopen my banking app and see that the money Kayce's father transferred last night has successfully been paid to the finance company.

Holy fucking shit. I honestly still can't believe how he just took care of it, without question. Even if it does leave me squirming a little that I didn't exactly tell him the truth, but then again, I don't need him fighting my battles with Kayce. As much as I'm still furious with the guy, there's no need to spoil his relationship with his dad any further.

The stupid mistakes I made with my ex are most definitely not his father's problem.

It's only a few minutes before I hear heavy footfall approaching and the overhead lights above the kitchen island flick on. The next moment, Colton Wilder wanders in, with messy hair and eyes still fogged by sleep. Only, he doesn't have a shirt on, and all I see is a broad chest and his jeans with belt undone at the buckle.

"Shit. Sorry." He takes me in, looking a little stunned to see anyone standing in his kitchen, and ducks into the laundry area just off the hallway. As he re-emerges, he's busy buttoning a flannel shirt, before rolling the cuffs to hit midway up his forearms. "I wasn't expecting—" He stops abruptly and shakes his head. Not bothering to finish explaining his half-naked appearance, while I'm busy trying to look anywhere but the direction of his belt still hanging loose at his groin.

For some reason, that sight is winding a curl of heat low in my belly that has absolutely no right to be there.

This is my ex's dad I'm staring at, as if I've never seen a man before.

It's not even five in the morning.

What the fuck is wrong with me?

Hearing the coffee stop running, I quickly grab the pot to pour into a mug from one of the cupboards. Sliding the cup across the counter to him, I figure he looks like a black coffee kind of cowboy.

"Here." As I look up, I catch a glimpse of his veined hands threading the leather through his buckle and I'm glad for how soft the lighting is in here because my cheeks heat. I'm managing to make this all sexual and shit, while the poor man is simply trying to get dressed. After saving my ass last night and offering me a temporary job, the least I could do is act appropriately.

Christ, if he's Kayce's dad, then that means he's old enough to be my father.

Although, this cowboy looks far younger than his years.

No. Nope. *Stop it right now.*

He accepts my offering, but as he raises the mug to his lips, he pauses before taking a sip, looking at me over the top with wariness in his expression. "You didn't spit in this or something, did you? That's the kind of thing Kayce would do when he's had enough of my shit."

I gnaw on the inside of my cheek, shaking my head as I turn and reach up on tiptoes to grab another mug. Putting all my focus into pouring my own.

"No. Just coffee... I don't really know how else to say thank you for everything yesterday, Mr. Wilder." Considering I have no money, a busted car, and no way of getting out of here—oh, and add that to the fact he somehow got me through hyperventilating and feeling like I was on the cliff's edge of losing my mind. There are about a thousand things I want to say, but I don't know where to start, and honestly, his sternness and broodiness is kind of intimidating. He's impossible to read and I don't know how he'll be now that we've both had a night to sleep on the events of yesterday.

Will he want me gone? I'd barely been here two seconds before he accused me of getting knocked up and coming searching for Kayce like some kind of gold-digging hussy. I don't know if I've forgiven him for how crude he was about the whole thing. But then he solved my financial crises on behalf of his son, and talked me down off the ledge of the worst panic attack I've ever experienced, so right now, I'm all at sea with this man.

Like I said, I don't know what to expect once dawn breaks over Devil's Peak.

"Christ, call me Colt... none of that Mr. Wilder shit. And don't mention it." Sipping his coffee, a long silence hangs in the kitchen while I secretly squirrel away the preening feeling that comes with being asked to call him Colt.

Not Colton.

Not Mr. Wilder.

Just, Colt.

It's such a ruggedly sexy name, and my knees go a little weak. He's doing all sorts of wonderful things to my body simply by standing in his kitchen nonchalantly sipping coffee at four in the morning.

Colt is intensely attractive, without seeming to know it.

"If I was a bit rude..." He juts his chin in the direction of my belly, and my already warm cheeks start to flame. One hand reaches for the hem of my sweater on reflex, tugging it down to make sure it covers my high-waisted jeans. Ok, at least he realizes he was an asshole about it, even if his apology skills could use some serious work.

As we stand across the large wooden island from each other, I feel the words bubbling up. Whether I stay here or not is still to be determined, but I can't have him thinking things about me that aren't even remotely true.

Plus, I'm already doubting he's actually serious about any of this.

"Can I be very clear about something? I'm not pregnant and Kayce and I have been over for—well, it was never anything serious." I set my mug down on the counter and twist my hands in front of me. I hate confrontation and this feels like I'm being the worst kind of imposition. "Look, I understand completely if you've changed your mind—"

"You said you are a worker, didn't you?" He cuts me off and gives me a hard stare. Challenging me in the gray light of this kitchen that now feels about ten times smaller than it did a minute ago.

"Well, yes."

"As of right now, that's what I need. A worker. My son isn't exactly reliable around the place—but I suspect you've seen enough of that yourself to know what I mean—and I won't be able to get in any new help on short notice between the road shutting again and being this close to the start of the year."

I shift on my feet. Somehow I still feel like he's doing me a favor, and we haven't even talked about money, and I just don't know if this is a good idea.

Especially considering the way I can't stop staring at his scruffy jaw, or the honeyed tint to his eyes, or barely restraining myself from watching the corded muscles flex in his forearm as he lifts his coffee to his lips.

"But, I couldn't take your money *and* also take up space in your home." It's too much. What he's suggesting seems like way more of an imposition on him.

"You said eight weeks, didn't you?"

I nod. "That's the minimum time for a placement to count, in order for my supervisor to sign me off."

"In my book, that's nothing. I've had a busted nose that lasted longer."

"Just—" God, I don't know how to explain this to him. I desperately need money, and I need to get certified, but I also usually work extra bar shifts to pay for Evaline's care.

"Spit it out." He's got that impatience flaring again. I suspect this man doesn't have a very long fuse, and for a moment, the girl from the cafe's warning comes back to my mind.

You're a bit young for him, ain't you?

I hastily swallow a big gulp of coffee.

If the beasts up there don't eat you, the wildlife might.

Oh, shit. What if Kayce and him don't have a good relationship because he was abusive? What if this guy is a sadist or likes to prey on women who wander up this mountain all alone?

I already know he can gut a deer and carry a carcass across his shoulders like it weighs nothing.

There are a million places to bury a body up here.

Maybe I've made a horrible decision and should take him up on the offer of riding one of the horses down to Crimson Ridge instead. Who knows when Kayce will get back, and in the meantime, it will just be me all alone up here with...

He sets his coffee down with a thud, a suddenness which makes me jump. Spreading both hands wide on the counter, he fixes me with a gaze that could strip paint.

"Do we have a problem here? Because I've got no issue leaving you to stumble your way back down the mountain in the snow without my help. I'm busy enough, and ain't got time to be messed around."

His dark hair falls in his eyes and I feel about two inches tall beneath the weight of his threat.

"I'm not lying about anything." I wet my lips. Not technically. Just leaving out vast amounts of information. When you learn the hard way never to trust anyone, it's a shitty habit to break.

"Then hurry up, because I don't have all fucking day."

God. This man is like riding a bronco. Just when you think you've got a handle on his mood, he flips on you.

"Where I was heading, Shipton, I was going to have to pick up extra hours bartending on top of my job at the stables. It's what I do to get by financially, until I'm qualified and I can apply for full-time veterinarian positions after graduation."

He's quiet, and between the silence filling this kitchen and the way he's studying me, I'm feeling wholly unnerved.

"So, like I say, it's all a lot of bother and a burden on you... and I can't ask you to give me that amount of work, or pay." The words rush out of me and I want to sink through the floor.

"There's work needed to be done here from sun up 'til long after sundown. The way I see it, if you're here and one of the herd gets into trouble over the next eight weeks, we've got a hope of saving them. I won't have to deal with it by putting a bullet between their eyes like every other year when the snow comes, and the closest vet can't make it up here because the roads are shut."

I'm blinking at him like an owl. He moves around to my side of the counter and scoops both our mugs up, tipping the dregs into the sink before sliding them into the dishwasher.

Colt towers over me, folding his arms across his broad chest. "I give you shit to do. You do it without question, and you do it properly."

All I can do is nod.

"You do that, I'll pay you full-time wages, bed and board, plus any overtime."

Holy shit.

"But—"

"You got a better fucking offer lined up?"

My heart is thudding triple time inside my chest. There's got to be a catch here somewhere, but I can't go looking a gift horse in the mouth.

His jaw tics. "Didn't think so."

With that, he stomps out of the kitchen, and I trail after him like an obedient puppy.

Colt Wilder is short-tempered, growly, and impossible to please.

No wonder he can't find any fucking help to work this ranch.

After spending a whole day trying to make myself useful, acting as his personal shadow in an effort to learn the ropes around here, I've discovered that it's like trying to read a book while the cover and pages are glued together.

Everything I need to know that would allow me to be more helpful is locked away behind a surly demeanor and a smattering of occasional grunts.

But even though I spend most of the day biting my tongue, I can't help but feel overwhelmed with the beauty of this place. The air is crisp and biting, with a thick layer of soft snow covering the ranch several feet deep in places.

I'm guessing there are more tasks to do today than usual, with the snowfall overnight, including things like shoveling the yard, salting it, and clearing pathways between the house and the stables.

The horses need fed and watered and I'm secretly already in love with a glossy black mare, Winnie, who has a white spot over one flank. She searched my jacket pockets with nibbling, velvety lips as soon as I came near her stall, and I make a mental note to bring treats on my return visits.

From what I understand, I'll be spending a lot of time here looking after the twenty or so horses. They're the lifeblood of the ranch. Providing transport to the places up here that vehicles can't reach, along with herding cattle. Some are mostly used when tourists come during summer to go on treks and trail rides around the property. Apparently, that is what occupies a big portion of Colt's time over the warmer months.

I'm also going to be somewhat of an odd-job laborer, cook, cleaner, and basically all-round ranch-bitch.

I honestly can't stop grinning to myself like I've won the lottery. If I'm getting my vet training hours ticked off, and I'm getting paid the equivalent of what I'd earn serving drinks in a scummy strip joint at one in the morning, I'll happily shovel manure all night long.

Sweat clings to my lower back beneath the multiple layers safeguarding me against the cold. Shirt, sweater, heavy jacket, the thickest and warmest items I own bundle me up to keep toasty while working outside. It's late in the day, and we've barely stopped. I've shoveled snow, hay, horse shit, and now we're heading down to some of the further paddocks to feed out the cattle.

Colt drives us down there in his truck, with the powdery snow apparently not too thick to prevent taking his giant vehicle.

The wide black heads and matching noses of the cattle all turn to greet us as we draw close to the gate, and I can see their hot breath on the crisp afternoon air, along with the steam rising off their backs. Their fluffy ear tips are speckled with white flakes, and a few of them let out bellows, looking mighty interested in what we have to offer.

They've got snow piled on top of their thick coats, a great sign that this herd is in optimal condition.

"Feed's over there. I'll usually handle this on my own, but it doesn't hurt for you to know the drill." Colt jumps out of the truck and goes about firing up the tractor and loading a giant round bale from the stack lined up outside the fence.

When I see him start to head toward their paddock with the feed, I head over ahead of the machine and unlatch the gate. The cows are eager to see him and it makes me smile. He obviously doesn't have a huge herd here, so I wonder if he's got more of a farm-to-table type operation going on. Maybe organic? This place certainly isn't massive in comparison to the sizable ranches in other parts of the country.

I lean on the wooden rail, with clouds of white forming on each breath, as he feeds out the stock in a wide arc until the bale has been distributed across the snow. The hay is still tinged with green on the inside and creates a stark contrast against the thick coat of white covering their paddock. The animals dig in quickly, enjoying having something to eat until a time when there's enough snow melt for their grazing pasture to be exposed once more.

The sight of Devil's Peak sits prominent in the backdrop and as I take a deep inhale through my nose, for just a moment I feel like this might actually work out ok.

Colt parks up the tractor and trailer unit. I'm expecting us to carry on our way, but as he walks toward where I'm making my way back to the cab of the truck, he's got a thundercloud hanging over his expression.

My stomach does a little flip, but not in a good way. This is an *oh, shit, what did I do wrong* kind of feeling.

"Latch the fucking gate properly. If you're going to be here, you need to be attentive, or there's going to be hell to pay if you leave a gate open and my cattle escape during the night."

I'm standing beside the cab with one hand on the door handle, stunned at his outburst.

Now I'm the puppy who's just been spanked and has no idea what for.

With my heart in the back of my throat, I make my way on numb feet over to the gate. Something as simple as being told off about a latch shouldn't make me embarrassed, because I've been on plenty of rural properties. I know the basics and I'm not stupid. It's ranch-life and livestock 101. *Always shut a gate behind you* kind of common sense.

I reach the offending gate and see that he's right, of course the grumpy prick is. Straight away it's clear the latch hasn't caught properly, even though I was certain it had done so. It's hanging a little loose, and all it would take is for a curious beast to nudge against it, and the thing would pop open. Only, it's not my fault because the damn gate is heavy, and I see now how it has gotten caught in the snow and pugged up mud turned to ice on the ground. Under normal circumstances, I'm sure it closes easily, but in this weather, it's clearly got a trick to it—one that I don't know because I've been here all of five minutes.

Silently, I wrestle with the gate and curse Colton Wilder under my breath until the latch finally slots firmly in position.

Once I've triple-checked the damn thing, I stomp my way back to the idling truck, doing my best to rein in my desire to breathe fire all over the insanely hot, brooding cowboy behind the wheel. I need to focus on being a good worker and keep my eyes on the task at hand.

Job. Money. Apprenticeship hours.

My threesome of needs that this man is so generously providing.

But when I slide into the warm cab, my emotions are immediately rag-dolled all over the place. It's full of traces of *him* in here, and in that moment, I realize as his scent of leather and hay and something citrusy hits me, I'm going to need to figure out a way to deal with the fact I'm up here all alone with a very off-limits man.

One who infuriates me as much as he sets my pulse racing.

CHAPTER 7

It's been a whole fucking week.

One spent doing my best to find something—anything— to focus on, other than the gorgeous girl currently sitting across the kitchen island from me eating an omelet and sipping her coffee, while she scrolls her phone.

Wi-Fi has been patchy as usual, and fortunately the power has only dropped out a couple of times for short periods. I've shown her where to stack wood both close to the house and inside so neither of us have to go far to load up the fireplaces. She's split kindling, neatly arranged supplies, and even offered to cook our meals. Insisting that it's the least she can do to help more.

Meanwhile, when I remember, in between all the other shit there is to do around this place, I've shown her how to run the backup generator in case we lose power completely and where to get fresh water if pipes freeze.

I also gave her a run-through of our radio system. It's what we rely on up here year-round, since cell coverage is non-existent and Wi-Fi barely works outside of my office. My brief instructions covered how to contact the ranch vehicles kitted out with a handset, the mountain patrol, and the sheriff. All those 'emergency situation' types of necessities that Layla needs to know about because god forbid I get myself into serious shit, but ranch life is tough. All it would take is for one of the cattle to crush me against a gate or for my horse to roll. Too easily things can go south. Accidents happen in the blink of an eye.

While we were going over the ways to contact the outside world, I went to mention Storm, but something halted me. Without any good reason, my mouth opened and then snapped shut.

I realized at that moment I didn't want him to know about Layla, or at least, the asshole inside me doesn't want *her* to know about him. I immediately bristled at the idea she might take an interest in what she saw... or whatever the equivalent of speaking with someone over a radio handset might be.

Either way, I didn't fucking like it, so I conveniently forgot to tell her about my friend and closest person nearby who *should* be her first port of call in case of emergency. She doesn't need to know anything about Stôrmand Lane, nor about the fact he used to be a rodeo star. Doesn't need to know about his stupid fucking tattoos that I've seen first-hand act as a pussy magnet everywhere he goes, and certainly doesn't need to be anywhere near his charming *gruffness*.

Nope. For now, she's got plenty of emergency contacts if required. Anyways, we had plenty more crap to go over on how things run here on the ranch.

Fortunately, the girl with green eyes is a quick study and it only took a day or so before I could leave her the horses. Those idiots all seem to love her.

Or at least, what she sneaks out to them in her pockets.

They never get enough attention from me usually because I'm too damn busy, and I see it in their big liquid eyes that they're gobbling up all the crooning and petting and brushing they're getting these days.

Lucky assholes.

I finally had a reply from Kayce, he emailed me one line saying he'll be back once the roads are cleared. What a first-class prick. He might be my own flesh and blood, but I'm not going to shy away from calling it shit if it stinks. How this girl ended up with him is beyond me.

She's stunning, and I can't seem to stop stealing looks at her, even though I know I shouldn't. Which inevitably leads to me barking something in her general direction, just to try and scare her off because fuck knows what I would do if she turned around and looked at me the same way.

Kayce is out partying, chasing the next high and likely a warm bed to fall into, meanwhile this girl is putting in a full day's work without so much as a peep. She shows up, gets on with it, and doesn't have much to say.

Which suits me fine.

I'm so used to my own company that the silence is easy for me.

Being busy is a godsend. It's the dangerous thoughts about this girl—those ones that bubble up at times when I least expect them to—that I'm most concerned about.

"We'll take the horses and ride out to check on the furthest paddocks today now the snow has thinned." I stand up, and she's right there, ready to go. Tidying up quickly after herself and slipping her phone in her back pocket. I don't know why kids her age always feel the need to have their phones on them. It's not like the damn thing gets service up here anyway.

"I get to ride?" Her green eyes light up, and I have to duck my head.

It's so fucking hard not to want to touch her when she looks like that. All flushed and excited and full of vitality for life, the kind that got burned out of me so long ago, it's a distant memory.

Maybe it got stubbed out of me like the cigarette butts my grandpa used to put out on the back of my head right after he wailed on me for just breathing wrong.

I grumble something resembling an agreement, and head off out the door. Shoving into my boots and yanking on my hat.

She follows, quietly doing the same with her own work boots, but I feel her eyes stray to me every so often. I hate that she's curious about me, even though I'm a fucking dickhead. There's nothing good that can come of being interested in the darkness that lies beneath the surface of Colt Wilder.

Layla seems to have rebounded well enough after that first night—we collected her things from her snow-bound car, which I'll get onto towing down to the shop once the road is finally clear —and I haven't wanted to pry any further as to why things over-whelmed her the way they did.

Jesus, I know well enough the way the mind can be a terrible place to be.

Right after Kayce was born was when the attacks used to hit the worst. I'd find myself losing it over the smallest thing. Hearing a loud noise, or another baby crying, or the thick perfume of lilies delivered to congratulate new parents who had no business being parents at all.

I never wanted to have kids. Does that make me a terrible person? But when you're raised by a man who loved nothing more than to lose himself in a bottle and then smack his own grandson around just so he could feel like a big man, well, it changes your perspective on what you want from life.

The truth is, I was just a kid myself when Kayce's mom came on the scene. I wasn't interested in her bullshit, but she wore me down, and when you're seventeen and dealing with years of neglect, there inevitably comes a moment when you finally let your guard slip.

It was meaningless. Only ever meant to be a *one time* thing. She told me she was on birth control, and who fucking knows, she either lied or wasn't reliable enough taking it. Either way, despite the fact I've always insisted on using protection to be certain, it didn't fucking matter. In the end I was doubly fucked. The condom broke, and Kayce arrived, and I felt like my life was over before it even began.

But you're not supposed to think like that, are you? Everyone expects you to be happy, and I don't regret his life, but I had to learn to reconcile how I imagined mine would be with the reality growing in front of my eyes week by week.

Then I went and fucked it all up more by convincing myself that my own kid would be better off without me. I had no one but a messed up grandfather as a role model. Who was I to be a parent? I hadn't even turned eighteen yet, and back then, I could barely afford to buy myself my own pickup.

Shawn went off to the Midwest, with big dreams of her perfect life as a new mom and making a fresh start, and instead, she drowned herself in pill bottles rather than being a parent. We weren't in contact much so the years trickled by, as they do, without me suspecting anything.

It wasn't until Kayce was too old and hated my guts too deeply that I found out how shit of a job she was doing. Offering to have him come and live with me did nothing, the kid didn't even want to know me by that stage, and I don't blame him.

So, when I got the call a few months ago that he needed a place to land and someone to help him out, I couldn't say no to the person I'd failed so many times before.

Now? Now, what am I doing? I'm staring at his girl's ass while walking into the barn and fighting back the urge to pin her against the stalls while I sink into her.

"Saddle up Winnie and Peaches. We'll take the girls out." I fiddle with my hat. Lifting it enough to dig my fingers through my hair before shoving it back on.

"You got it, boss." Layla scurries off to get them both ready and I can see multiple sets of ears prick up and follow her as the horses watch her work.

I grit my teeth, because it's taking everything in me not to do the same damn thing.

After I've successfully worked out some frustration shoveling hay and cleaning out a couple of the stalls while Layla's been busy, I wipe my hands on my jeans. She's leading both horses toward me, drawing nearer to where I've kept to myself over by the main doors.

She's got her plump bottom lip tugged between her teeth, and fuck me, everything about her is so sexy. How my idiot kid could let a girl like that go, I have no idea. If I were twenty years younger, she'd have been the girl of my fucking dreams.

Hell, she is right now.

Only problem is, I'm old enough to be her father, and I can't cross that line. Kayce and I are on tenuous ground. If I even think about going there with this girl, I'll ruin any hope of ever reconciling with my son.

But there's no harm in spending time with her. I just have to keep my shit together.

"We'll need to go as far round the perimeters as we can get, depending on the snow."

"Ok." She's got that breathy fucking rasp in her voice again as she gazes up at me. Her long, coppery hair is in two loose braids today, and my mind is going to very bad places now that I'm seeing her up close like this.

The kind of dirty places where her hair is wrapped in my fist.

What was that about keeping my shit together?

"You might be a horse doctor, but now's the time to see if you're a fair rider."

She gives me a coy smile. "I can hold my own."

"Good. Need a hand?" I reach around and stroke the warm neck of Peaches. She's a gentle horse and careful whenever we take guests out for trail rides over the summer. But this girl is short, and I have no idea whether she's ridden a horse of this size before.

"Maybe the first time." She's got a little flush high on her cheeks. I hate myself for constantly cataloging all these little details.

This feels like the day at the gas station all over again. It's too easy to slip into being like this with her. When it's just the two of us, and talking to her feels as smooth as honey.

Which is why I've tried to leave her alone as much as fucking possible this past week.

She shifts around to grab the reins in one hand and hold the saddle with another. I'm moving behind her, and all of a sudden, it's clear this was an insane idea. Her jeans are tight over her ass, those perfect thighs are right in front of me, and our hips are barely a breath apart as she lifts a foot into the stirrup.

I reach down and my bulk covers her back. We're so close my lips are right at her ear and I feel the way her breath hitches when I clasp my fingers around the top of her boot.

"Go easy on me, ok?" Layla breathes.

I don't know what comes over me, but as I help swing her up into the saddle, the words are out of my mouth before I can stop them.

"I promise, I can be gentle."

WE SPEND the day going around the outermost paddocks on the ranch, checking for any needed repairs and storm damage. Layla is more than comfortable on her horse, and that at least settles me a little, knowing she'll be fine to do more jobs unsupervised, now that I've seen she's competent and can ride in these conditions.

I decide it's safest to retreat into my shell after giving myself the biggest fucking talking to of my life.

Why I can't seem to keep it together in her presence is ridiculous.

She's just a hot little cunt parading around in front of me, that's all it is.

We finish up the day separately, I leave her to the barn, and I deal with other crap on my list that needs my attention. My evening check-in with the roading crew by radio lets me know the road is cleared nearly halfway up the mountain, and the team should be done all the way to the ranch within the week.

I drag myself through the shower quickly and then throw on a clean pair of jeans and a tee. I'd usually wear a lot less than this, but seeing as I'm battling my self-control with a gorgeous young girl in my house, wearing clothes seems like a prudent decision.

Real fucking mature.

Not like my dick is half-hard the minute I walk into the kitchen, and she flashes a smile at me over her shoulder.

After we've both eaten—her on her phone and me keeping my eyes trained on the meal in front of me—she stretches and makes a move to clear both our empty dishes.

"Sit your ass down. I've got these." I reach over to grab hers.

"It's fine, I don't mind." Layla tries to clutch the plate while perched on her stool at the kitchen island. I've got a dining table, it just never gets used. This has always been the place I prefer to sit and eat and Layla seems to feel the same way.

"You cooked."

She lets out a little laugh and finally relents, allowing me to yank the plate away from her. "The things you don't realize until you see the alternative."

I'm not sure I know what she means, but I'm not about to ask either.

"I'll leave you to the horses tomorrow while I head down and sort out that busted fence in the western paddock." As I rinse the dishes and stack the dishwasher, I'm aware she's moving around behind me but I focus my eyes firmly on the sink and the current task keeping my hands busy.

"I can handle that." She sounds tired, and suddenly, I'm a little worried I've been pushing her too hard. Kayce tells me all the time I'm a miserable old bastard, which is about right.

"You sure?" I turn around and rest my back against the sink. My eyes fall on her, and oh, fuck I really wish I had stayed exactly as I was. She's stretching up on tiptoes to reach for a cup from the cupboard, and her cropped sweater has ridden up, showing off the perfect rounded curve of her hips and ass, a strip of soft, pale skin above the waistband, jeans suctioned tight in the exact spot where her pussy is. Her back arches and her long braids hang down, and my filthy fucking brain devours the sight of her.

I'm more screwed than I thought because she turns and looks at me over one shoulder, catching me in the act of openly watching.

"Could you grab one of the tall glasses for me, please?" She twists herself and flattens her back against the counter.

I swallow heavily.

"Of course." Why is my throat so scratchy?

Crossing to the spot where she stands, I step into her small frame. Layla doesn't move, and I don't want her to. I keep my eyes on hers and reach up, which leans my body so close I can smell the jasmine and pear scent of her shampoo. There's a heat and tension thick in the air between us, and not for the first time today, I'm forgetting the reasons why I shouldn't be looking at her like this.

My fingers close around the cool, smooth glass, and I pluck it down for her.

"Thanks." Her voice is barely a whisper and I see her eyes flicker to my lips for just a second.

My dick jerks.

Blood rushes south in a way that it has no fucking business even daring to.

Fuck. I'm such an asshole. She's my son's territory, or at the very least, is meant to be with a guy his age, her age, and that reminder compels me to step back rather than grab her chin and taste those pouty fucking lips like I want to.

I'm a piece of shit for even looking at her.

What the hell am I even doing getting so close? This was a mistake.

If I'm ever going to have a relationship with my son, or have any chance of helping him make better choices with his life, I can't give into whatever this thing is that hovers in the shadows between us.

She's too young for me. I should know better.

There's this thing called loneliness, and I really need to take the opportunity to find someone else the next time the roads are clear to get rid of this tension with. To fuck the past few months of filthy fantasies I've been having about this girl out of my system.

Because the very soft and feminine-looking young woman standing before me, looking back at me with big eyes, is not where I need to be sticking my dick.

CHAPTER 8

Layla

My earbuds blast something with a heavy beat that makes working in here even more enjoyable. I'm almost happiest when I'm alone and left to do my own thing, which I always thought was a flaw about myself for a long time.

Doing things on my own has always felt more comfortable. Girlfriends would try to take me shopping with them when I was in my teens, and I never felt like I fit in. I'd go back later on my own and that's when I would find the things I wanted, by myself.

I guess that makes me a little bit faulty in their eyes? Why I never really found a group of girls to become friendly with. Like I was separate from the pack somehow.

Suppose it's also why Kayce and I were never going to work—his possible lack of being able to keep his tongue out of other girls' mouths aside—because he lives for the glow of people. It energizes him.

Whereas I needed an entire week to recover after a single night out. I'd enjoy myself, absolutely, but it was afterward that I'd gladly crawl inside my shell and stay there, not leaving my apartment unless absolutely necessary. Or until my next shift arrived.

Out here on the ranch, it's all too easy to slip into the fantasy of what life would be like. Being with someone who understands what it's like... who craves space and solitude, but also wants to enjoy being alone, together.

My nostrils flare, I can't allow myself to think like that, even for a second.

But holy shit, Colt could give a girl a break. This morning I caught a glimpse of him wandering around shirtless on his way to the laundry. I don't mind that he forgets, I can't imagine it's easy for a man like him to go changing habits he's been set in for so many years.

However, it's a *lot* of rugged man to withstand being around. Especially when my pulse triples each time I catch sight of him halfway dressed.

He didn't notice me sitting in the lounge with my coffee and Kindle while I warmed up in front of the fire. And my greedy fucking eyes ate up every inch of his muscled torso.

Colt isn't super cut like those health and fitness bros with eight packs that look airbrushed. He's broad-chested, with the sexiest indentations on his stomach showing the outline of his abs... and then there's that v I want to lick, dipping below his jeans.

He's got muscles honed by years of working hard and definitely could toss a girl like me around with ease.

But he's off limits.

I don't know what happened between him and Kayce, but he obviously sees me as his son's property. I saw the same war in his eyes last night in the kitchen before he pulled away. An expression that said he feels the intensity between us too, but nothing can happen.

There is no *Colt* for me... or dreams of being his lover... or even playing the role of forbidden fruit. The kind of temptation he knows he shouldn't touch but can't help himself.

He's too honorable, and I'm too much of a good girl.

But, fuck, if I didn't wish there was another time and place for us where the invisible lines keeping us from giving in to that electric pull didn't exist.

"Feeling better today, Ollie?" I smooth over the nose of the sweetest, most docile of the horses. She's the one they use for novice riders over summer because absolutely nothing can mess with her calm. Yesterday, I noticed her favoring one leg, so I wanted to get a good look to make sure there wasn't any infection or injury to be concerned about. The farrier Colt uses has left plenty of notes from his last visit, which I've been flicking through to make sure there aren't any past issues that might indicate a more serious situation I need to keep an eye on.

Ollie simply bats her long eyelashes my way, gives a snort, and walks up and down the barn perfectly for me as I study her gait.

"Nothing to worry about, huh?" I run a hand over her shoulder. "Looks like a good night's sleep and a few extra treats this morning has got you feeling brand new."

Now that I know Ollie isn't in need of any urgent treatment, tidying the barn today is my goal, and it's physical enough that I can keep the distraction of thinking dirty thoughts about my ex-boyfriend's father at bay. While the Wi-Fi doesn't work out here —to be honest, it only works in about two spots inside the house on a good day—I've been able to take some videos on my phone of the other horses being goofy, and with any luck, the internet will be strong enough for me to upload a couple of things to my Instagram when I check in on messages from Sage later tonight.

Guilt gnaws at me that I haven't found the right way to explain my situation here. Which is one hundred percent me being caught in my own head about it all. Surely I can just casually mention that I'm working for Kayce's father without revealing my decidedly non-innocent thoughts I've been having about him?

I'm so busy getting in the groove of sweeping up that I don't notice anything behind me until I feel one of my braids lift off my back. Whipping around, I'm expecting to see Colt's dark features, only, my face falls as my eyes meet with an unfamiliar sight.

A man with short, crew cut brown hair is smiling at me with white teeth, and hungry eyes.

"What's this we have here?" His breath smells like cigarettes, and I rear back in shock.

My eyes dart around the barn, and I pull my earbuds out.

"Who are you?" And where the fuck is Colt.

"Old Colton, eh? Thought he always went out of town to find himself a hot, young piece of ass." The smug look on his face widens as he leans up against the stall. His blue eyes are icicles, and he's busy looking me up and down like a slab of meat. "Obviously, this winter, he's decided to ship in a perky young thing to bounce up and down on his cock at night."

Oh my god. This guy is crude and gross, and I feel violated after twenty seconds in his presence. He looks to be maybe thirty, and probably turns girl's heads wherever he goes. But his personality is foul. Is this one of the supposed beasts who lives up the mountain? Because he sure as shit seems like one.

"What do you want?" My grip tightens on the handle of my broom. If I really needed to, I could smack this guy in the balls with it if he tries anything. What I would give right now for cell phone reception and the ability to shoot a quick text to Colt to find out where he is or how far away he might be from the house.

"Name's Henrik. I'm just calling in for a welfare check with the snow and all. Usually, we don't worry too much about old man Wilder, but now I know there's a pretty young thing like you running around up here, I might just have to drop by more frequently." He lets out a laugh. "Make sure you're being fed right." He raises his eyebrows suggestively, and I fight the urge to gag.

Ugh. This guy is a sleaze and makes me want to go take a shower.

"I'm working the ranch this winter as an employee, and I'd be more than happy to find Mr. Wilder if you need to speak with him." I'd like to shove this broom so far up his ass, it comes out his nose. How dare he talk to me like I'm some kind of winter fuck-bunny shipped in to occupy his time.

"Well, if you're not Colton's property, then I'd love to take you out on a ride sometime. See how good you look in a saddle."

Ew. Not in a million years, jerk off.

"No, thanks."

"Aw, come on, I'll take you out to the Ridge. Show you a real good time."

"Well, I'm not interested, so if you don't want to talk to Mr. Wilder, then I'd better get on here, and I'm sure you've got other properties to carry on to with your *welfare* checks..." I jerk my head in the direction of the open barn doors.

The horses stamp, and one of them lets out a low whinny.

Even they've had enough of this guy.

"You sure, girlie? How can I help change your mind?"

"Give me one fucking reason why I shouldn't beat your skull in for harassing my staff, Pierson." Colt's growl echoes through the barn like thunder.

A flutter of butterfly wings kicks up in my stomach at the sound of his voice.

Colt easily has a head on this guy, and it's clear who would win in a scrap between them. But whoever this dickhead is, he doesn't get the message that it's time to leave.

"Just making conversation is all. This sweet little thing was about to give me her number."

"No, she fucking wasn't." Colt has put himself directly between the man and where I'm standing, and my pathetic little heart is doing skips and jumps at the way he's protecting me.

It's ok, I still have my feminist card tucked in my back pocket. Having fought, and won, plenty of battles like this on my own in the past, this sure as hell feels nice to have someone standing up for me for a change.

"In fact, she was pretty clear when she turned you down the first time, or were you too busy sucking yourself off to hear her."

My cowboy protector is bristling. I'm sure he's grown at least a foot in height.

Pierson raises both hands. "Jeez, whatever. Girls like her are probably lesbian and shit anyway."

Oh my god. If Colt doesn't kick this guy's ass, I will.

"Get the hell off my property. You want to do a welfare check in the future? Pick up the radio instead, or so help me, I'll put a bullet in both your knees."

Colt stalks after the man, making sure he's saddled on his horse and escorted well past the boundary while I hang back in the yard, watching after his broad shoulders.

When he seems satisfied the asshole is long gone, he finally comes back over to me. With eyes like a midwinter's night, tension billows off him.

"He touch you?" Colt's jaw tics furiously. Stopping a foot or so in front of where I'm hovering just outside the barn, he folds his arms and looks me over with an intensity that sucks all the air from the space between us.

My hesitation possibly just signed the man's death warrant.

Colt advances on me, and I'm hastily backing up until my spine collides with the wood exterior beside the double doors.

"Answer the fucking question, Layla."

"Not really." I can't even breathe with how murderous this man looks. "He grabbed my braid is all." I twist the end of my hair between my fingers to show him it's fine and I'm fine and suddenly I feel like the whole thing has been blown out of proportion.

"I'm ok. I've dealt with bigger creeps than him." I try to show him how easily I'd like to just laugh it off. Because it's the truth. Guys at the bars I've worked in have done much worse, attempting to grope me and try it on when they're wasted, when they think they own the bar and my body because they've been buying rounds and filling my tip jar all night.

"Anyone tries to come at you again, you tell me." Colt's fists clench and unclench as he grits his teeth, but he steps back and heads for the house. I'm left clutching my stupid little broom, and my mind is trying to catch up with what just happened.

He's mad at me, and I don't understand why.

Dinner is a silent affair.

Colt wolfs down his food in record time and yet waits for me to finish eating before he pushes his stool out. The man eats about three times as fast as me, I swear, but always sits quietly, respectfully, until I'm done. He clears up our plates, but still hasn't spoken a word since that moment outside the barn earlier.

I can't help but feel like I did something wrong today, even though I know I did everything I needed to do jobs-wise, and obviously the run-in with that creep wasn't my fault.

But even still. The silence tonight feels charged.

So when he grabs a beer and heads for the lounge without even looking at me, I admit defeat and head off to my room. At least the internet has worked long enough for me to stack my Kindle with my favorite smut, and I'm hanging out for a long hot shower.

SAGE:

> Hellooooo, my mountain goddess. Are you all good? Please confirm proof of life ASAP or I'll be forced to don snow shoes and come trek through the Montana wilderness to find your corpse.

> PS. My delicate skin will hate you forever if you make me come down there and get chapped and wind-bitten.

> > I'm alive, Sergeant.

> > Smell like horse shit, mind you.

> Oh good. I know nothing makes you happier.

> Boned any hot cowboys?

> > Who says 'boned' these days?

> Oh, I'm sorry.

> Let me grab my urban dick-tionary

> Fucked

Shagged

Rode like a bronco

...Take your pick.

eye roll emoji

Rude.

Also, suspicious.

Are you avoiding my question with your overuse of that particular emoji?

No. I haven't.

Criminal, really. Your tits deserve some lovin'.

Is your boss hot?

I'm picturing older... skillful with more than just a rope and a horse, if you know what I mean.

I SUDDENLY FIND my heart in the back of my throat. So far, I've neatly side-stepped the exact details of my snow-bound employment. Sage knows I was coming up this mountain in search of Kayce, but for whatever reason, the actual words to the effect of *hey, bestie I'm stuck here working for my ex boyfriend's insanely hot father who totally flirted with me when we first met* have yet to come out of me.

But the truth is going to come out sooner or later about this entire scenario, and as I chew my lip, it quickly becomes apparent that it will look a million times more damning if I don't tell her.

Oh, god. I'm really doing this...

Nope. Stop that right now.

> I haven't had a chance to give you all the details, but the ranch is owned by Kayce's dad.

DOTS BOUNCE ON THE SCREEN, and my thoughts race in time with the tiny fluttering icons.

> And?
>
> Points for being a property owner, business owner, and cowboy.
>
> Tri-fucking-fecta.
>
> Perfect opportunity for hot revenge sex for all the shit that douchebag has put you through.
>
> Daddy has obviously got his shit together... unlike Kayce.

> I love you, but I am not even dignifying that with a response.
>
> Off to shower.
>
> Bye, Sarge.

> YOU DIDN'T ANSWER MY QUESTION?!

I LEAVE my best friend on *read* and swipe out of our message thread. There is no stopping Sage once she's on a mission to dig for information on my love life, and I'm sensing immediate danger by letting her get a sniff of blood in the water with the circumstances I've currently found myself in.

While I might, eventually, one day tell her the whole ridiculous tale, for now, it is far better for my own sanity if I don't start entertaining conversations about Colt.

There is already far too much going on in my imagination when it comes to the off-limits cowboy in this house.

Wanton thoughts and daydreams. Certain lingering fantasies.

Holy shit, my body heats and pussy clenches at the memory of the vivid sex dream I had about him last night. My submissive side and breeding kink is alive and well, it would seem.

Blowing out a breath, I plug my phone into its charger then reach up to tug my hair out. Crossing the room while wrestling both braids loose, I untangle them with my fingers before scooping the chaos of curls back up into a top knot. Winter, tiredness, and being all out of sorts means there is no chance I can be bothered trying to wash my hair tonight, it'll have to last another day of the dry shampoo treatment.

My ensuite is pretty much an all-in-one tiled square, with a deeply inviting bath recessed into the wall at one end, and an open glass partition creating a wall to contain the shower on the other. The third wall has a toilet, vanity, and big mirror.

I've never had such a nice bathroom in my life.

On my list to ask Colt tomorrow, if he's in a talking mood, is whether or not I'm allowed to run the bath. I'm hesitant to use it without knowing his rules about conserving water during winter storms up here. Reaching into the shower, I flip the water on and quickly get undressed. The stream from the detachable head pummels my aching muscles, and I groan at how good it feels to wash off the day of sweat and horses and the run-in with Henrik slimeball Pierson.

God, no one has ever protected me the way Colt did, and I think he somehow altered my brain chemistry. I've never been attracted to the idea of being someone's possession before, but the way he guarded me and threatened that prick... *fuck*. It was super hot, and even just thinking about it again now, I can feel the slickness between my thighs. There's a tension winding low in my core. What is a girl to do in the face of so much testosterone?

Especially when no good can come of allowing these thoughts to spill over into reality. I need to keep this job, and I need to not fuck things up between him and Kayce.

I slap the shower off and get out. More than a little turned on.

Why is it so hard to stop thinking about him when I know I shouldn't? It's like my pussy has been hijacked by a cowboy twice my age, and she refuses to calm the hell down.

I wrap myself in a giant man-sized fluffy towel and pad over to my suitcase lying open on the floor. For whatever reason, I still haven't unpacked my things. I'm in limbo where instinct and past experience tells me I should be ready to hit the road at any second.

To be prepared for the moment the roads are clear and my boss decides I'm not worth the hassle of keeping around.

In spite of all my anxieties and misgivings, my room is warm and cozy, overlooking the porch and snow-covered vista that glows with a luminous white sheen. A quarter moon hangs low in the sky, casting an eerie silver glint across one side of Devil's Peak.

Slipping into my comfiest sleep shorts and soft cotton cami, I toss the covers back and go to climb into bed, realizing with a groan as my ass hits the mattress that my Kindle isn't on the bedside table. After a quick scan around the room, it hits me. I remember leaving it down in the lounge this morning.

Fuck's sake. Tilting my chin to the ceiling, a gurgled noise of frustration comes out. I'm so tired, and cannot be bothered having to get redressed just to go a few feet down the hall to the lounge.

I creep over to my door and open it a crack, listening for where Colt is in the house. But everything outside my door is dark and blanketed in a heavy silence.

He must have gone to bed while I was in the shower because I can't hear anything and none of the lights are on. So I creep quietly down to the lounge on bare feet.

When I get there, I spot my Kindle lying on the coffee table straight away and snatch it up, preparing to spin on my heel. Only, goosebumps erupt across my bare skin when it dawns on me that I'm being watched.

Looking up, I see Colt sitting in one of the large armchairs beside the glowing embers of the fire. With knees splayed wide, he fills out the leather seat like it's a throne.

His handsome features are lovingly stroked by the long shadows of the room. As he takes a long swig from his beer, my entire body clenches, all while his hooded eyes remain locked on my figure.

"You gave me a fright." My voice comes out more than a little breathy.

He shifts his knees a little wider but doesn't say anything. Just rubs his thumb along the neck of the amber bottle as he rests it on one thigh.

"Is everything ok?" The air swirls with tension. He's sitting down here with only the dark for company, and I can't help but feel like I've intruded on something.

My bare toes curl into the carpet, and instantly, I'm very, very aware of my appearance. The way these tiny shorts barely cover my ass or my pussy. How my thin-strapped cami scoops low and shows off an expanse of cleavage. The way my nipples are hard and rub against the wafer-thin fabric every time I shift my weight.

"How old are you, Layla?" His voice is deep and alluring and tortured all at once.

"Twenty-five." I hear myself say the words barely above a whisper.

He studies me in silence, and I can't move. Or maybe I don't want to. Did that please him to hear my age, or make him madder with me? Does it piss him off that I'm young in years, even though I feel like I've lived more in my two decades than most people do in a lifetime?

There's a part of me that wants to hide, because Colton Wilder is a force of nature that shouldn't be messed with. But there's a more dangerous and demanding part calling to me from the deep.

I want this man to see me.

Burnt orange embers smolder in the fireplace while Colt takes another long drink from his beer, and I feel my body ache and plead for attention.

Through the darkness he's fixated on me, arresting me with that stern gaze. He's looking at me with the kind of voracious appetite that only means one thing.

This man desires what he sees.

Would he ever cross that invisible line to take what he wants? I don't know, but one thing I'm certain of, is that the longer I stand here, the more we're both tiptoeing toward the edge of something forbidden.

My chest rises and falls, breasts feeling heavy and full as his eyes continue to roam freely, dragging across my body, leaving a trail of crackling sparks beneath my skin in their wake.

"Go to bed, Layla."

There's a warning in his voice that makes me shudder, like he can't be held accountable for what might happen if I don't obey his order.

And his words echo after me, long after I've retreated down the hall. Long after I've closed my bedroom door with my heart in my mouth and my Kindle clutched to my chest.

His burning stare is still imprinted on my skin as I lean heavily against the doorway, panting into the darkness. When I squeeze my eyes shut, I wish it was his hands and body on me instead of just his gaze.

I'd give anything for it to be so much more.

CHAPTER 9

There's a satisfying thunk and splintering noise as I bring the ax head down.

Sweat beads at my temples, even though it's below freezing, and I haul the next log to be split onto the block in front of me.

I've been at this for an hour. Nightfall is closing in, and the longer I spend here, the closer it inches toward another endless, cold night. Each time the wood gives way below the metal head, I can't help but picture it being that fucker Pierson's neck.

God-fucking-damnit, now that one of them knows Layla is here, I'm going to have them both sniffing around whenever they think I've turned my back.

Men who like to use their good looks to prey on unsuspecting victims. There's more than enough evidence of the sick shit they do to women unlucky enough to fall into their grasp. Yet, the Pierson brothers have never been charged.

The thought that he'd dared set foot up here on the fucking pretense of a welfare check makes my blood boil. What's worse is that I know he'll be back, and there's nothing I can do when those two sick fucks are so deeply embedded in every part of Crimson

Ridge, pretending to be good people, like a cancer on this fucking community.

Just like he was.

Maybe Hayes was right. Maybe I should report them for the shit they've been responsible for up here over the years. The kinds of issues, damage, and spates of vandalism that I've never been able to confidently prove who was responsible for over the years, but I've always known it was Henrik and Alton Pierson.

Yet, even though I've known... guilt has stopped me from ever seeing it through and finally doing something about it. My connection to them makes it all so goddamn complicated.

All I want to do is make amends for my grandfather's sins, but these assholes make it impossible to do so, or to move on.

I bring the ax down again and the two bits of wood fly in opposite directions, before I bend down and toss them over onto the stack beside me that has grown much larger than I need it to be today.

Part of me knows I'm hiding out here.

The worst part of me nearly wrestled free of its leash last night.

Seeing her walk in wearing next to nothing was a temptation I nearly gave into. With her curves and smooth skin and wide green eyes looking back at me as if she fucking liked what she saw. The girl doesn't know shit about me. If she did, Layla would run a mile and I'd never see another glimpse of her silky head of hair ever again.

There's a reason I've been stuck on this mountain for years on my own.

Women I come across enjoy a fuck, an orgasm, and then they move on with their lives. They take one look after the glow has worn off from the sex and decide they want more than to be stuck with someone like me.

I don't blame them.

Just as I place the next round of wood in front of me and swing the ax in the air, I hear it.

A shout. *Layla.*

"Colt." Her voice is high-pitched. Frightened.

The ax clatters to the ground as I grab my jacket and head in the direction of her voice.

"*Colt.*" She's yelling louder, swinging off the back of Peaches as I round the corner of the barn.

"Layla?" I shrug my jacket on, and my eyes are all over her, looking for injury. Her eyes are hanging out of her head, but she's moving ok, rushing toward me. That's when I notice the blood on her hands.

"Where are you hurt?" My instinct is to grab her face, but I stop myself, instead I grip Layla's shoulders as soon as I'm next to her.

The girl is trembling.

"Layla, talk to me."

"It's the herd. Some are hurt." There's tears in her eyes.

"How bad?" My mind is already running back over all the fences I checked and trying to remember if there's something that I missed.

"I don't know. There's blood, and I was trying to keep one of them from making it worse—I needed to get supplies, and I couldn't call you." Her words come out a mile a minute.

"Get the kit. Whatever you need. We'll take the truck."

She swallows, nods, then heads to grab the equipment.

As I secure Peaches, I'm trying to figure out how I've got bleeding cattle in the middle of winter when I was only just down there earlier feeding out, and everything seemed fine.

My jaw is clenched so tight I'm pretty sure I hear a pop as Layla reappears with the kit, and she tosses it all in the back tray of the truck. I've already got the ignition running, and as soon as she's in her seat I take off in a spray of gravel across the yard.

"I'm sorry—" Her fingers twist in her lap and they're coated in thick, sticky red smears.

"Not your fault."

If I hadn't spent so long splitting wood trying to get my head on straight, I would have been there.

"There's at least three of them hurt that I could see." We bump over ridges in the track as I steer us towards the paddock. It's almost dark now, the headlights bouncing over the fence below us in the dwindling light.

"You did the right thing coming to get me." My fingers tighten on the wheel.

Up ahead, I can see the shadowy outlines of the cattle, and we pull up to the gate with a skid. Layla is out of the cab before I can say a word.

As I pull the truck closer, the sweep of headlights reveals tracks of bright red in the thick layer of snow coating the ground.

Layla rushes toward where she's got three of the cattle penned together using some temporary rolled-up fencing that I keep lying around down here. At least she had the sense to keep them contained, otherwise fuck knows how long we'd be out here in the dark trying to find them.

From how much blood is lying around, it could have been fatal if we hadn't gotten to them before morning.

"I couldn't see any others, but there might be." She lifts the box with supplies out of the back of the truck behind me and I reach under the seat to grab us each a headtorch. Then I fetch the spare halter and rope I keep in the back of the truck.

"Here." I hand her one of the flashlights, and flick my own onto high beam so I can get a good look at the cattle.

The three are already lying down, which will at least make my job easier, and as I approach one of them lets out a snort followed by a low noise of protest.

"Easy, girls." I keep my voice low as I walk around the edge of the temporary pen Layla created. She's got them in a kind of half-circle, using the paddock fence on one side to keep them together.

As I squat down and adjust my light I can see the stains of copper and brighter red across the snow beneath them.

Each has what looks like a shallow gash across their flanks, just at the height of one of the fence posts. Shallow enough that it looks like a protruding nail has done the damage where they've maybe rubbed up against it, but it's hard to tell and the amount of blood is possibly making everything look worse than it is.

Of course it's suspicious they've all been injured in the same manner. My spine stiffens knowing, but not wanting to admit out loud, what the obvious explanation for this bloodstained situation is.

"I'll get the first one restrained, you separate the other two with a bit more of that fencing." I direct Layla and she's doing exactly as I ask. The first one I manage to fix the halter on and put my weight down to hobble her on the ground, doesn't put up much of a struggle. This small herd is used to being handled and being around people. They're not exactly tame, but they don't scare easily either.

Layla brings what she needs over, and quietly sets to work while I force my weight down on the heifer. She kneels in the snow and examines the laceration.

"I don't think I need to shave it. I think it just needs to be cleaned. Maybe antibiotics just to be sure." Layla digs around in the kit, searching for what she needs, but I can see her hands are shaking. Either from the cold or the shock or both.

"Do what you think is best." I trust her judgment. From what I can see it's just a small gash and while I'm still trying to figure out what caused it, that is going to have to wait until we've dealt with these animals first.

Layla works quickly, despite the cold and the darkness settling in. Our breaths fog up in the icy air and the rumbling beast beneath me lets out the occasional soft bellow.

We repeat the same process for the second animal. With Layla making speedy work of cleaning up the wound and making sure nothing is embedded that might cause further infection.

It's the last one we get to that seems to be putting up more of a fight. Once I've wrestled them beneath me, making sure they're secured, Layla starts to examine the site where the blood is oozing from and sucks in a breath.

"This one is worse than the others." She presses carefully around the edges.

"How bad?"

"She'll be ok, but needs stitches." Layla sounds calm, but I can see it's only on the surface.

"Ok."

"Colt—" She starts to falter. In the bone chilling wind here in a paddock under the cold eye of Devil's Peak, this is the last place I want her to have to be right now, but this is the reality out here and she's going to have to face it.

"Layla." I adjust my position and lean closer to her. "Get it done."

Her green eyes flicker up to mine, and the glow of our head lights illuminates the plumes of white from each of our breaths where we're hunched close together.

"I've never done this before... like this. In a proper holding pen, or chute in the daylight, yes. But not in the dark when I might fuck it up."

"Do you care about this animal, Layla?"

She breathes a little harder. "Of course I do."

"Then I know you can do it. Because you care enough to do the job properly."

"But—"

"Did I hire you for nothing? No. You're the one with the fancy vet schooling, and I'm just a cowboy who can hold this heifer down while you stitch her up. Unless you want me to go back up to the house and get my rifle and put her out of her misery."

Her face contorts, and I see her nostrils flare slightly. She reaches for the needle and suture thread, but her hands are still trembling.

Without thinking, I grab hold of her fingers in my free hand and squeeze tight. She's so fucking soft under my touch, and I almost groan at the feel of her beneath my rough hands.

"I don't want to disappoint you," she murmurs.

Little does this girl know, she could never.

"You won't. Now, just take a deep breath for me, baby."

Her eyes search mine, but she does as I say. Taking a long, shaky inhale.

"And out." She blows a white plume into the space between us.

I stroke her palm with my thumb, and then guide her hands over to the wound.

"Just focus on one stitch at a time. I'm right here, and I'm not going anywhere."

CHAPTER 10

I t's well after sundown by the time we make it back to the house. Even though it's not late, it feels like we were down in the paddock for hours.

Colt orders me to go shower and warm up. I don't fight him.

The after-effects of the adrenaline, shock, and worry have sapped my energy, and I spend a lot longer under the warm spray thawing out than I normally would.

When I get back to the kitchen, I'm surprised to see Colt is also freshly showered, and not only that but he's rustled up dinner for two from somewhere.

"Don't get too excited." He says gruffly as the steaming hot stew is slid in front of me. "Just leftovers from the freezer."

My stomach lets out a loud rumble.

"I'd have been happy with Ramen, but this smells amazing." I dig my spoon in and the taste is pretty much heaven. Colt is obviously a damn good cook because the beef is tender and seasoned to perfection.

The man across from me looks horrified.

"You don't like Ramen?" I slurp stew off my spoon.

"That's not food."

Noted. Cowboy mountain man won't be joining me for a bowl

of instant noodles any time this century. I hide my smile in my dinner and we both start to inhale our meals. Today has been a lot, and my body feels like it's been run over by a truck and trailer.

"Beer?" He offers after standing and starting to rummage inside the fridge and I nod with a mouthful.

Colt settles down with a drink for himself across the other side of the island and passes one—already opened—to me. As he leans back to take a swig with head tilted, I watch on, captivated. His salt and pepper stubble and strong throat bobs when he works down a swallow.

God, he's nice to look at.

I take a few more bites of food, and maybe it's the alcohol working fast and helping me to feel a little looser, but there's something I can't quite work out. There aren't any photos of family or a woman or anything personal in this entire place that I've seen —and I've definitely done my share of snooping when I've had the chance.

"Tell me this, Colton Wilder. Why maintain such a big place if it's just you up here lording it over Devil's Peak?" I smirk a little over the top of my beer.

He glances up at me, and doesn't exactly smile, but I see his lips twitch.

I have to shift a little in my seat because that tiny flicker in his expression makes my pussy clench.

"It's not exactly a pretty bedtime story." His tone is light, but the creases around his eyes tell me this is territory he doesn't easily venture into.

"I don't mean to pry. You don't have to share if you don't want to."

Colt runs his tongue over the front of his teeth.

"An exchange is fair." He tips the lip of the bottle, pointing the neck at me. "Answer one question for me first, Layla."

My eyebrows shoot up into my hairline. What does he want to know?

"Okayyy..." I take the bait. Apparently I have no self-control when it comes to wanting to please this man.

"I've been sitting here wondering... what does a twenty-five-year-old need to pay for so desperately, that she's rushing like a bull at a gate to finish her vet certification, and work night shifts in grungy bars on the side?" He sits back and crosses one arm across his chest, dangling the neck of his beer between thumb and forefinger with the other.

I pick at the hem of my sleeve for a moment.

He waits for me to start talking.

Blowing out a long exhale, I shift around on my stool.

"My mom had me when she was young—too young." I hesitate, ducking a glance his way and see that he's waiting for me to carry on. "I guess she felt like her youth was taken away, so spent mine chasing after what she thought she missed out on. I never met my dad, and the procession of guys she dated came and went with the seasons."

Colt is studying me quietly as I talk, his hazel eyes watch me take a big sip of my beer before I continue.

"My aunt was the one who would pick me up after school, make sure I'd eaten, run me to dance classes and weekend recitals. She would let me stay with her for weeks, sometimes months at a time. I love her so much, and it always felt like I was on holiday when I was with her. Looking back, at the time, I was too young to think anything of it, but one day, I came home from school, and the guy sitting on my mom's couch was looking at me with the same eyes he used to give her when they first met."

It's hard not to move around more in my seat under the intensity of Colt's gaze.

"That's the last day I lived with my mom."

"Your aunt took you in?"

I tuck a strand of hair behind my ear. "Evaline made sure I didn't go back there again."

This is the hard part. The bit that always makes me choke up when I try to find adequate words to explain it.

"Except, by the time I finished high school, she'd already started forgetting things. Getting muddled up easily, you know." I scratch at the label on the beer. "They called it early-onset dementia, and it took my aunt away before I knew which way was up."

Colt clears his throat, and I reluctantly meet his eyes. I don't want his pity or his charity, but I hope he understands why this is so important to me.

"You pay for her care, I take it."

My lips thin as I nod again.

The clock on the wall ticks and we both sit there for a long moment.

"Now you've heard my happy bedtime story, let's hear yours."

Now it's Colt's turn to take a long swig of his beer.

"There's not a lot to tell. My parents died in a car crash when I was a kid, too young to even remember them, and it was left up to my grandfather to take me on."

"Here at the ranch?"

Colt makes a noise of agreement.

"Grew up right here. Or *survived* growing up here, I should say."

My throat tightens as I see the tension in the jaw of the man across from me, having to revisit memories I'm presuming he'd rather leave locked away.

"He might have owned this ranch, but he was a mean son of a bitch, the kind who liked to take his anger out on whoever was closest. When I was old enough to understand why our cattle always ended up broken, I started to pick fights with him. At least that way he'd take it out on me rather than innocent animals."

Colt chews over his thoughts for a moment.

"I was fourteen when I put my first bullet through a heifer's forehead. She was due to calve anyday and so badly injured she'd never have survived."

The backs of my eyes sting. I want to crawl into his lap and hold him.

"When that man hung himself, the real devil of Devil's Peak

was finally gone. Kayce had only just been born, and I spent the day knocking down the rotten old farmhouse that used to stand on this very spot instead of going to the sick bastard's funeral."

My chest aches just listening to him. But I don't want him to stop talking. I feel like there's a chance I'm the only person in the world Colt has ever spoken to about this.

I'm unsure what kind of spell has descended on this kitchen tonight, but it's as if we're suspended, dangling out of time.

He chuckles darkly to himself over the top of his beer. "Spent nearly thirty years taking this place from a broken, run-down piece of shit, and erasing that fucker's legacy. Hopefully, one day, when I move on, this place will be sold to some savvy person who will come along and make way more money than I ever have off this ranch."

"You didn't build it for you?" I'm heartbroken for him, but at the same time I think I just fell head over heels for this man and everything he has worked so tirelessly to achieve.

Colt shakes his head. His unruly dark locks falling across his eyes make him look younger. It's only when you see the flecks of silver in his beard that it gives away his age.

"Figured this place was always going to be a tourism opportunity, not a ranch that could compete with the big boys. So I built something that could be good for that. I dunno, accommodation for rich folk who like to chopper in and prance around on horses for the weekend or some shit."

"Like a dude ranch?"

Colt shudders and scrunches his face up. "I swear if anyone calls this place *that* in my vicinity, I'll have a fucking aneurysm."

He gestures for me to pass over my empty bowl. I'm guessing our little heart-to-heart has come to a conclusion, but I pick it up before he can try to do my dishes for me. While I kind of like how easily we seem to split chores around here, tonight feels like the kind of night when we can each clear up after ourselves.

"I've got it." I flash a small smile, then duck my head.

When I cross to the other side and join him beside the counter, my attention is drawn to peer out through the dark in the direction of the cattle. His broad shoulders fill the space in front of the sink as he rinses out the containers that must have had the stew in them, as well as his own bowl.

"They'll be ok. You did an excellent job out there."

My stomach does a little somersault at the unexpected compliment. Standing beside his large frame, I can't help but be drawn in by the look of his soft t-shirt that looks like a second skin on him. My fingers itch to reach out and touch the well-worn cotton.

"Only because you talked me off the ledge... *again*." It's the truth. I wasn't sure I could do any of what I did tonight if it wasn't for his steady presence grounding me. Suturing livestock while indoors with all the equipment to hold an animal still during broad daylight is one thing. Being covered in blood and out in the snow and in pitch black is another.

His jaw tics.

My blood starts to heat, the alcohol settling comfortably in my veins.

"I like how you talk to me."

He silently scrubs at the containers in the sink. My eyes don't want to stay off the way the map of veins on the back of his hands glisten, highlighted by the water.

"Thank you for trusting me." I'm standing too close, I know I am. But he's not moving away either, and the heat between our bodies draws me in.

My thighs squeeze as that all too familiar ache starts to rise.

I know what I heard out there tonight.

Whether he meant to say it, or perhaps it just slipped out by accident in the heat of the moment, I don't know.

But I want to hear him say it again.

"I liked how you spoke to me, *tonight*."

Colt goes still.

"It must be hard up here dealing with things like that on your own." I'm being way too fucking bold, but after hearing a little of his life and the beer and the warm glow I'm coated in, surely there might be a chance he's feeling the same way I am.

His big paw reaches over to take my bowl from my hands, but I shake my head. "It's ok. Let me."

I reach into the sink beside him, and our bodies fit together side by side. He stiffens slightly, but doesn't move away. As I feel my hip press against his thigh my heart kicks into overdrive.

Suddenly, the kitchen feels like a furnace, and my pulse hammers in my throat as I watch his hands rest on the edge of the sink. He's letting me get close. Too close. His scent and heat fold around me like a blanket I want to burrow under and stay wrapped up in.

Warm water rushes over my hands as I clean off the bowl, and then turn the faucet off. Without it, the kitchen is so quiet, all I can hear is blood rushing in my ears and the faint howl of the icy wind whipping past the windows.

Colt is standing in front of the dishwasher and I angle my body toward his, still gripping onto my stupid bowl like it's the only thing stopping me from putting my hands all over this man.

"Does it get lonely up here?" My whisper sneaks out as my head tilts back and I'm consumed by his darkened gaze. His pupils are the deepest crevasse imaginable, as he looms over me.

Reaching out, he takes the dish from my hands, placing it on the bench beside my hip.

Oh my god.

There's a force drawing our bodies together that I can't fight as he shifts his weight and plants one hand on the other side of my body. Caging me in against the sink.

His eyes drop to my mouth and my chest is rising and falling faster with every second we're locked in this forbidden moment. I feel him—his power, his masculinity, his damn intoxicating scent of leather and raindrops. There's a flood of wetness between my thighs, and my underwear has surely gone up in flames.

My tongue swipes over my bottom lip.

Colt latches onto the movement with a fierce, hawk-like gaze.

Just as his jaw flexes, as he lingers with precision on that spot where my lips are parted, a burst of noise crashes through from his office just off the kitchen. The radio explodes into life, making me jump, and Colt's head whips in the direction of the intrusive sound.

That's when a familiar voice crackles down the line, making my stomach plunge through the floor.

"Yo, Dad? Are you there?" Kayce's voice is tinny but unmistakable on the other end of the radio handset.

About three things happen at once. Colt jerks away from me like he's just burned himself on a hot stove. I spin around and double over the edge of the sink, gasping for air. The world rushes in like a freight train.

Holy shit.

Holy shit.

Holy shit.

Whatever was just about to happen between us was most definitely going to happen, and I'm immediately scolding myself for being so forward.

I shouldn't have put Colt in that position.

He should have moved away.

We're both being reckless with how close we keep getting to the precipice—one that neither of us can come back from if we plunge over the edge.

Guilt thunders through me. Not because I still feel anything for Kayce. My concern is entirely for Colt. I'm flirting with him and pushing him, and that's the thanks I give the man. Someone who not only provided me with a job, solved my disaster with the finance company, and on top of all that, has given me a temporary roof over my head.

What the hell was I thinking?

I slide everything into the dishwasher and turn it on. Behind me, I hear Colt's low voice as he talks to his son over the handset. I'm guessing the vehicle Kayce has taken down to town has a linked-up radio unit like the one I've seen installed in the cab of Colt's truck.

"You've got a place to stay?"

The line crackles, and I can't quite make out Kayce's reply. When I dare to peek at where Colt is standing in his small office, I see his broad back and he's got one hand dug into his hair. He's illuminated by the glow of the small lamp, light spilling through the open doorway. With his other hand, he fists the radio handset close to his mouth.

"Road's going to be clear in about a week."

There's more muffled chatter from the other end.

I really want to know what Kayce is saying, so I carefully make my way closer and linger out of sight in the hallway with my back pressed to the wall.

"... Got something to take care of down here." My ex's voice floats out into the hall.

Colt lets out a heavy sigh. "Could have given me some fucking notice at least."

"Yeah I feel bad. Are you gonna be alright dealing with everything for another week on your own?"

There's a pause, and Colt coughs a little. "I've got help."

My heart skips a beat.

"Fuck, that's lucky. Is it Storm, or one of the other guys from down the Peak?"

Holy shit. Is he going to tell him I'm here?

"Not exactly."

Kayce lets out a laugh that makes the static go crazy. "Don't tell me you've got a chick up there?"

I clap my hand over my mouth.

"It's not like that." Colt grinds his words.

"Yeah, sure, Dad. It's about time you found someone. Though I can't imagine who would put up with your bullshit." Kayce has definitely been drinking. Even through the radio I can hear the buzz in his voice.

"Kayce—" I don't know if Colt is aware I might be able to hear their conversation or what, but he tries to cut in, only it's no use.

"Have I met her before? Is she hot?"

I think I'm going to die.

"Kayce." He snaps down the radio line. "It's Layla."

There's silence and only a faint hum of static.

"My Layla?"

No. Not *your* Layla, dickhead. I want to burst in there and scream at them both. But I'm rooted to the spot.

"What the fuck's going on, Dad?" He sounds pissed. Even though he has absolutely zero right to be. If anything I should be the one clawing his eyes out right now and demanding every cent he owes me, and now by extension, his father.

"Are you fucking my girl?" Kayce is drunk and mouthing off, and I'm stuck here in this hallway in a maze of indecision.

But Colt reacts faster than me. "It's not like that. She needed help, and I gave her a job. End of story. The kid turned up here looking for *you* the night of the snow, and her car broke down."

"So, what? You tucked her into your bed?"

"Watch yourself, son." Colt sounds like he's about to hurl the radio set at the wall.

"Then explain to me why the fuck you've got my girlfriend up there with you."

Jesus. This is a nightmare. Between the man I nearly threw myself at a few minutes ago calling me a kid, and my ex-boyfriend being a drunk, jealous asshole, I don't know what to do. Should I intervene? Would I be helping if I just try to talk to Kayce myself?

Does Colt really just see me as that? Some little girl who he's just tolerating?

"I'm not getting into this with you. Nothing weird is going on. I've got a fucking business to run, and you're not here to help me. So sue me for helping *your girl* out when you should have been here to look after her." I've heard pissed-off Colt make an appearance before, but this is on a whole other level.

There's more crackling down the line, and for a moment, I don't know if Kayce has hung up.

"Ok. Look, I fucked up, alright. But I gotta sort some shit out, and I'll be back as soon as the road is clear."

"Good." I hear Colt shuffle some papers around. "I know I've got a lot to make up for, Kayce."

"It's ok, Dad. We're cool."

There's a heavy sigh in the room next to me.

"Stay safe, alright?"

"Always do. Tell Layla I'll be there soon."

"Sure."

Is there resignation in his voice? Something indecipherable, perhaps.

I hear them start to say their goodbyes, and that's when I get the fuck out of there, making a quiet beeline to my bedroom. Hearing them talk just reinforced everything I'd tried to ignore. This is a man trying to do right by his son, and I'm in the middle messing everything up.

Colt's right. He's got a business to take care of, and I now understand a little more about the vision he's built—the hard earned legacy he's crafted here—from the ground up.

I can't be the one that comes between him and his own son, and I refuse to be a distraction.

My goal here is to get through the rest of my weeks in this job. Get my reference to send to my supervisor, and move on.

No more inappropriate midnight run-ins with Colt Wilder.

CHAPTER 11

Layla

I t's been almost a week since our near miss in the kitchen, and I've been so good.

Until today, that is.

I swear, it's like Colt knew I was feeling proud of myself for staying well away from him and keeping myself occupied like the good little ranch hand I'm here to be.

The barn has been my safe-space to spend as much time in as possible with the horses, distracting my mind that wants to wander to thoughts of the cowboy sleeping just down the hall. I've been posting videos and photos of the horses, who are funny and sweet as all hell and seem to adore having my undivided attention heaped on them. Meanwhile, Sage is doing her best to flood my inbox daily with as many *riding* related puns as possible.

At night I've perfected the art of making dinner then excusing myself to go and read before Colt has even sat down to eat.

If he's got thoughts about my disappearing acts, he's keeping them to himself.

Mind you, the man has hardly been around. So I suppose we're approaching this whole awkward tension between us in much the same way.

But now, we've taken the horses to head out to some remote

part of the property together and it's the first real time we've spent around each other since that night when I definitely flirted a little too hard with the line in the sand.

Apparently the road will be clear tomorrow, and the weather has been settled all week. The sun has been shining the last few days, which means the snow has steadily melted little by little.

"You don't say much, do you?" Colt turns in his saddle. His black cowboy hat affixed on his head making him look as dashing as ever against the crisp blue sky overhead.

I give him an arched eyebrow. This man is telling me I don't talk much? The pot is busy throwing stones at the kettle from inside his glass castle.

My silence becomes an intentionally stubborn thing. Which makes him shake his head and look away, but not before I glimpse, spot the moment a tug threatens at the corners of his lips.

Colt readjusts himself in his saddle, and I have to drag my eyes away from the way his jeans hug his ass to perfection.

He's your ex-boyfriend's father—and your boss—I remind myself for the hundredth time.

This man is so far off-limits he might as well be galloping across the surface of the moon.

Except, in my head at night there's a sordid little fantasy world where he and I are drawn together in the dark. Which is exactly where those thoughts have to remain.

"Here will do." He slows the horses to a stop and hops off. I follow suit, still a little unsure of what we're doing out here among the pine trees and banks of snow still thick around the trunks at ground level. We've finished up with mending holes in fences and checking on the perimeter at the far reaches of the ranch, and instead of heading back as I expected us to, we've ended up here.

I'm even less sure why we needed to bring his rifle for this.

Uncertainty sits like a lead weight in my stomach.

What I want to be doing is hiding in the barn, grooming the horses and listening to them munch their feed. Not be out here in the wild with a wolf I can't seem to resist no matter how hard I try.

My only line of defense has been to avoid him.

Which I certainly can't do all the way out here.

"There's a target over there." Colt points towards a shape hidden amongst the trees. When I shield my eyes and squint, I can see faded rings of paint on it, and the wooden stand is riddled with holes.

"I don't think I need to learn this." I'm stroking Peaches' neck and trying to find an excuse to head back up to the other end of the property. Far, far away from Colton Wilder.

"Yes. You do." He grunts. Starting to load the rifle.

My palms are more than a little clammy.

"Get over here." He's trudging off toward a mound in the snow.

I don't want to follow him.

"Layla."

"I'll just watch." It's not like I need to know how to use a gun anyway.

Colt fixes me with one of his death glares. "Layla." He repeats my name, and it's so full of venom, I shiver.

"Fine." Grumbling under my breath, I make my way to where he's standing.

The next thing I know is I'm on my belly, lying in the snow, and I've got a rifle in my hands while Colt stands over me. I've tried three shots, and each time, I've missed completely.

I'm hopeless.

My toes are numb.

He's going to think I'm a failure.

I drop my head and blow out a breath. "I told you. There's no point teaching me this."

Colt looks down at me with something that definitely looks like disdain.

Maybe it's better this way. Having him hate my guts is going to make it a lot easier to keep my feelings tucked away out of sight over the next few weeks until I finish working here.

"You're not even trying."

"Well, I don't need *this* particular skill in order to do my job, do I?"

Colt drops down onto his haunches and grabs my chin. Yanking me to face him, which makes me yelp. His grip is rough and demanding, and it honestly shocks me a little to feel his touch.

Sparks fly beneath my skin where he's pinching my face.

"You see that point out there, with the big trees and the rock?"

My eyes flicker to the side, in the direction he's indicating. I nod when I catch a glimpse of where he's alluding to. It looks like it would make a gorgeous scenic lookout, with a stunning spot to watch Devil's Peak from at sundown.

"Round here, that's known as the Ridge. If one of those assholes tries to tell you he wants to take you out there, you'll know he only wants one thing."

I'm struggling to see what this has to do with shooting a gun.

"Do it again." He pushes my face back towards the target.

"I can't."

Behind me, I can hear Colt's teeth grinding. I'm expecting him to storm back off toward his horse and leave me here to wallow in my feelings of inadequacy. But then the snow crunches beneath his heavy weight and the next moment he's lying beside me.

Oh, god. I can't handle having him this close. The scent that is so perfectly him captures me with the swirl of leather and masculinity.

He positions himself with his arms wrapping my body from behind.

I feel like I'm going to crawl out of my skin.

My body is a traitorous little bitch, who starts to preen and swoon and heat up as his weight shifts at my back.

Colt's mouth is so close to my ear, I can feel his breath brush the fine hairs around my face. I'm instantly a puddle. All my efforts of the past week have flown straight out the window leaving me right back there in the dark of the kitchen with him staring at my lips.

"If you're out here on your own, or if something happens to

me, I have to know you can look out for yourself, Layla." His lips graze the shell of my ear, leaving a swarm of butterflies taking flight low in my belly.

He repositions my hold on the rifle, making small adjustments to my stance. Talking me through the small details like breathing, finding my target, and remembering to breathe again.

"Find the sweet spot, and take your aim."

I line the target up. Painfully aware with every shaky breath that Colt is so close to me. Then I squeeze.

The shot goes off.

I hit the target.

"Good girl." Colt's rich voice and warm lips are right at my ear.

This man is going to be the death of me.

"I don't know what you think I need to protect myself from," I murmur. Soaking up his closeness and the way he feels lying here with me like this. As if our bodies just know intuitively how to fit together in the most natural way.

He shifts, disappearing from my side, and I wince at the loss of his heat and weight covering me.

"It isn't what... it's *who*." Colt straightens up and does that sexy thing where he runs his fingers through his hair before putting his hat back on, and then his hazel eyes hold mine.

"If anyone tries to touch you ever again, don't hesitate to use that gun on them."

I BARELY MAKE it through the rest of the afternoon in one piece.

By the time we've ridden back to the yard, every jolt and shift of the horse beneath me has stoked a fire in my core that refuses to be ignored.

My clit throbs, and I'm so turned on I hastily throw together a meal. Leaving it simmering on the stove, I scribble a note letting

Colt know to help himself when he comes in from wherever he's disappeared off to on the ranch.

I can't be around him tonight.

The way he pressed himself against me and got so close was like he purposely wanted to push me just to prove a point.

It was as if he wanted to punish me in some way. Or put me through a test.

Lo and behold, I'm a slut for my ex's father, and I failed that class. Miserably.

Having a shower and hiding out in my bedroom seems like the only options left for me at this stage. I run the water to let it heat. Huffing and yanking at my jeans, socks and sweater, I strip down in the bathroom as steam begins to swirl.

Grumbling to myself, I kick all the offending clothes to land in a heap in the corner.

My entire body feels like a raw nerve ending.

As I step beneath the sluicing water, I let out a shuddering sigh. The thudding on my skin has my eyes dropping closed and I just stand there letting it wash over me from head to toe. I should probably be doing my usual hair care routine, or exfoliating thanks to the dry-ass winter climate, or making sure to hurry up and not spend too long in here.

But right now, I can't bring myself to do anything because all I see is his face.

There's nothing but the lingering scent and heat of him damn near imprinted in my brain. Even though there is no possible way that I could be detecting his presence, it still feels like he's right here beside me.

Seeping through every crack in my defenses and infiltrating my sanity.

I'm a fucking mess.

My eyes flutter open and I grab a handful of body wash from the pump dispenser. Being more than a little forceful with the way I slam down on the top. Why, of all things, did he have to insist on teaching me to shoot a gun? Why would he demand I learn how to do that and act like he was studying me for weaknesses the whole time?

It feels like he's just trying to find a reason to kick me off his mountain or something.

To prove that I really am just a waste of space and a girl who needs to be sent packing. Worse still, on top of all that tumultuous emotion, is that he views me as belonging to Kayce.

Trying to prevent my mind from imagining what he's doing right now is impossible. Is he in his own bedroom, doing the same as I am? Would he dare come and confront me and ask me why I've snuck off without talking tonight.

Would Colton Wilder walk into this shower and take advantage of the fact he has a young woman under his roof?

Oh, god. Just the thought of that makes my thighs clench and the pulse in my clit intensifies. All of a sudden, I hear it. I hear the sound of the door click, and the brief draft of cool air hits my skin as someone—him—enters the bathroom.

There's a moment when I spin around, wide-eyed and ask him what he's doing in here...

But that tiny, frail protest is eaten up when he advances on me. Closing in with his bulk and his strength, he's got me trapped between his body and the wall.

One hand shoots out to brace against the tiles in front of me, and the tumbling roll of water from the shower flows over my front. My nipples are hard and sensitive as the shower teases each tight bud.

His hands are on me. At my back, he's solid, immovable, leaning over me and roaming those rough palms down to seek out that hidden space. Fondling the soft swell between my thighs.

My fingers dip down, as I lean up against the tiles. Screwing my eyes shut, I feel the slippery wetness that has been building all day in his presence.

We both know we shouldn't be in here like this. He hasn't said a word, because he knows this is crossing a line. One that we absolutely cannot step over.

That's when, just as my middle finger presses forward, parting my pussy lips, sliding over my clit, I hear his voice, rumbling in my ear. "No one needs to know."

The roar of blood fills my awareness, and my nails scratch against the wall.

A whimper falls from my lips as I work my finger to rub firm circles over the bundle of nerves.

"Shhh. That's it. This is just our little secret." I hear Colt's voice and imagine it's his thick finger playing with my soaking wet pussy.

Heat floods me from head to toe and has absolutely nothing to do with the water pouring down. I'm teetering on the brink as I bite down on my lip. Trying to be the good girl for him that he wants. He's coaxing me to be quiet for him. Not to let anyone hear that he's in my shower with me, getting me off.

My breathing grows more and more labored, and my forehead drops against the smooth surface of the tiles. A quiver builds in my thighs as I feel the wave cresting. My finger rubs frantically, circling my clit in just the way I know is going to get me there.

God, the ache is exquisite and unbearable.

I need to get there.

Right. Fucking. Now.

Bright sparks flood behind my eyes and I feel the moment everything clenches, chased by the wave breaking over me. Silent gasps, with my mouth hanging open accompany the slow, circling touch as I continue to work over the swollen bud. Drawing out the rolling pleasure.

All the while, the ghost of the man hovering over me stays there.

But when I open my eyes, it's just me in this lonely shower.

I'm alone.

And I hate that I can't do anything about it.

CHAPTER 12

There's a special place in hell reserved just for men like me. Someone who should know better than to fuck his fist every night thinking about the hot young cunt just down the hallway.

The girl who belongs to my son.

Now, here I am, trapped in the confines of my truck cab as we make our way down the mountain for the first time since Layla barged into my life two weeks ago.

Her busted car is hitched on a trailer so we can drop it at the mechanic in town, and it's going to be a massive day of picking up all the supplies we'll need.

The road is likely to be cleared long enough to get everything done, but there's no telling when the next storm front might move in.

Besides, at this time of year, the road to Devil's Peak lives up to its name. Conditions are less than ideal after a heavy snowstorm, and there's always the risk of rockfall or slips with trees coming down.

My usual rule at this time of year is that it's safer to stay put and I don't intend to hang around down here in town any longer than I need to.

At least having two of us to get everything done will make it a quicker ordeal than usual. Thank fuck, because it's not like my own damn kid is going to make himself useful, from what I can tell. I haven't heard from him since the night he called up on the radio. I'm going to presume he'll drag his sorry ass up the mountain once he's sobered up. We'll probably get back tonight and find him propped up on the couch.

I can't say I've missed not having to deal with his crap lying around. Layla is like a mouse, I hardly notice her at times, even more so since she's hidden out in her room all week.

She says she's got a good book, but I know she's avoiding me.

Which has been a blessing and torture all at the same time.

Things got way too close for comfort that night, when all I wanted to do was drag her into my bed.

So now I'm just the fucking idiot who can't stop thinking about shit I have no right to. The squeeze of her tight little pussy wrapping around my cock as I pump her full. Watching my seed spill out of her. Hearing her breathy moans when I suck on her perfect tits.

Fuck, definitely straight to hell. I scrub my hand over my mouth.

This girl is a walking temptation for me, and I'm dreading the thought of what tomorrow's bonfire is going to be like. It's why I couldn't put off teaching her to fire a gun any longer. If there's going to be any hope of her surviving the next six weeks up here when I can't keep an eye on the girl every minute of the day, she's going to have to be able to deal with any jerk-offs who come sniffing around. The Pierson brothers are my biggest concern.

Something tells me they're not going to stop until they add Layla to their trophy collection of unsuspecting victims.

"Where to first, cowboy?" Layla smiles across the cab at me as we reach the outskirts of town. Her brightness only amplifies the scowl I'm wearing.

She's a ray of fucking sunshine, and I'm the thundercloud about to unleash all hell at any moment. My temper is already frayed just coming down here.

The place is full of vehicles and noise and people.

It's exhausting, and I can't be fucked dealing with idiots.

"I'll drop you at the store while I unhitch your car round at the mechanic's."

"You don't need me to come? I mean, it is my car, after all."

No. I really, really don't need those grease monkeys leering at her ass or trying to chat her up in front of me.

"You start getting all the things on that list. It'll be quicker if we split up."

She twists her lips and studies the hardware supplies we need to collect. "What if I don't know what something is?"

"You're a smart girl, aren't you?"

That makes her cheeks turn a little pink, and she looks like a fucking wet dream whenever I compliment her. Christ, I must be sick because I keep doing this to myself.

Right now, she's in the passenger seat of my truck, and all I want to do is drag her into my lap and unzip her jeans.

My cock twitches, and I've never been more relieved to pull up outside the hardware store in my life.

"I'll be back soon as I unload the trailer. Just grab a cart and start loading, anything you can't find I'll help with when I join you."

"Got it." She bites her lip and slips out the door.

As she rounds the hood of the truck, I watch the way her ass fills those high-cut jeans to perfection, and the cropped sweater she's got on skims the waistband showing off all her curves before she shrugs into her coat.

Fuck.

I roll my window down. "Layla," I call after her, and she spins around.

"Did I forget something?" She frowns and slips her phone into her back pocket.

Shit. I absolutely did not think this through, but I'm sure as hell not going to let her walk in there like that.

"Come here." I hop out the door quickly and look down at her, before casting a quick glance up and down the empty sidewalk.

"You'll need this." I take my hat off and drop it on her head. It's a little big for her, and even though she looks gorgeous in anything, fuck me, the sight of her wearing my jet-black hat sends a rush of blood to my dick.

She reaches up to touch the brim, readjusting it slightly on her head, and her green eyes sparkle.

Which is why I don't even bother trying to explain why I just did what I did, yet still hop back in the cab feeling like a fucking king.

Even if she's not my girl, I can at least lay a claim on her so no asshole around town dares to look twice her way.

Turns out, having two people to tackle the list of supplies and picking up hardware and groceries makes it a fucking breeze. Especially when that person is the girl beside me loading the last of the bags and boxes into the truck.

We're done a good couple of hours earlier than I expected, and while the sun has already dipped behind Crimson Ridge, the forecast for tonight is clear. It should stay above freezing, too, which means the road will be fine for my truck to get back up the mountain.

Laughter and a couple of squeals pierce the fading light. Layla glances up as a group of young girls spill out of a car down the street and file into the bar.

The Loaded Hog is the only place in town to get a meal and a drink, and from the looks of it, business is doing well tonight.

I shove my hand through my hair. Of course, it's a Saturday.

This is the kind of shit girls her age want to be doing. Not loading horse feed and wire into the back of my truck after dark.

Not having me work her to the bone seven days a week.

"You want to go in?" I nod in the direction of the music and lights twinkling from the beer garden out front.

Layla looks over and then back at me, shaking her head the way she does.

"No, we can get back."

I lean up against the truck.

"Don't you want to go out with people your own age? You know, to enjoy a drink or something?" What am I even offering? To drop her here and come back and pick her up like I'm her chaperone or some shit?

She worries her bottom lip. "God, no. I've been there and done that. I've always worked in bars since my early teens. There was always an after-after party to go to where I made enough bad decisions for one lifetime. That was how I met Kayce." Her eyes fall and she sounds a little self-conscious to even bring his name up.

My jaw clenches at the reminder of their connection.

"That night was probably the last time I went out, actually. The old crowd I used to run with convinced me to go with them to someone's stupid birthday party, for old time's sake, and then one too many shots later..." She stops abruptly there.

Which is fucking fine by me, because hearing about how the girl I currently cannot stop imagining in my bed, fell into the arms of my son, is hideous.

And is probably the exact reason I decide to try and erase that image, by suggesting the worst idea possible.

"Well, I'm starved and there's no way I'm waiting on cooking dinner when we get home." I lock the truck and start heading for the bar, leaving her to have to jog behind me just to catch up.

"Don't we need to go... the roads being icy and all that?" She jerks her thumb in the direction of Devil's Peak.

"Not tonight. It'll be fine." I hold the door open for her and a flood of music and raucous chatter mixed with the sour tinge of beer greets us.

"You're sure?" She looks curious but wary, hesitancy in her body language.

That's when it registers and can't help but feel like a dick. This girl is probably counting every dollar, and here I am forcing her into a bar when she probably doesn't even want to spend an extra dime until she's got her car fixed.

"Get inside. I'm paying."

Her lips tip up, and she ducks under my arm, but then turns around, almost bumping into me.

"Wait, here." She tugs my hat off. "I'm sorry, I forgot I had it on all day."

I fix her with a stern look. If there's any place she needs to be wearing that, it's inside this bar. Every part of me demands to sit it right back on her silky copper curls and order her to leave it on. But instead, I fist it with a grunt. Because the words I want to say and what I'm actually allowed to say aren't fucking compatible.

I don't wait to see the bemused look she gives me. Instead, I grab her by the wrist and tug her behind my back, heading straight for the safety of the booths. It's busy, but not too crushed yet since the night is still young. Fortunately, I don't spot anyone I know other than a few vaguely familiar faces. But that's the added bonus of life up the mountain, I keep to myself and it suits me just fine.

At least I won't have to face introducing her to the likes of Storm or any of the Hayes brothers. Those pretty motherfuckers.

Layla is giving me an odd look as I reluctantly let go of her arm, gesturing to slide into the booth. I take up the other side. Opposite each other, seems good in theory, but also makes it damn near impossible not to stare at her.

She keeps whatever it is she's thinking to herself.

There's a group of young bucks around a bar leaner nearby and I can already tell they're looking at her. She's fresh meat and easily the prettiest thing any of them will have seen since winter began.

Two minutes ago, this girl was wearing my hat. My eyes drop to where it sits on the empty length of the booth seat beside my thigh. Clearly, letting her take the damn thing off was a mistake because these fresh-faced cowpokes can't stop staring her way.

Maybe this was a stupid goddamn idea after all.

There are already menus on the table and after a few moments a server comes over, who must be all of eighteen with bleached curls and bright red lipstick.

"What can I get you?" The girl eyes Layla with open curiosity before giving me a look that lingers a little too long.

"You'll know what's good here... can you order for me?" Layla's green eyes meet mine, and she pushes her menu my way.

I don't know what fucking caveman part of my brain lights up at that request, but it feels damn good. Like she trusts my judgment or some shit.

Once I've ordered and food eventually arrives, we've both got burgers and fries, and I've got a beer in hand. Layla's been quiet, but she seems happy to people-watch while we sit here and finish our meal. I suppose I should be better at talking, but the music has gotten louder the longer we've sat down and more bodies have arrived, filling the floor. Some are dancing and it's turned into a Saturday night feel.

Do I even fucking remember the last time I did anything like this?

Being twenty-something years old feels like a lifetime ago.

"I can't help but notice, it looks like you're planning for a party, Mr. Wilder." The girl across from me rolls her lips together.

Fuck, it's impossible not to stare at her mouth.

"How so?" Clearing my throat, I shift my weight.

"Well, that's an awful lot of BBQ for me to try and eat on my own." Her head cocks to one side, green eyes sliding up to meet mine briefly, before flitting away.

Oh, right. The bonfire.

"Got some guys coming up to the ranch tomorrow."

"Really?"

This isn't a conversation I'm prepared to have. Every year when I host this, it's just me up that mountain. Thinking about what all those cocky sons of bitches are going to get ideas about when they get one glimpse of her green eyes, her pretty mouth...

Christ. My teeth clench and I fist my hat.

"I'll go settle up." Sliding out of the booth, my every concern for what lies ahead tomorrow is confirmed. I immediately feel the room full of eyes land on Layla as she slips out and follows behind me. My fingers itch to grab hold of her, to feel the soft underside of her wrist beneath my callouses again, but once earlier was risky enough to set tongues wagging around this place.

Just as I'm digging my wallet out, a voice slides up alongside my shoulder.

"Long time, no see, handsome."

CHAPTER 13

Layla

At the sound of the female voice ahead of me, I glance up from my phone. I'd been scrolling through a few of the comments left on my latest video of me and Peaches from the other day in the barn. It's fun posting the horses, and I've always liked sharing a bit of a diary of my work with animals across my different vet placements.

A long time ago, I'd probably have sent a quick check-in text to my mom in a moment like this, not that she ever used to reply to them, but after going full *no contact* when I hit my twenties, it has honestly made a world of difference to my mental health.

Sad. But it's true.

I can see notifications from Sage, and there are a handful of comments on my latest photos on my Instagram I managed to upload when the internet was reasonably solid last night.

One girl has asked where the ranch was and just as I'm in the middle of typing a reply to let her know where Devil's Peak Ranch is located, that's when the voice distracts me.

Colt had been all sorts of brooding and quiet during our meal, even though it was his idea to come here and eat in the first place. Not to mention how abruptly he avoided my question about why we'd just loaded his truck with enough BBQ meat to feed an army. So, when he said he'd go settle the bill, I was kind of relieved.

Too much time spent sitting two feet away from Colt Wilder is enough to have my ovaries misbehaving like little sluts.

I also cannot understand why he keeps insisting I wear his hat today.

There are rules about cowboy's hats and the fact my ex-boyfriend's father gave me his... well, I can't let myself read too much into it. My horny mind is already up to no good.

Wear the hat, ride the cowboy, and all that.

But then again, it carries his scent, and I feel like I've been harboring a naughty little secret around town this entire day. That I'm the girl wearing this cowboy's hat even though he's absolutely off-limits.

Does he not know? I mean, he is kind of a hermit and doesn't use the internet or social media...

However, that train of thought is derailed by the urge to claw the eyes out of the woman who currently has her tits shoved in his face. She's not a lot older than me, but must be at least in her early thirties, and everything about her screams that this woman is ready to walk out of here with a man on her arm tonight.

She's got an amazing figure, and that body-con dress wrapped around her shows off every flawless inch. Olympic volleyball players have got nothing on this woman. Tall, statuesque, leggy. Absolutely everything I am not.

I'm busy trying to watch Colt's reaction to the six-foot model fawning all over him in a way that is far too friendly to have just met five seconds ago, while also wanting to vanish into the crowd like smoke.

I have no right to be jealous.

He's my ex's father for Christ's sake. My boss.

If anything, I should be over the moon for him at the prospect of meeting someone here tonight.

And that's when it slams into me.

Is that the whole reason we're here? Why he was so insistent about coming to have a meal before leaving town in the first place? It feels like a Rubix cube has started to slot various matching colored pieces together in my mind... oh, my god. He was planning to meet up with a woman while the roads were clear and I've been so caught up in my obsession with him that I couldn't even see it.

Before I know what I'm doing, I spin on my heel.

Right into the broad chest of a tanned, dark-eyed, cool drink of water.

There's no denying this guy is very nice to look at. But he is certainly not the cowboy I want to be in the arms of, so I make a polite face and try to excuse myself past him.

"I've just spent half an hour trying to work up the courage to ask you if you'd like a dance." He flashes a dimpled smile at me.

My eyes flit sideways to find Colt still waiting to pay. The woman is still talking to him, and the line of the bodies between him and the bar is thick. He's going to be there for a while.

"Have you now?" I tuck my phone into the back pocket of my jeans and give him a look up and down.

Maybe I'm feeling petty. But if Colt came here to chat up women, then why the hell can't I say yes to a dance?

"Did I ruin my chances by waiting too long, or did I completely fuck up by not waiting long enough?"

Oh, he's cute enough alright. Pretty close to my age from what I can tell, maybe a year or two older. His clean-shaven, perfect jawline look might make some girls go all whimpery, and the cologne he wears is pleasant, but it still doesn't do anything for me.

"How about you let me decide after a dance." I give him a small smile, not trying to be flirty or coy, but going for a strong, *friendly* kind of vibe. This isn't going to lead to anything, but a dance might help take my mind off worrying about whether I'm going to spend tonight listening to that woman scream Colt's name as he fucks her brains out just down the hall.

"Sounds fair. But take a shot with me first?" He winks and plucks a glass filled with clear liquid off the leaner beside us.

ELLIOTT ROSE

Shooting my more than a little jealous gaze back to Colt, all I can see is the woman's hand placed on his arm. That's the final push I need to be a whole lot of reckless for once. I toss the shot, and reach for another. Chasing the burn straight down with a second.

"Atta girl." The guy laughs as I cough, and my eyes water.

Holy crap. I literally did the one thing in all my years bartending I never usually do. *No accepting drinks from unknown men.*

Fuck it. Maybe having my memory obliterated tonight might be a nice relief from all this longing for the man I simply cannot have. Colt is on the other side of the room. It's not like this young cowboy can cart me off while comatose and draped over one shoulder without his noticing.

Do I want to dance? Do I want to get drunk? I don't even know.

Before I can change my mind about the proposition of a dance, he's got a firm hand around my waist and one of my hands wrapped in his warm palm. We're moving among the other couples all dancing to the country music blaring and I can't help but feel my skin prickling.

Is he watching me?

My dance partner is pretty good and I'm kind of enjoying this little opportunity to focus on something other than money and work and not fantasizing about my boss slash ex's dad. But the sensation only intensifies the longer the song goes on, and as we turn, I feel the air rush out of my lungs.

Colt's eyes are possessive, watching me from the same spot I left him, and I can see that he's in the process of shoving his card back into his wallet. If he had a shotgun hidden over there, I wouldn't be surprised.

Fucking hell, I'm single. It's like I have to keep reminding myself that I'm not doing anything wrong. I'm allowed to dance with someone, and there's nothing preventing me from saying yes to this guy.

But his hands don't feel right on my body.

126

His scent is pleasant, but it doesn't cause a mad fluttering in my chest like I get whenever I'm encased in the rich scent of rain and leather belonging to the man currently committing murder with his eyes.

The song peaks and winds to a close and the vodka hums sweetly beneath my skin. I'm pretty sure I hear the guy with his hands around my waist ask if I'd like to go grab a drink with him at the bar, but I don't even get a chance to put words together.

Colt grabs me by the hip, and looks like he's about to smack the other man in the mouth. As he hauls me out of the guy's reach, his expression is furious.

"That's enough. We're fucking leaving."

Propelling me through the crowd, his bark is at my back, and I have to fight the urge to laugh out loud at the irony.

The attitude of Colton Wilder is something else. Manhandling me, like I'm some kind of disobedient dog.

My fists clench, and I'm too busy calculating the odds of me being able to successfully connect my fist with his jaw to notice anything else as we leave the bar.

CHAPTER 14

Layla

I'm tipsy, exhausted, and pissed off. Better yet, there's a man-sized bullmastiff beside me who looks set to snap the steering wheel in two.

While my fists are balled in my lap, I've run through a mental checklist of every scathing insult I can imagine hurling at the man occupying the driver's seat.

The silence between us is as gritty as the rough road beneath our tires for the entire trip back up Devil's Peak.

Colt slams us to a halt when we arrive in the yard, leaving the headlights on so that we can unload the perishable supplies. I'm really fucking hoping he doesn't intend on forcing me to get all the hardware and other crap out of the back of the truck while it's cold and dark.

But I wouldn't put it past him, in his current mood.

Colton Wilder: alpha asshole. He's acting like I'm the problem here, as if I'm running around inviting attention left, right, and center. When all I want is for one single shred of it from him.

Although, I'm so angry with him for embarrassing me like that, I'll gladly go another week without seeing him. Hell, he can spend the next six weeks out of my sight for all that I care.

"Kayce." He bellows as he carries a box of groceries through the back door.

Oh, fuck.

Between the long day, and the shots, I had totally forgotten that Kayce was coming back up the mountain today.

Well, that's going to make it extremely fucking easy to steer clear of Colt. Even though I don't want to have to spend time with my douchebag ex, he'll be a good buffer between us for my remaining weeks here.

As I reach in and drag out the final box containing the fresh produce we picked up today, I glance around the empty yard. It's only Colt's truck that I can see parked out here, and I furrow my brow trying to put my finger on what looks out of place with this scene.

If Kayce was back, he'd have a vehicle here... wouldn't he?

I make my way inside and I can hear Colt crashing around inside his tiny office. The box he carried in has been dumped on the island in the kitchen, so I roll my eyes and start putting things away in the fridge and pantry. He obviously expects me to do this part, I guess since I'm the one who insisted on doing the majority of cooking for us these days anyway.

He can go back out in the cold and unload whatever else he thinks needs taken care of tonight.

I'm done.

Ready for this day to be over and to crawl into my big, lonely bed.

Colt is still in his office, and I glance at the stack of supplies, waiting to be put away in the kitchen.

Whatever. He wants to hide out there tonight? I'll get this job done and be gone to bed any minute.

I run my fingers through my hair a couple of times to shake it loose, along with an attempt to dislodge all memories of just how damn good it felt to wear his hat earlier and get back to storing the groceries.

While I'm in here, I hear Colt head outside and turn off the truck, before he stomps back in, barging through the kitchen without looking at me. I nearly have to jump out of his way as he reaches up into one of the high cupboards and drags down a bottle of whiskey. He roughly splashes some into a glass, picks it up, but then slams it back down on the bench. Without even touching the damn thing, or taking a sip, Colt disappears again, empty-handed.

Jesus. This man is as bull-headed and temperamental as they come.

My nostrils flare.

It's not often that I lose my temper, but right now, Colt is acting more like a four-year-old than a man in his forties. Not that I know for certain how old he is, but I'm guessing he's somewhere around that age—having pieced together Kayce's birthdate and knowing the two of us were born in the same year—I can only assume that Colt must have been pretty young himself, maybe seventeen, eighteen at the most, by the time his son came along.

Which is what spurs me on to do the most thoroughly passive-aggressive tidy-up of this kitchen it has probably ever seen. Including tipping out his untouched drink abandoned on the counter. By the time I'm finished, the fridge has been cleaned, there's not a single dish left unwashed, and every surface has been polished.

I'll earn every fucking dollar of my paycheck, and when I'm gone, this man will never have to worry about seeing me again.

When I flip the lights off in the kitchen, I see the glow of the fire illuminating the lounge. Of course, Colt is in there, sitting with his head lowered and his forearms resting over his knees in what must be his favorite night-time-brooding chair.

I curse my body for the way it remembers how he looked at me the last time I crept in here late at night.

"Kayce isn't here." He says, talking to the floor but aiming his words at me. There's an ugly sneer in his voice.

Logically, I knew that. It was pretty obvious, but I had been too busy rage-cleaning to bother looking around for his drunken ass. He's not who I want to be seeing.

"He's not coming back anytime soon, Layla. Sent a message to say he's got some things to take care of in town."

"Fine," I bite out. At this point, I'm tired and beyond caring. The money shit with Kayce isn't time-urgent, it's really his father he owes it to now anyway.

"Thought you'd want to know." Colt tilts his head up to look at me. There's a curl to his top lip, like he's waiting for some kind of reaction.

"Ok." I shrug. Ignoring the way his dark hair falls across his eyes.

"Guessing you want to go back down there." He narrows his eyes. "To him."

Oh, for fuck's sake. We're back on this bullshit again?

That puts a fire under me. I cross the open plan space and get right up close, folding my arms. "Like I told you. There's nothing between me and Kayce. I'm not his girl. I'm not his property. What I *am* is someone who is here to do the job I was hired for. So I'd really appreciate it if you quit jumping to conclusions about me and my life."

My pulse thunders in my ears.

Colt cracks his knuckles as he looks up at me.

I realize I'm almost standing between his knees, but I'm not backing down. He's got to understand this once and for all, that I'm not Kayce's girl and I'm not going to be made to feel like it's my fault every time another man looks at me.

"He says otherwise. Says you're his." There's a warning and an ugly snarl in his voice.

"Well, I hate to say it, since he's your son and all, but he's an idiot, and he's probably got about ten girls he calls *his*. I'm sure as hell not one of them."

The man in front of me is wound so tight, I think something in his jaw is going to break.

"That guy with his hands all over you at the bar sure as hell thought you were his."

I roll my eyes. A burning log lets out a loud pop as we remain locked in this standoff.

"No more than that woman wanted you to be hers. She seemed awfully friendly."

Colt launches out of his seat and I have to crane my neck just to hold his fierce stare. I'm frozen, and he's impossibly close. His scent washes over me, and a tingling sensation spreads right through to my fingertips.

"I don't give a fuck about random women who try to talk to me in a bar, Layla."

He looms over me, and oh, god. My core tightens at the way he says my name. The insinuation is right there, screaming loud and clear into the silence of the darkened room.

He doesn't care about receiving attention from a woman in a bar, because there's someone else he *does* want it from.

"Kayce is my son." His voice is a strangled whisper.

There's a wild fluttering in my throat where my pulse should be. Every inch of skin beneath my sweater and my jeans feels electrified.

"I'm supposed to do right by him." He pauses, and his eyes drop to my mouth. "I'm trying my fucking best to do right by him."

"You are." My throat is so damn tight, and I feel the way his eyes bore into me. Warmth seeps low in my belly and my clit throbs.

"Then tell me why every night is a battle, Layla. Tell me why I have to damn near lock my own door."

"Why would you—"

His gritty noise cuts me off. "Because I'm in so much trouble when it comes to you. Tell me why the fuck I'm spending every night talking myself out of visiting the bedroom just down the hall of the most gorgeous woman I've ever laid eyes on, just to see how she tastes."

My breathing is heavy and shallow as my chest heaves. Those

shots from earlier are still making themselves known in my veins. "Is that my lips, or somewhere else, cowboy?"

Colt lets out a groan mixed with a growl, and my breathy words are hardly out of me before his hand dives into my hair.

"Fuck it."

His mouth crashes against mine.

Oh, my god...

My pulse races up the back of my throat as he sinks into me, consuming my mouth, with his tongue swirling heat right through my body. He's so overpowering, as his hand slips into my curls and the other fists the waistband of my jeans to hold me steady. Warmth pools low at the junction of my thighs. It's all I can do to moan as I'm kissing him back before I even have a chance to realize I've made the conscious decision to do so.

Holy fuck.

Colt tastes like the crisp night air and glow of the fire rolled into one. I can't breathe as he holds me against him, and everything feels so fucking good. His body is so solid and powerful pressing against me.

I want more. I *need* more.

My body is so damn hungry for his, I want his mouth on me. To taste me everywhere like he threatened to. I want him to own me and keep me in his bed, and I don't want to resurface, ever.

"Fuck. Layla. I can't stop this. I can't fucking fight it," he says the words against my mouth, like it's paining him, before slipping his tongue past the seam of my lips again. The stubble of his beard drags across my skin, and I can feel the slickness of my pussy soaking my panties.

"Tell me to stop." He kisses and nibbles my bottom lip, and I whimper with each gentle tug.

"Please don't." I cling to his strong forearms. Letting out a tiny gasp when his grip on my hair tightens against my scalp.

The hand he's been using to hold me by my hip now slides to the front of my jeans. I moan into his mouth with a pleading noise as he pops the button on my fly. Keeping my bottom lip tugged between his teeth, he yanks the material open. My spine bows under the force, and my core clenches in anticipation.

Colt spins me around so that my back is against his torso, and his hot mouth sucks down on the sensitive spot right behind my ear.

"Oh, god." I'm moaning at how good it is to finally have his lips and hands and body on me. All I can do is arch my neck to give him more access, and he works the zipper of my fly down. The metallic noise sends a flurry of goosebumps across my skin, and my nipples are hardened points rubbing against the lace of my bra beneath my sweater.

He runs his teeth across the curve of my shoulder, licking and sucking, and biting a dizzying path. The rigid length of his erection rubs up against me through his jeans. The feel of him is too much, too spellbinding, and nowhere near fucking enough all at the same time.

"Jesus. Fuck." His hand shoves down the front of my jeans, and his fingers graze the spot just over my clit, pressing against me through the drenched, silky material of my panties.

"You're so fucking wet." Colt sounds angry. His mouth is hot at my ear, and he starts to rub me over the soaked fabric. My breath falters while he keeps massaging my pussy, and sucks my earlobe into his mouth.

His other hand is hungry, sliding up inside my sweater, blazing a trail across each inch of my bare skin he touches for the first time before grabbing a handful of my aching breast. Kneading and squeezing and pinching my tightly furled nipple.

"Please. Don't stop." I'm begging and whimpering as he teases me, feeling like I'm going to explode. The ache is unbearable, and my hips start chasing his touch in search of relief.

I'm so high on this man right now, I just want everything and I want it immediately.

"Touch me." *Properly*. Silently, I'm willing him to cross that forbidden line for us. To slip inside my panties and let me feel the roughness of his fingers sink against the most intimate part of me, like I've been craving for this man to do ever since I first laid eyes on him.

Colt grinds against my lower back. His cock is rigid and thrusts against me as he grips and rubs the fabric covering that tiny bundle of nerves. The way he's expertly massaging my swollen, needy bud has me melting in his arms.

"This is all for me?" He grunts against my neck. I feel his fingers slide down further, hard and low inside my jeans, cupping the drenched material against my entrance.

I whimper and nod. "All for you. *Only you*."

Colt curses. In that moment, it's like something shifts inside him. It's as if reality bursts through the front door with a flurry of ice coating the two of us, and he tears himself away. Yanking his hand out, he pushes himself off. Backing away from me while panting.

Meanwhile, I'm left with a chill sweeping through me right down to my toes.

"*Fuck*." When I turn to face him, one hand is shoved in his hair, and his wild eyes sear into me with longing. "No. We can't do this."

I take a step nearer, but he scrubs his other hand down over his mouth and shakes his head. Warning me not to come closer.

"Why not?"

When his desperate stare meets mine, Colt's features show the strain of everything about our circumstances.

The lines in his face show the intricate mess of unwritten rules we just bulldozed through, and shouldn't have.

"I'm sorry. Is it me? Something I—" Faltering a little, words abandon me. Maybe I'm the problem here. Perhaps I'm not what he wants after all.

That brings Colt rushing back to me, at least. Fisting the hem of my sweater, it's like he can't bring himself to risk touching me again, but can't fully let go either.

"Look at you, baby." He lets out a low growl. "Jesus Christ. The things I want to do to you."

My cheeks are flushed and my lips still tingle from the force of his kisses. The scratch of his beard feels as though it has imprinted itself, indelibly left a mark on my memory. In the flicker of the low flames I see the creases deepen around his hooded eyes. My fingers itch to reach out and stroke those fine lines, to press at them in an effort to smooth them away. To maybe be that person who can help ease the burden of what he carries alone.

"But we shouldn't." My eyelids squeeze shut. This cannot be happening. It's so fucking unfair I want to run out into the frozen night, drop to my knees, and scream until my lungs burn.

"But we can't," he echoes.

I feel his knuckle tilt my chin up, and the pad of his thumb rubs over my puffy bottom lip.

"Layla... look at me." His voice is low as he speaks my name. When I open my eyes, all I see through my damp lashes is his own battle raging beneath the surface. That sight makes it worse. Makes it so much more fucking unbearable to know that he wants this as desperately as I do.

"You're perfect and beautiful, but right now, I need you to do as I say, baby."

I hate how much I love hearing him call me that.

"Go to bed. Don't stop. Don't pause. I need you to do that for me."

He knows he can ask this of me, and of course I'll be good for him. Because he knows I want to please him and if I don't obey him right now he'll never forgive himself for giving in to this thing between us.

I want to be so fucking good for him.

My face cracks as I duck my chin away from his touch, and I wrap my arms around myself. His stiff grip relents, with his hand dropping away from my sweater. Unbuttoned jeans hanging loose over my hips are a taunting reminder of what nearly unfolded in the shadows and firelight.

Reluctantly, I head away from him and toward my room. *Just as he asked.*

As I reach the doorway to my bedroom, I can't help myself,

sneaking a long look back down the hall. When I do, all I see is the sight of his broad frame. Colt stands in the gloom gripping the mantelpiece above the fire with two hands and his head dropped down between his shoulders.

My tortured cowboy.

CHAPTER 15

The snow is falling again, and my resolve is seconds from burning to ash.

As of this moment, I know the way Layla tastes and the tiny noises of pleasure she makes as I fuck her mouth with my tongue.

What I want is to learn every single sound she makes when she's falling apart beneath me, and my cock is buried inside that sweet little cunt of hers.

Jesus. Fuck. Her scent is still on my fingers, and she's consumed every single thought I've had since last night.

Everything moved so fast.

How the hell can I justify my actions? One minute I'm arguing with her about whether or not she's still involved with my son, and the next minute I'm trying to rip her jeans off and eat her pussy till she screams.

What kind of a fucking father am I, if I can't keep my hands off what doesn't belong to me? Off my son's girl?

Layla is the most stunning woman I've ever come across. Our connection goes beyond just being drawn to her magnetic pull on my body. Spending time enjoying her company is just so damn easy... and that might be the most terrifying part to all of this.

She's also the only person I've ever felt such an intense attraction to. I'm insane for this girl. My dick is permanently hard whenever she's around, and it's becoming impossible to find reasons to remove myself from her presence twenty-four hours a day.

Especially when we're in the depths of the longest, coldest nights of winter. When I'm battling myself at every turn because all the ways I want Layla is utter madness.

When all I really want to do is let myself into her room and give her the kind of goodnight kiss that lasts 'til sunrise.

I brace myself on my knuckles. Staring at my craggy features in the bathroom mirror.

What the fuck does a pretty young thing like her see in a grumpy old asshole like me, anyway? I've got grays in my beard, and silver starting to streak a little on one temple. My hands are rough from working this goddamn ranch for thirty years, and my soul is in even worse shape.

She could have anything... and anyone in life.

Yet, the way she melted into me and wanted me last night was the most exquisite torture.

"You're a real piece of shit, Wilder." Glaring at my reflection, I wish I could punch myself in the jaw for being so reckless.

When I got home and saw the single line Kayce had emailed me, I just about got in the truck and took off back down to town, with my only plan being to kick his ass. Not because I care about the fact he's not working or spends his time drinking or whatever the fuck it is he's doing to waste his life. No, the reason I lost my shit was because *I knew*.

I knew if he didn't return, if he wasn't here, keeping my hands off Layla would be impossible. If I'm stuck up here buried in the snow with only her to tempt me every day, that's going to be an enormous fucking problem.

At least if Kayce was around, I thought it would be ok. That I could make it through the next six weeks without my cock trying to get inside her at every opportunity.

Christ, I'm so fucked.

Before, it was just this unspoken thing between us, where we'd both fallen into a pattern, pretending we didn't feel the attraction that day we met at the gas station.

I shoved that interaction in a box and tried to throw away the key the second I found out who she was and that she just so cruelly happened to be Kayce's ex.

There wasn't any other option. Because a father trying to make amends is not trying very fucking hard if he's got his tongue down the throat of his son's girlfriend. Even if she considers things long over between them, it's obvious Kayce is still hung up on her.

Yet, here I am, spending most of my day imagining what her cunt tastes like.

I stab my fingers into my hair and look down. My cock is tenting my briefs just at the thought of Layla, as per goddamn usual. If I don't take care of this, it is only going to make for an extremely awkward day ahead.

Not to mention we've got the bonfire tonight, which means that between the annual winter round up of the cattle happening today, the BBQ I'm set to host later on, the ranch is going to be swarming with pricks sniffing around the property all day and night.

My teeth grind, as I shove off the sink. Flipping the shower on and stepping out of my briefs. There's already a dark patch on the navy-blue cotton where my dick has been leaking.

I step under the spray and rest a forearm up against the tiled wall. My other hand pumps some body wash from the bottle on the recessed shelf and I wrap my fist around my rigid length.

My eyes squeeze shut as I stroke myself from root to tip. It's a well-trodden path I'm on, one that is coated in the dark shame that comes with knowing I'm fantasizing about a girl far too young for me.

The whole time my fist slides up and down my cock, all I see is Layla on her knees between my thighs.

She's looking up at me with those big doe eyes of hers glowing with the shades of green the forest turns in spring.

Her pouty little mouth is right there, and as I collar her slender neck, she darts her tongue out to lick at my tip.

My chest tightens, and my dick jerks in my hand.

As my grip works up and down, it's her lips that struggle to close around me, but she's determined to take every inch. Her tongue glides, swirls, traces underneath my length.

She's such a good fucking girl for me, taking me deeper and deeper, until I'm tapping the back of her throat as she swallows around my tip. I squeeze and massage her throat each time and feel her moan with pleasure beneath my palm.

I'm pumping faster. Tingling builds low in my spine. My stomach clenches, and the vision I have of her is so visceral as she bobs up and down. I even watch, entirely captivated, as her cheeks hollow.

My balls tighten.

Holy fuck.

My hand strokes harder, my release loading, her soft moans still ringing in my ears from last night, as if she's right here in the shower with me. She looks so pretty, taking all of me. Hums around my length. Sucks me harder, and all I can imagine is the sight of filling all her holes, leaving no part of her unclaimed.

The filthiness of that image, of my release spilling out after fucking her bare, is what finally does me in.

A grunt bursts out of my chest, and thick ropes of cum shoot forward to paint the tiles in front of me as my cock jerks with the force of my climax.

I feel like I just ran a mile. My head spins, heart thunders, it's too good and almost too much at the same time.

Apparently, my self-restraint is non-existent, because even though I collect myself and hose the streaks of evidence pointing to my shameful obsession off the shower wall, I can already sense that it's not enough to satisfy my interest. It's bad enough that she's technically my employee, and here I am, forty-two years old, acting like a horny teenager.

This shit has got to end.

Throwing the extra layer of her past with my son into the mix makes me feel like a real asshole considering the depraved sorts of ideas occupying my mind.

Dangerous goddamn ideas that I've never experienced in my entire life, but when it comes to Layla, they've risen to the surface unbidden.

As much as I don't want to, I have to face reality today. The spillover of me losing control like I did last night makes resignation sit heavy in my gut, knowing that I'm going to have to put in a really big fucking apology. Most of the early hours of this morning were spent laying awake worrying that she was going to have disappeared under the cover of darkness. Lying in bed, my hearing was attuned to every goddamn creak in the house—could have sworn the front door clicked shut about three times.

I wouldn't have blamed her. Seeing the crushed look on her face as soon as I stopped things between us was nearly enough to have me going back on my word. I'd rather stab myself in the eye than be the person who causes her to have tears in hers again. She deserves so much goddamn better.

Better than I can offer her.

And that's the entire dilemma I'm in... I want her to have the moon and the stars and the sun itself, but I don't want anyone else to be the one giving it to her because I am a selfish, old bastard.

When it comes to Layla, it turns out I'm possessive as all hell and barely keeping that side of me on a leash. That girl would flee this mountain and never return if she knew the messed up way I can't stand the thought of anyone else even looking at her... the ways I can't stop myself from fantasizing about claiming her.

Which only reminds me of the shit show that today is likely to be, not to mention tonight.

Any minute now, there will be a bunch of randy bastards crawling all over my ranch. Most of them are good kids at heart, but they are all at an age where they have nothing better to do than chase after something pretty. Putting the girl currently under my roof and my care, firmly as the cherry on top of Devil's Peak.

My fingers itch with the need to shove the barrel of my shotgun between their teeth until they get the picture.

None of them are going to lay a fucking hand on her, or I'll cut them off and send them down the mountain bleeding out.

I've barely got my jeans belted and my shirt buttoned when I hear noise coming from outside.

Trucks pull into my yard, and the tightness in my chest strangles me like a vise. Looks like this morning, I'm going to have threatened half the mountain with murder before I've even had my coffee.

CHAPTER 16

Layla

I don't usually sit out here in the mornings. Most of the days fill up too fast for me to sneak a moment to sink into one of these ridiculously comfortable outdoor armchairs and take in the vast beauty that is Devil's Peak, wrapped in her cloak of snow like a winter queen.

Of course, it was no surprise that I hardly slept last night and have been up since long before the first purple streaks of dawn caressed the wide horizon stretching out in front of me.

This ranch is breathtaking, achingly beautiful, yet I feel like I'm drowning under ten feet of water. There's hardly a scrap of oxygen reaching my lungs. Life is cruel and unfair, and the worst part is that I care about Colton Wilder too much to hurt him by forcing something he refuses to act on.

I don't know where that leaves us for the next six weeks that I will be working out the remainder of my placement. But for a solid hour last night, I spent my time going back and forth between packing and then unpacking my small, ratty suitcase. I almost gave up on trying to make this situation work, figuring it was for the best if I were to cut my losses and contemplate finding a new job elsewhere.

Then, I realized my only option for leaving was to either steal a horse, or his truck, and both would inevitably lead me back to him... So I'm once again stranded on the top of this mountain with snow gently drifting down from the sky above and the insanity of it all keeps laughing in my face.

Fat, puffy snowflakes coat the wooden railing in front of me like mounded sugar. Kayce really wasn't joking when he said the roads might be closed most of the winter.

Out here on the porch, the Wi-Fi occasionally musters enough strength to work. This morning is one of those days. Scrolling through my posts I've shared of the horses and a couple of quick videos around the ranch, I see they've been picking up a little more attention than normal for my account.

Knowing how many other people are swooning over the horses being complete fools makes me smile.

I love getting to show off their individual personalities. They really are a bunch of starlets in their own right. It's something I secretly wish the ranch could promote more, but I'm guessing since Colt is allergic to the internet, that job would fall to Kayce and, well, he simply doesn't give a shit.

SAGE:

Any update on the *hot cowboy you won't talk about* situation?

I know there is SOMEONE.

My third eye is tingling, bitch.

I SUCK IN A BREATH. All I can do right now is pretend that there is, in fact, a cowboy in the picture. Keeping it unspecific as all hell is my last line of defense against my best friend who is a bloodhound on the scent. I'm resigned to the fact I'm just going to have to work overtime to throw Sage off the trail, because, as much as I desperately want to spill my guts and tell her every little detail about how insane last night was, I am most definitely going to need to lie to her. No good can come of letting her know what happened between me and Colt in the dark and the firelight.

Butterflies start to riot on fluttery wings in my stomach, and I find myself absently running my fingertips over my lips. Is it possible they are still tingling from the scrape of his beard and force of his hot mouth devouring mine?

> There's nothing really to tell…

Dots erupt quickly on screen as Sage types frantically.

OMG.

BITCH.

I KNEW IT.

> We met at a bar last night. Yes, we kissed. But sorry to disappoint, I don't know that there will be anything more than that.

> He's busy, I'm busy up here at the ranch.

> How's Evaline been lately?

Oh, good. Deflecting to the ONE TOPIC you know I won't side step.

Very uncouth of you. Dirty tricks, freckles.

Maybe those cowboys have been teaching you a thing or two after all.

Aunt Evie is a delight, as always, and obliged me with an hour of puzzle time the other day. She's doing fine, babe.

> Thank you.

> I miss you both so fucking much, you know that right?

> Well, of course you do, I'm the whole package.

> And whatever, you can't be missing my ass that much. Tell that to the tonsils you were exploring last night.

> Don't think you can avoid giving me more details. I expect a play by play.

As I wrap my fingers around the warmth of my coffee and try to figure out what to reply, I hear crunching gravel beneath heavy tires and around half a dozen trucks not dissimilar to Colts pull into the yard. My moment of peaceful 'figuring out what the fuck is happening in my life' is broken, and I'm assaulted by every good-looking cowboy in Crimson Ridge.

I knew there was something happening here on the ranch today, but it would seem that Colt has neglected to inform me it would involve a bevy of sharp-eyed men poured into tight jeans. At first, I watch them with curiosity, like a flock of playful wolf cubs, some roll out of their trucks, teasing each other and joking around. A few shove at each other's shoulders in that roughhousing way guys always seem to want to do with their buddies.

They haven't noticed me yet. Stretching and exhaling long plumes of white into the crisp wintery air as they shake themselves out after however long it has taken to drive here. I'm guessing they're locals, judging by their familiarity with the ranch, they've got an air about them that says they've been here a hundred times before.

My eyes catch on one man who seems much older than the others. He's come on his own and wears a tan colored hat slung low, shadowing his face while leaning against the grill of his truck. Observing the group, he stands quietly with folded arms.

What I do see is an expanse of ink. A large, tattooed rose and script climbing up his neck from beneath the fleece-lined collar of his jacket. His body language is so different from the others. Stern and composed, reminding me of Colt in many ways.

Before I can thoroughly analyze how this particular cowboy seems to be so at odds with the others who have just arrived, one of them spots me, and the atmosphere switches immediately. It's still playful between the younger guys, only now the snowy air has become charged. They each eye me sharply, enjoying the prospect of what they all presumably see as easy prey to chase. I'm not surprised, considering each of these pups looks like they could feature on a billboard advertising toothpaste or men's underwear.

They're cocky and gorgeous, and don't they all know it.

Except, just like the man I danced with briefly last night—oh, god, I still can't wrap my head around the events of last night—they do nothing for me, and all I want to do is laugh into my coffee at their boyish eagerness.

There's only one cowboy who turns me into a panting mess and he's currently missing in action.

My thighs clench as a memory of his tongue against mine drifts in, followed quickly by a pool of heat low in my stomach when I feel the ghost of his teeth tugging against my bottom lip.

A long, drawn-out sip from my mug hides my blushes.

"Heard rumor the view up here had dramatically improved this winter." One of the guys leans casually on the railing at the bottom of the steps. Tipping the edge of his cowboy hat in my direction, I almost snort at the cliché move, but he seems sincere about offering those country boy manners in my direction.

"I bet a hog in a dress would look good if you've only had this crowd to look at all winter." I gesture around the group of them with a smile. While I don't want to come across as flirty with these guys, I also want to hold my own up here. Even in school, I always found it easier to be 'one of the guys' rather than make friends with other girls. But this is no playground. Behind those wide grins

149

and fitted wranglers are cowboys with much hungrier appetites indeed.

They're all frisky-eyed and cocksure of themselves, gathering by the railing at the bottom of the steps.

Of course, they're being utterly charming, even if they're each weighing their chances.

Only the solemn, tattooed, brooding one hangs back. My eyes flick over him quickly a second time, appraising the way he leans against his truck. Arms still folded. Heavy black combat-style work boots crossed at the ankle. As I sip my coffee, I see him bring a thumb up to rub his jaw, hints of a chunky silver ring and leather cuff peek out from beneath the sleeve of his jacket as he does so.

"You working here for the winter season, or what?" My attention is drawn back to the guys closest to the porch. I see the wheels spinning behind all of their eyes, as they race each other to some sort of imaginary start line. They're jockeying for position and attempting to establish if I'm fair game for them to pursue.

"Yup." I pop the p and stare them all down with my best *don't mess with me* expression. "I'm here on a vet placement for a couple of months."

"Hope the old bastard isn't riding you too hard." One of them quips, giving me a wink, while his mate standing beside him thumps his shoulder.

"How original." I tilt my head and raise my eyebrows.

The first guy laughs and gives me an apologetic look. "Ignore him, he wouldn't know how to have a conversation that doesn't involve his fist being wrapped around his dick."

"All I'm saying is that if the lady decides she'd rather not get locked up in this place surrounded by ten feet of snow... I have a spare seat in my truck ready and waiting to whisk you outta here. Your chariot awaits." With cowboy hat grasped in one hand, he puts on a fake bow, then flicks his friend in the nuts. Everything promptly erupts into shoves and some kind of play-scuffle in the middle of the yard.

"Thanks, but I'm good." I call out before taking another sip of my coffee. "I'm Layla, by the way."

"Pleasure to meet you, lovely Layla. Are you joining us with the cattle this morning?" Country-boy-manners sports a dimple to go with his pearly white smile.

"Oh, I'm not sure. I've got plenty of jobs I need to get done up here." That part is the truth, I don't know what else might be on my agenda today other than following the usual routine. Colt hasn't mentioned anything to me.

"Well, even if we don't have the pleasure of a lady joining us on the round up today, hopefully we'll see you at the bonfire later tonight?" The one leaning on the rail sounds a little too keen and my gut twists into a tangle. There's absolutely no reason for me to be worried about him taking an interest, but I don't want to give Colt the wrong idea, either.

Especially after we established last night that he is clearly not pleased with the thought of any man coming near me. His son, or otherwise.

My mouth opens, but I don't get a chance to answer, because the door crashes open. There's a hurricane of messy dark hair, and a set of glaring hazel eyes taking in every single one of the cowboys gathered in the yard. The snarl on his upper lip already fixed in place as if they are all dead meat.

I swear a smile plays on the lips of the tattooed one, barely visible beneath the dipped brim of his hat.

"Told you pricks to get the horses and meet me down there." Colt barks as he aggressively stomps into his work boots. "Does no one fucking listen around this place? I'm not paying you to stand around talking."

More than one of the guys gives a knowing look my way, but they're obviously well-versed in avoiding the wrath of Colton Wilder.

There's a shuffle and some murmuring, and some of the group move off toward the barn. Others head for a handful of the vehicles. They must be making use of the horses to round up the cattle today. Mr. Pearly Whites gives me another little touch to the edge of his hat as he swings into the cab of his truck.

Their engines roar into life, and one by one, they jolt off over the muddy track in the direction of the far paddocks where the cattle are located. A chorus of voices drift on the snowy air as the others head toward the barn. Meanwhile, flakes of powdery snow silently fall thicker and faster. It has barely started sticking yet, but I imagine if conditions carry on this way by tomorrow, the mountain road will become even more treacherous, perhaps even impassable.

I begin to wonder if we might get cut off from town again, barely five minutes after the crew managed to open the road all the way up to the ranch entrance.

Colt hasn't left to join the others. He's thumping around, looking for something in his truck, and I guess this is the moment when we have to face each other in the cold light of day.

I take a steadying breath, and walk down toward his parked vehicle. Why do I feel like I'm having to coach myself through this? Nothing to worry about, we can both be professional. I'm just checking in with my boss.

Totally professional. Not at all like this is the man I begged to touch me and make me come not even twelve hours ago. The man who left my pussy tingling and whose bulging cock I can't stop daydreaming about.

My stomach is a riot of fluttering wings as I approach the hood, my coffee still clutched in my hands. Something about this feels like trying to coax a feral dog out of hiding.

He could come gently, or might need a muzzle.

"Uhh, do you need me to help with the cattle round up today?" I try to keep my voice cheery. Like I would sound every morning when I slide him a cup of coffee across the kitchen island, or offer to fix us both breakfast.

Not like a girl who can't stop thinking about his tongue pressing into my mouth or what he said last night.

Then tell me why I'm spending every night talking myself out of visiting the bedroom just down the hall.

"No." He doesn't even look my way. Just continues to ransack the cab of his vehicle looking for god knows what.

Okayyy...

"Are you sure you don't need more help? I honestly don't mind?"

Colt slams his palm into the outer panel of the truck so hard I'm certain there must be a dent left in the metal. The force of the noise makes me jump.

"Christ, Layla. Just do your fucking job." He pins me with a glare that is all too familiar by now, but no less intimidating. "And if I catch you trying to sneak off and get out of doing your duties by leaving the stables today, I'll put you over my damn knee."

"So this is something Colt puts on for you boys every year?" I'm sitting on the flipped-down tailgate of someone's truck, watching the flames dance in the huge bonfire set up by the cowboys earlier this evening. Plumes of orange sparks soar into the inky black sky as logs crack and spit out bursts of heat.

"You betcha. Every year around this time. We pitch in and help him out with the midwinter check on the full herd, and in return he throws a BBQ and bonfire. It doubles as a thank you for the mountain road crew." The polite cowboy I met this morning stands with an elbow propped on the side of the truck and has a beer in hand. Turns out his name is Brett and he works across a few different ranches around Crimson Ridge.

What has surprised me the most about this bonfire tonight is that this is evidently a thing Colt puts on annually, purely out of the goodness of his heart. Considering he's ready to march people off his property at gunpoint and threatens to kneecap them like some kind of cowboy gangster, I'm struggling to believe what I'm hearing.

There are new layers I'm discovering to Colton Wilder every day, it would seem.

"Are there no other women on Devil's Peak, or what?" I glance around the gathering of men—some of whom I recognize from earlier, and others I assume must be the roading crew who have shown up. But it is decidedly an all-sausage affair, and I'm sure they are all more than conscious that I'm the only female present.

I certainly am.

"Well, there hasn't been a woman around up here before, so wives and girlfriends never bothered coming along. I guess it just became a routine after a while."

Clumps of snowflakes continue to drift down, one lands on my face, instantly melting against my cheek.

It's more than a little magical.

And there's never been a woman here. Before me.

I can't let myself fixate on that detail, it doesn't mean anything. In fact, all it proves is that Colt keeps his women elsewhere, and they don't feature in his life beyond the bedroom.

Oh, god. I promised myself I wouldn't think of Colt and his bed and agonizingly long, snowy nights in that house, knowing he's just a couple of doors away from mine.

Especially not after how much of an asshole he was earlier.

You can bet I spent the entire day doing every single one of my jobs to absolute perfection. There's not a patch left un-mucked or unattended to. Each stall is completely spotless. I'll be sure to fill all the horses in tomorrow on how much of a grouchy dickhead their owner is. I'm pretty sure they're all on my side by now, anyway.

The tack room is gleaming, the chicken's coop has never looked better, and I've stacked wood like a woman possessed.

It was only once I knew I'd ticked off everything without a shadow of a doubt that I followed the smell of BBQ and woodsmoke to join the gathering. Colt can't accuse me of not doing my job, and I'm certainly not going to sit up in that house all on my own.

The way I've worked today, I've earned a drink and some company to chat to. The generous second helping of whiskey I've poured myself is giving me a perfect glowy feeling all over.

All the while, as I sit here chatting with Brett and sip on my drink, I can feel his eyes on me. Even though I can't see Colt through the darkness, I know he's here, but he's being too much of an asshole to approach me, or talk to me today.

We make small talk. Chatting about Brett's life in Crimson Ridge. That he's lived here, or thereabouts his whole life. I explain a little about myself, but in all honesty talking about my upbringing usually makes people uncomfortable, so I'm an expert at keeping on asking other people questions about themselves.

Deflecting attention is something I've grown accomplished in.

Shitty mom I cut out of my life and Aunt who raised me but has advanced dementia and doesn't recognize me anymore aren't usually the topics strangers want to get into while enjoying a few drinks and casual conversation. Plus, I kind of like getting to pretend my life isn't a trainwreck. Certainly, up here at the ranch, it is easy to *forget*.

An orange glow throws enough light to illuminate the immediate circle around the bonfire. Other than that, it's all heavy shadows and silhouettes, making it impossible to see anyone's faces as we gather out here in the snow.

Eyelids drooping, limbs growing heavy, Brett's voice cuts through my daydream.

"You all good there, Layla?"

God, this drink is hitting me hard and that's when I scrunch my brows with realization. I've been so determined to work my ass off, I haven't eaten anything all day. Between the lack of sleep, full day of work, and freezing cold, I'm more of a lightweight than usual.

Actually, I'm probably way more drunk than I intended to be.

"Yeah, I'll be back in a sec. Gonna grab a bite to eat." I hop off the tailgate and figure I'll fix myself some food up at the house.

I'm sure there are some leftovers to toss in the microwave, that'll soak some of this liquor up nicely. Besides, as much as it has been nice chatting and all, the man I would really love to be snuggled up next to in the flatbed of a truck won't come near me.

Everyone's vehicles are parked in a circular pattern spread out around the fire, so I weave my way between a couple of them. Just as I wander between the two parked furthest from the fire, I sense a figure up ahead in the darkness.

A waft of stale cigarette smoke hits me, and my stomach sours.

Whoever this is, he's blocking the way, and I'm either going to have to squeeze past or double back on myself.

The way he just stands there makes the hairs on the back of my neck stand up.

"Layla, isn't it?" The shadowy outline of the man readjusts his stance, leaning up against the passenger door.

"Uh. Hi." I don't want to be rude in case this is one of Colt's friends, but it feels weird that he's over here hanging around alone. Maybe he's just taking a piss.

"Headed off by yourself in the dark?"

Something in this man's energy is setting off alarm bells in my tipsy brain.

"Nowhere, I was just—" I go to step backward, but he closes the distance like a viper. His hand wraps around my elbow.

"Ah, no need to run off, now."

I do *not* want this man touching me.

"Take your hand off me, please." I try to keep my voice calm. Years of dealing with drunks in the bars I've worked at kicks in on reflex. Just be firm with them, but not dramatic. Don't provoke them, but stand your ground. Remove yourself as safely as possible. The bartender's handbook for dealing with grubby men who think that because they're at a strip club, it means they can lay hands on the women working there.

Right now, I don't have a burly bouncer to intervene. Not that they ever paid too much attention to the lowly barbacks, they were mostly far too focused on the girls working the stage or the customers on the main floor.

"Don't be like that, we're just talking."

"No. You're talking, and I'm leaving."

"Why don't you have a drink with me over here?"

Bile forms in the back of my throat.

"No thanks."

"You seemed happy enough to have a drink with Brett at his truck, surely it won't hurt to do the same for me."

All I can see is the outline of his head, but I can't make out any features. It's pitch black and the snow trickling down from the heavy skies overhead ensures there's no moonlight to see by.

"Listen. I'm not interested." I yank my elbow, but he tightens his grip.

"Come on, girlie. It'll warm you up. I promise you'll enjoy yourself much better once you've had a drink with me."

Yeah, one that's probably been roofied, judging by the way this guy is acting. I don't really give a shit anymore if this is supposedly a friend of the other men here, I'd rather not stick around to see what he's like when he's *really* friendly.

"I said, no," I growl.

"Layla?" One of the other cowboys from earlier, whose voice I sort of recognize, comes up behind me. One part of me is relieved, while the other is spitting mad that this dickhead doesn't have the word 'no' in his vocabulary, or understand its meaning.

That's when I hear the unmistakable sound of a gun being cocked.

"Get up to the house, Layla." Colt's tone drips with cold aggression.

He's disguised in the shadows when I turn toward the direction of his voice, but I can sense the tension rolling off him, bouncing between the sides of the vehicles we're all crowded in between.

At first, I'm relieved as all hell when I hear his voice. Then as I tug my arm out of the dickhead's grip and step back, I get slapped around by Colt's next statement.

"You shouldn't even fucking be down here. Let alone wandering around drunk in the dark."

Excuse me?

My fists clench by my sides as I fight back the urge to start hurling insults at him.

He's barking orders before my whiskey-soaked brain can come up with anything to say. "Grange, I'm gonna need you to go on up to the house and make sure Layla gets safely inside. If you so much as take a glance her way while you do so, you'll be picking lead shot out of your balls for the foreseeable future, you understand?"

"Colt—" I don't know what I want to try and say, but this feels like the moment back at the Loaded Hog when I danced with that guy all over again. Another scenario when I'm the one being chastised for something that isn't my fault.

Grange—the only man in this situation who actually seems concerned for me—mutters something in agreement. I find myself stomping away, leaving the tense standoff without so much as a backward glance, with alcohol diluting my blood, using my phone as a flashlight.

"You don't have to coddle me." I snap as the man traipses after me, keeping a respectful distance.

"And risk the hell I'll have at the hands of Wilder if I don't do exactly as he asked? No, thank you."

"He's such a controlling asshole." I grind my teeth. Talking to myself more than the man behind me. "I'm fine now, see?" I sneer as I slap a hand on the wooden railing, giving him an exaggerated bow to show that I've safely made it to the house as instructed.

"He might be that, but with good reason." Grange gives me a sympathetic look, then dips his hat. "I'll just wait here 'til you're safely indoors, Miss Layla."

"Fine." My eye roll is unnecessary, but the whiskey and confrontation have jumbled me into a mess. Apparently, the way I'm choosing to handle this situation is to be petty.

As I stomp my way up the steps and head inside, making sure to lock the doors behind me, I sure as hell hope Colton Wilder doesn't have a key to get in and ends up having to sleep out in the barn with the horses tonight.

I JOLT AWAKE.

A sickening clench in my gut makes itself known straight away, wondering if something startled me from sleep, or if I've woken up for no good reason at all. Lying still, I strain my ears for a hint of anything that might be the reason I find my heart fluttering madly in my throat.

The room around me is so dark I can't see my hand in front of my face, yet it feels like it's swimming a little all the same.

Events from the day before, and what happened immediately before I got into bed, come flooding into my mind. God, was it really only yesterday that I sat out on the porch with my coffee?

Not just that, but was it truly only one night ago that things escalated wildly out of control with the man whose house I'm sleeping in?

Christ, the man did me a favor by getting me away from that creepy guy, but the way he went about doing it somehow made my hackles prickle and my defenses sit up.

It felt like the moment when he accused me of getting knocked up by Kayce all over again.

Colton Wilder certainly has a way with words.

Lying there in the dark, I gnaw on the inside of my cheek for a while. Did the sound of him coming back to the house wake me up? I reach over and fumble around, slapping a hand in the direction of the bedside table, before successfully tapping my phone's screen. Numbers glare at me through the dark, telling me it's two in the morning, and while I don't know how these bonfire nights usually go, I don't exactly picture Colt as being the type to indulge in benders around the campfire lasting through the night.

That's more Kayce's style, and the two Wilder men couldn't be more different in that regard.

God, I need to stop comparing them.

Now that I've had a little bit of sleep, I wince at the thought that maybe I locked Colt out of his own house in the midst of my drunk, petulant state of mind.

Guilt weighs heavily on my chest. Cowboys rough it in all conditions, and that man is as tough as nails, but shit. What if he's trapped outdoors in below-freezing temperatures, and I'm the heartless, sulky bitch who barred him from coming inside?

I slip out from under the warm covers, tugging the loose blanket from the foot of my bed to wrap around me as I go. Crossing the carpet, the sliding door off my bedroom overlooks the dark porch. When I crack the curtain, I can't see shit, but there's still an orange glow of embers off in the distance where the fire has burned down.

There's one way I can know if he's back for certain, so I creep out into the hallway. The low sensor lights pop on, letting me see just enough to make out the room my eyes are immediately drawn to. It's a space in the house I'm hyper-aware of at all times, whether his door is open or closed, whether he's in there or not.

Straight away, I can see that his bedroom door is standing wide open. No lights come from within either.

Crap.

Now, I really feel the churn of guilt.

There's still just enough alcohol in my bloodstream that I don't stop and think. I just move. Perhaps it's the late hour, or the instinctive fear of something gone terribly wrong, or call it fucking intuition. I can't simply crawl back into bed without checking, without confirming with my own eyes. So I wrap myself tighter in the blanket and set off through the house.

Scanning around, there's no sign of life in the office or kitchen.

The fire in the lounge has burned right down overnight, and I spot that his hat and jacket are missing from the hooks.

God, what if he's frozen to death out there, or something worse happened with whoever that guy was? Guns and alcohol and angry men are not a good combination.

But I haven't heard any gunshots.

I don't think.

Oh, my god. What if that's what woke me up?

My heart is wedged in the back of my throat as I unlock the front door and prepare to step out into the bracing chill. Even from where I'm standing in here, it's obviously quiet outside, there's no wind, and I can make out the silhouette of puffy snowflakes fluttering down just beyond the edge of the porch.

The glow of the bonfire is all I can see, and I wonder if maybe Colt is still down there? I'm not dressed to be outside at all, but even so I twist the handle and hover just a moment.

What's my end game here? I'm hardly intending to venture out into the elements, but I find myself peering with all my might through the glass panel beside the door to see if I can make out any sight of him.

I slowly ease the front door open on silent hinges before a deep voice startles me.

"Where do you plan on going, dressed like that?"

CHAPTER 17

Layla

T he dark rumble hidden in the shadows makes me jump a mile. As I spook at the sound of Colt's voice, the door slams shut, sounding like a thunderclap going off in this quiet space.

"Hoping one of them is still there?"

Holy shit. He sounds... I don't know. Aggressive isn't the word. Territorial perhaps? Like I imagine a wolf guarding their pack would bear glistening fangs in warning.

Either way, a flurry of goosebumps runs along my arms that has nothing to do with the witching hour, or the cold lingering outside.

Tugging my blanket tighter around my shoulders, I step in the direction of Colt's words. This is the part where I shouldn't engage, I should take my ass straight back to my bedroom. This little excursion confirms what I needed to see for myself, and I've determined he is inside and safe and not frozen solid somewhere out in the snowfall.

Though I can't seem to rationalize what I should do, with what my feet actually do. Which is carry me closer to where he's sitting.

Colt is over by the giant bay window of the lounge. He's seated on a dining chair, looking out over the endless blackness outside.

The blinds hang open, and the inky starless sky filled with a million swirling snowflakes consumes the entire vantage point.

He doesn't flinch as I step toward him. Gaze remaining trained on that window with his broad shoulders that seem to fill half the room. I see he's still wearing his hat, with a coat slung over the back of the chair, but that's when my eyes tick down and catch on the glint of metal. There's a shotgun laid across his lap.

Jesus.

"Planning on sneaking out in the middle of the night?" He's not even bothering to look my way, just tilts the glass clenched in his hand up against his lips. Staring out into the night like there's something he's expecting to see at any moment. Something he's lying in wait for. "Might be unwise, considering it's well below freezing by now."

I shuffle on my feet and realize that I really did just roll out of bed without thinking. Beneath this blanket, I'm only wearing what I had fallen asleep in: a thin oversized t-shirt, knee-high socks, and underwear.

When my brain is completely sober and not so strung out, she has got a heck of a lot of explaining to do in the morning.

"I heard a noise." Darting my tongue out to wet my lips, I try to get a read on his energy. It's challenging with him at the best of times, and we still haven't properly cleared the air after last night. "I was—"

"Sure you did." Cutting me off, he drawls those words, lifting the whiskey to take another sip, while his other hand rests over the long barrel.

Heat prickles across my chest. The insinuations are thick in the air tonight, and I'm done with Colton Wilder's bullshit. Why this man keeps circling back to this same old tune is beyond me. Even if all this is just an act and his way of trying to convince himself he shouldn't want me, the thinly veiled accusations still sting. It doesn't matter that none of it is true. He doesn't need to push his own crap and whatever skeletons might lurk in his past onto me.

"That's honestly what you believe? You really think I wanted to be with any of them?" Rounding on him, I step in between his spot on the chair and the windows. Inserting myself directly in his line of sight.

It might be the middle of the night, and there's almost nothing illuminating this room except for the embers glowing in the fireplace, but I see the way his eyes sharpen on mine.

I don't wait for his answer.

"Oh, of course. Because I'm just a slut who will open her knees for anyone, right?"

My nostrils flare. The words I've been biting back ever since he first accused me of wanting to take off down the mountain, to chase after his son, start flowing.

"Because I'm just some stupid girl who wants it wherever I can get it, and I don't care who gets me off?"

I step right up to his spread knees. Heat and liquid courage courses through my veins giving me the freedom to unleash all the thoughts I've had bottled up and am now ready to hurl his way.

Yes, I want to be good for him and listen to him and please him, but I also have a fucking spine, and he should know after what happened last night that I'm just as tangled up in this thing between us as he seems to be.

"I'll tell you right now, all the nights I had guys offering to buy me drinks at the bars I worked in, and who begged to come home with me, and offered to be my Daddy... I never once said yes to any of them. Even the ones who got handsy. Even the ones who threatened me if I didn't say yes."

His gaze is thunderous, tension pulses in his jaw.

"Especially not assholes who corner me in the dark and refuse to let go of my arm like that jerk earlier." I'm aware of how close we are, with me standing between his knees, but this is the dance we do, and I can't seem to want to hold myself back from being drawn to him.

There's a force that is Colton Wilder, and I'm completely at his mercy.

"You want to know why I'm sitting here?" His voice rumbles

165

through the air. Gravelly and heavy with the late hour and touch of alcohol.

I nod. Clenching my fists tight on the edges of the blanket. "Yes."

"The thought of one of them sneaking back up here, after liking what they saw a little too much, is more than I can handle." He pokes his tongue against the side of his cheek, moving the weight of his focus up and down my body. "The pretty young thing who they only see as a notch in their belt and an opportunity to steal."

"That's not going to happen."

Colt makes a warning noise. "There's shit from the past that you don't know about, Layla. So, believe me when I say, there are men who would absolutely try and take the most valuable thing up here. By force if necessary."

I suck in a breath. "I'm not valuable."

The man in front of me shifts and knocks back the last of his drink before setting the glass down on the floor beside his chair. With his big paw, he reaches out to rub the hem of the blanket, keeping his darkened gaze on mine.

"You don't get it, do you? Every single fucking asshole with a pulse around here wants you."

It's like the air instantly crackles to life the moment his fingers connect with the soft wool. He hasn't touched me, but the proximity and nearness of him sends an ache pulsing through my core.

"That doesn't mean I'm anything special."

He clutches the blanket tighter in his fist. "Layla." His voice is thick and acts like a line straight to my pussy when he says my name. "They only see one thing when they look at you." Colt's lips curl in a snarl.

I wish there was a way to prove beyond a doubt that I don't care what they see. But this man won't take what he wants, and I won't force him to do something he'll regret. Wretched tension and longing bind the two of us together in the shadows.

Unwrapping one hand from my blanket, I reach out and nudge

the brim of his hat up with my forefinger. Tipping it back, allowing myself to melt underneath the heavy intensity of his stare, I exhale. "I'm not looking their way, cowboy. There's only one man I'm interested in, and he's one I can't have. So, what does that make me... a pathetic slut, or a masochist?"

He squeezes his eyes shut for a moment, before letting out the sexiest groan, the sound reaching out and humming in my blood.

Liquid fire pours down into my toes as I finally breathe life into the words we've both been feeling and can't seem to find a way to express. I'm back in that place where I know I'm being too brazen in talking to him like this, but the truth is clamoring to burst out of me.

I don't want Colt to remain under any kind of illusion. How badly I want him to know... that I'm completely and utterly disinterested in anyone but him.

The foolish, pining mess that I am for this man.

Maybe, just maybe, there's a way we can play in the shadows while they linger around us, just a little longer. Before dawn creeps in and things have to go back to how they were before.

"Do you like what you see?" I drag my bottom lip between my teeth. Giddy, fluttering hope occupies my chest.

Colt sucks in a sharp breath. A warning, maybe. "You know the answer to that."

That gruff tone and those glittering, darkened eyes combine to send a throb intensifying between my legs. His hand is so close to touching my thigh, the skin tingles with each agonizing second of lingering proximity.

"What if you didn't have to cross a line, but could still take what you want? What we both want?" I bite my lip harder. There's no mistaking the fact he hasn't let go of the blanket. He wants me to stay right here, so close he must be able to hear my pulse thumping in my throat.

"*Layla*." The rough way he exhales my name sends an explosion of butterfly wings in my stomach. "I've spent my whole life being selfish, I can't..."

"But you want to?"

"Yes. When it comes to you... so badly, I don't think you want to know."

My stupid little heart does a kick, and my stomach swoops, and I turn a blind eye to all signs warning me to beware the dangerous cliff edge I'm inching toward.

Fuck it, this is insanity, and I'm lost in this forbidden moment, buried beneath the snow and the time of night when things can so easily be hidden away.

"I heard a saying once..." My fingers unclench from the blanket, allowing it to fall open and reveal my figure. Reaching out, I lift his hat off his head, setting it on my own, not missing the flare that catches light behind his honeyed eyes.

"You touch a man's hat, you're either planning to fight them or fuck them. So, which do you want with me, cowboy?" Colt takes in my appearance, giving my scantily clad form a long look. I don't know if it's too dark for him to see my hard nipples through the thin material of my shirt, but every inch of my skin incinerates as his eyes roam freely.

"Plan on fighting?"

He makes a gravely noise in the back of his throat. Another warning.

"You willingly placed your hat on my head... so, is the real reason you gave me yours in town the other day, the second option?"

He sinks fingers into his hair, mussing those curls up more and goddamn my knees go weak. "I'm not a good man, Layla. Don't say shit like that when you're out here at night... dressed in..." Colt drops his hand to scrub over his mouth. "Fuck, when you're walking around tempting me."

Every part of him is coiled tight.

I'm a fool for him.

"You know some of the bars where I worked..." I let go of the blanket completely, allowing it to flutter to the floor around my ankles. "We were hired as entertainers."

He doesn't just look at me, he consumes every inch of my body. As if this is the first and last time he'll get the chance to properly lay eyes on me ever again.

"Were you a stripper?" The question barely gets past his gritted teeth. It's obvious he hates the idea, but is too curious to stop himself from demanding the answer. His fingers ball into fists on top of his knees, fidgeting as if it's taking everything not to reach forward and grab the backs of my bare thighs before he settles on clutching the edge of the seat on either side of his hips.

My eyelashes flutter. I'm recreating in my mind all the times I observed this exact scene play out while I poured drinks for hour upon hour. "No," I admit, "But I learned a thing or two watching the other girls who did perform."

There's a flicker of relief in the hard lines of his face, only for the briefest moment, before it vanishes and is once again replaced with a stern glare.

"You should go back to bed. You're going to freeze wearing only that."

I reach for the gun and try to gently move it off his lap. Hoping to god he's not going to turn it on me and march me out of here for taking things this far.

"I'm warm enough." It's the truth. Right now, my skin feels like it's burning up.

Colt's fingers tense around the barrel of the shotgun before I can lift it. "We can't do this, baby." His voice drops to a whisper. Even though he's saying one thing—those words laced with grit and sex and in that deep voice I dream about—he leans over to place the gun on the floor beside the chair.

I swallow heavily, plucking up even more courage at that tiny indication that he's joining me in this game.

"Nothing is going to happen. Just pretend with me... this is exactly how it would be if you walked into a random bar one night when I was working. Imagine we're just two strangers. Imagine what it would be like if you paid for a private dance."

He tenses up instantly. "I'd fucking drag you out of there."

There's a coy smile that dances on my lips. I devour the way he's so possessive, his hair all tousled around his face, his jaw flexing.

"Ah, but you can't." I tease. "Remember, the clients aren't allowed to touch. You're only allowed to look."

"That's a big goddamn ask." Based on the way his eyes keep flicking up to where his hat rests on my head, then back down to my bare thighs before fixing on my mouth, this is almost too much for him.

Well, fuck. It feels nearly too much for me, too, but I can't walk away from him. Not tonight.

"It's ok. We don't have to do anything else, but this."

He sucks in a ragged breath as I hook my arms around the back of his neck, and ease forward to straddle his lap. Everything feels so heightened, from the scratch of his jeans against my skin, to the heat radiating off his chest, to the scent of him that I want to nuzzle into.

"Jesus. Layla." He's looking down at the spot where my shirt has ridden up, exposing my soft thighs and lace covered pussy. One hand scrubs over his mouth as his gaze bounces back to meet mine.

"I love it when you look at me, Daddy."

A storm explodes in his eyes.

"Do you like it when I call you that?"

"*Fuuuuck.*" He groans and tips his head back. Giving me a long, hooded stare that makes my clit throb. "I don't want to say."

I nibble on my lip, and let my fingers run through the short hairs on the back of his neck. "You're so sexy when you make that noise."

We're both breathing heavily in the darkness, and desire blooms the longer I spend straddling him. My pussy is soaked, resting above the bulge in his jeans. Beneath me, he's rock hard, and it would only take the smallest, teensiest roll of my hips to give my body the friction it begs for.

"God, I want to fuck you so bad. I want to be buried inside your cunt this entire winter."

My teeth catch my bottom lip as a whimper escapes me. Sweet Jesus, this man can talk dirty and I'm going to be putty in his hands knowing that's what he's keeping hidden away behind his broody exterior.

"Is this what you're wearing all the time underneath your jeans out on the ranch? These slutty little knee-high socks?"

"Maybe." Cocking my head to one side, I study him for a long moment and then lean forward until my aching nipples brush against his chest, lips ghosting against his ear. "Or maybe not, and I like knowing you'll be asking yourself that question every time you watch me work."

He curses under his breath.

God, my pulse is flying with the headiness of being this close to him. Pulling back, I peek at him from beneath a curtain of lashes. "Should I leave them on?"

"Yes." His gruff command makes me shiver.

"What else do you want?"

"Christ. Layla. You're killing me."

"It's ok... you're not touching. All you're doing is watching." I slide my arms off his shoulders, and bring them to the hem of my shirt. His eyes track my every movement as I toy with the edge of the fabric, lifting it just a little.

Colt doesn't know what to do with his hands. He's trying so fucking hard not to touch me, and part of me just wants to grab his big palms and place them on me somewhere, anywhere, will do. But in this game where we're bending the rules to the point where they might shatter, I have to behave. As much as I really want him to pick me up and throw me down on the floor and rail me senseless.

He swallows heavily, the strong line of his throat bobs as his eyes stay transfixed on the spot where my pussy is. "I'm going to hell."

"I'll be right there with you." I breathe. "What do you want to see next?" My fingers inch the hem of my shirt higher, and with the other hand, I tease the lace at the waistband of my underwear, pushing it down ever so slightly.

Colt's nostrils flare as he fights a silent battle with himself, watching my hands like a hawk the entire time.

"Show me those perfect fucking tits." His cock jerks beneath me when he finally speaks, his voice husky with desire.

A shudder of pleasure rolls through me, and I hook the thin cotton up to rest over the tops of my breasts. I hitch in a breath, exposing myself fully for the first time. They hang full and heavy with need, and I want him to rip free of his self-restraint, to paw me, and play with them so goddamn bad. If he would only lean forward, close that small distance and take one into his hot, wet mouth.

"Fucking hell." That delicious noise he makes when he's turned on makes my pussy clench.

I allow my fingers to roam over my soft flesh, caressing and teasing and stroking, while my nipples turn to diamonds. The little moans coming out of me are breathy and desperate as I cup and pinch both of them beneath Colt's fearsome gaze.

God, I could die from the way he's studying every needy motion of my fingers.

The thick hardness of him presses up into me between the layers of his jeans and my barely there scrap of lace. It would take almost nothing for him to unzip and tug the soaked fabric to one side and thrust up into me.

My face must say it all because he makes a strained noise.

"I'm barely hanging on to decency here. There's too much filthy shit going through my mind for you to be looking at my cock like that."

I whimper and tug harder on my nipples. Fixating on his mouth as he turns my body molten, dirty-talking me into a soaked mess.

"What else do you want?" As I keep pressing him to tell me every illicit detail, my words are shaky, raspy, and don't even sound like myself when I finally manage to speak.

Colt shifts his hips beneath me as he readjusts himself in the chair. "Baby, I want to fuck you so badly. I want these tiny lace panties balled up inside my sheets every morning, and I want your sweet cum all over my tongue."

His words wash over me, leaving me panting.

Holy fuck. I'm clenching and damn near ready to lay myself down right here on the floor at his boots and beg.

"Mmmm, god." *A tug on my nipples.* "I want that too." *A roll of my hips.* "What else?" Grinding myself down on the firmness of his jeans works my desire tighter.

"I want to slide my tongue inside your sweet little cunt while you're asleep. Have your body fall apart while you're still dreaming, then shove inside you." He hisses as my hips shift over the head of his cock. "I'd fill your pussy up so fucking deep you'd never be able to forget me."

With how swollen my clit is, the friction sends electric sparks flying down to my toes. I'm perched in his lap, with my soaking wet core rubbing over him, and my fingers teasing my sensitive tits. It's going to take next to nothing for me to fall apart if I actually touch myself in front of him.

But I don't know that he'll let it get that far, if how rapidly he pulled away last night is anything to go by. This could all end any second now, the moment Colt's conscience comes crashing in. How long will he allow us to stay trapped within this carnal bubble?

Will he halt this madness before we tumble over the edge, swallowed up by this illicit moment? Right now, only the snow falling outside bears witness to the dangerous game we're playing.

"Layla, baby. That's it, keep making a mess of me," he murmurs, eyes transfixed on the place where I'm pressing down over his length. Through the dim light, I can see the tension in his neck and the strain on his face with each shift of my hips.

"Do you want to look?" I whisper, skating one hand down the soft swell of my stomach, until I play along the outline of lace. Letting my fingers rest over the top of my aching clit for a second before sliding over to the edge. Just low enough that if I hook the side, I can tug them and reveal exactly how needy I am for this man.

"*Fuck*." His hand lifts, and then hovers in the space between us, before he drags it over his mouth with a dark groan. "I don't know. I don't fucking know, baby. If you let me see your cunt, I'm going to want inside you. I'm going to want to eat you until you're begging me to stop. But I know I won't be able to stop. There's no going back for me once that happens and I'm not going to be able to keep myself from fucking you in every one of your sweet little holes."

Well, holy shit. The moan that drops out of me is pornographic.

The mouth on this man. He coats me from head to toe in a dizzying, wanton kind of temptation—the kind that screams and demands absolutely everything he just promised.

"It's yours if you want to look. I won't tell anyone." I rub a little harder over the outside of the lace. My eyelashes flutter as the liquid heat settles low in my stomach. I'm not even sure I can feel my toes anymore.

"God, you're the sexiest fucking thing I've ever seen." Colt's intense stare at the spot where I'm working myself smolders like the embers of that bonfire still burning outside. His praise glows hot and carnal straight through me and sets a fire in my veins.

Another whimper escapes me, every thick inch of him feels tempting and sinful beneath his jeans.

"Slide your fingers inside from the top, baby. Don't show me or I'm going to lose my goddamn mind." He growls and my stomach caves as the vibrations roll through my body. I do as he says, slipping beneath the waistband and dipping my finger through the slickness to make contact with my clit.

"Jesus. You're fucking soaking wet, aren't you?" He sounds almost angry, as I nod and my breath hitches as I finally make contact with the aching, swollen bud.

"That's it. Rub that spot in nice slow circles for me."

My mouth hangs open as pleasure rapidly gathers momentum and my pulse thunders in my ears.

"You like that middle finger?"

"*Mmmfuck.* Yes. God. I'm so close already." I whine. My hips are rolling and my fingers pinch my nipple and all I can focus on is the hunger written all over Colt's face. Every tiny, desperate movement beneath my panties is in response to this man's attention as I work myself and the crest of the wave draws nearer.

"Fuck. *Fffuuuck.* That's it. Just like that, eyes on me while you give it to me like a good fucking girl."

His rough words and coaxing do me in. I fall apart with a moan as my orgasm curls up from my toes and sweeps me away.

"Fuck. Baby. I'm gonna come."

Beneath my pussy, I feel his hips jerk. His cock pulses where he's pressed tightly against me as his own release takes hold. Colt's eyes squeeze shut, lips curling into a grimace of pleasure, and we're both breathing hard, mouths only inches away from each other in the darkness.

Holy shit. I've never felt anything that intense before, and this man didn't even touch me.

We both sit there, allowing our hearts to stop galloping, and the headiness of the moment drapes over me like the softest blanket. All I want to do is burrow into his chest and beg for him to take me to his bed. The need to have his strong arms wrapped around me is almost overwhelming as I fumble my way back into my body.

I don't want this moment to end, but it has to.

That was all this was ever going to be.

A brief moment when we could suspend reality and indulge in something we both know can't happen.

I let the hem of my shirt fall and pull my hand from my underwear, feeling the wetness of my cum drag up against my overheated skin.

Even though this was our midnight bargain, I'm desperate for more of his rough kisses. To have him steal my breath and kidnap me to that illicit place where all I want to do is submit and worship and be filled by him. My eyes bounce between his lips, his strong brow, his molten eyes. I see the moment that hazel gaze drops to my mouth, before he takes a deep inhale through his nose.

His self-restraint wins out, and my stupid heart squeezes with longing.

"Layla." There's a heaviness and weariness to his tone. "You're a goddamn dream, and I don't ever want to wake up, but you're gonna have to do what you did for me last night. You're gonna have to, because I'm not a good man and I just don't trust myself right now."

I nod. Slowly. Shakily. Still foggy and high after my orgasm. "Ok," I whisper, and ease back off him. Biting on the inside of my cheek.

My legs are unsteady as all hell, but I bend down to scoop up the long-forgotten blanket and bundle it against my chest, taking one last look at the man I'm torn in two by.

There's an ocean of desire staring back at me as our eyes lock, but I can't push this any further. It has already gone too far and there's every chance Colt already hates himself for letting this temptation lure him in, even if he didn't do anything more than watch me.

I'm the first to drop my gaze. Taking his hat off, I place it over his knee before ducking my head.

Once again, I'm the one to walk away, because he asked me to, because I want to please this man against all my better judgment and hope that things could be somehow different between us.

As I crawl into my bed with a tightness in my throat, my pulse thrums in my neck when I hear his heavy footfall follow not long behind me. For a tortuous second, I swear his footsteps pause right outside my door, before disappearing, fading away in the direction of the lounge.

Resuming his guard over me while I sleep, as I lie burrowed beneath the sheets covered in my own arousal, with a burning in my chest for wanting a man that I simply cannot have.

CHAPTER 18

I'm so fucked.

That girl is going to be the death of me.

Every time I turn around or close my eyes, she's there.

And I can't stand myself for all the tiny details and moments that make me want her. How she looks at me with big doe eyes and nibbles her lip when she doesn't think I'm looking. Every curve of hers is hugged by those goddamn jeans I want to peel slowly off her body, and the way the cropped part of her top rides up when she has to reach for something. How she hums to herself while brushing the horses and murmurs to them with that raspy little purr in her voice.

The one that goes straight to my dick.

What's worse, is I know the exact shade of forest green her eyes turn when her hot little cunt grinds in my lap, and rolling climax drags her under.

All around us, the world has turned white. The snow is piling thicker day by day as we've danced around each other for the past week. Avoiding the girl under my roof has been the only way to keep my sanity in all of this. It might be the least mature thing I've ever done in my life, but acting like ships in the night has been a hell of a lot easier than trying to have a conversation. So I've stayed wrapped in silence, coming and going when I know she won't be there.

What the fuck am I supposed to say to Layla after what happened between us?

There were so many lines crossed that night, and I should have been the one to put a stop to it the moment she wandered in, wearing next to nothing. But that selfish, jealous, asshole part of me took everything she offered and didn't make any effort to say no.

Jesus, I'm nearly twice her age. All it took was one flutter of those eyelashes, and I was convinced to lose my morals within seconds. Ready to damn near risk it all just for a taste.

Not that I think I had any to begin with where the beautiful girl living under my roof is concerned.

We both pass through the house in a strange routine, one where each of us is painfully aware of where the other is and what they're doing. Like the faint footfall I can hear from my room as she pads down the hallway for a glass of water late at night. Or the dinner she leaves out wrapped up for me on the bench when I've stayed out after dark doing shit I really don't need to be doing. Even though we're sleeping just down the hall from one another, and working the same few acres of this ranch, neither of us dares to encroach on the other's space.

Or maybe Layla is just so sick of my bullshit, that she's come to her senses, and this is how it will be until she leaves this mountain.

The moment she takes her sweet scent and soft presence and leaves me for good.

What it comes down to is that I want her. There's nothing complicated about that, only the longing and twisted loathing of myself for desiring her. I fucking hate the circumstances we've been tangled in, and if I was a worse person, I'd have said fuck it, and given into this thing between us back on day one.

Even though I shouldn't want Layla, there's no way I can turn off the flood of desire that courses through my veins all day long.

Just thinking about her is misery and agony and pleasure all mixed up, churning, whirring around in my brain.

I'm a piece of shit father is what I am.

Unfortunately, for my sanity, today is a job that requires both of us. I even put a call out on the radio to some of the guys who might have been able to come give me a hand checking the cattle, but none could get here in the current conditions. I don't blame them considering the forecast for later today is for a whiteout.

No one needs to be risking their neck, not when I've got someone right here who is more than fucking capable of riding out with me.

It's just that I've been putting off the inevitable of having to spend time together.

Right now, I'm radioing the final person who might have a chance of getting up here, but deep in my chest, I already know he won't be able to.

"Oh good, this isn't you calling me from jail then?" Storm's familiar chuckle comes over the radio.

"Don't start with me, Stôrmand." My fist grips the handset. "Not in the mood."

"Well, after watching you threaten Pierson off with your shotgun the other night, I thought this might at least be a thank you call, seeing as I made sure those two fucked off down the mountain."

I suck in a deep breath. "Yeah, thanks. Didn't need to be getting my ass locked up for taking matters into my own hands."

"Are you finally gonna file a report with Hayes? File that trespass order we've talked about a hundred times? You've got more than enough cause."

"You know exactly why I can't."

"Colt, you gave them an offer of equity, even though you shouldn't have even given them two minutes of your time, and those two shit-for-brains assholes spat in your face. You don't owe them anything, and you sure as hell don't need to atone for the sins of that asshole. He's long dead and buried, and you can't keep carrying guilt because of what he did. You're just as much of a survivor as the others."

"Didn't know you were giving out free therapy sessions on the side there, Storm."

I hear him laugh through the crackling of the line. "So if you're not in cuffs with the sheriff, and you're not wanting to talk about why you should be getting those pricks put away, to what do I owe the pleasure of this neighborly chit-chat?"

Pinching my brow, I ignore his taunting. "Don't suppose you could make it up here before this next front rolls in."

He's silent on the other end for a moment. No doubt checking the conditions outside.

"You know as well as I do, I'd be there any time of day or night if you needed... but this one looks like she's gonna be a real bitch."

Storm's right. I know he is.

"Yeah, don't worry. I'll handle it."

There's a static-filled silence.

"What about the girl?"

"Mind your business."

"Just saying, she couldn't stop looking for you around the bonfire." My gut twists. Storm is too goddamn perceptive for his own good at times. "Also, couldn't help but notice that you might have been ready to shove that shotgun down someone else's throat, too, even before Pierson turned up. All for letting her sit pretty on his tailgate and get a little friendly."

"You didn't see fuck all."

His laughter echoes through with a tinny crackle. "Sure, old man. You're absolutely right. I didn't see a thing."

HEADING INTO THE BARN, my heart bucks around in my chest like a bronc trying to unseat its rider. After talking with Storm over the radio, I'm keyed up, hoping like hell it was only the fact he knows me so well after all this time that gave him any clue there might be something more between me and Layla.

Something more than has any right to exist.

The scent of cedar and hay alongside the soft snorts of the horses greets me. All their curious sets of eyes peek out and follow me, giving me the exact looks that tell me they know my secrets.

Of course, it doesn't take long until I find the gorgeous girl who is mucking out the furthest stall. A pink flush coats her cheeks, and her headphones are in as she works.

Which means I get to stand here like a fucking pervert watching her bend over, just so I don't give her a heart attack creeping up from behind.

My cock thickens the moment I'm near her, like some damn automatic response to her presence. I've spent the better part of the day fighting off the need to see her and the rest of it willing away an erection just at the memory of her grinding in my lap.

When she had me shooting cum in my jeans like some sort of randy teenager.

Now, I've got a front-row seat to all her curves and softness.

Layla doesn't hear me approach, too caught up in what she's doing, and the music she's listening to drowns out the scuff of my boots against the ground. So I knock on the wooden framework, as if I need to fucking announce myself at my own ranch.

She jerks up and spins around, snatching one of her earbuds in the process of doing so. Her lips drop open a little as she takes in the sight of me and my breath catches in my chest. A giant hand reaches in to squeeze a tight fist around all my vital organs at the moment our eyes lock on one another for the first time in a week.

This is the power Layla Birch has over me. What this girl does to me, without even so much as trying, every single time. I'm so fucking fucked.

"Hey," she says softly, her lips roll together while plucking the other earbud out, too. "Is everything ok?" I see the way a tiny crease furrows her brow, but she hesitates to step any closer.

Damn it. This is my fault. The fact that in her mind there has to automatically be something wrong to warrant me coming and seeking her out is telling enough.

"No, no. Nothing's wrong." I wrap my palm around the back of my neck. Feeling prickly and clammy all over. Like my tongue is too damn big for my own mouth. "Just need you to come down with me to help check the cattle before this front sets in."

"Ok." Her eyes drop, and she sets the shovel aside.

"We'll need to take the horses. Snow's coming down thick out there."

"Sure." Layla edges past me, keeping herself as far away as possible as she passes through the opening to the stall.

I hate the way her eyes stay fixed on the floor and that I'm the asshole who has made this such a difficult thing to endure. All I want to do is reach out and catch her hand as she scoots past, to hook her pinky finger and tug her into my chest.

But I do the rational, sane thing and don't maul the girl half my age right here in the middle of the barn. Because I'm a gentleman.

A. Real. Fucking. Gentleman.

Between the two of us, we saddle up our horses, side by side. In a silence that aches in my bones, only the little whinnies and snorts and munching sounds of the other horses in their stalls surrounds us. Outside, there's an insistent howling and swirling as the conditions continue to deteriorate.

As much as I'd love to put this off, or just go on my own, the reality is that I need Layla to come with me so we can get the cattle checked and fed before it's too dangerous. I don't need either of us to be caught out by thickening snowfall while down in the far paddocks.

Up here, it could be life or death if you don't respect the laws of Mother Nature.

She's up on her horse, rugged up for the elements without so much as a peep, and I follow suit.

"Layla—" I venture.

"Let's just go. I'm sure the weather is only going to get worse."

She shuts me down efficiently and I get the sense she's retreated into herself.

There are a thousand things I want to say, but instead, I grind my teeth and take the lead. Once we're both out of the barn, the biting cold and whipping snow feel like razors against my skin. I turn in my saddle to catch a quick glance at Layla and silently confirm she's right behind me. All I get is a dip of her chin, but not her eyes.

I can't fucking stand it.

My mind is anywhere but focused, which is going to be a massive problem if I can't keep it together for the time it takes us to get down there and get shit done promptly.

As we make our way through the deepening snow, I'm quietly calculating how much more time we've got together up here: just over five weeks. Out of that, it's going to be at least another two before the mountain will be reopened again, given how thick and fast this storm has come in.

Burying my face in the collar of my jacket, I blow out a long breath. This is exactly what I'm used to—silence and being alone on top of the godforsaken mountain, working my ass off day in and day out. So I just need to suck it up and get the fuck over whatever this obsession is that keeps festering away inside me.

Layla is here to do a job. I'm going to make sure she gets her hours signed off, and at least I can sleep at night knowing I've helped the girl out.

Somehow, in five weeks' time I can try to rid my house of the wisps of jasmine and pear after she's taken all her things and left an old man like me buried in the snow with my misery.

As we reach the cattle, they're already lined up, waiting close to the gate. Snow coats their ears and flanks, and plumes of white stream from their wide noses. Layla doesn't even have to ask, just heads straight for the gateway while I head over to load up the tractor with a large bale.

Everything is white as far as I can see, and there's a threatening sky, full of heavy-set ominous clouds rolling toward us.

Devil's Peak has retreated out of sight, completely obscured by the weight of the storm approaching.

I slide off and hitch the horse, making fast work of the usual routine. With Layla to man the gate and check round the cattle while I'm feeding out, it doesn't take us long to be done. Thank fuck, because the snow is damn well pelting down by the time I've gotten myself back in the icy cold saddle.

"Let's get the fuck out of here." I reach forward and give Winnie a pat on the neck, dusting some of the snow off her mane. Her haunches flinch, and she snorts, clearly unimpressed with the need to be out here in the first place.

"Layla. We gotta move." I glance up at the sky again and see that the front is bearing down on us. Snow whips around my face, and the cold stings every exposed part of flesh. It's deteriorating quicker than the forecast suggested, and that makes my gut churn.

While we have a lot of easy-to-identify markers to help make our way back to the yard, I don't like the idea of risking being in a total whiteout. Shit can go sideways real quick, and I'm not taking any chances.

I have to squint against the force of the wind, and clumps of white determined to haze my vision. She's on her horse, but not moving away from the gate.

"Layla." My bark in her direction is loud, even to my own ears. While I don't want to sound pissed off, now isn't the time for any of us to be fucking around. And even though I deserve every second of her silent treatment, there's also a time and place for her to be pissed off at me.

That's when I see her slide off her goddamn horse and go back over toward the gate. She's fumbling around with the latch, and I can barely make out a faint, blurry outline of her from where I am.

Jesus. We're both going to get caught out down here with no shelter and every possibility that neither of us will make it back to the barn or the house in one piece.

Growling under my breath, I urge Winnie back in their direction, and my heart pounds. I've never been particularly worried about myself up here, I can handle my own, but knowing that she could get hurt—lingering in a blizzard, when we need to fucking move—my teeth are grinding themselves to dust at the mere thought.

I need to get her to safety, but I don't understand why she's not listening to me.

"Layla. For fuck's sake." I'm outright shouting now. Against the wind and the force of the snow falling and trying to drown out the thundering sound of my own pulse in my ears as I hit the ground.

Crunching over ice and powder, I'm jogging in her direction, with all sorts of curses and threats on my tongue, when I realize what she's doing.

Layla is tugging and hauling on the gate that's become lodged in the pugged-up, frozen mud, and she's trying with all her might to get the latch to slot securely in place.

I feel my stomach drop down into the soles of my boots.

She's following my fucking orders from when I tore strips off her that first day.

Right now, I don't know who to be more furious at. Myself for being such a goddamn asshole, or Layla for being too proud to ask for help.

Reaching out, I try to grab her upper arm and drag her off. "Fuck. Layla, leave it. We need to go."

"No." She fights against my hold. Shrugging me off with gritted teeth.

"I said leave it."

"NO. I've almost got it." Her small frame tries to wrestle to lift the gate, as the freezing wind slices right to the bone.

"You're going to get both of us fucking killed." I don't care about any sort of self-imposed boundaries I've tried to put in place about getting close to her again. Right now, it is about getting to safety, so I do the only thing I can do considering the circumstances.

My arm snakes around her stomach, and I haul her away.

Dragging Layla back into my body and toward the horses. She's fighting me and hitting at my arms like a woman possessed.

"It isn't secured." Her gloved hands try to wrench my grip off her waist, but I've got her clamped against me like a steel bar. "They might get out." Layla's furious voice resonates straight through her layers of clothes and into my own chest as her small frame thrashes beneath my hold.

Clumps of snow layer her eyelashes and stick to her mouth, and a part of me wants to wither up and die inside that this girl is trying to be good for me. She's trying so damn hard to be perfect, for bullshit I growled at her about weeks ago. Is there any worse fucking feeling in the world than this? The only reason I said what I said that day was because I felt like I was losing my mind, being trapped together in the front seat of my truck and unable to reach for her the way I wanted to.

"The gate can fucking wait. Now get on the damn horse." I keep her trapped against my chest, fighting against the snow and the cold seeping through my bones. Meanwhile, my blood is a raging inferno running through every inch of my skin.

Layla makes a strangled noise, crushed against my front. "Why do I care so much what you think of me?" She spits against the wind. "All I seem to do is want to try not to disappoint you, and yet it's never enough."

"You are enough." My voice comes out cracked as I shove her in the direction of the horse. I want her with me, tucked against me, and in the face of a storm rolling in thick and fast, I'm losing the will to resist.

"No. I'm not. I'm not enough for you. I never will be."

This isn't about the ranch or a fucking gate anymore.

"We'll fix it tomorrow," I grunt. Not giving her a choice. Being rough and forceful and manhandling every inch of her in order to throw her up to the front of the saddle, quickly tying the other horse to pony behind us, before swinging up directly behind her. It isn't ideal, two people on one horse is damn hard on an animal. But it's a straight shot back to the barn, and I don't like the idea of Layla spiraling out here where I can't physically hold her tight.

She's still determined to fight me. Trying to growl and slam an elbow into my gut in an effort to get back down.

"You just want me to suffer." She squirms and moves against me, and blood rushes to my groin. We're in the middle of a whiteout, and I'm stuck somewhere between crippling panic like I've never known before for this girl's safety and the overwhelming need to wrap my fingers around her neck and crush her mouth against my own while we freeze to death out here.

"Fuck you. Fuck this place. As soon as I can, I'm leaving." She snarls and tenses in my arms. Her entire body is rigid with anger and the cold, and I'm the sick asshole who is soaking up every moment of being so close, in spite of the insanity of our circumstances.

Yeah, and I'm hard as stone against the thickness of my pants. There might be a whole lot of winter layers in the way, but my cock reacts, thickening with each jostle of our bodies against one another.

I'm angry at myself. I'm angry at the universe for cursing me with the knowledge that Layla exists. I'm angry with my shitty son for treating her so poorly that she'd even look twice my way.

Leaning forward, I make sure my mouth is right against her ear. "Maybe all you are to me is the punishment I've been long overdue for being selfish." I grit out. "Maybe I'm the biggest asshole you'll ever meet who wants you to suffer exactly like I am."

"Well, you got your wish." Her coldness matches the bleak winter landscape of this mountaintop, and I should be relieved. I shouldn't be cursing to myself, while gripping the reins tighter, urging the horse to move faster. There are so many reasons for me to be overjoyed that the beautiful girl pressed against my torso has woken the fuck up and realized what an irredeemable bastard I am.

But instead of all that, something is stirring in my gut like a damn hurricane.

There's a tingling beneath my skin that won't go away. It buzzes and hums with every moment we draw closer to the peak of the barn, cedar planks and iron lettering partially obscured by white, barely standing out against the sky thrashing with snow and wild wind.

We reach the entrance, and I launch myself off the back of Winnie before we've stopped moving. We're still covered in snow, and flurries eddy around my boots from the open doors. These horses need warmth and to be fed and the tiny girl glares down at me from her position high on the front of the saddle, shaking. Not with cold, but with a desperate kind of anger and rejection.

The grim line of her plump mouth sends a sucker punch straight to my ribs.

I grab the reins of both horses and lead them further inside. Layla's eyes bore into my skull from where she's seated.

"You're right. You *are* too old for me. Bitterness has consumed you and shriveled up whatever used to beat inside your chest." She sneers in my direction. "You're going to rot up here hoping that tomorrow you might wake up, and you'll suddenly be free of the guilt you've been carrying around."

That's right, baby. See me for what I really am.

There's no denying that I deserve all of her frustration and more.

I reach up to roughly grab her, lifting her by the waist and setting her on both feet, and she shoves against my chest. "Don't touch me."

There's nothing but the sound of heavy breathing between us, and the gentle clip of hooves and chuff of breath as the horses settle in their stalls.

"Get inside the house, Layla." My throat tightens, and my jaw works overtime not to do the very thing that can't be undone if I cross that line. Reluctantly, I let go of her hips and tug my gloves off one by one. Studying every facet of her face as if it's the last time I might see this girl look my way.

Her green eyes are nearly glowing, with wisps of hair plastered against her wet cheeks from the melted snow. Those pouty lips of hers are stung a deep shade of dusky rose by the freezing temperatures, and my brain immediately connects that color with the sight of her hardened nipples.

"I'll deal with the horses. Go." I turn away—no, wrench myself away from her and start making work on Winnie's tack. Trying to focus entirely on the horse in front of me, and not be lured into looking over to where Layla is still standing.

Fixating on getting these horses cared for is about the only thing holding me together right now.

I want her.

I want her so badly it aches.

Yet, she's not mine to hold, or whisper to, or soak up her smiles.

It's the most fucked up thing I could have ever done to let myself get even a taste of her. It'll torment me for an eternity, and maybe that's the devil's bargain I've been cursed to endure living here on this mountain.

Alone.

I've had one taste of forbidden fruit, and now I'll be trapped in my own private hell with the faintest dream of her whimpering into my mouth and melting for me as I rubbed over her soaking wet panties.

Fucking fuck.

For a moment, I run my palm over the horse's long neck. Gathering myself, with head bowed to somewhere and somehow find it in myself to do the *right* thing. To be a good father. To not fuck up this girl's life because I'm being a selfish bastard. To take a last, deep inhale before I go over to the other stall and repeat this process.

I give her a final pat before straightening up and turning around.

But I don't even get five paces before I realize Layla is still here. She's standing in the middle of the barn with a bridle in hand and her eyes narrow on me. Behind her, I see that she's finished up while I've been lost in my head, and the horse in the stall behind her has already been taken care of.

"Thought I gave you an instruction." I grind each syllable like it's personally offended me.

She cocks her head ever so slightly to one side. "This is my job." Stating it with that same ice queen tone as before.

It slices like a motherfucker, but I can't help silently urging her to continue being like this. To forget about anything she might have found interesting in me and move on with her life.

"The job was to go inside." Get warm. Get dry. Get away from me and my fucked up obsession. Leave me out here to drown in my vat of longing surrounded by the sweet notes of hay and self-hatred.

"No. You don't get to ignore me for a whole week and then yell at me." She glares back. Green eyes glowing with emotion. "You freeze me out every time. You did it that day I first came here. As soon as you found out who I was, you turned to ice. It's the same thing now, and I know you'll do it again."

"Well, that's who I am. Sorry, sweetheart, but I can't change." The snarl is out of me before I can halt it.

"That's bullshit, and you know it. You've chosen to be that way, and you can choose differently."

My heart pounds in an erratic rhythm. "I don't know what you want from me, Layla." How else am I supposed to survive this? To deny this thing between us that shouldn't happen? How the fuck am I supposed to survive her?

I stride over, fully intending to swipe the bridle from her hands, but Layla tries to pre-empt me. She attempts to turn around and head for the tack room herself, and I shoot a hand out to catch her elbow.

"Leave it." I hear myself hiss the words through a clenched jaw. "Just go."

Layla spins towards me, and our bodies collide. I'm still holding her arm and even though she's glaring at me, there's no attempt to try and shake me off this time.

"I said," she thumps the heel of her palm against my shoulder, but the action is soft. Too soft. The way her hand sits over my chest is more like a caress. "Don't. Touch. Me."

We're tangled together in the middle of this storm, and instead of shoving me away, her fingers curl against the shell of my jacket.

Layla's big eyes hover on my mouth, tongue darting out to wet her bottom lip.

She swallows heavily, and her hand moves between us to grip the v of my collar.

"*Please*." Her throaty rasp is hardly more than a whisper.

I lift the bridle from her other hand, and there's a soft thud as the leather drops to the floor, and I've officially lost my mind because my fingers reach out to slide into the hair at the base of her neck. Tightening my hold, I yank her head back ever so slightly, and a tiny gasp rushes past her lips.

"Please, Colt."

Hearing her say my name in that breathy little voice, fuck. I'm going straight to hell. That moment is when the last tenuous thread of my resolve snaps.

With one hand still fisted in her soft curls, I crash my mouth against hers.

CHAPTER 19

I devour every little whimper Layla makes against my mouth. Madness roams freely through my veins as I dive into the gorgeous girl in my arms with every selfish desire to take and take and fucking take, running wild. There's no holding back as my tongue presses past the seam of her lips, invading and demanding. But she softens and opens for me like the good fucking girl she is and tangles her tongue with my own.

The soft, sweet noises she's making are a nectar I could feast on for eternity.

My grip is punishing and must be stinging her scalp, but right now, I'm not necessarily in control. I'm stealing her breath and devouring her lips, and the way she moans and presses up against me is going to echo in my brain for a lifetime.

She winds her arms tight around the back of my neck. Digging her nails into my nape... and she kisses me back without any restraint.

Fuck. Yes.

I pinch her lower lip between my teeth and tug on it, dragging a moan out of her that has my cock jerking. I've been hard for this girl all week long, so it's no surprise that I'm leaking inside my pants just from a single taste of her.

When I draw back a fraction, Layla stares at me with a glazed look in her eyes. She's flushed and panting, and her lips are that deep, dusky, rose color that drives me insane.

"You don't want me to touch you?"

"No." She bites down on that bottom lip of hers so hard it might bruise. Her eyes are hooded, and there's a dark tinge of conifer green coloring her gaze as lust takes over.

"How badly do you *not* want me to touch you, baby?"

Layla lifts her hips, arching against me. "So bad."

"You don't want me to taste you?"

Her tiny moan is filled with need. "*No.*" It's a barely-there prayer that means the complete opposite of what is coming out of her mouth.

I back her up until her shoulders slam against the wooden stall. It's not exactly warm in here, but my skin is on fire and there are far too many layers of clothes standing in the way of what I want.

My hands glide up beneath her jacket, seeking out the waistband of her jeans, as I drop my lips to kiss along her jaw. "I wouldn't want to go against your wishes. If you're telling me you don't want me to put my tongue inside you, or to lick your cunt until you're screaming, then I'd better not."

"You wouldn't." She exhales a shaky breath before sliding her nails higher up the back of my neck, tipping my hat onto the floor. Layla hums and digs her fingers tighter into my hair to hold me against the column of her neck.

God, I'm obsessed with having her fingers roam over me. I'll never wear that goddamn hat again if it means having her tugging on my hair and guiding me to rasp my mouth and beard all over her slender throat.

As my fingers find the button above her fly, her hips chase my every move. She tilts to give me better access, and I suck down on the sensitive spot below her ear. With each hot glide of my mouth over her pulse, I feel her blood quickening beneath that impossibly soft skin. It matches the furious thudding of my own heart, a thief determined to break its way out of my ribcage.

"Baby, I want to taste you." *Kiss.* "Fuck you." *Lick.* "Consume you." *Bite.*

"Colt. Oh, god." She shudders with each word. Then the sweetest and horniest noise escapes from her as I start working her pants down over her hips.

"This is just to take the edge off." I brush my lips over hers and suck her bottom lip until she's writhing with desire. It's too fucking cold out here to get her undressed properly. "I'm not leaving this spot until I've tasted your sweet little cunt."

Resting my forehead against hers, I brace one arm on the wall above her head and finally—fucking finally—dare take a glance down at the sight of her exposed to me for the first time. My breath shudders as we both look down, following the path of my other hand. She's so unbelievably soft, and pink, and glistening wet. Jesus. My thumb glides over her pussy lips, caressing and dipping into the slickness between her thighs. It's like every fucking fantasy I've had about this girl has come to life.

The sensation of having her, feeling her bare like this, is almost too much. My eyes drop closed for a moment as a dark groan escapes me.

She presses her plush lips against the stubble on my throat, her tongue darts out and laps at my skin with a whimper. "Yes. Holy shit. *Colt.*"

I feel drunk on the way she keeps saying my name.

"Fuck, you're so fucking wet." My dick aches as my thumb slides further in and swipes over her swollen clit. When I brush against the pouting little bud, stroking her pussy, Layla jerks a little. "Why are you so wet?" It comes out like a gritty curse.

This is surely my own personal hell. Because it was bad enough when I knew she wanted to kiss me back. It was pure torture seeing her look at me and fall apart while grinding in my lap. But now this? Now I know exactly how swollen and dripping her sweet little cunt is beneath me? Well, that singular glimpse is going to goddamn destroy me.

Her teeth graze my skin, panting breaths fan across my neck, a wildness clings to her energy. She's so tightly wound, I need her coming apart on my tongue right fucking now. That way I can get us inside and take my time, but this moment right here isn't about anything but chasing a release we've both been building toward for weeks.

Months, if I'm being honest with myself.

Fuck it all, because honesty feels a lot like doing the right thing, and if I scratch at that thought too long, I'm going to remember exactly why this is a terrible idea.

So I do the thing I shouldn't do, and lower myself down on my knees in front of her. Grabbing hold of her hips. Painfully fucking aware of how soft and perfect Layla is compared to my calloused, weather-beaten hands.

"Last chance, baby." I gaze up at her, hovering my mouth so close to her pussy, it's taking all my willpower not to feast on her without hearing the words that are going to spell my final damnation in this.

The scent of her arousal washes over me, and she's so damn sweet. It's a heady thing knowing that she's wet and needy and aching for this just as badly as I am. The fact that we're both in this torture together feels like a secret kind of fantasy. One we can both disappear into, suspending time just for this moment.

"I want you, so fucking badly. But I've never—I usually can't— Not like this."

Jesus. I'm torn right now. Do I hate that no one has ever treated this girl the way she deserves, or do I love that I get to be the one to ruin her for anyone else who might come after me?

I'm enough of an asshole that it's definitely the latter.

"You're going to shatter on my tongue. Then we're going to go inside, and I'm going to take my time worshiping this pussy." Dragging my mouth over her inner thigh allows me to greedily soak up the way she whimpers with pleasure, feeling the rasp of my beard.

"You don't have to."

I nip at the soft swell of flesh with my teeth, drawing a gasp out of her, before soothing the spot with my tongue.

"This is exactly where I want to be. I've been dreaming about having my mouth on your pussy for months." I growl against the inside of her thigh. That's not a lie either. Since that first day, I've had dreams about her, and as much as I tried to fight them, wiping Layla from my mind was impossible. Confirming just how much of a terrible person I am, because once I *knew* who she was, it only got filthier, more depraved, more focused on filling and marking and spending my release inside her.

Her whimper fills the air.

"Fuck, Layla. Tell me to stop." I blow gently over her pussy. "Baby, please just tell me to stop."

She shakes her head. Mouth flushed, lips swollen, her cheeks pink from both the cold and being flooded with arousal.

"I can't. I want more." She begs, and my dick kicks at the desperate sound. "*Please.*"

My teeth and beard graze her inner thigh again. "What do you want more of?"

"Everything. You. Your mouth. Oh, god." Layla pushes her fingers into my hair, and it's that touch of her fingertips that drags us both over the line we shouldn't be crossing.

I part her pussy lips with my thumbs and close my mouth over her clit. There's not much room to move with her pants only just pulled down over her luscious thighs, but I intend to explore every inch of this girl tonight. This is just the start of all the things I'm going to do to her.

All the ways I'm going to pleasure her.

Layla bucks against my mouth as I suck down. She's moaning and begging and tugging on my hair like a goddamn angel above me. The filthiest kind. One that doesn't mind getting her halo dirty down here in the darkness with me.

She tastes so fucking sweet, with her arousal coating my mouth and soaking my face. I lap at her and run my tongue through her seam, keeping her spread open so I can fasten down on the part of her that draws out the horniest little noises. My cock is begging to burst out of my own jeans, leaving me damn near humping the air as I drag my tongue up and swirl around her bud.

"Fuck. Oh. God." She starts shuddering above me, and I keep my eyes on her as I do it again. And again.

"Eyes on me, angel." I hum against her clit, then nip at her pussy lips when she doesn't immediately meet my gaze. Demanding her attention because I'm fucking addicted to watching this girl come already.

When her hooded, lust-filled eyes open, she can't help but let her eyelids flutter under the weight of her orgasm bearing down. Sucking on her clit, working her with my tongue, my fingers dig tighter, branding themselves into her hips. Helping to hold her upright as the force of her climax comes racing up to claim her.

"Colt. Oh, fuck. Oh, yes."

I go in for the kill.

"I'm—I'm coming. I'm coming." She chants, and her eyes hold mine in the most erotic fucking sight I've ever seen as her mouth hangs open and her body convulses above me. Layla's fingers remain clenched in my hair with the effort to hold herself up, and I know right then I'm more fucked than I thought.

Because I'm going to want this every day.

I'm going to want her out here, surrounded by the scent of cedar and leather, and I'm not going to be able to resist watching her come for me pushed up against this wooden wall looking like a goddess.

Giving her one final long lick, I ease backward and tug her pants up. Settling them loosely over her hips, before placing an open-mouthed kiss on the damp fabric covering her heat and perfect wetness. Jesus, the way this girl just fell apart on my tongue has got my dick so hard I have to adjust myself as I push up to my feet. My balls are throbbing—aching with the need to come.

But we can't do any more than this out here, we'll both freeze, no matter how good it feels to be lost to the dizziness of this stolen moment.

Layla's still floating somewhere on the waves of her orgasm, and it's the most beautiful damn thing I've ever seen. I brush some loose curls behind an ear before tilting her chin up with one knuckle, and she damn near purrs. I'm fucking ravenous for her, and it's taking everything in my self-control not to start ripping her clothes off right here and to shove her down in the hay.

Bracing one forearm high above her head, I lean down, seeking her out. Pressing a heated kiss against her lips until tiny fingers grip the front of my jacket. That's my cue to grab the backs of her thighs, lifting so she can circle her legs around me.

She flings her arms around my neck and dives against my mouth, harder and more demanding this time. Moaning as she melts and swirls her tongue, sampling her own sweetness there.

"You've wrecked me." I nibble at the sides of her lips and over her jaw. "Now I know what your cum on my tongue tastes like, I'm never going to get enough of this." My fingers knead her ass as I hold her tight and start walking us in the direction of the house.

"Then we're a match." She trails hot, wet kisses up the side of my neck in return, and Christ, it feels too addicting. "Because I *want* to be ruined by you, Colton Wilder."

I groan as she sucks on my pulse point. Hearing her say shit like that is simultaneously the best thing, and the worst fucking thing, considering our circumstances.

"I'm not good for you." I rasp against her ear. My blood hums, writhing and darting around like a wild creature ready to be set loose from its cage.

Layla feathers more kisses along my jaw, making my dick throb in anticipation of where we're heading. This forbidden moment is rushing up with the force of a hurricane to consume the two of us.

The perfect girl in my arms pauses to speak against my mouth, firmly tugging on my hair so hard I let out a growl.

"*Good* is not what I need." She sucks on my bottom lip as we make it to the front door, snow flurries dancing all around, wind howling in both our ears. "What I need is *you*."

CHAPTER 20

Layla

We barely make it inside the door before Colt has me pinned against the wall.

His mouth is a searing brand against mine, and I chase his tongue with desperate noises I didn't know I could make. We tear at each other's clothes, tugging on zippers and buttons, and bump into one another with the effort to shed the winter layers we're both wearing.

I feel like I'm burning up inside my skin.

Jackets thud to the floor one after the other, and my sweater is tugged over my head, leaving me in my bra and jeans still unbuttoned from out in the barn when Colt made me fall apart like no one else has done before.

I've never had a man make me come like that.

The sight of Colton Wilder on his knees with blazing eyes staring up at me while his tongue ran perfect circles over my clit will forever be embedded in my memory.

No man has *ever* looked at me with anything approaching such intensity.

My fingers yank at the hem of his shirt impatiently, I don't want to try and navigate buttons. I just want it off. I want this man naked right fucking now.

Colt senses my urgency and undoes the top couple of buttons with expert hands, before reaching behind his head and tugging everything off in one pull. Leaving his hair ruffled and wild and so achingly sexy.

"Jesus. You're so fucking gorgeous." Colt brushes the backs of his knuckles over the swell of my breasts and down my stomach. Goosebumps and flutters follow in the wake of his touch.

I move my palms to hover over his bare torso and pause. I've seen him half naked like this before, when he's forgotten his shirt and wandered around in the gray light of morning. Yet, this moment somehow seems like I'm overstepping by finally putting my hands on him.

Why is my mouth so dry? I hastily work down a swallow. My eyes bounce everywhere. From his sculpted shoulders, to his chest, down to the muscled outlines ridging his stomach. He's so fucking hot I can't even breathe.

"Can I touch you?" It comes out as a throaty whisper. God, I want to climb all over him. But I'm nervous as all hell.

The solid, powerful figure in front of me is a man, and I've clearly only ever wasted my time with boys.

Colt rests his palms up against the wall on either side of my head. Caging me in with his strength and warm scent. "You can have whatever you want, sweetheart."

His words glide over me like silk. Drawing me into him, like we're magnets, unable to remain apart. My fingers find every groove and dip and defined line, tracing over Colt's warm skin with a fever running through my veins.

I'm pretty sure I whimper because he's here and not running from this—us. And Colt's body is absolutely worth worshiping.

Holy shit.

"Fuck." His voice is husky as my fingers glide closer to the muscled v leading to his waistband. We're both breathing heavily, looking down at the path I'm tracing. One that leads right to the bulge where his cock stands hard and insistent against his fly.

I nibble my bottom lip. Fully aware that we're right at the brink of no return. The moment when my stupid moral compass decides to make itself known. "How does this work? We shouldn't … we shouldn't be doing this?"

Colt's stomach caves a little under the brush of my fingernails, following the dusting of dark hair leading below his pants.

"I'm a selfish asshole. Don't you think I know... that I shouldn't be anywhere near you right now?" He lets one hand drop and runs the length of my arm with the rough touch I'm ready to plead for more of. Immediately. "But I'm going insane with the need to have you, angel. So you tell me what you want. I'll take whatever fucking crumbs you're willing to throw on the floor."

My heart thunders in my ears as he reaches for my unbuttoned pants.

"The storm—the roads." I falter.

Colt's fingers hook below the loose waistband, tugging them down to expose the lace edging of my panties. "It'll be at least two weeks before they reopen," he murmurs.

My mind is spinning with pleasure and need and poor decisions. That means at least a couple more weeks stuck up here all alone with Colt and no way anyone can get in, or out.

"So we've got two weeks?" I drag my teeth over my bottom lip. My eyes flit up to meet his and the racing sensation in my chest intensifies.

His pupils are fully blown, and the sizzling lust in the air between our bodies is matched by the crackling in the giant fireplace. Neither of us needs to say it out loud, but we both know. We both understand what that means.

The clock is ticking until Kayce returns, and whatever this forbidden thing is between us has to end. It has to, because I can't stay here, and he won't risk further ruining his relationship with his son.

"Two weeks." Colt's jaw flexes.

"Two weeks."

I nod slowly in return. Repeating his words.

Hazel eyes slide down my body. Leaving a burning trail in their wake, roaming hot and hungry across the softness of my aching breasts and swell of my stomach.

I take in a shuddering breath.

He leans closer, hovering his lips over mine while circling the front of my neck with one strong hand. "I expect you in my bed every night." His fingers squeeze lightly over my throat, and my eyelashes flutter. "If that's all I get, I won't settle for anything less than having all of you."

A needy, whimpering noise rises up my throat beneath his firm hold.

This man has me quivering with desire under the possessiveness of his grip and his desire.

"That had better be a yes, Layla." Another squeeze punctuates his words.

I wet my lips and nod. "Yes."

That one small word seems to be the final straw for Colt. He hauls my body against his in a way that I don't think I'll ever get over, lifting me so effortlessly and carrying us both across to the lounge.

My horny brain is entirely hung up on the feel of his heated skin pressed up against mine, the way his scent winds a coil around me and wraps me up, how his muscles are so firm beneath my trembling fingers.

He's so steady and sure, while I feel soft, melted, reduced to a puddle.

Colt is so goddamn capable. What would it be like to have a man like this take care of me? It's a dangerous thought—one that I quickly push aside. This is sex, only. Don't go getting it twisted, Layla.

I'm tumbled down over the end of the couch, and my instinct is to try and push myself upright. But Colt takes command and presses a firm palm beneath my shoulder blades, tipping my body forward to greet the couch, exposing my ass in the air.

Holy shit.

This man is trying to kill me.

My already flushed cheeks turn into an inferno as I feel his presence right behind me, peeling my jeans off my legs with so much careful precision, it feels as though he's unwrapping me. Once they hit the floor, he lowers to his knees again, staring at every single curve and stretch mark from up close.

"Goddamn woman, that ass of yours has been tempting me since you first stepped foot on this mountain."

His voice is gravel and velvet and makes my toes curl.

"Colt..." My voice is muffled against the cushions and I try to squirm away from his scrutiny. It feels so wrong, and yet, at the same time, hearing how he appreciates my body is messing with my brain chemistry.

"Unless the rest of that sentence is *please eat my cunt until I forget my own name*, I don't want to hear another word." His fingers glide just along the crease below my ass, tracing the sensitive skin at the top of my thigh, before hooking beneath the edge of the fabric seated against my skin.

Tugging my soaked panties roughly to one side, he lets out a low, gritty sound.

I make a strangled noise of protest.

"You—You don't have to. You've already had to do that once."

"Had to?" Colt's so close I feel his rough words against my exposed pussy. He makes a disapproving noise, then bites my ass so hard I squeal. "Did some fuck-face with a small dick make you feel like you owed him if he ate your pussy one single time? Like you had to make it up to him even though he never made you come?"

Oh my god. Every inch of my skin has gone up in flames. I can't handle this. Colt is staring at the most intimate part of me, pointing out what idiots I've let myself fall into bed with up until this moment. His own son included.

"I'll tell you now, I intend on spending as much time as possible licking this sweet little pussy of yours. And I'll gladly spend all night with my head between your thighs without you touching me once."

I whine and jerk against the couch as he bites me again. A fragment, a spark of an idea flares to life inside me when I think about him leaving bruises on my skin. There's a hint of something, a faint tingling sensation that races through my veins... I hope to god when these two weeks end I'll be covered in his marks.

"There is no *having* to do anything, I've been craving this, Layla. I'll eat you for every meal. You are goddamn beautiful and the sweetest fucking thing I've ever tasted. So, let me take care of you until you're shaking and soaking my face like a good girl."

There's no more talking or wondering. Colt's wicked mouth is on me, leaving me a quivering mess, gasping and whining as he sets to work. He presses his tongue into me, then alternates that by sliding two fingers inside, and I'm hopelessly at his mercy.

I'm quaking, so close to coming another time—something I didn't know my body could do in such quick succession. There's not much I can do except dig my fingernails into the cushions below my head and let out a string of ungodly noises. Each flick and suck of his skilled tongue, along with the scratch of his beard against my sensitive skin, drags more whimpers and moans to the surface. The hardened buds of my nipples drag against the inside of my bra as they're pressed into the couch.

My legs shake when he spears his tongue inside again, humming against my pussy, seeming to love the way I'm losing it above him.

Fuck, this man has already ruined me, and I haven't even caught a glimpse of his cock.

This time, he draws back, right as I'm dangling on the precipice of falling apart. Leaving me lying there breathless and with my pulse pounding between my legs.

Warm arms band around my middle, drawing me upright, so that my back is against his broad chest. Colt seeks my lips out, tilting my head, devouring every drop of my soft moans. Forcing me to taste just how thoroughly coated in *me* his mouth is.

"I expect you to be right here and completely naked by the time I get back, angel."

He growls, nips at my jaw, then his heat and his strong arms—the only thing keeping me upright at this point—are gone. Leaving me a panting mess, awkwardly standing in the middle of the lounge.

I flutter around in place, trying not to collapse and to get my bearings. Working my way around the couch, I end up somewhere close to the fireplace. Without knowing what else to do, I toss a few fresh logs to build the flames back up.

God, I'm so not good at this.

When Colt saunters back into the room, his big hands are working on unfastening his jeans. Hazel eyes drag down my body in a leisurely sweep, while his tongue pokes against the side of his mouth. The corner of his lip tilts up, and the sight of him looking like some sort of sex-god, cowboy rogue, is entirely too much for me to handle.

"I—Uhh—" Apparently, he tongue-fucked all my brain cells out of me, because all I can do is stare at his groin.

He's in total command.

I feel painfully naive.

What I do notice, other than the way his corded muscles in his forearm flex as he unzips his fly, is a foil packet peeking out from one of his hands that he must have gone to find.

Of course, the sluttiest part of me kicks up a silent protest, demanding to feel this man bare. I'm on birth control. I'm all clear. I will happily drop to my knees and politely whimper my request to feel his cock pulse and unload inside me. But knowing that he's already had one run-in with an unwanted pregnancy in life, who could blame him for always using a condom.

Colt prowls towards me from across the room. "I won't ever say no to fucking you while still wearing clothes, angel, but right now, I'm greedy enough to want to see every perfect inch of you."

Oh, right. Getting naked... *for him.*

"Ok," I breathe out. Insanely turned on and more than a little shaky, I retreat a step as he closes in.

Reaching behind me, I unhook my bra, letting it drop to the floor. Another step and I'm backed up against the wall. This feels even more sensual, the fact he's demanding that I undress *for him*, while drinking in the sight of me. Colt has slowed everything right down, and it's only ramping up how needy I am to have him.

He sucks in a ragged breath as my nipples tighten even more under the weight of his gaze.

"And those soaking wet panties."

Each frantic thud of my heart is in the back of my throat. Biting down on my lower lip, I hook my thumbs under the lace and lower them to the floor. While the man in front of me palms himself through the front of his briefs. His pants hang loose around his hips, revealing that trail of dark hair below his navel and muscled v disappearing below the waistband.

With every agonizing second, he devours the sight of me. It's like nothing I've ever experienced before. Until now, I've only ever had sex with the lights off, fumbling around in a bed, covered up by sheets. No man has ever taken the time to watch my body like this.

I can't decide if I want to be swallowed up by the floor, or lay myself spread out for him and let him drink his fill all day long.

"Christ." There's a deep rumble that comes out of his chest. "How the fuck am I supposed to get anything done around here for the next two weeks?" Colt is right in front of me now. Reaching to grasp my chin between thumb and forefinger, his molten gaze brands me just like the proximity of his body does against my nakedness.

He drags his thumb over my bottom lip, then presses down. God, I crumble beneath the possessiveness of that tiny action. Forget being naked while he's still half-dressed. All this man needs to do is grip my chin and tug on my lip, and I'm ready to kiss his boots and plead for his cock.

Colt must read my mind, because the lines around his eyes

crease a little, and there's a renewed heat behind his hazel stare. I can't help but shiver the longer he crowds me like this and doesn't give me what I want so badly.

"Cold, baby?" His voice is raspy.

I shake my head. "God, no."

Amber flecks spark and glow brighter around the inner ring of his eyes. It's an honest answer, too. There's so much heat pouring off his bare chest, I feel like it's about a hundred degrees in here. My pussy is screaming for him, and my blood is racing in time with the force of the storm outside.

A low rumble fills the space between us. "I'm going to try and take it slow with you, sweetheart... if I do something to hurt you, promise me you'll tell me." Colt's hands move down to where his erection strains against the front of his briefs, and my greedy eyes track every second.

The moment he pushes down the waistband and his cock springs free, I let out a soft whimper.

Jesus. Fuck.

I knew Colt had a big dick, but this... he's thick and long and the smooth length is veined. I'm salivating at the size of him, while my pussy is already clenching in anticipation of whether or not this man is going to split me in half.

"Holy shit." The whisper falls out of me.

He makes quick work of ripping the foil and rolling the condom over his massive cock. All the while, I'm squirming and staring and going out of my head with the anticipation of having him inside me.

I don't want to go slow anymore. I want this man to pound into me and have me screaming this mountain down.

"Hold on tight, angel." Colt reaches behind my thighs, hooking me around his waist and my arms around his neck. My back is shoved up against the wall, and I'm pretty sure if it wasn't below freezing outside, this is exactly how things would have ended up in the barn.

Then he's nudging at my core. With his jeans slung low on his hips, fisting the fat head with one hand, he guides himself against my entrance. It's impossible to take my eyes off the spot where our bodies are about to join together in the most carnal way.

He presses forward, notching the tip just inside, and I gasp at the stretch. I'm soaking wet and so fucking turned on after having his tongue in my pussy, that he slides forward easily. Stilling and holding there, with just the head breaching me.

"*Fuuuuck.*" I dig my fingernails into the back of his neck. My pussy walls are already fluttering, adjusting, welcoming this man inside me for the first time. The sight of him, hard and slowly pressing forward has my eyes nearly rolling back in my skull. He's so fucking big, it pinches a little, in a good way, but even still, I've never experienced anything like the size of this man.

"God. Colt. I don't know if it's going to fit."

Colt makes the sexiest groaning sound ever. One that vibrates straight through into my chest.

"It'll fit, baby." He bends his head and sucks my earlobe into his hot mouth, sinking a little deeper as he does so. "We'll make it fit." The pleasure of how good his lips feel, while my body adjusts to him, nearly undoes me completely.

"Breathe for me. Just like that." The gravel in his voice and scrape of his beard against my throat is intoxicating. "Relax, I'm not even halfway in yet."

"Oh, god." I whimper. Melting against him as he keeps licking and sucking down on the sensitive spot beneath my ear.

He keeps working me like that, rough hands hold me tight, as his velvet words pour against my overheated skin and my body welcomes him deeper and deeper.

I'm only vaguely aware that I'm moaning and tugging on his hair, my hips starting to shift of their own accord. Waves of sensation and pleasure roll through me in endless succession with each new shove forward. Colt works himself in and out with pulsing thrusts, each time sinking further inside my pussy.

"That's it, baby. Look at you, taking me so well." His praise coats me from head to toe as I arch into him. Everything feels tingly, and I'm floating, gliding as my almost-orgasm from before dances back into reach.

Colt groans as his hips finally meet mine. "Jesus. Fuck."

"Oh, god." I feel so full. Forget ruining me, this man is going to imprint himself upon my body in a way I'm never going to be able to forget.

"Are you ok?" His lips move against my neck. I can feel the strain in every muscle of his shoulders as he's holding himself still. Letting me stretch around him.

"Please. It's so good. You feel so good." Fuck me senseless, *please*, because a thought has already begun to dangle on the edge of my lust-soaked mind... I don't think two weeks is going to be enough with this man.

"You have no idea."

His voice draws me out of getting lost inside my own head. Shifting his hips back, sliding almost all the way out, I'm then treated to the most insane, incredible sensation as he punches forward. Both of us groan while pleasure shoots through me, making my toes curl. And that's when he really fucks me. Time slows down, and there's nothing but the slap of our bodies together, the filthy sound of my wetness, and the desperate noises I make while clinging to him.

I don't stand a chance against how good this feels, with my climax thundering toward me.

"That's it, beautiful. Let go for me." Colt slides his thumb down between us, finding my clit and rubbing firm circles. Moaning and clenching around him, I'm dragged beneath the wave almost immediately. He expertly captures my mouth with his own and soaks up every ounce of my climax, every whimpering noise.

He fucks me straight through my orgasm, maybe into another, I don't even know, but the drag of his cock against my walls is drugging. Colt slams into me until I feel him tense, his thrusts start to lose their rhythm, and his grip grows punishing.

"Fuck. *Fuuuck*. Angel." He grunts a delicious, dark noise that I want to curl into and wrap myself in, then I feel his cock swell, and he buries himself deep. Colt's erratic breaths and biting kisses are matched by his release sweeping through as he fills the condom.

I'm officially lost to this man. Clinging to his neck, with our hearts hammering between us, gladly buried beneath the drifts of snow trapping us here together.

CHAPTER 21

Layla

"Stay right there, baby... keep that pussy warm for me." Colt hits me with the sexiest fucking look, and even though it's all ice and snow outside, I melt as quick as a popsicle on hot pavement. Sinking back on my elbows, the soft blanket I'm bundled in beside the fire cushions my body.

He kneels before me, reaching to toss another couple of pieces of wood on the embers, before leaning one powerful arm on either side of my hips and brushing his mouth over mine.

I'm struggling to not straight up whimper every time his beard drags across my skin. The rough glide is so damn sensual, my thighs squeeze together, knowing *exactly* how good that same kiss is when his mouth is in other places.

"You're not done?" I tease.

"Not even fucking close." He nips at my puffy bottom lip, and when he pulls back, I can see that he's already thickening, nearly hard again, with a prominent bulge in the front of his briefs.

Holy fucking shit.

We haven't yet managed to leave the lounge. After fucking me senseless up against the wall, he laid me out in front of the fire with my legs thrown over his shoulders and had me coming on his tongue. Again.

If I thought I was in trouble with fantasizing about this man, now that I've had a glimpse of what he can do to my body, I might be a lost cause for eternity.

We might've agreed to two weeks of allowing this intensity between us to play out, but there's a spark burning deep inside my chest that already knows I won't ever find another man to compete with the cowboy currently striding half-naked out of the room.

God, his body is incredible.

I'm left gaping after him, unashamedly eating up every flexed indent along his spine as his muscles do their thing. A small laugh dances on my lips because he's still wearing his jeans. Something about knowing this man was too busy giving me orgasm after orgasm to get fully undressed is immensely fucking hot.

As Colt disappears off into the kitchen, my stomach decides to let out a grumbled protest. What is the time even? It's so hard to tell with how dark it is outside and the storm raging around the ranch feels like being stuck inside a snow globe being shaken around.

For whatever reason—one that I'm not prepared to examine too closely—I don't feel ready to be separated from him just yet. So, I bundle my naked self up in the blanket and tiptoe across the lounge. There's a trail of clothes strewn along the path we obviously took once we made it inside. Each discarded item of clothing I come across serves as a replayed memory—moments that cause my cheeks to heat pop back up in wickedly vivid detail.

Colt's flannel shirt lies in a crumpled pile on the floor in the hallway, and I can't resist the temptation to put it on. If I'm only going to get a momentary glimpse of indulging in everything *Colton Wilder,* then screw it, I'll steal all his clothes for the next two weeks. He wants me in his bed every night? Surely, I'm at liberty to enjoy spending as much time wrapped in his scent and potent masculinity as possible.

Once I've shimmied into the fabric—which, holy fuck, smells so insanely good my pussy is already perking up with joy—I follow him into the kitchen. There's something heating in the microwave, and my taste buds are doing little cartwheels in anticipation.

I must make a noise to that effect because my rugged cowboy glances over his shoulder at me.

Then does a double-take at my appearance.

A five-alarm fire explodes across his eyes as he rakes over every inch of my body, tracing the length of his shirt down to my bare legs.

"Well, there goes my plan to keep you naked, but can't say I'm going to protest, mind you. That's a hot fucking sight... it's gonna be hard to forget seeing you freshly fucked and wearing my shirt anytime soon." Colt grabs the steaming container and swipes up a couple of forks, joining me around where I'm standing on the other side of the kitchen island. "Can I convince you to wear either nothing or only that for the next two weeks?"

Cocking my head to one side, I give him a smirk. "Not unless you want me losing a limb to frostbite while I'm taking care of the horses. Can't imagine that would look too good on my resume."

He shakes his head, and instead of heading back to the lounge like I'm anticipating, he drops the food onto the table and reaches for me. With one fluid motion, that is far too smooth for my sanity, he hoists me up so that I'm seated on the countertop.

"I suppose I can make allowances for outdoor activities." He's got an amber sparkle in his irises, and those crinkles around his eyes make their appearance as they tend to do when he's teasing me. Just like that very first day we met at the gas station.

Jesus. Do not go falling head over heels for this man over his eyes.

The way my heart is fluttering around and has grown wings inside my chest, I don't want to dare admit it might already be too late.

Colt steps between my knees, picking up the heated bowl of leftovers to hold in one big hand. It's only lazy macaroni I made yesterday, but day two cheesy carbs have never looked so appetizing.

Especially when there's a bare-chested cowboy between my legs handing me a fork and sharing a meal with me out of the same bowl.

It's kind of cute and insanely sexy all at the same time.

"Aren't you cold?" I stab some pasta and gesture at his nakedness. Not that I'm complaining, but it's a whiteout beyond the kitchen windows, and even though it's toasty warm in here, I don't want him catching a chill because we've been too insane for each other to worry about clothes.

He digs around the bowl with his own fork and shakes his head. "No. Especially not when I'm about fifteen minutes from being buried inside that sweet little pussy of yours again." Popping the mouthful, he chews his pasta, looking particularly sinful as he does so.

Goddammit, I can't stop the creeping blush spreading up from my chest.

"You're going to kill me. Flaunting *that* and a filthy mouth, Mr. Wilder." Twisting my lips, I lean forward and spear some more macaroni.

Colt makes a rough noise.

Apparently, we've both just had the same visceral reaction to those words that just slipped out.

I have to concentrate hard on eating and not imagining being on my knees addressing him as *Mr. Wilder*.

"Says the beautiful girl sitting in my kitchen with a body like *that*." He pointedly takes in my figure as he echoes my words.

Well, shit. If I didn't already want this man to do wicked things to me all night long, he's just guaranteed that I might beg him to.

"You know, I'm rather impressed..." I point my fork at his handsomeness, in hopes of distracting myself from the way my body is heating up the longer he stands this close. With his jeans scraping the sensitive insides of my knees, I'm pretty sure this is just another round of foreplay that he's calculated to perfection. "Turns out you do know how to form proper sentences after all."

Popping another mouthful, he chews it while raking his gaze

over me. Purposely taking his fucking time as I begin to squirm beneath his lingering stare.

"And here I thought you were a quiet little thing, until my tongue is in your pussy, and you're suddenly very vocal."

"Oh, my god." I blush so fucking hard and swat at his muscly arm. God damn, this man is carved from granite. "Says the man who didn't say a single word to me for an entire week, but miraculously becomes the king of dirty talk." All I can do is peek at him from beneath my lashes.

Colt's lips tug at the corners, and his eyes dance with honeyed flecks swimming amongst the hazel. He looks so boyish and charming it makes my pathetic little heart swoon.

"The king, hmm?" He sets the bowl aside, then reaches for my chin, grasping it between his thumb and forefinger, before leaning down and brushing his lips against mine.

Sweet Jesus. My heart is officially plummeting like one of those freebasers. Only, I have no parachute strapped to me and the rocks below are rushing in at light speed.

"I like the idea of you being my queen," he murmurs against my lips. "One who loves to rub her pussy all over my face and shatter around my cock like a fucking dream come true."

There are no words. My brain has gone blank. All I'm capable of at this point is staring back with what I'm certain are big cartoon hearts in my eyes.

If I've got any hope of surviving this, I need to firmly ignore that first part about being his queen. He doesn't mean that. This is just sex. A release for both of us after so much tension and longing.

I can't go forgetting who I am and who this man is and that our time together is painfully finite.

"Are we done eating?" There's a ragged noise as I clear my throat, but I'm basically just in a trance. Ready and willing to worship at the altar of Colt Wilder—sex god and rugged fantasy made flesh.

"Food? Yes." He lets go of my chin, sliding firm hands underneath my ass, effortlessly lifting me, and I have to throw my arms around his neck to steady myself. "You? No. I'm nowhere near satisfied, angel."

He ignores my squeal and carries me through the house, clinging to him, inhaling big hits of his woodsy scent like a woman possessed. It's only when we get to his bedroom that things tumble into focus all over again.

This is real. This is happening.

He actually wants this... with me.

Seeing the inside of his bedroom for the first time feels so natural, yet at the same time I can't hide the grin that threatens to overtake my face. There's hardly time to glimpse more than a quick look at the neatly made bed with stone-colored soft coverings and white sheets I want to sprawl in, preferably while being spooned by this gorgeous man. Big sliding doors out onto the porch. No clutter. But we're already in his ensuite bathroom before I can really absorb it all.

When Colt sets me on my feet, there's something I know I definitely want. My fingers snag the waistband of his jeans before he can move away in the direction of the tiled walk-in shower.

"Since you've taken such good care of me..." I'm channeling every ounce of confidence I can muster as my fingers work his button and fly. Biting down on my lower lip, my gaze holds his hooded expression. "Now it's my turn."

I'm back in that moment we had together when I was in his lap, and there was silent tension rolling around us like a forcefield. Colt wants this. His pupils grow with lust as he watches me, but something also tells me he's not used to someone willingly taking care of him in this way.

"You want to get on your knees for me, angel?" His voice is thick with longing and so fucking sexy.

Nodding, I ease his jeans down past his hips, and he takes over to kick them off, then shucks his briefs. When I sink down in front of him, the sight of his cock is enough to have my thighs clench in renewed anticipation.

In this light and at this angle, impressive feels like barely enough of an adequate description to do him justice.

I've definitely never been with a man this blessed in the dick department before.

My eyes must say all of that, or maybe I accidentally blurted it out loud, but the man standing before me clears his throat. One calloused palm glides along my jaw, guiding me to look up at him.

"Need a towel for your knees, baby?"

God, this man. I nod and wait in place as he grabs the world's biggest and fluffiest-looking man-towel so I can kneel on it rather than the hard tiles.

As he stands back in front of me, his hard length bobs with a glistening bead at the tip, and that's when I see it. My brows furrow a little, and my fingers lightly trace the markings on reflex. Silvery lines and puckered, stretched skin extend down his right thigh. It looks like a series of old wounds. Ones that have long since healed, but must have happened as a child, and from the looks of them were never properly taken care of. As I glance a little closer, I see some similar markings on his left thigh. Interspersed with scar tissue is what appears to be old burn marks, too.

"Part of my not-so-pleasant bedtime story." He gathers my hair on top of my head and watches me as I take in the pain of his past.

No words can make any of it better, but I want to show him how sorry I am for what he's been through. While ensuring he's under no illusion that I'm bothered by the sight of his scars at all. He's gorgeous, and these are a part of him, and he's so fucking strong and secure and deserves to be utterly worshipped.

Leaning forward, I place a kiss over the largest area of puckered skin that sits on the front of his thigh. Then, feather more kisses, tracking down along the path of whatever wounds and awful things happened to him so long ago.

Colt's fingertips brush against my scalp; he keeps hold of my hair, but it's not rough or tugging. Just commanding enough that it sends a shudder through me.

Then there's no more waiting for this, I'm desperate for a taste of this man. As I wrap my fingers around the base, his thick cock jerks in my grip.

I run my tongue to trace his veined length, before swirling around the head. Tasting the saltiness of him while his musky scent wraps around me. As I work to take him deeper, I realize there's a faint hint of *me* on him too, and holy shit, that makes my clit throb.

God, this is every desire come to life, and I pretty quickly lose myself in the way I'm wrapping my lips around the velvety feel of him and sucking down.

Hollowing my cheeks, I dip further forward, focusing on relaxing and breathing through my nose and anything possible to navigate the fact that this man is so fucking huge.

I'm turned on as all hell. Having his cock filling my mouth perfectly and gliding across my tongue is stirring up a wildfire low in my stomach. My pussy clenches and hums, knowing just how mind-altering it is to have him stretching me and filling me, and thrusting deep inside.

Well, fuck. I'm a mess of saliva pooling around the corners of my mouth within seconds, and I can't help but moan around his length.

Which leaves Colt shuddering and murmuring all sorts of praise above me. He tells me how beautiful I look, how well I'm taking him, how my mouth is every dirty fucking fantasy he's ever had.

I might be on my knees for him right now, but I feel adored in a way I've never experienced before.

"Fuck. Layla. I can't hold back with you." My eyes water, but tip up to meet his fierce gaze above me. Digging my fingers into his thighs, I hum around his cock and guide him to do what we both want right now.

He lets out a rough noise. "Tell me if it's too much... *fffuuck.*" Slowly, his hips start to pump forward, and his eyes drop closed.

Yes. God, yes. Seeing this man swept up in the throes of pleasure all because of me is officially my new favorite thing in the world.

One of his hands leaves my hair, and wraps around the front of my throat, collaring me and massaging over the column of my neck each time he thrusts forward.

Holy shit. *Holy shit.*

An avalanche of sparks and heat rushes through me as my clit pulses with an intensified rhythm. This is the side of him I know I'll crave. That powerful, in-command kind of dominance that leaves me feeling cared for while under his control.

I want to relieve that ache so badly, but I'm hanging on to his powerful thighs, allowing Colt to chase his pleasure and floating on the headiness of this moment.

"Look at you, angel. Your mouth wrapped around my cock like you were made just for me. Look how well you take me. Taking everything." With each thrust forward, he hits the back of my throat, and I swallow around his tip, soaking up each time he lets out a deep, resonant groan at how good that feels.

"I bet you want to play with that pretty little pussy of yours, don't you? You're squirming and looking so goddamn perfect. I bet you're already soaking."

I'm pleading with my eyes. Yes. That's exactly what I want.

The noise that comes out of me with my mouth full of his dick is slutty and desperate.

"Maybe next time, but right now, I need to fuck you and be buried deep inside your cunt when you fall apart for me."

Well, in that case...

He draws out on a wet pop, sliding the hand up from my neck to swipe at my puffy lips. The look on his face is so fierce, filled with something that I could only describe as raw, unfiltered desire.

It's addictive to think that this man has the most gorgeous hazel eyes, capable of looking at me like that.

For a moment, I wonder what he sees in mine. But I can't go letting my heart get tangled in this. Right now, it's racing at a frantic pace, and I'm prepared to chase the high of this next orgasm while being filled over and over by this man.

"Get in the shower. Face the wall." He presses down on my bottom lip again. All firm commanding energy, the kind that sucks the air out of my lungs.

"Ok," I breathe out, probably sounding exactly as dazed as I feel.

I slip out of his shirt, and get up on more than shaky legs. Making my way to the shower, which is a replica of my own, I turn on the water. Steam starts to billow and as I do exactly as he said, my palms brace against the wet tiles.

This is so much like the fantasies I've had while on my own; a shudder of anticipation rolls through me. Waiting for him naked like this feels thrilling.

His presence sweeps in behind me as the warm water sluices over my skin, and he tucks my hair over one shoulder. Plush lips and the scrape of his beard slide along the curve of my neck and trail a hot, wet line up my skin to suck down on my thundering pulse point.

Does this man have any clue of how gone I am for him? I hope to God I don't blurt out something like confessing my undying love, because there was every chance I might have done so earlier when he was sucking on my clit until I whimpered his name over and over and over.

"I'm gonna be between these pretty thighs all night." He rasps against my ear, as his body fits in behind mine, angling me just how he wants. Colt guides himself to my soaked entrance, rubbing the rigid head of him sheathed in a new condom through my slickness before he presses the tip in.

"Oh, god. Oh, god." I moan. Arching my spine and spinning out of my head already at that stretch that feels so fucking incredible.

"Squeeze me just like that, my perfect girl." Colt presses forward, and I can't help the whimpers tumbling past my lips. I'm begging and pleading and wanting him to fuck me senseless. But he's going so torturously slow. "Christ, you're so fucking tight."

Colt fills me and withdraws right to the tip, keeping me pressed against the shower wall, with my spine curved so he can sink so deep I'm seeing stars instantly. There's a spot he hits that has my body clenching and gripping him in ecstasy, one that I didn't know was even possible for it to feel *this good*.

"Give it to me, angel. Then I'm going to have you in my bed, and you're going to give me one more."

"Fuck, I'm so close." My toes curl, and my clit throbs, and I'm panting—spiraling toward the edge of this next climax with each pump of his hips against my ass.

His hands roam in tender caresses, over every inch of my soft flesh. Colt maps my body, tracing the crease at the tops of my thighs and over the swell of my stomach. Finding my aching full breasts, he pinches my nipples until I'm crying out with pleasure. All the while, that wicked mouth unleashes a torrent of dirty talk in time with each slow, deep thrust of his cock. Combining to unravel me into a million fractured pieces.

As the warmth of the shower beats down, he slides one hand over my pussy, and finally—finally gives me the relief I've been aching for.

"That's it. I can feel you squeezing the life out of me, angel. I know you're close. You're doing so well." Colt talks me through it, dipping a finger through my pussy lips to rub firm circles over my swollen clit, and I'm flying, soaring. White-hot sparks travel up from my toes, and the warmth of his voice right at my ear takes me over the crest. This time, my climax thunders through me, and I'm a whimpering, shaking mess.

"Such a good girl for me."

His praise is right there, sliding over my heated skin, flowing with the ease and fluidity of the shower as he keeps pumping slow glides in and out of my channel. Massaging my clit, he guides me down from somewhere way up in the midst of the clouds high above the ranch somewhere.

I don't even think I'm fully back to earth when I feel the shower cut off, and Colt pulls out of me. Wrapping me in a towel,

I'm tugged into his bed. He hasn't come yet, but exactly as promised, proceeds to spend the rest of the night between my thighs.

Leaving my heart fluttering a wild, pathetic rhythm that answers only to the name of this cowboy.

CHAPTER 22

Layla

Waking up, there's no hiding the smile that immediately finds itself at home on my lips. I feel like I must have spent the whole night grinning because my cheeks are sore.

Actually, make that, my entire body feels sore... but in a deliciously, filthy way.

Colt certainly made true on his promises of not getting much sleep.

With teeth dragging across my bottom lip, I brush my touch over the imprint of his fingers left on my hips. After the shower, he tugged me down on top of him once we'd finally made it to the bedroom.

"Ride me, angel. Give me one more."

Holy shit. The man dragged yet another orgasm out of me, when I was certain there was no fucking way my body could possibly reach one more climax. Only, this time when it claimed me, the sensation was slow and rolling and languid, picking me up and spiriting me away as he let go with his own release.

I'm more than a little groggy with the lack of sleep. It feels like his hands were on me, and his giant cock was buried inside me only a few moments ago, yet as I turn my head, stretching like a cat beneath the thick blanket, my hulking cowboy has vanished.

There's only the hypnotizing scent of him, and the unfamiliar feel of his soft bed linen to cradle me this morning.

If it could even still be considered morning.

My head pops up off the pillow, scanning the room and listening for any hint of where Colt might be.

But everything is peacefully quiet, with no wind howling or creaking sounds roaming through the house like I've become accustomed to whenever there's a storm front whipping across Devil's Peak.

Wriggling around, I move to toss the covers aside and go in search of something to wear—because I am most definitely still completely naked and in the bed of my ex-boyfriend's father—when my eyes fall on the sight of my phone on the bedside table, a note tucked beneath it.

I don't remember where I left my cell last night. Colt must have fetched it for me, and my heart does backflips and cartwheels that he didn't want to wake me, but that he's gone to the effort of leaving this right here for me to find easily.

Do not go reading anything into it, Layla.

The attempt at sternly talking to myself does nothing to deter my silly little heart from giggling and skipping circles inside my chest.

His handwriting is kind of scrawling, but easily legible. Black ballpoint on a lined sheet torn from a spiral notebook with the top of the page all ragged where he's ripped it out.

It's so very... him.

'Gone to take care of the stock. Consider this an official day off, especially since your demanding boss kept you up all night.'

Forget trying to keep my cool. Colton Wilder flirting with me over cute handwritten notes left beside my pillow in the morning... that's my goddamn weak spot, right there.

I check the time. Shit, it's already 10 a.m.

No wonder he needed to go take care of things around the

ranch. Here I've been lazing in bed, while he's gone off braving the snow and cold. Part of me feels insanely guilty, but after the way last night took such an unexpected turn, maybe this is his way of giving himself a little space. An opportunity to gain a clear head.

God, I hope he's not having second thoughts. My stomach quickly knots itself at the idea he might be wanting some time to *think* and come to the inevitable conclusion that falling into bed together was a massive fucking mistake.

Sucking in a deep breath through my nose, I decide now is not the time to start overanalyzing. Last night was the best fucking sex I've ever had. Even if it was a one-time-only thing—the mere thought of which just about makes me whimper like a pathetic fool—there's no denying our chemistry.

Everything was perfect and scandalously hot.

A girl can only dream of being indulged so expertly by a cowboy sex god.

Once I've found a towel and padded back to my own room, I make quick work of showering, pulling on some leggings that do wonderful things for my ass paired with a cropped sweater I can always count on to make me feel cute as hell. Taming my wild hair is out of the question, so I settle on a stylishly messy bun.

Glancing at myself in the mirror, I can hardly believe how far and fast things have changed since last night. My cheeks heat at the thought of seeing Colt for the first time... but even though I'm nervous, there's also excitement zooming around behind my ribs.

I'm all giddy over a certain cowboy who is nearly twice my age and my ex-boyfriend's father.

Holy shit, who am I, and what did I do with Layla Birch—good girl ranch hand?

As the promise of coffee and food lures me toward the kitchen, I can hear the sizzling of a pan and there's a mouth-watering smell of bacon drifting to greet me.

But, the moment I spy his broad shoulders from the back, my nerves kick up.

How does this work? Am I allowed to go up to him and kiss

him? Do we kiss? Outside of sex and getting naked and being out of our minds for each other, how do I treat this cowboy?

Colt turns around with the pan, and his expression doesn't really tell me anything. Last night, when we shared our bowl of reheated macaroni and he stood right there at the kitchen island between my knees, he was flirty and more seductive than can be good for my health.

Here, now, in the mid-morning light, he's standing on the far side of the bench looking like he wants to melt the cup of coffee in front of him with the powers of the mind.

"Hey." I wander over to the pot he's already made. While my eyes feel like they're hanging out of my head, in desperate need of said caffeine, I'm also more than a little uncertain of how we do *this* part. Busying myself with pouring a mug, a glance confirms that he already has his own, so I retreat around the other side of the counter and slide onto the closest stool.

This man is unreadable at the best of times, and while I'm not going to tolerate poor behavior from him, I also have compassion for the fact that what we did would be a lot for him to process.

Fuck my life for being such a goddamn empath all the time.

There's no turning that sucker off.

"Thanks for letting me sleep... I could have come and given you a hand." I fiddle with the cuff of my sweater as I watch him fix a plate. An empty one sits beside the sink; his own breakfast already eaten.

"It was only feeding out, easy enough to do on my own." He doesn't really look at me, and I'm shifting around uncomfortably in my chair.

I could have sworn the note he left beside the bed for me was playful, a little flirtatious even. So why is he looking like he wants to hurl the frying pan across the kitchen?

Maybe I read it all wrong between us.

"Colt... if you need..." I barely get the words out before he cuts me off.

"Layla." My plate gets slid across to me, loaded with bacon and

228

a couple of fried eggs, and smelling all kinds of delicious. Except, the man in question hovers and then leans forward, bracing himself on the countertop with his fists.

Goddammit, at this rate, I'm going to crawl out of my skin.

This is it.

This is the moment he tells me it was all a bad idea, a terrible idea even, and that he's going to pack me off on a horse down the mountain.

"We're going to have to have a real fucking adult conversation." His jaw flexes a couple of times.

Oh god. I feel shaky. I knew in my logical mind that there was every chance this might happen.

"It's ok, Colt." Resting my mug on the counter, I keep my fingers wrapped around it, even just to give myself something to hold onto. Warmth seeps through my fingertips as I try to find adequate words.

But there are none. So, I blurt out what I probably—most definitely—should not be saying. "Last night was amazing. Incredible. I just thought... fuck... that maybe this might have been fun for more than just that once, but I don't want you to feel uncomfortable, so..."

My words die in my throat when the cowboy in front of me advances so fast I'm left a little dizzy.

Within a heartbeat he's standing right beside my stool, spinning me around to face him. Colt is so close that I'm consumed by his scent and heat and brawn that fills every morsel of my awareness. His flannel shirt is rolled up his arms, revealing those corded muscles and network of veins. It takes so much fucking willpower not to grab the hem of the fabric and tug his body against mine.

"What the fuck are you talking about?" He looks at me with flashing eyes, and in those honeyed depths, for a second, I see a dash of a deeper emotion. Concern? Surely not.

"I just—uhh—I'm assuming you were about to say how terrible this whole idea was?"

"Layla... Fuck..." Colt shakes his head while scrubbing a hand over his stubble. "No, angel, what I'm trying to say here is that we've got a *supplies* issue." His brows pinch together.

My pulse intensifies. Relief and some other weird sensation pours into my veins at hearing him call me *angel* and that he's almost touching me again.

"A *supplies* issue?" It's my turn to look bewildered.

That's when Colt erases any thought from my mind. He makes a soft noise in the back of his throat, then runs the knuckle of his forefinger over my cheek. Using that same hand, he glides down, tracing over my skin, before tipping my chin up to meet his stare. With one fist braced on the back of my stool, he lowers his mouth to meet mine and steals me away in a soft, divine kiss. One that feels warm, comforting, with a faint hint of coffee on his wetted lips. As he treats me to such an exquisite moment, the tingling scratch of his beard sends a wave of arousal straight through me.

I'm instantly transported to all the places his mouth, and that beard, made their acquaintance with other parts of my body last night. Then again in the early hours of this morning.

"That should have been the first fucking thing I did when you walked in here, I'm sorry. I'm completely shit at this." He brushes his lips over mine again before drawing back.

Excuse me while I collect myself. This man has got me busy dissolving into a puddle on the kitchen floor.

"You're not shit at this." I somehow remember how to form words.

"No—Yes—I am, Layla. I've spent the past couple of hours in my own fucking head, then seeing you walk in here looking too gorgeous for words made me realize that we need to have a serious conversation."

I blush profusely, and somehow attempt to keep my cool.

"About?"

"There's something I didn't really think to factor in."

"And that is..." Tilting my head to one side, I wonder what on earth he's about to say.

"Protection." Colt practically chews the word and spits it out.

I have to bite the inside of my cheek to stop from laughing out loud. He looks so fucking serious right now, and while I get it, I really do, it shouldn't be quite as dramatic as he's making this out to be.

"You're saying that..."

"Layla, trust me when I say that I'm going to struggle to keep my hands off you these next couple of weeks... and I haven't got anywhere near the number of condoms for all the ways I plan on taking care of you, sweet girl."

A smile tugs at the corners of my mouth as I flutter my eyelashes over my coffee in his direction. "And that's what you're all twisted up about in here?"

"Call me old fashioned, or just too damn polite for my own good, but don't you think it's fairly important to talk about?" He crosses his arms and gives me a stern look, the exact kind that leaves my clit pulsing.

"No, I do... and I truly appreciate it. I just can't say that was what I expected we'd be discussing over breakfast."

"Well, in my eyes, it sure as hell is a serious chat we need to be having. Not while it's in the heat of the moment, and I'm two seconds away from getting my mouth on your pussy."

I have to take a hasty gulp of my coffee, with my cheeks flaming at the words *mouth* and *pussy* coming from this man, never mind the fact that I most definitely am ready for more of that kind of treatment. Preferably as soon as possible.

"Ok, cowboy..." He wants an *adult* conversation, then I'm more than happy to lay it all out on the line to prove to him just how much I want this. How much I want him, even if it's only for the short amount of time I'll be able to enjoy having him. "I'm on birth control, and I'm all clear, just so you know. I got tested before winter... and, well... you're the only person I've been with since then."

He still looks pained, and closes his eyes as he clears his throat. "I wanted to ignore it this morning when I pulled open the drawer in the bathroom and saw I only had a couple of condoms left."

Opening his gorgeous eyes again, he holds my gaze and shakes his head a little ruefully. "Little did I know the last time we were in town, that should have been one of the *supplies* I restocked. But I wasn't exactly expecting to be doing anything but fucking my fist in the shower every time I thought about you."

Rolling my lips together, I peek at him from beneath my lashes. "You think about me when you touch yourself, cowboy?" God, that is the sexiest fucking admission I've ever heard.

"Only you have that kind of power over me, Layla." Colt pauses for a moment, then steps into me again, and I hope to god he's feeling the same magnetic pull to be touching constantly as I'm being tortured by. "You have for a long time now. Longer than I want to admit, because I really shouldn't have been looking at you that way, but I couldn't fucking fight it."

Colt's heat and scent wash through me, and I nearly goddamn whimper as his knee slides between my thighs. He's got a hunger in his hazel stare that is enough to make me forget about food and coffee. To forget about anything other than begging him to get me naked again, spread me out on the counter, and have me for breakfast.

"Well, how's this... you're the only person I've thought about, too."

His chest makes that seductive, rumbly noise, like a storm rolling in, and he grabs hold of my chin. Trapping me exactly where he wants me.

I'll gladly stay pinned here. Hell, this man could hog-tie me right on this spot on the kitchen floor, do whatever he wants to me, and I'd say *thank you.*

Lowering his head, he speaks against my lips. "Fuck, that's hot. I think I'm gonna need you to show me what that looks like." Then his tongue slides against mine, invading my mouth and commanding me with the kind of kiss I'll be left dreaming about for years to come.

I whimper into his mouth, because it's honest to god the only thing I can do. My blood turns to white-hot sparks flying through my veins, and every nerve ending dances with joy at the way he presses against my body.

God, I want his weight on top of me. I've only had one night of this man, and already I'm craving the sensation of being pinned beneath his bulk and strength.

Things start to build, he sinks deeper into my mouth, exploring hands begin to fist and squeeze the soft material at my hips, my waist, the swell of my thighs. Just as I think we're definitely going to follow the road of desire to its inevitable climax, Colt pauses and makes a primal noise, something part growl and part groan against my mouth.

"Holy shit. Angel, I gotta go finish up the crap I've got left to do." He rests his forehead against mine, surely able to hear my frantic pulse fluttering in my throat. "As much as I can't think of anything fucking worse than walking away from you right now, I have to go."

Swallowing heavily and trying not to sound completely porn star worthy, I tuck a stray curl behind my ear and collect my sanity for a second. "I can help, if you need. Let me get dressed and I'll come give you a hand."

Colt gives me a crooked smile that melts my brain. "No, you stay right here." He brushes his thumb across my kiss bitten lips. "You've more than earned a day off. Rest up, eat your breakfast— that has now gone cold, might I add."

I glare at him. "Whose fault is that? *Mr. Condoms and Important Sex-Talk.*"

He grunts a short laugh. "I plead innocence. Besides, I want you naked and in my bath when I get back... and I'm sure you'll keep yourself busy reading one of your horny books."

There's a spluttering noise that comes out of me, and I damn near fall off my stool. Absolutely no way did this man just say those words.

But Colt's hazel eyes glow with boyish mischief. "Oh, don't think I don't know what you've got on that innocent-looking little device of yours."

"What do you know about the types of books I read?" I'm incredulous, but have absolutely no right to be. He's correct. My Kindle is brimming with the most deliciously smutty books imaginable.

"Oh, I'm sorry... reading *serious literature* over there every night, are you, angel?"

Shaking my head, I nibble on my bottom lip. "You really never cease to amaze me, cowboy. I thought you preferred to stay cut off from society up here on your mountain."

"I know a thing or two. The guys, they talk about what their women are reading." He's mighty pleased with himself. Smug Colt is next-level sexy. Damn him, he makes cockiness look so, so ruggedly good.

"Bet they do." Rolling my eyes, I give him a poke in his muscled chest.

That earns me a searing look and a squeeze of my hip, but he steps away, readying himself to venture back out into the snowy vista blanketing the ranch.

"Oh, wait. If I'm not allowed to come help, then you have to take this out to the horses." I hop up and grab a couple of carrots from the stash I've been keeping. "You'll need to apologize to my friends that I'm not around to give them their dose of attention today... you can explain exactly why I'm not there."

As I hand him the carrots, Colt cocks his head to one side before his gaze drops appreciatively down my body. "I think they already had a pretty good preview as to why, last night."

The tips of my ears heat.

He runs his tongue over his bottom lip.

"Remember what I said. I'll be back in a few hours." Glancing at the carrots I've pressed into his big palm, Colt shakes his head before turning and heading out the door.

Leaving me to a day spent swirled up in mountain-retreat-luxury. The kind of snowed-in dream I could have only ever dared to imagine. Some kind of faraway wish, the kind girls like me only get to sigh over wistfully in movies. As I reheat my breakfast, stoke up the fire, and float around this beautiful home, I can't help the smile that keeps creeping across my lips.

This man might live alone in the middle of nowhere, but his taste is immaculate. Everything from the sleek black finish on his truck, to the finely laid stonework wrapping the fireplace, to the flannel shirts that compliment the flecks of amber in his eyes.

His life is a work of art. This ranch is a giant, awe-inspiring canvas.

And somehow, for the briefest of moments, I've managed to steal just the tiniest slice of this paradise and the man who comes with it.

CHAPTER 23

S team puffs in two plumes to greet me and big, glossy eyes fix me with a reproachful stare.

Even the horses know I'm a terrible fucking person.

I shouldn't be doing this. There are a litany of reasons why I'm the world's worst father and an even worse boss, but holy shit, as much as the word 'shouldn't' keeps resounding in my brain like a goddamn siren... absolutely *nothing* about being with Layla feels wrong.

Embedded in the core of my bones, I only feel a kind of warmth and contentment with her in my arms that assholes like me aren't supposed to know about.

We aren't the kind of men who get to enjoy soft kisses or whispered words. We're not supposed to know how the supple glide of delicate skin feels beneath our roughened touch.

Holding out the end of the carrot for Peaches, I rub her neck as her velvety lips and whiskers brush my palm. Thieving the treat on offer, she immediately nudges at my shoulder to demand more.

That's how I fucking feel too. Like I want to march straight back into that kitchen and demand so much more from the girl I've already taken from over and over since last night.

"I goddamn know it, ok," muttering as my fingers stroke the

long nose in front of me. The horses give me their huffs of disapproval. All of them are just as fucking grumpy as I am that it's only my presence they've got for company today.

But I've got to somehow keep my sanity and not lose myself to this incessant need to dive into Layla Birch. At least being out on the ranch, among the piled snow and icy winds, there's not much time for letting my thoughts drift.

I needed to be busy. Needed to keep my hands occupied with something that didn't involve tearing her clothes off and pressing bruises into her hips.

So, putting myself on ice for the day is about the best option I've got, until later, that is.

Because I know the moment I set foot inside that house again, there's no stopping what comes next. I'm too fucking far gone, having already lost the battle with myself to keep my hands off her.

Now I know how she tastes, how she moans when my cock hits that deep spot inside her sweet cunt. Fuck, her whimpering little noises are my absolute undoing. The way her body responds to me is like a bloom unfurling after the darkness of winter, and that shit is addicting.

I drop my forehead against the warm, earthy scent of Peaches' neck in an effort to collect my thoughts. She nibbles the seam along the shoulder of my jacket while I'm there because she's never going to pass up the opportunity to tug and pull at me. Demanding in no uncertain terms to have her new best fucking friend come out and groom her and croon over her and make her feel special.

When the irony is that I'm no fucking better than any of these horses. Just waiting for the moment her lips curve into a smile against my collarbone and those tender fingers slide into my hair at the back of my neck.

Although, somewhere in amongst all the insanity of what we're doing, I'm painfully aware of my responsibility to put an end date on this.

Two weeks.

Two fucking weeks.

A timeline like that... feels like a precious gift, and a goddamned cursed chalice, all rolled into one.

Get it out of my system. Find a way to fuck away all the longing and wanting of this girl who can't be mine without completely destroying someone else—someone who is deeply important in my life—even if we aren't exactly on solid ground yet. What a fitting bargain for the likes of me, who has wound up living out my days on Devil's Peak.

Even though she's a drug I keep chasing, and I'm already imagining all the filthy fucking ways I can have her over the next two weeks before it ends, it has to be this way.

Turning my attention to the horse's stalls, I'm immediately drifting back to that moment in the kitchen, replaying our conversation from earlier. Goddamn, when I was feeding out the cattle this morning, before heading back to cook breakfast for her, there was no avoiding getting lost in my own bullshit inside my head.

Of all the situations, I didn't anticipate *this* being the thing I'd nearly lose my damn mind over.

I've never fucked anyone without a condom.

In all my years, I've always been careful to avoid a repeat of my past misfortune. After the way things turned out with Kayce, my trust was destroyed, and no matter who or what the women since then were to me—some stuck around for a short while, others were just sex and a release and nothing more—I stuck to that rule hard and fucking fast.

There was no way I was about to tempt the same mistake twice in this lifetime.

Now, the longer I'm out here, shoveling, sweeping, and finding an unending list of things to do that might just keep me busy for another few hours, I've mulled it over. Torn the situation apart, put it back together, reconfigured it fifty different ways and I'm still not entirely certain it's the decision I should make.

But fuck... it feels right with her.

She wants this, and if I allow myself to stop and breathe life into the words clambering up my throat with the determination of a bull rider hanging on for dear life. *I want this, too.*

A heavy exhale gusts out of me.

Jesus.

Scrubbing a palm over my face, my eyes scrunch closed. All the depraved fucking thoughts I've been keeping at bay since that day at the gas station are lined up, ready to bust through the crack in the dam. My mind is splintering with need and selfish wants that should be kept firmly in the category of *no fucking way.*

But it's only pure, unfiltered desire that runs a course through my veins. I want to feel her bare and to have her wrapped around me so fucking bad. I want to fuck her and watch the expression on her face as she tumbles over the edge while my release spills inside her. To pull back and see the dripping evidence of where I've been. To feel the slickness coat my fingers and her channel as I push my cum back inside.

Layla is the only person I've ever felt this way about. I knew it from before the moment I first touched her, before we kissed that night. Not because I want to get the girl pregnant. Christ, no, that's the furthest thing from my mind, and it sends an unbelievable dose of relief through me to know she feels the same way.

No, it's nothing remotely connected to that. If I had to put a word to it, it's the sense of ownership. There's something feral and fucking primal in knowing I'll have marked her in a way that I haven't ever done before, and holy shit, if that doesn't trigger a beast inside me that has no right to be there.

A wild creature has come roaring to life, and I've got no hope of taming it without feeding into the insistent desire, that primal goddamn urge, it hungers for.

Now, here I am, ready to risk it all for the girl with big green eyes I can't help but see whenever my head hits the pillow. When I look out over the forested slopes, I'm constantly comparing those mossy flecks around the innermost rim where her pupils meet that verdant coloring. Whenever I walk into the barn and catch a hit of her fragrance drifting toward me, there's no denying the hook that tugs from deep behind my ribs, dragging me to be near her.

To put it bluntly, I'm screwed. And don't I know it.

After a good couple of hours, I'm still berating myself. Even as I finish up with the horses and their long necks crane to watch me through curious eyes as I exit the big wooden doors. Even as I readjust my cap backward, lifting it to dig my hands through my hair for the hundredth time before shoving it back down on my head. Even as I kick my boots off and hang my jacket when I reach the house.

This is madness, and I'd be out of my fucking mind to even consider this.

Which is why I head straight for the bathroom, where I just know I'll find my good fucking girl, exactly where I told her to be waiting for me.

SURE ENOUGH, the moment I walk through the doorway, feeling the gentle wave of humid warmth, I catch the first sight of her in that oversized tub and know I never had a goddamn chance of denying this.

Every feral instinct roars to life, and all I want to do is fuck and fuck and fuck. To fill her up and hold her against me while feeling her fluttering heartbeat find a rhythm with my own.

"Hey." She's lying back with her curls piled on top of her head, looking like temptation and heaven and everything good that I should never be allowed. Flush sits high on her cheeks, and her eyes are hooded, relaxed, gazing at me with a softness in her expression that I'll be replaying forever in my mind's eye.

My dick is hard as a rock, leaking, just at the sight of her.

The water is fairly deep in that sunken tub, but I can still enjoy every gorgeous inch of *Layla*. Her peaked nipples sit just at the water's surface, and my eyes feast on the sight of her floating like a mermaid, ready to tempt me willingly into the depths.

"Looks cozy in there." There's absolutely plenty of room for the two of us.

She hums. Nods and relaxes against the lip of the tub. "Was everything ok after the storm?" Those stunning green eyes suck me in, two deep pools I want to see looking back at me every single day.

"The cattle are fine, just hungry bastards. The horses told me to fuck off, and won't answer to anyone but you... traitors." I tuck my hands in my pockets and rest my ass on the vanity, hooking one ankle over the other. Content to lean back and simply enjoy watching this girl for a moment.

"Will they be sending you an official complaint?" Her lips curve into a coy grin. Cute and alluring, and my dick is screaming at me to get naked and dive into her.

"Something like that. Apparently, I'm shit at grooming, do a terrible job at cleaning up their stalls, and not even promises of extra treats tomorrow was enough to satisfy those miserable bastards."

"Well, when you speak so highly of them... I can't imagine why." Her eyes glimmer in the dim light.

"They'll survive. How was your day off?"

I love that she's not shying away from allowing me to enjoy her body on display beneath the gently rippling water. Layla doesn't try to cover herself, and damn, it's sexy as all hell.

"Restful... my boss did keep me up pretty late last night." Her teeth catch her bottom lip.

"Sounds like an asshole to me."

"Oh, you have no idea. He's extremely demanding, too." Her blush turns a deeper shade, and those perfect nipples stiffen as water laps around the tight buds.

Fuck, she's gorgeous.

"What a dick."

"At least he's got one or two redeeming qualities."

"Yeah?" My eyes rake another full sweep over her figure and I lap up the way she's starting to squirm beneath the weight of my gaze. Especially when I linger on the spot at the junction of her thighs hidden deeper below the water level. "What might those be?"

"Well, for one... he's pretty skilled with his hands."

My eyebrows raise, and I'm fighting back the urge to cross the tiles and show her just how fucking skilled my hands want to be right about now.

"Sounds promising. What else?"

"I don't know if I should say." That husky edge to her voice appears. The one that has my dick jerking to attention whenever this girl talks in a way that is part innocent, part seductress, and wholly, Layla.

"Maybe he wants to know."

Her teeth sink into the plumpness of her bottom lip as her sooty eyelashes flutter a little. Good, she's just as turned on as I am.

"Well, he walks in wearing this backward cap, and that is *definitely* a highly favorable quality."

I have to fight the smirk that threatens to escape. "You got a thing for my hats, baby?"

Layla nods at me, eyes going a little glassy as the tension and heat builds between us.

"A cowboy in a cap? That's sexy. Hit me with the backward cap? You've got me wherever you want me." With a hard swallow she keeps on squirming and squeezing her thighs together. I'm about two seconds from relieving that ache I know is building there. "Now you know all my secrets, Mr. Wilder. What are you planning on doing about it?" She sounds all breathy and that's the moment I make my move.

Pushing off the vanity, I cross over to the bath and sit on the wide edge. It's tiled and built into one side of the bathroom with an ample ledge surrounding the tub. I've never been more fucking pleased it was designed with this particular feature.

My flannel sleeves are already partly rolled up my forearms, but I fold them a couple of inches higher to hit my elbow.

"You hungry, angel?" My voice drops low as I watch her lips part and her eyes trace the movement of my hands.

Layla drags her gaze up to meet mine, stares at me for a long second, then nods.

"You want to get out of that bath and eat?"

She shakes her head.

"Comfortable?" I ask, dipping my fingertips just below the surface, swirling the water a little.

She shakes her head. "Not with you all the way over there."

"How about I make you more comfortable, then? Would you like that?"

"Please." It's barely a whisper that floats off her lips and echoes around the damp tiles.

I slip my hand below the water, keeping her locked in my gaze. Layla's breathing shallows, her chest rising and falling with little panting breaths that tell me just how horny she is.

When I glide up the soft swell of her thigh, starting from the sensitive spot inside her knee, she jerks a fraction. A tiny whimper escapes, and I'm already planning my next move.

Can I fuck her right here in the bath? Sounds like a goddamn perfect idea.

My hand slides higher, and the moment I reach the softness of her pussy, I'm fighting back the urge to groan. She's so fucking aroused, dripping and ready for my touch, just like I hoped. Slick and slippery and already swollen with desire.

"I guess I need to wear my cap backward more often if this is how wet your sweet little cunt gets." With my other hand, I hook below her knee, sliding a palm down the slope and curve of her calf, until I catch her ankle. Keeping my eyes locked on hers, I gently ease her foot out of the water and hook her leg over the edge of the bath to rest across my thigh, opening her right up for me. My fingers slide through her slit and dip into her entrance, before dragging up to circle around the pouting bud that's waiting for my attention.

As soon as I brush over that bundle of nerves, Layla bucks beneath my touch and lets out the sweetest, horniest noise. One that is going to become my mission to have her making again once my cock is buried inside her.

"Tell me what you want from me, angel." I rub firm circles over her clit and devour the way her pupils dilate, pleasure starting to wash through her veins.

"I want you. I need you inside me."

Wrapping my grip tighter around her ankle, I press into that pleasurable spot below her calf that I know will have her melting. A shift of my other hand is all it takes, I sink two fingers inside her slick pussy, and her eyes flutter closed on a moan.

"You gotta tell me the truth, baby. You talked a mighty big game this morning in the kitchen, but you've had all day to think about this, just like I have. Now, I need to hear you use your words."

She's so silky and wet, and her tight channel sucks my fingers deeper with every moment I work a little harder inside. I want my girl draped over me and burying her teeth in my neck while I fill her up. I want to be able to see every perfect fucking expression playing on her face as she squeezes the life out of my cock.

As much as I'm desperate for this, I won't do anything unless she tells me in no uncertain terms. The words need to come from her lips.

"Colt..." Her whine hitches in her throat as I start scissoring my fingers, working her and getting her ready to take me. She's so fucking tight, her pussy is like a velvety glove around my digits, but I don't want to dare risk hurting her.

I add a third finger and she arches for me like a goddamn dream. Those nipples are dusky pink and lovely, stiffened to tight, furled peaks.

"Play with your tits, show me how you love them being teased."

Without hesitation, she pinches and plucks at them. My balls throb watching her, feeling her grip my fingers tighter.

"I'm not going to give you what you want until you tell me. I gotta hear you say it, but not because you think it's what I'm wanting. I'll give you anything you need, as long as it's the truth." I start fucking in and out with my fingers, her body rocking, cradled by the water's buoyancy.

Layla devastates me with a hooded stare, pouty lips, and nothing more than the slightest rasp in her sultry voice.

"I want to feel you with nothing between us. Please let me know what it's like to have all of you. I haven't stopped thinking about it all day."

"You want to be dripping with me, angel?"

Her cunt tightens around my fingers immediately, and a soft moan fills the air.

"Yes. Oh god, yes. I want that."

"You gotta be specific. Tell me exactly what you want."

Layla is right on edge. Her fingers work her nipples relentlessly, pussy walls fluttering around my fingers. Shallow, panting breaths laced with needy little noises rise up.

Goddamn, this girl is a vision.

"Please don't use a condom. You don't need to when you're with me." She whimpers and bucks her hips against me. "Fuck me bare, cowboy. I want to feel all of you. I want to feel the way you fill me with your cum."

Jesus Christ. I'm nearly choking as the filthiest words tumble out of this beautiful girl, and I'm fucking done for. Her back bows as I work my thumb over her clit and plunge in and out of her, hungry for the way she unravels perfectly. Moaning and shaking and clamping down on my hand, she pinches her hardened nipples.

I hold her leg, insisting that she stays open for me even when she tries to wriggle out of my grasp and draw her legs together, massaging her through the come down. Or maybe not even that, I'm too fucking greedy and don't give her much of a chance to land

—before I fully realize it, I'm already working this beautiful girl harder, that precious next climax firmly set in my sights.

But I have to drag myself off her. If I'm going to do this, I've at least got to get rid of my clothes. My dick is a steel bar, ready to feel every soft undulation of her silky channel wrapped around me.

With teeth gritted, I pull my hand away, but not before sucking down on the taste of my perfect girl and enjoying every second that she soaks up the sight.

"You want me raw inside you? So fucking sweet when you're begging, angel."

Layla arches her back and the warm water laps around all her curves, forming shimmering, iridescent dress fitted to her nakedness. A transparent swirl of steam and droplets runs over wet skin, caressing the swell of her stomach, the crease at the tops of her thighs, the fullness of her breasts.

"Are you getting in, Daddy?" She flutters those eyelashes my way, and there's every possibility I'm going to struggle to last long. This girl has got me ready to blow in my jeans, for the second time in my adult life.

"Don't even think about moving; of course I'm getting in there with you." Reaching up, I flip off the cap and then fumble my way through the top few buttons before dragging my shirt up over my head. Why couldn't this have been summer time? It'd be much more goddamn convenient if I could have us both wearing next to fucking nothing all day long. There are always far too many layers of clothes between us, and I'm inwardly cursing the fact I can't insist on Layla wearing dresses or skirts or something that is much better suited to all the places I want to take her on this ranch and sink inside her.

If I only get two weeks of memories with this girl, I'm going to make sure I've had her in every single place possible.

Christ, it hits me square in the chest that I already know one particular place I want to steal Layla away to and hide out for a short while. Problem is, I doubt we'll have enough time to get there.

ELLIOTT ROSE

Ditching my jeans and briefs, I stand over the bath and fist my cock for a moment. What kind of heaven is this, where I can slide into that water with her and feel her and be with her in the kind of way I never should be allowed.

Even though it might be a fever dream, I'm going to take it in both hands anyway. Damn whatever miserable, lonely future lies in store for me. This is a moment in time I'll forever have, and she's the girl who is willingly giving it to me.

Fuck, I definitely do not deserve someone as perfect as Layla.

"Get in here, cowboy," she purrs at me and shifts around, which means I fucking do as she says without another second's hesitation.

The water's still warm, and besides, my skin feels overheated just being near. Our limbs tangle as I ease in, guiding her to straddle my thighs, and my cock juts up between us. Layla dives against my mouth with fingers threading into my hair, that small action causes my mind to go blank.

It's her and only her that consumes me as she makes those sweet little noises into my mouth. Soft curves fitting against me like our bodies had been mapped out somewhere in the goddamn universe an eon ago.

Kissing Layla is a privilege I don't plan on ever taking for granted.

Why is it that the person who feels so fucking *right* to be with, is someone I cannot have? Someone who I'm unable to keep. A beautiful creature being gifted my way for such a painfully short time. Leaving nothing but a stolen, snowbound secret between us.

"Colt..." Her soaked pussy rocks against my length, and it's so close and intimate and searingly hot right here, locked together. Water sloshes quietly, cradling our bodies in time with a rhythm that seems unbelievable, considering it's been barely twenty-four hours since we first crossed that invisible line.

It feels like I've already known this girl for a lifetime longer than anything as simple as a single night tangled up in bedsheets.

"You want it? It's all yours." With one hand, my fingers dig into

248

the swell of her hip, with the other I stroke tendrils of damp hair back off her forehead. Cupping her jaw, I trace across the dusting of freckles high on her cheeks with my thumb. "Take it from me. Fuck yourself down on me, and show me just how much you want this. Because I've been dreaming about having you for far too long." Might as well confess it all. At least that way, she can know without any doubt that this isn't a hasty decision on my part. "Right now, I feel like I'm in a dream... one that any second now is going to come crashing to a halt in a painful moment if I wake up and discover this isn't real."

Layla grinds harder against me, a hazy shade of emerald-green dancing in her eyes as they blow out with the pleasure of how good it feels rubbing her pussy all over my length. "You've dreamt about this?" Those puffy lips have deepened to the perfect rose color from the scrape of my beard.

Definitely. Too often for my own sanity. "More than I should probably admit, baby."

"You wanted me?" A little moan slips out as she shifts her hips, and the head of my cock nudges her clit.

She likes hearing me tell her, and I'm nothing but a slave to doing whatever the fuck makes this girl happy.

"Layla, if I told you all the ways I've had to deal with keeping my hands to myself..." We both groan as she reaches down and wraps her hand around me, stroking my dick and tapping it repeatedly against that bundle of nerves.

Jesus. My hand cupping her jaw slides down to fit perfectly around the front of her neck. I've got her pinned by the hip and the column of her throat, and I'm going to goddamn fall apart if I don't get inside her right fucking now.

"I'm so close." She whimpers, and like a damn artwork seated in my lap, lifts herself and guides me to her entrance.

My entire body lights up as I feel everything. Heat and slickness and delicate fucking skin. I have to focus on breathing through my nose in an effort not to start rutting up into her, because this right here is like nothing else. Tensing my fingers against her flesh, I watch pleasure wash through that captivating green gaze.

"Oh god... keep doing that." Her lips part.

"You like my hand round your pretty little neck, baby?" My grip isn't tight, I'm not restricting her airflow, but she moans as my fingers wrap a firmer hold.

"Mmmhmm. God, yes."

Where her drenched core presses against my tip is so fucking hot. She's so unbelievably wet, so ready to take me, and the sensation of her entrance welcoming in the crown of my dick makes my eyes want to roll into the back of my head.

"Oh, fuck. Oh, god." Layla breathes hard. Pulse fluttering beneath my fingertips like a hummingbird taking flight.

"*Fffuuuck*. Angel, that's it." Months upon months of obsession, of insane thoughts about filling her sweet cunt, finally break loose and roar into my consciousness.

I grunt and my balls draw up tight, already primed and ready to unload. Ready to spend inside her with that one goal in mind that doesn't make any sense, considering my past, but is brought to life by Layla.

A desperate need for ownership.

Marking. Claiming. *Breeding*.

As she lowers herself, her walls stretch around my length and the rippling sensation of her velvet heat molding to me feels like a flood, a torrent of primal obsession racing straight to my cock. My eyes bounce between devouring the expression on her face, and the place where her soft pink cunt swallows every inch, where my bare dick disappears deep inside her.

Pleasure flares and builds down low in my spine. Hissing noises come out of both of us, and Layla fucks herself down on me with a steady rocking of her hips as she slides lower to settle her weight fully.

"Fuck, oh my god..."

"I know, baby." My fingers flex slightly.

Her eyes drop closed as she feels it, too. She's so full and at this angle she's nearly fully impaled, sunk all the way to the hilt.

"God. You're so big."

"That's it, angel. You're doing so well. Look at you stuffed full, taking all of me." As if she was goddamn made just for my cock to nestle inside her and rock together like this. Wrapped in the steam, my drifting consciousness is only dimly aware of how easy it is to lose hours when I'm with her.

"Colt—" She part-whispers, part-whines, and that's when I feel every muscle tighten. Her slick channel squeezes around me and I'm barely hanging on.

My fingers dig tight into her hip. This girl has already got me seeing stars.

"Christ. I'm not gonna last long like this. God, you feel too fucking good."

"Please. I'm so close. Please come inside me."

"Fuck." This is every filthy imagining wrapped around me, and I tug her down to my mouth, keeping my fingers tight on the column of her throat as she sinks against my lips. "Ride me. Fuck me like I know you want to take it—hard and fast, angel; we can go slow after, because I'm nowhere near done with you."

Her lips hover over mine as she pants against my mouth. "You're so deep... oh god... oh god."

"Just like that. Holy shit." It feels like being squeezed by the tightest fist imaginable. Those luscious thighs work over me, hips rolling beneath my grip.

"Colt—fuck—come with me."

"Don't worry, baby. I'm right there with you." Trapping her bottom lip between my teeth, my hand snakes to fit between our wet bodies and seek out the pouting bud of her clit.

She cries into my mouth with unrestrained pleasure, and I feel every fucking thing. I'm buried so deep inside her and I couldn't care less that this time everything is brief and desperate, because I intend on fucking every single part of this girl and marking her up. Over and over.

Whimpers and moans float between us as it's coming. My climax builds and loads, ready to pulse forward, in unison with the force of her grip on my length. A grunt wrenches from somewhere deep in my chest as searing waves of heat flash and spark, and a surge like nothing I've felt before rockets through my belly.

"*Ffffuck.* Fuck."

Layla falls apart on a shuddering roll of ecstasy. Sobbing out mumbled words while pinched in the brutal hold I've got on her bottom lip. "*Oh god. I'm coming. I'm coming.*"

"Angel. Oh, fuck. *Unnghhh.*" I'm lost to the driving need that flies through me. My balls draw up and my cock swells, and a torrential sensation pours through my groin. Tight. Desperate. Hungry. The most incredible feeling of release takes over as I fill her up.

My dick pulses, and somewhere along the way, Layla has buried her face into my neck. Her teeth sink into me as her cunt keeps squeezing and I can't seem to stop coming. Goddamn. The girl in my lap who shouldn't be there. Who I shouldn't have my hands wrapped around. Who I shouldn't have allowed myself to be inside. Who is now pumped full of my cum, my seed, and moaning my name.

There's nothing but pounding blood in my ears and my heart trying to escape my chest as we float in the forbidden moment of all of it. Me. Her. Us. The knowledge that we've already crossed the line, but we've now gone too far, well past the point of no return. Yet, a path connects us in a way that I've never had with anyone else before.

An immediate sensation roars in, demanding my attention, even in my out-of-body state.

I don't want anyone else to know Layla like this.

She belongs to me.

I can't let her go.

Even though I have to.

A curse that I've been given and have to damn well learn to

survive, now that I've allowed myself one sip and gotten drunk off the poisoned chalice of knowing what it's like to claim her.

"Come here, angel." My throat feels raw. Like I've bellowed myself hoarse, and for a brief moment, I wonder if the deafening pounding in my ears was me actually roaring out loud just now.

"Mmm... god... that's the hottest fucking thing I've ever experienced." Layla sounds drowsy after her orgasms and so goddamn precious. Her plush lips and little darting laps of her tongue trail a hot, wet line up the side of my throat. Feathering kisses across my jaw until our mouths seal together.

My cock certainly isn't interested in taking a break, because the moment our tongues meet and slide forward in another round of sensual connection, it rears to life once more. All the blood in my body flows back south, and I feel my length kick in response to the way she rubs her sweetness all over me.

She moans as I suck on her tongue.

"I wanna be deep inside your cunt all night long." Roaming my palms along the length of her spine, I reach down to cup her ass. So fucking pliant and soft, and even though she's still impaled on me, I feel the way her back bows and chases after my touch as I knead her rounded flesh.

"That's all I want." She gasps and tightens around me as I toy with her ass. Spreading and parting her, but not playing with her, yet. Just enjoying the sensation of seeing how perfectly we meld together.

"You want more, angel? Want to be filled up again? Want more of my cum dripping out of you?"

A shudder of pleasure runs through her in response. As she shifts slightly, I can feel the welling of sticky release sliding between our bodies pressed against each other. I'm struck by the thought that next time I want to watch. I want to see what it looks like for this girl to be coated in the evidence of me, and the urge to swipe it up and push it back inside that tight channel is a damn headrush.

I have no idea what this beast is, or where the hell it has come from, but it's feral for my girl.

"Yes. *Please*." Layla nods against my throat, and I don't know what the fuck I'm going to do after these two weeks are up.

But for right now, I sink deep, and much like the storm and snowfall that has isolated us up the top of this mountain, I disappear into her pleasurable depths until morning breaks over Devil's Peak Ranch.

My lips find her ear, and the words flow as easy as silk.

"Anything you want."

CHAPTER 24

Layla

"Excuse me? Is that any way to treat your favorite person?"

Winnie snorts and gives me another insistent nudge, demanding more attention and scratches behind her ear, so I indulge her, of course.

"I'm trying to clean up. You're not helping with your constant neediness, you know."

She gives absolutely zero fucks and explores my pockets like she's some sort of raccoon bandit with grabby hands, not a thousand-pound horse with all the subtlety of a brick wall.

"Your boss isn't going to be happy if I'm not done soon." That's only partially true. I don't think Colt could care less if I was back late because of the barn or the horses. However, he most certainly will come and drag me inside if I'm not done by the time he returns from the work he's been attending to. While I've been getting things done up here around the stables and the yard, he's been down on the far boundary mending fences.

My pussy clenches in anticipation of seeing him after going our separate ways for the day. Not that it's been all that long. The man had me coming on his tongue and moaning his name in the small hours of this morning.

It's been a week of nothing but indulging our curiosity in one another, and holy shit, a girl could get used to being at the mercy of Colton Wilder.

My cowboy fucks like a god and treats me like a princess, and I'm so painfully fucking aware that our time together is coming to an end.

I've officially fallen for my ex-boyfriend's father, and it's the cruelest reality that the mountain road is liable to be reopened any day from now onwards—we've had a run of clear, warmer weather, and by all accounts, the roading crew is making excellent time with no setbacks to report.

I've sent up a quiet prayer every damn day that something might swoop in to impede their steady progress.

Hello, it's me, Layla... again. Any chance of sending another storm front through on short notice so I can continue to be stuck in a snowy paradise with a man twice my age and his giant dick?

"Fuck them and their efficiency," I mutter out loud, and Winnie makes a noise of agreement. Or maybe she's being a judgy bitch. I don't know, but these horses have seen far too much of my half-nakedness in the past week. So it could go either way, really.

Colt likes to surprise me out here, and it's the biggest turn-on ever when he unexpectedly catches me working in the stalls.

We've managed to fuck on just about every surface. Having a sexy as hell cowboy bending me over while growling in my ear that I take his cock so well and look so pretty full of his cum? My cheeks heat just thinking about how much that makes me needy for him all over again.

Turns out, when you both have a kink that you've never previously explored with someone else... there are a lot of reasons to keep indulging in that fantasy with one another.

"Stay still, angel." Our foreheads drop together, damp with sweat, coming down after the haze of frenzied fucking on the kitchen counter. He presses my knees as wide as they can go, reaching between us to swipe up the welling evidence of him at my entrance. With sucked-in breaths mixed with fluttering heartbeats, we both stare, transfixed and insanely turned on as he pushes those two thick fingers back inside.

"Fuck. Daddy. That's so hot." My pussy clenches, ripples in response to my rugged cowboy pressing into me, still sensitive and desperate for more.

"Christ. Look at you. Stretched around my knuckles. Leaking cum," Colt murmurs hotly.

His cock is already halfway hard.

I'm halfway to begging him to pump me full of his seed again.

I have to shake myself of the daze threatening to tempt me back into memories of him using my body in the way we both get off on.

Can I be addicted so fast, so soon?

It's a dangerous thought, because I know even allowing myself a single thread of that kind of thinking is going to weave a noose of bad-fucking-news.

This thing between us could be over any day now, and my stupid heart squeezes at the notion of not being bundled in Colt's arms at every opportunity.

I'm not a complete idiot. I agreed to this, knowing the risk of allowing things to happen while we were snow-bound up here on top of this mountain together. As much as it pains me to admit, I strolled into this arrangement with my eyes wide open to the reality that Colt will never choose me over his son, and I care about him too deeply to ever expect him to.

As much as I want to be selfish, that's just not how I'm wired, and like some sort of good girl martyr, I'm not going to come between him and Kayce. I know what it's like to have an absent parent, and even though Kayce is a fully-grown, partially functioning adult, he and Colt deserve to be able to have a relationship in the long term.

Holy hell, but if I don't have it in the worst possible way for this rugged man.

The butterflies currently kicking up in my belly are a lovely little reminder that my feelings have taken on a very treacherous shade. Where I'm not just at risk of being swept up in this man, the danger is I've already drifted far out to sea, no longer in sight of the horizon, with nothing but a will to keep treading water and hold my head above the surface.

All I want is to stop and allow myself to sink, to fall, to be surrounded by his warmth and scent and capable arms.

I'll gladly drown in a single drop of him.

Checking the time on my phone, I know it'll easily be another hour before Colt is likely to get back. It's not yet that point in the afternoon when the daylight vanishes like water down a drain, and the weather lately has held resolutely blue-skied and brimming with sunshine.

Something I *should* be grateful for, rather than ice and wind and atrocious conditions for the cattle to have to endure out on the ranch. But my heart pouts at this feast of spring-like weather all the same.

Colt will most likely take every minute of daylight he's given to get these jobs done out on the furthest reaches of the property, so I might as well make myself useful until the time when we can heat up dinner together and lose hour upon hour exploring each other in front of the fire.

There are a few jobs I've been meaning to get to around the back of the barn. We've got a stockpile of extra wood and kindling located back there and I keep intending to do a big restock of fire-wood close to the house. Ever the gentleman, Colt had told me not to worry about it and leave it to him, but I'm a big girl and I can handle lugging some wood around.

Heading out the main doors I take a hard right and follow the side of the barn that is furthest from the main high-use areas. In all honesty, I never see Colt coming around here either; it's a place where an odd assortment of ranch debris lives. A graveyard of wood and wire and the kinds of occasionally useful things on a working ranch that need to be put somewhere in anticipation of a rainy day.

The snow around this side hasn't melted fully. It's shaded nearly all day back here in a strip between the barn and the tall stand of pines, with the left-over remnants of the last storm banked up in places. Back when I first arrived, this was one of the locations Colt showed me to get supplies from if needed, so I'm careful to pick my way toward where I know the wood is stockpiled at the far end, not wanting to twist my ankle on something hidden beneath the layers of ice and snow.

As I reach the stack of cut logs, I spy the wheelbarrow that I'll be able to pile up and run a load to the house with. If I start with the kindling and then tackle the larger-sized pieces, that should be a reasonable amount. No one wants to discover wood supplies have dwindled when it's pitch black and the weather has turned to shit.

One less job for Colt to have to worry about. That man has got more than enough on his hands around this place at the best of times. The sun is still hovering low in the sky, it's the perfect opportunity to get this done.

Swiping the residual snow and ice off the wheelbarrow, I set it beside me and turn to the wall of wood. It's heaped taller than me, and the smallest pieces have been carefully layered at the top. Of course, the cowboy up here on his own most of the time has stacked everything perfectly—only he's done so to match his own reach.

Which is much too high for me.

This is going to require some fucking ingenuity, because call it laziness or sheer stubbornness, but I'm not trudging all the way back to the barn to find myself a stepladder.

There's a round of wood hanging on the edge of the pile that I'm sure I can knock down, if I stretch. It'll do perfectly to balance on as a temporary height boost until I get through the topmost layer of kindling and firewood. Once I've removed that, the next one down is still over my head, but at least I'll be able to reach that from where I'm standing on the ground.

Looking like an absolute fool—and terribly mindful that I don't want to risk bringing down an avalanche of wood on my head—I strain upward to catch the edge of the log. I'll only need to bump it. The thing is hanging out over the front of the stack, and won't need much of a nudge for gravity to do all the hard work for me.

My fingers graze the bark, and it shifts a little but could be stuck thanks to all the ice back here. It's fucking cold and shaded around this side of the barn, but I'm determined to get this shit done. My toes already feel a little numb in my boots as I reach again and let out a curse as my fingers bump the piece of wood but it only dislodges a fraction.

"Come on, asshole," I grumble, and this time spring upward a little, swiping at the edge, which has the desired effect. The log loosens and tumbles to the ground. I'm not intending to catch it, so I let it fall with a crash, feeling mighty satisfied that I've now got myself a thick, heavy-set round of wood to use as a step stool.

Only as it hits the layer of compacted snow with a thud, my stomach lurches. Instead of the noise I'm expecting to hear, there's a slick sound and a clatter. Heavy-cast metal leaps upward from where it had been partially hidden beneath the blanket of white. Sharp layered teeth made of steel snap together.

A fucking bear trap.

Right in front of the wood pile and only a matter of inches from where I currently stand, now trembling.

Everything feels too confusing. My mind tries to piece things together in a flurry. Colt never mentioned bears or traps or anything of the sort up here on the ranch. Bear traps are illegal, aren't they? He certainly wouldn't take the trouble of showing me where this supply of wood was located and forget to point out something as dangerous as this.

If I'd stepped a foot to the side—If I'd stretched and lunged for that piece of wood only a tiny fraction to my right—it would be my leg currently mangled in those powerful, flesh-ripping teeth.

My hand flies up to cover my mouth as I suppress a cry. I'm chilled to the bone, too stunned to move. Too terrified to take a step or shift my weight. What if there are more of them hidden beneath the snow out here? As my wide eyes survey the layer of white all around me, the plummeting realization lurches in my stomach that I'm essentially standing in what could be a minefield.

It's impossible to tell what might lurk beneath the surface of the innocent-looking white blanket stretching out in all directions.

"Layla, you out here?" The sound of Colt's voice drifts from near the entrance to the barn. Oh, god. I don't know what to do. Fear has frozen me to the spot, like the icicles clinging to the pine trees behind me.

"Colt—" I croak out his name. Fuck, why do I feel like bursting into tears? I don't even think as I call for him, but it's only when he approaches round the side of the barn that my panic morphs into a different emotion entirely.

What if he gets hurt? I can't be the one responsible for him getting hurt.

"Wait. WAIT." My hands fly out, sounding like a woman possessed even to my own ears as I yell at him. "Don't move."

"Layla?" He strides toward me, and blood pounds in my ears as I have an instant meltdown watching his boots hit the fresh snow one after the other. Crunching footsteps that I'm certain are going to end in bloodshed with every step nearer.

"Stop... Stop walking. Don't come any closer." Tears prick the back of my eyes. I'm not good at any of this, and I'm so confused and shocked and don't fucking know how to handle this situation.

Thankfully, he stops and gives me a look from behind dark, furrowed brows.

"What's going on?"

"The snow. There are traps. Fuck. I don't want you to get injured. Please don't come closer." I'm an incoherent stream of babbling words.

My voice is too high-pitched and panicky, and Colt closes the distance between us, almost jogging, before I can stop him. "Layla, are you ok?" He's moving faster than I can do anything to change his mind, with concern written all over his face, and I'm urging him to stand still. Just fucking stop. Don't keep walking over here because I have no idea what I'll do if there's another set of those brutal steel teeth that snap up out of nowhere.

"What happened to you? Baby, show me where you're hurt." He's on me before I can do anything about it. His big hands cup my face while all the blood drains from my limbs.

"Don't move. Don't step anywhere. Just stay still." My fists grip the front of his jacket like I'm clinging onto him for dear life, and right now, he's the only thing holding me upright.

"You get hurt?" He repeats again, voice gruff but soft in his way that he always is. Always so endlessly caring as his hazel gaze, alert and filled with concern, flickers over my body.

"Traps." I stammer. "Under the snow."

"Traps?"

"Right there. I don't know how many." Each knuckle turns white under the force of how tight I'm clinging to his jacket, because I can't handle the thought of him stepping to one side. I'm certain that if I don't anchor him in place with every ounce of strength I've got, he's going to end up mangled and bloody and broken.

"Where?" His voice is so fucking steady. Sure and certain, and with an even tone that reaches into my brain and works some kind of magic because the grip of panic I'd been locked in seconds ago loosens its constrictive hold.

How is he able to talk me down off the ledge so effortlessly, every single time?

"By the wood. Please don't move your feet. Please stand still." God, the way my voice sounds so shaky when he's the picture of calm. How the fuck does he do all this on his own? He's as rock solid as this mountain, and I'm nothing more than a snowflake ready to melt at the first sign of inclement conditions.

Colt tugs me against his chest, wrapping one palm around to nestle between my shoulder blades, while the other strokes my hair. He smells like the horses and the open plains and sweat from his day's work. My knees just about buckle as that scent rolls through me, soothing and comforting as if it's his goddamn superpower.

"You're ok." The rumble of his voice comes through beneath my ear. "You left perfect tracks in the snow, baby. All we're going to do is walk exactly where you stepped before, ok? I'm going to go first, and you follow right behind me and that's all we're going to do. I've got you."

I've got you.

Words I can honestly say, hand on my shaken-up heart, I don't think I've ever had spoken to me before.

For my entire life, I've had to go it alone. Other than my brief time living with Evaline, and the way my aunt took care of me to the best of her abilities, I've never had anyone tell me it's going to be ok with that sonorous voice and steadfast energy. As he speaks, the words don't just flow out of Colt's mouth, his voice radiates off him like a fire emitting warmth and light and sustenance.

Squeezing my eyes shut, I nod against his broad chest. It takes everything in me to block out the three little words swimming around my brain. Words threatening to blurt out an entirely inappropriate confession of how deeply I've fallen for the man currently holding me and calming me.

"Let's get you out of the cold. Just step right inside my footprints. That's all you gotta do."

Something tugs behind my ribs and hooks me to him. Doing exactly as he says, we follow the track I cut through the snow when I first came around here. Daylight has all but vacated and made way for nightfall, with only a blackish-purple hue stretching over Devil's Peak as we reach the house.

Just like the night after stitching up the livestock, he tells me to go shower and quietly takes charge of organizing some food for us. I should be fucking stronger and should shrug this whole thing off, but the shock and cold have eaten away at my reserves of energy. Besides, I get the feeling this man would simply pick me up and toss me in the shower by force if I didn't listen to him.

When I return to the kitchen, he's not at the island like I

expected. Our plates have been heated and there are a couple of beers already opened, but then I hear him coming out of his office in the hallway.

Stopping in front of me, he takes my chin in between thumb and forefinger and studies my eyes. There's a solemness in his gaze, and I don't really know what to fucking say. How many times is too many times before a man like Colt realizes what a goddamn headcase I am and is relieved to be rid of me? Why do I seem to crumble in his presence? Or is it just a sequence of ridiculous occurrences, each of which he's been right there for.

Now I'm going to be forever stuck—the knowledge chafing my brain like sandpaper—knowing what it feels like to have someone who sticks by you even when you're falling apart at the seams.

What a cruel and unusual punishment.

"Feeling better?" His voice is low.

I nod. Once again, enjoying the roughness of his hands and the closeness of him too much for my own good. "Thank you..." I trail off. There's every chance I'll start crying again, and I don't want that.

"Let's get some food in you." Dipping his head, he places a gentle kiss on my lips, then ushers me toward the source of another incredible-smelling dinner he's reheated. Colton Wilder is my perfect man, and I've never fucking hated our circumstances more than in this moment.

After we've sat and eaten in silence for a while, Colt clears his throat. "There are cameras around the place, not that I ever have the need to use them much. But I keep some going over by the barn for the security of the horses, and around the yard, the front of the house... just a couple of spots where anyone coming and going can be captured on camera."

He scratches at his beard, not looking at me, studying the beer label on his bottle real fucking hard instead.

"There aren't any unusual footprints or tracks in the snow I've noticed. It hasn't snowed fresh in over a week. So whoever has been up here and laid that trap did so long before the last storm came through. Fuck knows why, or what for, but my gut is telling me it has something to do with whatever happened to the stock that day."

I fiddle with the hem of my sweater. What is he saying?

"While you were in the shower, I ran back through the older records. The cameras out there sense movement and detect when there's been something or someone pass by. A lot of it was just wildlife, but..."

"Someone has been up here?" I gasp. Not sure whether I'm more freaked out by the idea that there's been an intruder on the property, or that there's every chance whoever it was might have seen something between me and Colt during that time.

Oh, god. I suddenly feel like my stomach has flopped. It can't have been Kayce—he wouldn't be fucking with the ranch or the stock—but what if this person who *has* been here saw us together? What if they were to tell him?

What a nightmare scenario. For my ex-boyfriend to find out about me and his father through a goddamn stranger spilling secrets to him in a bar down in Crimson Ridge.

"Not just someone." Colt grinds his molars. "The footage is blurry, it's nighttime when the cameras caught the movement, but I know it's them."

"Who?" But even as the words come out of my mouth, I already can tell what the answer will be.

"Those Pierson assholes. I've every right to fucking shoot them on-site. Should've done it with Alton, the older one, the night of the bonfire."

The dots start connecting. "The stock were hurt right after that day one of them turned up in the barn."

Colt dips his chin. "Right after Henrik was poking around. Then the snow stuck that night of the bonfire, and hasn't cleared until these past couple of days. So whoever laid that trap did so probably the night we were all down at the fire, and whatever happened to the cattle was probably retaliation for being threatened. Those two fuck faces deserve to be in jail, and yet they're out here creeping around the ranch causing shit."

"But you've got them on camera, right? You could take the evidence to the sheriff of what they've done?"

He shakes his head and digs a hand through his hair, making it stand on end. "No. All I've got is grainy fucking shadows of two figures dressed in black and a gut hunch that has never let me down."

"But why would they do any of it... what makes you a target up here?" There's an uneasy feeling building in my chest. One that tells me this has everything to do with the way Colt sat up guarding the property—and me—that night with a shotgun in hand.

"They're bad people. Damaged fucking kids who only want to pass that poison on to others. That's all they want to do in return is hurt, because they're hurting."

"I don't understand. That trap could have seriously maimed someone." *You.* I want to shout it at him from across this counter-top. It was obviously set there with the intention of injuring whoever went out to collect firewood from that pile next. No prizes for guessing that it was Colt they were targeting.

"Layla." His voice is soft, but it's a warning to drop the subject.

"Why? Why don't you get on the radio right now? Even if you don't have the evidence it was *them,* you should at least be reporting that there's been someone trespassing and creating god knows what dangers on the ranch." I'm bristling on his behalf. The thought that anyone could come and disrespect him and his property and his livelihood, not to mention that they intentionally hurt his cattle, is making my blood boil.

He takes a long swig from his beer, while I stew in my seat.

"Colt. I'm serious. What are you protecting them for?"

That triggers a response. His hazel gaze lands on me, and there's a ferocity that sparks right there. Bright embers glow beneath his heavy brow. "You think I'm protecting them? Those assholes are exactly the kind of predators who like to drug girls and film them when they're out of their head, while they do whatever they want to them. They get away with it because they always manage to make it appear as though whoever they preyed on wanted it. Hayes has tried to catch them in the act before, but nothing has ever stuck to them. There's never been enough indisputable evidence."

I'm so confused and lost and angry on his behalf. I don't understand what this has to do with the ranch and the man sitting across from me isn't being forthcoming.

"Then why not report them?"

His shoulders roll back, and he shakes his head. "Just... fuck... there's history there, and even if I got on that radio to track down someone at this hour of the night to put in a report about trespassing, absolutely nothing can be done about it."

My lips press together as I watch him closely. "You've had shit like this happen before, haven't you?"

Colt holds my eyes, and there's an expression on his face I can't read.

"The important thing is that you didn't get hurt." His throat works down a heavy swallow as he looks me over, then pushes up to his feet, collecting our empty dishes.

As I help with tidying up after the two of us, I keep mulling over what secrets still roll around Devil's Peak and this ranch. What burden is Colton Wilder still carrying? As we settle into bed together, he tugs me against his chest, holding me tightly in his strong arms. I drift off to sleep listening to the thump of his heartbeat beneath my ear, with a wishfulness filling my mind that he didn't have to continue facing whatever it is that he carries alone.

Even though my time on this ranch is coming to an end, I hate that he'll be left here and that he won't have anyone to be steady for him, like he has been for me.

CHAPTER 25

I'm dreading the call that is going to come in any day now.

In fact, at any minute that handset tucked in the cradle below my truck's stereo could potentially crackle to life with the words I do not want to hear.

There's likely to be a cheery fucking asshole on the other end of the line, letting me know that the mountain road is cleared and that they'll be arriving at the entrance to the ranch, reuniting us with the rest of the world.

I've never felt more animosity toward the men and women who work to keep these mountain roads safe and passable. For the first time in all the years I've been living on top of Devil's Peak, I don't want them to arrive with their beaming smiles and friendly jokes and motherfucking helpful attitudes.

Not once have I ever felt this much longing to be hidden away and kept isolated from anyone and anything outside this ranch.

One more day. One more hour. That's what I keep begging to some fucking unknown entity as I let my whispers fly on the icy wind.

Layla is so close to slipping through my fingers, and I can't believe that the most desperately short two weeks of my life are coming to a close. I know *time* like the veins mapped out on the back of my hand. I've nursed broken bones and burns and been left with scar tissue that needed the best part of a year to heal properly. I've endured nine months of waiting for a child to be born— all while torn to shreds by the conflicting emotions his arrival would bring. I've hit my knees wishing for time to speed up, wishing for death to come calling, when there seemed to be no end in sight to the beatings or trauma, being a kid frightened half to death by the monster left in charge of my life.

Time is an asshole of the highest order, and we're close fucking acquaintances.

This fraction of a moment has disappeared as fast as the sun sets behind the Peak on a mid-winter's night. For only the briefest of glances, I got to bask in the brilliance of this girl, and now I have to go back to enduring the longest, coldest, most fucking soul-destroying darkness. Alone.

Even worse than that? She'll still be right here.

The girl of my dreams will be in a bedroom just down the hall from me, with her sweet scent still embedded in my pillowcase because there's no way I'll be able to bring myself to wash it. Every time I roll over, all I'll see is the lingering outline of her coppery curls fanned across my sheets. She'll be *everywhere*, and I won't be able to go near her.

A rock lodges in my throat knowing that the second we receive that impending update from the roading crew, Kayce will arrive back, and I don't know how I'm going to get through the coming weeks with him here at the ranch—having both of them in the same place—until Layla ups and disappears once her contracted time is over.

I'm not going to stand in the way of her future, because it's one that is radiant and filled with possibility. She deserves to have everything she's ever dreamed of, and it certainly doesn't look like wasting her life away in a place such as Devil's Peak.

Could we tell him? Sure. However, we both know Kayce is miles too immature to handle something like this. She knows it. Don't I fucking know it.

And I've got so much to make up for that I cannot put my own selfishness ahead of my kid's life. Goddamn, I would be the world's shittiest person and most fucked up human being if I didn't care about him enough to put our relationship as father and son above my own desires.

Maybe in another life.

Maybe sometime in the future, there's a miracle that this girl won't have gotten married and settled down with some nice guy her own age, and an old, gruff asshole like me could have a hope in hell of finding her again years from now.

But that's never going to damn well happen, and I know it.

That girl is too special, too brilliant, and too fucking beautiful. She'll have someone proposing to her and sweeping her off her feet and buying her every horse she could ever want within minutes of leaving this place.

I swear to god I hear a molar crack beneath the force of my clenched jaw.

"You want me to feed them today, cowboy? Let me ride that big ol' tractor of yours?" Layla gives my shoulder a playful nudge from her spot in the passenger seat and pokes her tongue out at me when I jolt back to earth.

I've spent the whole drive down to the cattle wrapped up in my own head with my fists strangling the steering wheel, and it's her teasing that grounds me back to the present moment. I mean, she's been quiet, too, maybe even thinking along the same lines as me. There are moments lately when I catch her staring off into the distance, lost in thought, or chewing hard on her bottom lip in that way she does when something is bothering her. But then she spots me and quickly shakes off whatever shadow has been hanging around and kills me with that sparkling green gaze.

A part of me secretly hopes that she's as tangled up in conflicted thoughts about our situation as I am, while another part of me wants her to head down that mountain and never give me a second thought.

That part of me is pretty goddamn tiny, though. In fact, it has just about withered away to nothing. The bulldog residing in my chest wants to snarl at any motherfucker who even dares breathe the same air as her for the rest of her life.

You know, the completely sane, normal reaction to having a girl half my age, who I absolutely cannot keep.

"Be my guest. I'll happily wait right here in the warm with this heater blasting." I flex my hands around the wheel, not missing the way her eyes snag on the place where my fingers curl. She's commented, more than one time, on liking my hands. God knows why; they're rough and cut up and been weather-beaten after all the years up here wrestling livestock and mending fences.

Fuck it, if she's gonna eye fuck me in this truck, I'll be a greedy dickhead and savor every last second before that final grain of sand trickles through the hourglass.

She twists her lips, cocking her head to one side. "Nope. Actually, that sounds like a much better idea. You go do your thing, while I hug this air vent, and enjoy the sight of your ass in those jeans."

I'm defenseless against this girl. So, of course, I shake my head and hop out, leaving her looking mighty smug curled up on the passenger side. Would this be quicker with two of us feeding out the cattle? Probably.

But right now, I'll let her watch me work and know she's keeping warm. Apparently, I'm an old fucking fool and have developed an addiction to having her eyes on me.

It takes me no time to load up, distribute feed for the herd, give them a check over—especially keeping an eye out for any injuries or hint that the Piersons have been back up here messing with my stock—making good time to jog my way back to the warmth of the cab.

When I open the door, the sound of static and a metallic voice makes my stomach plummet to the icy ground beneath my boots.

Layla's got the radio handset in one fist, and her wide eyes meet mine.

"Actually, Sheriff Hayes, Colt's just here..." She speaks into the radio and holds it out for me to take over the conversation.

"Hayes." I bite out. Damn near crushing the plastic in my hand as I slam the truck door shut behind me.

"Bad fucking news, Colt."

My stomach flips.

"Talk to me."

"I was just telling your ranch hand. Rock fall. It's worse than a couple of years back when that part of the valley gave out."

My mind immediately leaps back to the last time the road was nearly entirely wiped off the face of the mountain thanks to heavy snowfall and subsequent melt bringing down a landslide.

"What are you saying?"

"We've gotta source diggers and shit. Heavy machinery. I'm fucking sorry, man, hate to do this to you up there... but we can't get any further until all this rock is shifted and we can make sure the road is stable."

A drum beat thunders inside my chest. Probably shouldn't be feeling fucking giddy about the prospect of half the mountain sliding down the valley, but here we are.

"Your crew ok? No one got caught up in it?" It's taking everything for me to keep my voice level and not sound like I'm over the goddamn moon right now.

Out of the corner of my eye, I can see Layla watching me while I talk, and she's twisting her fingers in her lap, no doubt piecing together this conversation because she's quick as a whip this girl.

"Yeah, they're all fine. It happened overnight, and we only discovered it this afternoon once we got past the hairpin bend. I wish we could get to you faster, but this'll set us back another week I'm guessing."

One. More. Week.

My eyes meet Layla's, and she's giving me an expression that I can't read. Is she happy to hear that? Fuck. I don't think I could handle it if there was an alternative answer. She'd better be fucking happy to hear that because as of this second, the selfish

273

bastard inside me is crowing like every Christmas in my miserable life has come at once.

"It'll be fine. The ranch is well stocked, my deep freeze is full, you know I've always got enough to get through the entire goddamn winter if needed."

"Yeah, well, I still wanted to check in. Anything urgent, like a medical emergency or shit like that, you get on the radio and don't be a stubborn fucker, you hear me?"

"Got it. You'll be the first to know if I put an ax through my foot or one of the cattle breaks my ribs."

"Don't fucking joke with me, Wilder. I worry about your ass enough without you getting clever and thinking you've got a sense of humor all of a sudden."

"I promise, it's all good up here." As I say those words, I can't help but hold Layla's eyes. She's the good up here, and I'm so fucking relieved we've just stolen another momentary glimpse of time together. Or, at the least, I've managed to hoard this girl to myself for another week.

Another fucking week.

As I finish up with Hayes, my heart is thumping in the back of my throat. Setting the handset back in the cradle, I feel like I'm going to crawl out of my skin.

Do I even know a life where things aren't always hard? Horns and hooves. Metal gates and wooden fence posts. Bullets and knives.

And then there's her.

Layla is a constant reminder that softness and beauty exist. Wrapped up in feather-soft cotton and lace and the delicate fragrance of jasmine flowers.

Heat flashes up my spine, and the air inside this cab becomes electrified, like static, causing all my fine hairs to stand on end.

As I watch her tongue dart out to wet that bottom lip, she swallows beneath my gaze, a little cautiously, or like she's turned the fuck on. Holy shit, I'm hoping it's the latter because I'm ravenous for this girl, and waiting until we're back at the house isn't feeling like an option.

Turning to angle my body toward hers, I brace one hand on the dash and the other on the headrest beside her ear.

"Anything you wanna say after hearing all that, sweetheart?"

She flushes, pink decorates her cheeks, and pupils dilate as we sit here, while warmth blasts from the truck heaters, keeping the chill from outside at bay.

"They won't be able to open the road for another week?" She says it slowly. Sensuality in every little form of those words as they dip across her tongue.

"Nope. That ok with you?"

Teeth catching her bottom lip, Layla nods in reply.

"There's somewhere I want to show you tomorrow—a place I want to take you." I've imagined being able to go there, but it's at the far ridgeline of the ranch and the past two weeks went by so fast I just never got time to plan the trek. But now that I've been given a golden opportunity, I'm not going to miss out on this moment.

"Like the Ridge?" She's teasing, but sounds a little breathy, and I'm glad I'm not the only one feeling worked up right now.

I grunt. "Much better than the damn Ridge." Or at least I hope she thinks so when she sees it.

"Is it on the ranch?" She shifts in her seat, squirming a little.

Leaning a little closer, I nod. "We'll need to take the horses. Pack to stay overnight. Feeling up for a little adventure with me, angel?"

Layla's eyes bounce between my mouth and my gaze. My dick perks up at the hunger in her expression. A dangerous idea forms, one of saying *fuck it all*, and hiding her away in the place I would spend all my time if I could.

She adjusts herself in the passenger seat, then leans forward, reaching out to rub a forefinger along the rim of my hat. "Sounds like the full cowboy treatment." There's a smile tugging at the corner of her mouth as I let her flutter those long eyelashes at me.

"You know... the first day I saw you, I wondered what it would be like to get the cowboy treatment in the backseat of your truck."

My cock is immediately rock hard at the sound of that. This beautiful creature wants to fool around with me in the backseat? I've officially died and gone to heaven if that's the case.

"Is that so?" My tongue pokes against the inside of my cheek. Fuck being in heaven, this girl could tempt me into the flames of hell.

Nudging the brim of my hat up, Layla gets a real damn shimmer in her eyes, stealing it off my head before she settles it over her silky tresses.

Oh, it's fucking on.

"Mmm. I haven't had the full ranch experience, yet. Wouldn't want to leave without a chance to see what the view's like from back there."

A groan escapes me. "How fucking wet are you right now?"

Layla squeezes her thighs together and licks her lips. "Why don't you come over here and find out for yourself?"

"You wanna get dirty in my truck, sweetheart? If you're gonna sit there wearing my hat, teasing me with promises of getting inside your sweet cunt, then you better damn well show me."

Layla makes a soft little noise and unbuttons her jeans, shoving her hand down the front of her panties as my greedy eyes devour the way she writhes in my passenger seat.

"That's it. Drag your fingers through your soaked pussy. You're drenched, aren't you?"

My girl lets out a tiny whimper as her fingers find her clit, and I click my tongue. "No relieving that ache, not yet. Be a good girl and let me see." She pulls her hand back out, and I can see the sheen coating her delicate fingertips. Shit. My dick throbs, and I want to snatch her hand and suck down on her sweetness, but my girl is keen to play, and I know what will get her even more riled up.

"Taste yourself," I command. And ever the fucking good girl she is, her fingers pop into her mouth and she hums out a horny little noise. Flushed lips form an O around her knuckles, and I'm imagining that exact expression when her soft little tongue swirls along my length. Damn, I love the way my girl chokes on my cock like a dream, made intensely and maddeningly hotter anytime she does because I know just how soaked she gets, without fail, whenever my dick is in her mouth.

"Fuck, baby. Look at you. Dripping all over my seat because you're desperate for me to fill you up."

She whimpers around her fingers.

"Maybe I'll keep you on edge. Make you wait." I have zero intention of doing that, but it's fun to toy with her. She gets extra fucking turned on whenever I get growly like this.

But today, it seems, Layla has other games in mind. She hits me with a sultry gaze, then starts climbing into the back. Giving me the most enticing fucking view of her ass as she does so. "I guess I'll have to show you what you're missing, hmm?"

At first I don't move—can't for whatever reason. I'm still caught in a snare of disbelief that we've been given more time, while also feeling like I'm going to suddenly wake up and this will all be ripped away from me.

There's a stunning girl, panting and wet for me, in the backseat of my truck, and my blood turns to fire.

Giving her a stern look, one that tells her in no uncertain terms that I'm not planning on missing a single part of this, I climb in after her—because that's what I do. I follow this girl wherever she fucking goes, and I don't want her venturing anywhere without me. I can't think about it too much—about what comes after all of this because I'm going to drive myself insane if I allow that floodgate to open.

So, for now, I'm shoving it all to one side, like an absolute fool.

"Please, I want to feel you inside me... *please*." As she begs, I take in the image before me. One hand wedged down the front of her jeans, back braced against the door, my hat perched on her head, and it's the hottest fucking sight I've ever seen. I'm leaking, throbbing in anticipation of getting inside her, but it's too goddamn cold out here to strip naked, even with the heat blasting.

Wrapping a palm around each of her thighs, I kneel, kind of hunched over in front of her. Devouring every single movement of her fingers beneath the fabric, every moan dripping past her lips. "Baby, how's this going to work out here? As much as it kills me to say this because holy fuck, I want to, I can't strip you out of those jeans."

She bites her lip.

"I know..."

Pulling her hand away, she tugs the waistband looser, shimmying the material over the swell of her hips. "You know I love how deep you get when you're behind me. Imagine how good it'll feel."

The backseat of my truck has become hotter than the surface of the sun.

"Jesus, I want you naked and in my lap... want you riding me so fucking bad right now, so I can suck on your tits while you come all over my cock."

"Well, I want to be bent over in the back seat while you fuck me so good I forget my name, cowboy."

"Christ, sweetheart." Heart thundering, my neck heats, and I scrub a hand over my jaw. "Such filthy fucking words for such a pretty little mouth."

"Please."

Mossy green eyes mixed with that sultry word, that moment of pleading with me, well, that flips a goddamn switch. Hearing her say those words and give permission for this is too fucking tempting. She's too tempting for me. Even though there's absolutely no way I should be allowed this girl, or to be given the gift of her playfulness and sweetness and submission. She gives it to me anyway, and fuck if that doesn't light a fuse inside my chest.

Words are coming out before I'm able to stop them.

"You want my cock filling you up and a mouthful of that leather seat while I rail you from behind?"

"Oh god. *Oh god.* Yes." Layla twists around, my hat knocks off her head and lands in the footwell as she repositions herself. She's on her knees, ass facing me, looking like a filthy dream brought to life with her jeans stretched tight part way down her thighs.

"Do you want to be a dirty little cowboy cum slut for me?" My knuckle traces up the center of her. Finding the drenched patch on her panties and rubbing over the spot, before my fingers slip under the edge.

She whines louder as I make contact. Her oh-so-goddamn delicate, bare skin waiting just for me. Back arching, giving my fingers easier access to her pussy, my dream girl makes all the sounds that have my dick aching and my balls throbbing in response.

"Fuck. Yes. Use me. Please."

Holy shit, what is it about this girl that drives me into this caveman state?

"Is it too much?" My voice drops low and husky, checking in for a moment, as I palm her ass, squeezing her flesh with my other hand.

It's too easy to feel out of control, but I only want to say or do something that leaves her knowing exactly how much she's adored. Because every word I say to her, or every moment I sink inside her—no matter how hard or demanding and filthy that might be in the heat of the moment—it's only ever with the intent of worshiping her.

"No. It's perfect." Twisting her head to look back at me over one shoulder, she gives me her eyes. "It's so fucking hot—you're so fucking hot when you talk like that." She squirms and tries to fuck herself backward onto my fingers playing with her beneath those soaked panties, and I'm so close to losing it already with this girl.

"Good. Because if you're going to taunt me like this, begging to be railed right here and now, I'm gonna eat this sweet little ass first until you're shaking."

Roughly tugging the silky fabric to one side reveals how flushed and wet she is at the apex of her thighs. Layla's head drops against the seat as I spread her out like a goddamn feast. Every inch of her is on display just for me, and there's a roaring in my blood as I lower my head and soak up every quiver, every tiny noise of need. My nose roams along her crease, and my girl jumps a little when she feels me there.

I haven't done much more than tease her occasionally over the past two weeks, more intent on being inside her pussy every chance I've had, but there's no hiding the way Layla isn't shying away from letting me pleasure her like this. Fuck, it's so sexy.

"You're goddamn perfect, angel. This sweet little ass of yours has been tempting me for weeks. You gonna let me own all your pretty little holes?"

She makes a strangled noise, gasping and desperate, that turns into a sultry moan as my mouth explores her ass. Feeling how responsive she is to me only drives everything into more of a frenzy. I'm consumed by the need to make her legs tremble and have her pussy dripping so that when I shove my cock inside her, she'll be seconds away from coming apart.

Swirling my tongue over the bundle of nerves, I lick and suck and devour every choked-out noise coming out of her. God, it's the filthiest, most fucking perfect thing, and the thought of getting to have more of Layla when I'd been resigned to giving her up, makes my head spin.

"Colt—oh, fuck—" She's quivering and bucking beneath my tongue as I press harder against that little rosebud hole, exploring, worshipping, feasting on her like a man starved.

She pushes back, ever so slightly toward my face. "That feels—god, that feels so good."

Just as I suspected, my perfect girl likes it a little dirty. The whine in her voice goes straight to my dick, and I can't hold out any longer. I'm just about ready to explode if I don't feel her wrapped around me.

Pulling back, I give her ass cheek a nip, a warning not to move, then I'm fumbling with my belt and to free myself from my jeans. Every inch of skin feels alive and overheated. Someone has turned all my senses up to full volume, and the blood currently rushing around my body—mostly in the direction of my straining cock—is like jet fuel. Racing and raring and eager to pound into her so hard she'll be screaming my name.

Sliding her panties to one side, Layla's body is already more than ready to take me. Her entrance is so warm and soft and allows me to push forward on a wet glide.

Fuck. *Fuck.* It's already too good. Her silky channel is even tighter than usual because of her jeans trapping her thighs together, and I have to shove my way inside. We're both frantic, and this is going to go down as one of the hottest fucking moments of my life.

"*Mmmmfuck...* just like that." Her fingers claw against the seat. The way her head tilts to one side, allows me to see the deep blush covering her cheek, matching the darkened shade of her full lips. She's so perfect.

"You look so good taking me, baby." My voice is a growl, and I can't fucking help it. "Like you were made for me." Goddamn, her pink, swollen cunt grips my dick and swallows me inch by inch as I feed her my length.

She wraps around me like a vise, and I'm seeing spots and stars and the fucking Milky Way as I start pumping in and out of her.

"I want to see you dripping baby. To see your pretty little holes all filled with me. Do you like that idea?"

"God. I do." Layla moans and whimpers louder. "After..." Her face screws up with unrestrained desire as my cock hits that sweet spot. She lets out a soft cry. "After... I want you to push it back inside... please, please."

Christ. My balls draw up.

"Fuck, you're such a good girl for me."

She knows we both get off on that, and I'm lost in the mist of pleasure that claims us. Driving and pounding into her over and over as the truck rocks, my windows fog up, and I'm numb to anything else. Nothing exists right now outside of this cramped backseat except how good it always feels being with her.

Our joint climax builds and my balls tighten. Tingling races through my spine, and I manage to wedge one hand beneath the front of her panties as I hold her hip in a punishing grasp with the other. It only takes the first brush over her clit to feel her tighten around me and those flutters I'm addicted to start to ripple. As I circle that pouting bud, Layla falls apart beneath me.

"Coltohfuckohmygod." Shaking and moaning, her pussy milks me so damn hard, I'm tugged over the precipice right alongside my girl.

The rhythm of my thrusts falters, my cock jerks, and I'm unloading, pumping forward, spilling deep inside. I'll never fucking get over this feeling. Of nothing being between us. How my release fills her. How each slide of my dick is coated in the evidence of where I've marked her up, my seed painting her inner walls.

Holy shit.

Chest rising and falling rapidly, I don't know if I can even see straight for a moment. My hips thrust languid strokes against her ass until I bury myself to the hilt and hold myself there. Sweat dampens my brow and I fall forward, feathering kisses along the back and side of Layla's neck. She turns, gives me her mouth and we're both panting.

There are some very specific words that threaten to fall past my lips that I have to swallow back down. Because all I want to do is confess everything to this beautiful girl, and now is not the fucking time. Truth be told, there have been a hundred little moments I've felt this urge lately, only, the situation is intensified right here as I'm buried deep inside her.

Layla hums against my mouth, and it's the sweetest little purr of pleasure.

"How was that for the backseat experience?" I move to suck her earlobe between my lips and relish the shudder that rolls through her.

"Extremely fucking hot, cowboy."

"I like the look of you, full of my cum in the back of my truck." My teeth nip her ear, and I draw out. Holding her hips in place, I watch on as the evidence of me starts to well at her entrance. Layla rests her head against the seat, looking so fucking soft and satiated and blissed out of her mind. The feral thing inside me is roaring like a goddamn wild creature that I'm the one who gave her that.

"Stay still for me, angel." Swiping my fingers through the cum leaking out of her, I press two fingers back inside, and Layla lets out a whimper. Her spine bows, and she pushes against me. Yeah, she fucking loves when I do this, and it's the sexiest thing I've ever seen.

"Look at you. Loving being filled up and desperate for more." The husk in my voice sounds strange to my own ears. Repeating the process, each time I collect more and press back inside her swollen entrance. It's too easy to get lost in the fantasy of simply fisting my dick, fitting myself at her core, and pulsing into her again.

Based on the way Layla is shuddering and moaning softly, chasing my touch, I'd say she's feeling exactly the same way.

As I push my fingers past the second knuckle, coated in my release, her green eyes watch my face.

"You want to taste us, angel?" I'm slowly finger fucking my cum back into her and as soon as I say those words, Layla nods. My good girl opens her mouth and sticks out her tongue.

Her eyes glaze over as she feels me draw out, then push back in again, swiping up the slickness. Then I brace myself to lean over her back, slip those fingers past her soft lips, and allow her to swirl her tongue around. Cleaning me up, moaning softly as she does so.

"Goddamn, angel. You're not making it easy to do anything but wanna stay right here."

She gently nips my fingers, making a sweet little contented noise.

And even though I'm still floating, still coming back down, we can't keep lingering. The sun has well and truly set, and we both need to get inside into the warm. There's plenty of time between now and morning to have her all over again while spread out in my sheets.

Fixing her panties back in place and slipping her jeans back up over her ass to sit loosely over her hips, I pull her up and against me seated sideways across my lap.

"Are you ok? Was that ok?" I just want to hold her and kiss her softly for a moment. Even though I know we should get moving, she's still so pliant, and it always feels like a gift I don't deserve to get this side all to myself.

Layla's smile is a little dreamy looking and it makes my chest squeeze. She reaches up to thread her fingers through my hair and nods, "That was amazing."

Resting our foreheads together, my heart clatters around behind my ribs. So fucking lost to her. "Bath and food when we get back?"

"Sounds perfect."

Yeah. It fucking does.

CHAPTER 26

Layla

I've been unashamedly staring at my ex-boyfriend's father's ass for the better part of the last hour.

Holy shit, that man fills out a pair of wranglers to perfection.

The trail we've steadily climbed higher and higher along while on horseback is rocky, narrow, and snakes its way up a ridged outcrop located at the far reaches of the ranch. Much to my delight, I've been fortunate enough to occupy the second rider position while Colt has led the way for us.

Although I suspect Peaches knows exactly where she's going from the way her ears pricked up, and she has hardly needed any guiding. In fact, I've pretty much just been a passenger princess for this entire ride. With all the trail riding clients Colt has visit the ranch each summer, she must have frequented this track many times over the years I would imagine.

A girl can only dream of mornings spent like this. Blue skies overhead, a crisp, spring tinge to the air, and a gorgeous cowboy to soak up every moment with. Watching his broad shoulders, skill with his horse, seeing this man in his element—all of it is a blessing I don't intend on taking for granted.

Our destination is a mystery, but I was told to pack for a night away from the house. Wherever we're headed to I'm hoping, at the very least, there will be a fire I can huddle around. I'm certain Colton Wilder is fully immune to the cold, but my toes go numb the moment I so much as look at the snow, and I'm not built for roughing it cowboy-style while lying on a bed of dirt under the stars.

Maybe that's his plan all along—force me to have to cling to him for warmth. Not that I would mind that one little bit, thank you very much.

As the horses crest the final rocky outcrop, my eyes grow wide. What comes into my line of sight is beyond anything I could have imagined. There's a panoramic view overlooking the pointed tips of pine trees coating the mountain, while Devil's Peak sits on the far horizon. She prominently guards the main plateau of the ranch and I can make out tiny dark spots of the cattle happily grazing hundreds of feet below this elevated ridgeline.

That's when I spot the sweetest little A-frame cabin, a single-room type of accommodation that could probably sleep a maximum of four people comfortably from the look of it. Tucked in a perfect clearing, pretty as a picture nestled amongst pines and conifers and doused in enough sunshine to have the scene take on a sparkling quality. It's a breathtaking sight, with a few snow drifts still settled in shaded patches, giving the whole scene a sprinkling of winter wonderland dusted over the top.

A small stall for the horses sits just behind the lodgings, and as I try take it all in, the sound of bubbling water catches my attention. Just off to the side of the cabin a small stream runs through rock and alpine grasses.

I haven't even noticed Colt hop off his horse. It's only when his warm palm finds my thigh that I look down at him, all hazel eyes and dark, scruffy curls peeking out at me from beneath the black rim of his hat.

"What is this place?" My mouth hangs open. It's simple and gorgeous and immediately feels like Colt, even though I can't explain why I get that sensation tingling through my awareness, but this place has his energy. Much more so than the big fancy house down at the main part of the ranch.

His eyes most definitely have a cocky twinkle in them when he taps my jean-clad thigh again, encouraging me to swing my leg over and hop down.

"This is the cabin where trail riders come and stay during summer. Bring 'em up here for a night or two and let them get a taste of this part of the ranch. There's a few more tracks the horses are familiar heading further in that direction." Gesturing his chin towards the trees, Colt runs one palm down Peaches' nose as she nuzzles him with a snort. I can only guess there must be more stunning vistas to explore if this, right here, is anything to go by.

"It's beautiful." I'm turning in place, a touch giddy and entirely overwhelmed by everything my senses are trying to digest all at once. "Wait... how is there a running stream up here at this time of year?"

Colt takes the reins of both horses, leading them in the direction of the stall.

"Stick your hand in." Is all he calls over his shoulder.

It's a weird fucking instruction, but I'm bemused enough to do as he says. Tugging off my glove, I crouch down beside the edge of the babbling creek, and as I get closer, I can already feel it, without having to touch the surface. On closer inspection, I can see steam drifting in little clouds and wisps off the surface. Sure enough, as I gingerly reach my fingertips to scoop the gleaming, clear water, there isn't an icy bite to it that would be expected for this time of year and this altitude. Instead, the creek is as pleasantly warm as dipping into a bath.

"That's crazy." Muttering out loud more to myself than anything, I plunge my whole hand in. It feels incredible, and the further beneath the surface I dip my fingers, the warmer it feels.

"Now you know why this place is called Devil's Peak." Colt wanders back over to where I'm crouched down. "The whole mountain is filled with natural heated springs, and the groundwater here pours out hot as hell all year round. No matter how cold

287

it gets, that creek runs like it's got a fire lit beneath it. Damn good for the stock, too. Full of minerals and shit that keeps them healthy when they drink it."

Shaking my head, I can't help but grin. "That's really cool."

Colt's face looks even younger at this elevation, lighter somehow.

"Do you come here much?" I stand up and automatically lean into him, no better than one of the horses, tucking against that broad chest, circling my arms around his waist, and my eyes flutter closed when he automatically wraps me up tight in response.

God, I'm so fucking weak for this man.

"Over summer I'm here just about once a week, depending on the groups booked in for trail rides, but it's not the same when there's other people around. Usually I'll try to steal away on my own for a couple of nights here and there. Mostly spend time splitting all the wood that needs to be stacked ready for the colder months, but really it's just an excuse to be alone with my thoughts."

"You like it here."

I feel him nod above me, followed by a rumbly sort of noise, an agreement that comes out of him right beneath my ear.

"I lived in this cabin for a long time. Before the main house was finished, this was where I came after I knocked down the shithole that used to be my grandfather's house. Built this place, then spent a long time figuring out what the fuck I was going to do with my life." He flexes his fingers against my spine, keeping me tucked close and I could gladly just stay here wrapped in the leathery, spiced scent of him and the deep resonance of his voice.

"I loved the land too much to leave after he was finally gone. But back then, I was an angry shit and had started to resent this all because of the bastard I'd been cursed to live with. Being up here helped give me back what I loved most about the ranch after losing sight of what it meant to care for the land. This spot, right here, was where I hid for a long time."

Colt takes a deep inhale of the mountain air, while I draw in a deep, soul-quenching dose of *him*.

"After everything with my grandfather, then Kayce's birth. I didn't have anyone, or anywhere, and this place sort of spoke to me, so I stayed. At first, I judged myself for doing what I needed to do to cope, but then realized it wasn't hiding... being out here was just a part of my process to go through until I found what my soul needed to feel whole again."

This is my favorite version of Colton Wilder. I decide it right there on the spot. We've only been here all of ten minutes, and I can already tell this is my cowboy's true heart's home.

Therefore, it might just have become mine. Even if I can't stay here with him.

"To be honest..." He clears his throat. "This little patch of dirt saved my life."

I can't even begin to imagine what his past was like, but being here and having this peaceful, wild location must have been deeply healing for him.

"Well, in that case, I love it even more than I did five seconds ago." I tilt my head back and give him a grin.

If this is Colt's happy place, then it has just leapt to the top of my list of favorite places to be in this entire world.

A COZY FIRE lights up the cabin in an orange glow as it pops and snaps, emitting a delicious heat. We spent all afternoon checking over the exterior of the cabin for any repairs needed after the recent buffeting of storms and heavy snowfall. Even though I'm sure there was much more I could have done to be helpful, Colt waved me off.

Supposedly, that's why we've come up here. *Maintenance.*

Ever the pragmatic man he is, Colt tells me it's all part of his shuffle of jobs that need to be done regularly on the ranch over winter. Although, I'm certain it's more than that. He alluded as much last night in his truck, that he wanted to show me this place... and I'm clinging tight to that warm, gooey, ridiculous feeling occupying front and center in my chest.

Colt wanted to bring me here. To a place that holds such special meaning for him.

Knowing that, feels like I've been given a little peek behind the curtain of his carefully guarded heart.

Earlier in the day, he seemed happy enough to fuss around with a mental checklist of little details. Fastidious things like fixing down roofing tin and testing the wooden boards for rot. Stuff that I am very much clueless about and felt like I was only getting in his way if I tried to assist. My contribution was mostly just occasionally passing a hammer or a few extra nails, while I spent most of the time enjoying the view.

Both the muscular cowboy kind, and the mountain vista kind.

I'm guessing since Colt built the damn place with his bare hands, he's got a bit of a love affair going on with this cabin.

Well, if it isn't the biggest turn-on ever to know how endlessly capable the man currently at my back can be. We've already heated up and eaten the meal we packed to bring, making sure the horses were fed, watered, and warm for the night before coming inside ourselves. Colt has kept me tucked between his outstretched legs, and now there's just the glow of the flames and a contented feeling wrapping around us.

I love that being together like this is effortless. There's no need or urge to fill the silence. It's not awkward or uncomfortable. It's just enjoying each other's company and small touches, like how his thumb absently strokes my upper arm, while appreciating the peacefulness up here.

Although I'm sure this rosy-hued scene will turn a more heated shade before too long. The more time I sit with my back pressed against his strong torso, the more I enjoy the steady rise and fall of his chest behind me. A growing torrent of warmth hums to life in my veins with each soft glide of his thumb.

"Layla... I've got something for you." Colt's voice is relaxed and rich as honey when he breaks the silence. I stretch a little, then twist around so I can sit facing him, our legs kind of tangle with one another's when I do so.

"You brought dessert?" I tease. Curiously watching him lean back on his elbows onto the small couch behind him. We're both on the floor, using a pile of cushions and blankets for comfort in order to be closer to the fire, and even though there is a loft with beds, I much prefer this idea. It's a little nest-like, and the prospect that we might just end up fucking and spooning and sleeping in front of the fire feels mighty appealing right now.

Heat zaps up my spine.

Oh, yup, I'm definitely turned on by that idea.

"Well, for starters, *you* are dessert..." He wets his lips and devours me with hungry, hazel eyes. "But no, I wanted to give you something."

All of a sudden, that heated look he just hit me with morphs, and Colt runs his tongue over his teeth. If I didn't know better, I'd say he's a little hesitant, rubbing one hand up the back of his neck, and I swear to god, right before my eyes, a faint blush appears on his cheekbones. Sweet Jesus, I'm instantly the horniest girl alive, sitting tangled between the thighs of a rugged cowboy who is looking all sorts of gorgeous and flushed.

Sounding gruff and gritty, he shifts his weight. "It's a gift. Either an early one, or a late one, or fuck, I don't know." With a shrug, he adds. "You arrived after Christmas, and you'll be gone before March, so I wanted you to have it."

I'm blinking fast as Colt reaches one arm toward the end of the couch. Fisting his jet-black hat, this startling, gorgeous man nonchalantly leans forward, placing it on my head.

My brain vacates this plane of existence.

He stares at me with an expression I can't decipher, and leans forward, elbows on knees while rubbing a strand of my loose hair between his thumb and forefinger. All the while, studying me, like he's committing every inch of this scene to be stored away in his memory. Me seated between his thighs in a simple sweater and leggings. My curls over one shoulder. Fire dancing behind me. His hat seated on my head.

"But..." My hands fly up to the brim. I'm trying to form words of protest. "This is yours. You can't give me your hat? You don't need to be giving me anything."

He clicks his tongue at me. "Like I say... whichever way you want to look at it, take it either as a late present, or an early one, since you'll be gone before your birthday."

"How do you know—"

"Bosses gotta have their employees' records, don't they?" Colt tugs on my hair gently, a curve playing on his lips.

"I couldn't."

"Trust me. It looks much better on you, angel. Besides, I hear you quite like me in a backward cap."

Is that the sound of my heart exploding?

"Colt, seriously, you can't give me this."

The cowboy staring me down isn't in the mood to discuss the matter. He shakes his head and heaves himself up off the floor. Towering over me, he extends a hand and effortlessly hoists me to my feet leaving me swaying before him.

I'm breathless and awe struck and utterly confused. Trying to read meaning into whatever this gesture is and at the same time, willing myself to not read any meaning into it at all.

I don't know if my sanity would survive finding the answer.

But Colt sweeps all of that away when he tilts my chin and dazzles me with a sinfully hot stare. "Now for dessert..." His thumb sweeps over my bottom lip. "We're going outside."

"TWO TRUTHS AND A LIE, COWBOY."

Steam swirls to cloak our naked bodies, and the warmth of the water currently caressing my skin is absolutely to die for.

A girl could get far too used to this.

Colt had me damn near screeching when he showed me where we were headed. I accused him of being intent on murdering me and leaving my body out here among the trees, but no, in fact, there is a natural hot spring only a few short yards from the cabin. Another of the magical features of Devil's Peak I have since discovered.

I'm still wearing his hat—only natural, of course, after the way he ate up every second of me quickly shedding my clothes at the water's edge—and now we're playing a game that is very much leading us on a fast track straight to the *dessert* portion of tonight's little cabin adventure.

"You're thinking too hard," I mumble at him, splashing a little water teasingly in his direction. Colt is spending more time looking at my breasts than entertaining my game, and I'm being a shameless flirt, enjoying every second of his attention far too much for my own health.

"You'll have to go again. Help me understand the game, angel." He tilts his head to one side, eyes still fixed on the stiffened peaks of my nipples just below the water's surface. Goosebumps pepper my arms, not from the cold, but from being insanely turned on while trapped in his gaze.

Holy fuck, it's hard to resist climbing him like a tree, floating just out of arm's reach, with his hair wetted and water droplets caressing his beard and throat. I want to slide my arms around his neck and lick up every single one of those glistening beads coating his skin.

"Fine." Huffing out a breath, I give him a coy look. "I can't stand egg whites on their own... I've traveled to London... I broke my tailbone falling off a horse when I was seven."

"Too easy." Colt's eyes glitter, reflecting the scattered light of the lantern he brought out here. Overhead, the sky is pitch black, punctuated only by a brilliant carpet of stars. There's almost no moonlight to see by, with only a tiny silver crescent dangling close to the shadowed outline of the Peak.

"Oh, am I that transparent?" I flutter my eyelashes. "Didn't want to make it difficult for you, especially since I know you're still catching up to speed, old man."

He growls out something and lunges for my ankle below the water. I roll my lips together with a tiny squeal and tuck my legs up on the rock ledge I'm perched on.

"I see the way you leave your whites every time I cook eggs sunny side up. You've never been to London. So how'd you ass off a horse and crack your spine?"

"How'd you know I haven't been to London?" I feign incredulity. Placing a hand on my chest.

Giving me what amounts to the Colt equivalent of an eye roll, he shakes his head. "You and I are cut from the same cloth. We didn't have parents giving us the opportunity to travel overseas."

He's absolutely right, but I don't want to delve into our past hurts right now. "It is on my list of places I want to go someday..."

"Where else would you go if you had the chance to travel? And don't think I'm going to let you off without telling me about the horse thing either." He adds.

"Top of my list? Ireland, for that wild coast they have... wander around some Scottish castles... spend a summer exploring cute little Mediterranean fishing villages... lots of dream places really. I have a folder of photos I've saved, whenever I see somewhere beautiful online, I add them in there. Maybe one day I'll get the chance to visit in person."

Colt studies me. Listens. It's as if he's entirely uninterested in anything outside of what I have to say. "And the horse story?" His voice is all rumbly and low.

"Ahh... that one's kind of embarrassing, really. You'll definitely judge me, cowboy." I hide behind my fingers.

But his strong hands find mine, our bodies float closer together, wrapped up in the warmth and rising steam of the hot spring. He tugs my fingers away from my face and guides me to cling around him. God, he feels so nice to touch. I'm constantly in awe of how strong and sturdy he is, like every muscle has been finely honed over so many years of being Colton Wilder.

"Can't be worse than me getting kicked in the ribs by one of the mares when I was about five and didn't know better than to try and pretend to milk her like one of the cows." He chuckles.

"You didn't," I snort, and his eyes twinkle in reply.

"I did. Learned pretty quickly that you don't milk the horses." He nudges our noses together, then draws back. Taking the last of my brain cells with him as he does so. "Ok... broken spine?"

"Broken tailbone." I correct. "My Aunt was the one who arranged for me to have riding lessons each summer. Knowing I was horse obsessed and wouldn't shut up about them—that's how I learned to ride in the first place. All I had been doing was learning the basics, how to trot, to build my confidence, you know. They put me on a horse far bigger than I'd ever ridden before, for a group ride... well, I was too shy to speak up and wasn't ready. So when the group took off at speed, I was thrown real good and hit the dirt. It was all over and done within about five seconds, but I landed hard on my ass... hence, broken tailbone." Shrugging my shoulders, I grimace a little. Still feeling the ghost of the sting right at that particular point on my spine. It had been agony to sit down for months afterward.

"Yet, here you are. Back in the saddle like a proper horse doctor."

"Sure am." Holding on tight around his neck and waist, I'm very much feeling the need for this man to either fuck me right here, or to take me back to the cabin. But I want to hear his attempt at this game, since I've had several rounds telling him about myself. "Now. Your turn, Mr. Wilder."

He hits me with a fierce look. One that I know is a sure sign that I'm successfully winding him up.

Good.

There's a pause, his fingers dig into the soft, fleshy part of my hips, while he turns things over in his mind for a long moment. "The first day I saw you, I didn't want to leave the gas station... I could see your hard nipples poking through your bra the whole time we were talking... I've never eaten a sardine in my life."

I can't help but choke out a laugh, hitting his shoulder with my palm. He looks mighty pleased with himself, a small twist tugging at the corner of his lips as he attempts to maintain a straight face.

"You could *not* see my nipples. Oh my god. So that is obviously the lie."

"Is it?" He holds my eyes, kneading my flesh and sliding his hands lower down to cup my ass.

"So, you've never eaten a sardine. That tracks, and I can't say I blame you. They're disgusting." My tongue pokes out as I scrunch up my face.

That makes his lips twitch for a second, then his voice comes out all sexy and deep, and I know as soon as he opens his mouth, that if I wasn't already completely gone for this man, he's guaranteed that I am now.

"I honestly didn't want to leave that day, you know. Nearly turned around and came straight back a couple of minutes later. I even pulled off the road at one point." Colt admits.

"Why didn't you?"

"Look at you, baby. You've got your whole life ahead of you. What was I going to do? Selfishly roll back into that gas station and fuck your entire life up—like I'm currently doing, might I add."

God, I hate that he thinks that. "You're not. I'm a big girl. I can make my own decisions."

He clears his throat. "The only thing that stopped me was the thought that if I chose to put the truck back in drive, to keep on heading up here to the ranch, was that I would be thinking of someone else for a change. It wasn't just me being a selfish old bastard. If I did that, maybe there might be something good that came out of it."

"And then I turned up on your front porch." I can't help but nibble on my bottom lip as a smile creeps across my face.

"Like a fucking vision."

CHAPTER 27

Layla

"So... I was something good, then?" My fingers thread into Colt's wet hair. I'm practically grinding all over his abs, horny as hell and wanting my cowboy about a thousand times more than I ever thought possible.

Even though we only have a matter of days left.

Hours that are rapidly counting down.

Which is why every minute we have left together feels heightened in importance, like we need to be connected somehow. If I only have a handful of opportunities left to soak up everything this man can give, I'm going to greedily steal that gift with grabby hands.

"*Good* isn't even the word, angel. I'll have to come back to you when I find one adequate enough."

"Well, in that case, take me inside, cowboy." I tug his hair so that we're eye to eye. Steam rises and coats our damp skin, swirling around us, building and weaving with the heat from the pool we're soaking in. "Unless you've got plans to show me what you'd like to do out here? More games under the stars?" Wetting my lips, his proximity and solid form leave my heart thudding rapidly.

God, I'm going to miss having this man pressed up against me, naked. There are a lot of things I'm going to miss, and I'm not prepared to face that eventuality yet, so for now, I'll *pretend* and *ignore* and *forget* while being wrapped up in this man for another stolen moment beneath this darkened wintery sky.

Colt presses his mouth to mine, sliding our tongues together in a hypnotic connection. The kind that makes my skin feel like it's buzzing and coming alive all at once. His hands are hungry as they knead my flesh and press me against his hard length jutting between us.

As I moan and writhe and sink deeper into his mouth, I feel him play with my ass in the way that we both know will have me panting for him almost immediately. His strong fingers hold me open, and he strokes below the water with firm presses and teasing touches. The way he caresses me in that spot feels different, but safe with him.

Before long, I'm pushing against his fingers and moaning into his mouth as he strokes around the nerve endings. Colt swipes beneath me, gathering up the slippery arousal waiting there, then drags his hand back up to rub circles, applying a subtle pressure. It's just enough to breach my tight hole with his fingertip.

I see stars.

Humming against my lips, his voice is gritty and sinfully attractive. It's the kind of rumbly, commanding sound I'm going to be hearing in my ear forever more when I have to make do with recreating private fantasies about this man while all alone.

"You want my cock? You want me to fill this perfect ass with cum, too?"

Well, fuck. Yes. Yes, I want that. I want it with him, and it feels so right for it to be here and tonight, because there's no guarantee of anything beyond this additional slice of time we've stolen away up here.

"Please, Colt." Lapping at his mouth and being more demanding with my kisses, I try to convey exactly how ready I am for this. "I want it all."

"*Ffffuck.*" He drops his forehead and groans against my neck.

The sound reverberates along my pulse point, and I'm aching *everywhere* for this man.

"Then I've gotta get you ready to take me, angel. You're such a good girl.... always so fucking eager for me."

Am I ever. I'll happily be whatever this man needs.

We're moving, as he carries me through the water, then helps me out. Colt doesn't even bother with putting anything on, just wraps a towel around my shoulders and scoops up all our clothes plus the lantern. We quickly shove into our boots, his big palm firmly swallows mine, and he leads us the short distance back inside. My gruff cowboy slips my hand so neatly inside his hold, so secure, so warm, it makes my entire chest squeeze.

With every step closer to the cabin, my blood heats and races, and I don't even feel the cold air on this crisp, star-filled night. All I can focus on is the point where my fingers are threaded with those of the man beside me, and how much I'm hopelessly and ferociously in love with him.

He might as well have my heart tucked in his other hand, pressed against his chest with my sweater and leggings that I shed earlier, because it belongs to him. Answers to him. Has his goddamn name branded upon it forevermore.

We've hardly made it through the rear of the cabin, when Colt slams the wooden door, sets the lantern down with a thud, and pins me against the wall. It doesn't matter that I'm still partially wet from the hot spring, he drops our bundle of discarded clothes and rips the towel off me in a fluid motion.

I have to bite back a whimper. My heartbeat pounds between my thighs and the wild look written all over his face is enthralling.

He is simply captivating.

This ranch. The wilderness. How rugged and isolated everything is out here steals my awareness, and this man echoes all of that and more.

Colt drops to his knees in front of me, and this is exactly like our first moment in the barn all over again. Except, so much has passed between us. He's always known how to command my body, but now it's as easy as dragging his teeth over my quivering thighs. His beard scrapes across my skin, and he hitches one leg over his shoulder, exposing me fully to him.

"Look at you. Wearing my hat with the prettiest cunt, dripping wet for me." Colt fixes me with a hooded stare, and without wasting any time, his tongue presses into me. While this man holds my gaze, he licks over every ruffle and inch of softness, teases me, and has my entire body trembling in no time.

Clinging to his damp hair and digging my fingernails into his scalp, I'm just a string of desperate noises and begging sounds that tumble past my lips into the silent cabin.

As I'm beginning to climb and build towards the edge, Colt draws back, looking at me from just above my pussy with pure hunger all over his face. He licks his lips with a deep groan, and fuck, it's the sexiest thing to see how much this man takes his own pleasure from my body, because I can see he's wrapped a fist around his cock and is stroking up and down. A glistening sweep of pre-cum leaks from his swollen tip, and my core clenches, wanting him to hoist me against this wall and bury himself inside me.

"Turn around." He stays where he is, but gives me the kind of firm order to make my clit develop a heartbeat of its own. My knees are weak as he sets my leg back down and guides my hips. Slowly spinning me in place, holding me exactly where he wants me.

This man has already had his tongue in my ass before, but right here, right now, I feel a thousand times more wound up. Tonight, I know we're tumbling towards something new, and I'm both insanely horny for this man, while also unbelievably nervous about his massive fucking cock fitting inside that part of me.

As if he knows my brain needs to be switched off, Colt spreads me and nips at my ass cheek with his teeth as he does so. The sharp pinch makes me jump, and my palms hit the exposed planking on the wall. Rough wood grates against my fingertips, as his beard does the same to my hypersensitive flesh from behind.

Oh, god. When he closes his mouth over my seam and starts working and massaging my hole, everything blanks. Colt is a man possessed, rimming me and pressing forward with wet, heated glides of his tongue. Pretty quickly, my back arches for him, opening more, relaxing, and giving over every ounce of control.

I'm fairly certain there are animalistic noises coming out of me as he makes it feel so fucking good. His fingers slide a devious path beneath me, finding my clit and teasing that sensitive bud until I'm shaking.

Just as I'm moaning—coiled tight, and ready for release—he draws back again. Leaving me hanging with the wave about to crash right on top of me, and I whimper all too vocally. *Shit*. I'm quaking with need. There's a sheen of sweat coating every inch of skin as my veins race with fire instead of blood.

Did I just beg him to fuck my ass, out loud? I might have.

Colt runs his big palms up and down my thighs, dropping kisses over my soft flesh, and stretch marks, and parts of me that no one has ever worshiped so attentively before.

Being with this man makes me feel like the queen he said I was that day when he set me on the kitchen counter and fed me left-over macaroni.

My bare skin is quickly covered by the weight of his chest pressed along my spine. Plucking his hat—my gift of his hat, and whatever the act of saying he's given that to me means—off my head, he tosses it somewhere. His lips brush over my neck in a hot trail, sending goosebumps peppering tracks down my arms. Bringing his palms around the curve of my stomach, his touch roams over me, sliding across my skin until he finds my aching, full breasts and cups them. Pinching and tugging on my nipples, while his mouth works that spot just below my ear that has me melting.

"Colt." I whimper as he tortures my nipples. I'm so close to coming apart, and his expert handling of my body undoes me entirely.

"I know. You're doing so well for me, angel," he murmurs

against my ear. "We'll go as slow as you need to. Just talk to me, ok?"

"What if I don't want to go slow?" My voice is throaty and whiney, and I'm so fucking ready to come it's not even funny. All he needs to do is find my clit again and I'll shatter, I'm certain of it.

The noise that comes out of him is stern. Right now, he's in *Daddy* mode, and there are no complaints from me, except that he's edging me, and I'm equally obsessed and petulant at the denial of my orgasm so far.

"On your knees in front of the fire." He swats my ass, and that gets me moving. I don't ask questions, floating across the cabin, high on the tingling sensation bubbling through my bloodstream.

Sinking to my knees in the pile of cushions and blankets, Colt appears in front of me, a familiar-looking tube in one hand.

"Well, aren't you just prepared for all eventualities, cowboy." Lube wasn't exactly the first thing I thought of when packing for an overnight trip. Obviously, Colt has been having even dirtier fantasies about us than I thought, and internally I'm swooning and kicking my heels.

Having this rugged man hopeful that we might have been fucking all night long up here is a heady sensation. I might be on my knees right now, but it feels powerful to know that he enjoys being with me so much that he'd put a little thought and pre-planning into this. He organized everything from our meals to our bedding.

He's so fucking capable.

I'm so fucking in love with him.

Does he see the way I stare up at him with hearts forming in my eyes every damn time?

And, of course, this man kicks it up a notch when he turns on that filthy mouth he keeps hidden away.

"I've got the hottest thing I've ever seen naked and wet and spread out for me. Do you really think I'd let an opportunity like that go to waste, when I know you've been secretly wishing and hoping for me to fuck your ass for weeks now?"

Flush heats my cheeks. I should be embarrassed with how eager I always seem to be for this man, but he's right. I do want this with him. There's no shame in that, and he's not making me feel self-conscious in any way, either.

"Touch yourself, baby." He pops the cap open, squeezing some of the gel into his palm, before fisting his cock. The weight of his gaze rakes every inch of my body, my nipples furling tighter and stomach caving on reflex. "Use one hand to part your pussy lips and use the other to rub that needy clit. Show me how you play with that pretty little cunt when you're thinking about me." As he stands there, huge and veined, making my mouth water for a taste of him, he strokes over himself.

"Oh my god." I'm pulsing with desire as my shaky hands do as he says. Spreading myself open with one hand so he can see what I'm doing in the flickering firelight, while using the other to rub through my wetness. My eyes flutter closed as everything brightens and builds almost immediately.

The slick sounds of Colt gliding his fist up and down his length captivate me. Working himself while he watches me kneel at his feet, touching myself for him, creates a filthy backdrop, a moment so hot I can hardly breathe.

"*Fffuuuck*. Look at you." He reaches out and makes contact with my breast. Pinching one nipple, then dragging a finger up my sternum until his palm sits over my throat. A delicious shudder rolls through me as the weight of his hold settles in the spot that feels like it was designed just for him.

My mouth hangs open. Panting with pleasure, both at the way he collars me like that, and the frantic circles I'm making over my clit.

"You want to come, angel?"

"God, yes. Please."

His palm squeezes a little, sending my body tightening with need. "Not until my cock is inside you."

I just want to blurt it all here and now. It hangs on the tip of my tongue, to confess how I feel, to free myself of the self-imposed rule I've stamped in red ink all over my life that says I cannot tell this man I love him. My ex's father. Colton Wilder. The cowboy who has my heart, and who gets to keep it once I leave this place, even if he never knows that it will stay here with him.

This whole situation is going to be painful enough to say goodbye when I leave, as it is. Telling him those words is only going to make it unfairly and devastatingly harder. So I push them down, and my throat works beneath his palm, and I feel every second Colt feasts on that movement below his hand.

He falls on me, a man who is done savoring and watching. Tangled on a bed of cushions and blankets, this moment with him feels so perfect. So right. Glowing orange warmth streaks across our damp skin as the fire coats our nakedness and Colt slides inside me. Working his cock deep in my pussy while our mouths fuse together. Moans and nips and licks roll between us as the rocking of his hips against mine leads to the most divine sensation of being so fucking full.

Part of me still cannot comprehend how he's going to fit... even though I want all of him... but he's so overwhelming, even like this.

"You're such a good girl for me. I can feel how close you are." Colt's smooth voice draws me back into my body. Bracing one hand beside my head, he hooks one of my legs over his shoulder with all the confidence of a man who enjoys taking complete control of my pleasure. He brings the other lubed-up hand around to my ass and starts to work over my hole. My back arches with the increased flood of sensation and stimulation and oh my god...

"Oh, fuck. That's—" My words disappear into a moan as his thumb slips inside, easing past the ring of muscle, gently applying more pressure.

I'm a panting mess. His giant cock is buried deep inside me, and Colt dips in and out of my ass with a rhythm that leaves me in no uncertainty that my soul is going to vacate my body when my orgasm crashes through me.

"Play with your clit, angel. You look so fucking pretty taking my cock. Just like that." Once again, he's talking me through my climax as I follow his velvety words, and my fingers find that aching bud. A few circles are all it takes before that familiar tingling rockets up from my toes.

"That's it. Let go for me. Squeeze me tight." Colt thrusts deeper, and he presses further into my ass, preparing my body, as I'm whimpering and crying out with unrestrained pleasure. Everything feels much more intense, perfectly heightened with being filled like this.

"Mmmfuck. Baby. Look at you, made to take me like a goddamn dream."

After how expertly he's prepped me and edged me, I'm languid, entirely relaxed, floating somewhere up amongst those pine trees and stars in the winter's sky outside. Colt pulls out of me with a hiss, then drops hot kisses and swirls his tongue all over my nipples.

"Ahhh, god, right there." I'm chasing his hot mouth, loving the attention he's giving my sensitive peaks. It feels like he's dragging my orgasm out, extending it somehow. In the next moment I feel him sliding more cool gel over my seam, while his mouth sends me flying on waves of sheer bliss.

He doesn't push things too quickly, continuing to work me—first with one finger, then two. The whole time his wicked tongue caresses my breasts, then travels down my body to suck on my clit, before moving back up again. Colt drives a maddening, continual wave of pleasure through me with each suck and nip and torture of my pussy and my tits, while his fingers slowly scissor, letting my body adjust for what is to come.

I want to keep him. I want to lock myself away here with this rugged man and never see another soul as long as I live.

"Be a good girl and keep teasing that pretty cunt for me. We're going to go as slow as you need, angel," he says against my overheated skin, pushing my knees toward my chest, and I don't know if I can form coherent words but I'm pretty sure I start pleading again because he chuckles darkly and runs his tongue over my nipple.

Then the crown of him is there. He feels *huge* and demanding, and it's only the fact that he commanded me to keep rubbing my clit, that my body dissolves and the resistance gives way, and I feel the tip of him slip inside. There's a momentary sting at first, but it melts quickly as he holds still and allows my body to get used to the foreign sensation.

"Jesus. Fuck." Colt's head drops forward, and his shoulder muscles strain. "You're the tightest fucking thing, baby."

My fingers fly over my clit as he lets me adjust to the tip of him. "Oh god. *Oh, god.*"

"Breathe for me. Good girl." He coaxes slowly, being so gentle and gritting his teeth as we both feel the moment he starts to shift forward. Slowly working deeper. *Holy fuck.*

"It's—god—so full." My face scrunches. I'm trying my best not to tense up.

"Deep breaths. That's it."

I follow his words, taking deep inhales to allow my body to keep melting for him.

Sparks fly through my blood and I'm whining, whimpering, incapable of focusing on anything but the sting and small amount of momentary burn as there's a further stretch there, before everything morphs into pleasure.

"You're doing so well." Colt's voice is gravelly like he's barely holding on. "Fuck. Fuck, you're so goddamn perfect." His praise keeps rolling over me, and before long, he's starting to shift his hips more and more. Every movement he makes is so measured and gentle, and it's the most insanely pleasurable fucking thing being with him.

"Colt." I gasp as we eventually both feel him slide forward and seat himself fully.

"You ok, baby?" He rasps out and I nod, my eyes have long squeezed shut with the overwhelming fullness and strange sensations currently gripping my body.

"Layla, give me those pretty eyes. I need to see you, angel."

My lashes flutter, bringing everything into soft focus, and Colt is right there. Filling my vision, his irises are deep pools I readily dive into, allowing myself to be hit by the surging wave of emotion of it all. He's so powerful and commanding, and my heart feels like it leaps out of my chest right into his hands as he draws out, then slowly slides forward again. We both groan in unison, and there are no more words. Just the tremors of desire and heated pleasure as I drown in his hazel gaze, flecks of gold and shadow cross his face, and my mouth hangs open.

My cowboy has me trapped, tied up in his all-consuming form. With each gentle roll of his hips, each bunch and flex of his muscles, we're panting, entirely lost to the way our bodies find their pleasure together. It's so tender, he's so careful with me, treasuring me through every measured thrust, every second of being with him like this.

"Fuck. Baby. I can't hold out anymore." Colt grunts. "You're gripping me so tight. It's too good." I feel the moment his cock swells and the rhythmic pumping of his hips starts to falter.

"Please. *Please*." I'm already right fucking there, rubbing over my aching clit, and my eyes must tell him that entire story. He groans from somewhere deep inside his chest, a rich sound that flows right through into me, and that's my final push over the precipice.

I'm picked up and tossed around on a long, rolling wave. Fuck, if it was intense when he filled my ass with his thumb, now a whole new level of bliss has been unlocked. My climax leaves me quivering and shaking beneath his muscled form, as Colt drives into me over and over. Still taking perfect care of me, chasing right behind, his thick length jerks and unloads.

"Oh, god. That's it. *Unghhh*." Pulsing jets of cum fill me as he thrusts forward and then stills. My rippling orgasm grips him tight, and if I was floating out of my head before, now I've entirely disintegrated. Surrendering to every second. All I know is that my soul gladly wants to turn into a puddle beneath this man.

We get lost in a fevered kiss with Colt still buried deep—the kind of passionate, languid joining that perfectly reflects our need for closeness—murmuring against each other's lips. Sweat coats our skin as shivers of pleasure roll through, and it all feels absolutely unreal. I cling to the man coating me like a blanket, entirely blissed out and willingly ignoring anything that might drag me away from this moment.

I'll stay here, wrapped up by him and hopelessly lost inside him.

CHAPTER 28

As I swing into the truck cab, the familiar beeps and static-filled white noise ring out. Slamming the door behind me, I grab the radio handset calling for my attention.

We've not been back long. Layla took charge of dealing with the horses and shooed me off to go feed out the cattle. I gave them extra yesterday to make sure they could handle a little delay in my usual routine this morning, but I know there will be a line of wet noses and twitchy ears all waiting at the fence for me when I get down to the paddocks.

Holding the radio in my fist, I bark at whoever is trying to get in contact. Inwardly grimacing that it might be Kayce.

I'm filled with guilt knowing that I just spent the most incredible night, with the girl of my goddamn dreams, in the one place that feels like home to me... and if my son finds out, he's going to detest me for the rest of his life.

However, the voice on the other end, fortunately for my guilty fucking conscience, is Hayes.

"You must be busy up there, old man." He chuckles, the line buzzing. "Been trying to get hold of your ass for the past hour."

I pinch my brow. Do I outright lie? Or feed him half-truths? "Been up checking on the cabin at the ridge for damage."

Half-truths it is today, apparently.

"All good there? No trees come down? No rockfall?"

No. Everything was perfect. Including the girl who I had moaning my name and coming on my tongue at four-thirty this morning.

Every ounce of her sweetness still coats me, and I don't want to dare rid myself of any little thing related to *Layla*. Mostly because I'm terrified that it'll suddenly be the last time I've gotten to have her, and I won't have realized that would be it—that final finish line for the two of us.

"Can you hear me clearly, Colt? Is the connection cutting out?" Hayes jolts me back to earth.

"Yeah. Sorry. Everything was good." Letting go of the speaker button, I cough into my fist to clear my throat for a moment before holding it down again. "No damage."

"Shit, you had me worried there for a sec."

"How's the road looking?" I start the truck, put it into drive, and begin a slow crawl following the track, headed down toward the paddocks. Not really wanting to hear his update, but fuck, it's obviously why he's been trying to get hold of me.

"That's why I was getting in touch." Yup. There it is. "We're making good time, still on schedule for the end of the week."

My knuckles on the hand I'm steering with blanch around the wheel.

"Great." Everything feels fucking hollow. It's been almost forty-eight hours since he told me we had a week left.

"Best estimate, I'd say we'll be cleared up to your ranch, oh, say another four days."

I've never done mental math quicker than at this particular point in my life.

Another four days.

Three more nights.

At least seventy-two hours, maybe a little extra, if they run a day or so longer.

Jesus.

"Sorry we couldn't get it done faster for you." Hayes sounds so apologetic and I can't help but puff out my cheeks, blowing a long fucking exhale. It feels shitty lying to him, he's a friend, but honestly, there's no one I can tell about any of this without the risk of blowing up Layla's entire life and I'm not about to do that.

"Nah, you're all good." It's the best I've got. Settling for an easy reply.

We keep it brief, getting off the channel as he heads back to work supervising the roading crew and their machinery part way down this mountain, and I pull up beside my tractor.

Sure enough, there are insistent, hungry bellows coming from the cattle who all look at me with curiosity and more than a little impatience.

I'm stuck going through the motions. Repeating the same goddamn process of feeding out that I've done every day for far too many years up here. Through wind, rain, hail, and fucking snow. This life is harsh and somehow rewarding all at the same time. I don't know what else I would have wanted to do with myself if it hadn't landed in my lap through misfortune that I ended up here on Devil's Peak.

Something tells me I would've ended up working the land some way or somehow.

You just *know* when there's a thing that sits right within your bones. Like you've done it a thousand times before. That part of you will go on into whatever comes next after your time in the sun runs its inevitable course, and you'll end up using all those skills you've accumulated over lifetimes along the way in a similar fashion.

There's no denying when you've got a connection to the land that feels deeper than from solely *this time* around.

My hands recognized this soil and the correct fit of a saddle before I could spell or read or goddamn figure out how to count to a hundred without fucking it up.

I know it's not that way for everyone, which is why I've always tried to help others. To right the wrongs committed by my piece of shit grandfather, even if those who I've tried to help refused the hand being extended their way.

Yet, I've persisted, to my own fucking detriment, countless times.

Not only that, but I've wound up putting Layla into harm's way, all because I can't bring myself to be the one to pull the metaphorical trigger. I don't want to be responsible for protecting awful men like the Piersons, but my shit is so intertwined with theirs. And no one else in this community has ever come forward with anything concrete against those assholes, despite all the ways they've fucked over others time and time again.

So, why do I have to be the one to have to do it? To have it staining my conscience that I was the one to goddamn blow the whistle on their bullshit?

Hayes was the one who told me I need to let the guilt go. He's been ready to take action if I ever wanted to lay a formal complaint against them, if I ever provided solid proof they have been the ones messing with the ranch over the years.

He's looked me in the eye before now and told me that sometimes it doesn't make sense why we have to be the ones to see something like this through, but maybe this is the way I can finally set things right after what my own flesh and blood did.

You're not responsible for the sins of your grandfather.

Lost in my own thoughts, I've easily fed out and the cattle fall into a contented, munching rhythm in my wake. I'm back parking up the tractor and doing a quick visual check over the stock and the fencing before I know it.

They seem healthy. No injuries that I can see. Too many times mysterious things have happened to my herd, and I've only ever captured grainy night-time images on the cameras scattered around the ranch. Not enough concrete evidence of who was responsible, but with a gut knowing of who to lay the blame at the feet of, all the same.

Short of sitting down here every night with a shotgun, there's not much to be done.

Lifting my ball cap off, I dig my fingers through my hair, then tug it back down, flexing the brim between my palms.

That small action immediately brings the memory from last night, of Layla wearing my hat, back into focus. Dragging me away from horrible memories—away from stomach-twisting guilt—and into a soft place that feels too good for the likes of me.

The way her green eyes lit up with a spark that I hope to fucking god meant that she understood even a tiny part of the reason why I gave it to her. Because I'm serious. It wasn't just a stupid gesture that I'll take back later, I meant it. It's hers. I want her to take it with her when she leaves, and even if she never wears it again, knowing that she has my hat in her possession will somehow settle the raging unease that rushes to the surface any time I picture her not being here anymore.

I tried not to overthink it while riding up to the cabin yesterday. Ultimately, it sat right, and I've always trusted my instincts when something has felt like the correct kind of decision to make.

She didn't seem to hate it, so there's that.

As I slide into the front seat of my truck, the handset of the radio stares back at me, solemnly. It says one thing, and one thing only. *Kayce.*

The person who I really, really should be attempting to contact, even if he doesn't answer, or even if he's still off-grid and black-out drunk somewhere.

I'd be the world's shittiest father if I didn't at least try. If he does pick up, I don't want to have this awkward conversation—well, awkward on my part at least—with Layla around. And if he doesn't answer, well, then I can always try to shoot him a quick email when I get back to the house.

So, before I can talk myself out of it, I snatch up the radio and flick it to the channel that will connect up with the truck he's got down in town. There's a good chance he won't answer.

Ironically, as I put out the call for him, I find myself wishing he won't pick up.

Fuck. I really am the world's worst father.

Every second that goes by, where I'm met with only static and no response, relief settles in my veins. Rather than being overly concerned about the reason why he's not here on the ranch, or what he's been doing in Crimson Ridge this whole time, I'm the fucking asshole who is breathing easier in knowing that I don't have to face talking to my son.

My own fucking son.

The one who thinks of Layla as *his*.

Christ. What the fuck I'm supposed to do about this mess of emotion I'm feeling when it comes to this girl? Because it isn't just sex. It isn't just about getting her under me. There are layers and layers of depth to how I feel about her, and if our circumstances were different... Jesus... I don't know. I'd probably be thinking about all the ways I could guarantee that she understood I'd follow her around for the rest of my goddamn life, if she allowed me to.

Scrunching my eyes closed, I give the radio one final attempt. Still nothing.

The tightness in my chest eases, knowing that I don't have to hear Kayce's voice and get hit with wave after wave of guilt at lying to him.

Absently rubbing over my sternum with the heel of my hand, there's an ache there, entirely connected to the beautiful girl with copper hair and green eyes.

Sticking the truck in drive, I'm pulled back toward the barn. Back toward the person who I only have all of seventy-two hours left with. Everything else feels like it stands fucking still around me. The mountains, the grass, the pine trees watching over this entire ranch.

Right now, none of that matters, and all I want to do is be within arm's reach of her. Even if all I do for the rest of the day is muck stalls and cart horse shit around while listening to those bastards stomp and whinny and beg for Layla's attention. I'll gladly spend the day with her.

"So... you built this place."

She hits me with those mossy green eyes, glinting in the light of the fire as we eat dinner. Sharing out of the same bowl, settled side by side on the floor.

"I did." Scooping up a mouthful of reheated stew, I see the wheels turning in her mind.

"All on your own?"

I nod. Finishing chewing and letting her keep giving me those eyes. One part wonder held in them, one part disbelief. I've never had anyone share that kind of expression with me... I think it's something that could be described as pride, but I don't know for certain. My selfish fucking heart wants to believe she's proud of this tiny, ultimately meaningless thing that I did so many years ago.

It's only a cabin. Just bits of wood and nails and tin.

Even so, I feel a swelling in my chest that she seems to understand it does *represent so much more than that to me, at least.*

"Feels like a lifetime since then." Shrugging, I stab at another piece of tender meat. Coming up here on my own, I usually pack pretty simple things. The kind of meals that you can throw in a pot over the fire, not having to worry about cooking or anything like that. I'm usually so fucked after a day of splitting logs and maintenance, hammering and checking the roof for leaks or damage, that it's a struggle to do much more than chuck something over the hot plate on top of the firebox and inevitably fall asleep on this very couch.

"This is your sweet spot," she murmurs. Eyes soft and holding my gaze. Everything about her is so fucking soft.

Reaching out with my knuckle, I swipe a bit of rogue sauce from the corner of her mouth, bringing it to my own to lick off.

"What do you mean, angel?" My eyes fixate on that plump curve of her lower lip. The way her cupid's bow sits elegantly below her nose. Every little detail of this girl feels like a constant reminder that I should be paying more attention. Committing these unique little features to memory, while I still have the chance.

"Your sweet spot." Layla tilts her head to one side with a tiny smile. One that settles in the fine lines around the corners of her eyes. How I know when she's truly smiling. "You said it that day, and it's stuck with me ever since... You've got to find your sweet spot, and take your aim."

ELLIOTT ROSE

My own words from that day with her, lying in the snow, teaching her how to fire a gun come rushing back.

"Sounds pretty wise. Don't know what kind of asshole would be saying shit like that."

"Well, you can be pretty damn wise when you want to be, cowboy." *Layla shakes her head, outright smirking at me now. "And for the record, this place is incredible. I'm glad you took your aim and found your sweet spot up here."*

Her words, and our conversation from last night echo in my mind as I reach the yard, gravel crunching beneath the truck's tires when I pull to a stop.

It's the cruelest fucking irony that I've found more than one sweet spot in life. One that I'd gladly spend all my time hidden away in, away from the world, where everything feels calm and simple and so easy to be at peace.

The other is with the girl walking through the double doors to the barn toward me, leading one of the horses outside.

CHAPTER 29

Layla

"Oh, god."

A loud moan falls past my lips. My hot breath fans against the wooden stall in front of me. I'm whining and arching as Colt rubs over my clit.

He's fingering me mercilessly, right here in the middle of the barn, and I've already fallen apart once for him since he cornered me.

Right now, my knees feel like they're about to give way. It's only my palms braced against the wood, and Colt's arms wrapped around my body from behind that prevent me from sagging to the floor in a puddle of pleasure.

"That's it, angel. Give me another, then I'm going to pull these pants down and fuck you until you're filled with me again."

I can't help the desperate sounds coming out of me. "Fuck. Fuck. I'm nearly there."

"Dirty fucking girl, leaving those black panties hanging on a hook for me." He's got the scrap of lace in question shoved in the front pocket of his jeans, after strolling in here holding them in one fist, looking like he was going to eat me alive. "You've been out here with nothing on underneath these leggings all morning, baby?"

"Mmm... yes." My eyes scrunch closed. Two thick fingers dip inside me, while the heel of his palm works my clit, and I'm only just hanging on. Another climax races toward me, but Colt is clearly in the kind of mood for torture. Intent on wringing as many orgasms as possible out of my body.

Not that I'm complaining.

After we got back from the cabin yesterday, he hardly left my side. It was unexpected, but I can't say I was anything but a swoony bubble of bliss having my rugged cowboy working along-side me and the horses all day.

So, I might have decided to play a little game this morning, to see how long it would take him to notice the pair of lacy panties hanging on a hook in the middle of the barn. Which is how we've ended up well on our way to fucking in the middle of the day.

I've got hardly any time left in this fantasy before the mountain road reopens and the cold, harsh light of reality comes flooding back in. Might as well make the most of it while I still can.

"Feel how wet you are. Already dripping." He grunts against my ear. Two fingers plunging deeper to the point where I'm seeing sparks and flying on a waterfall of stars with how perfectly he works my body. "Your sweet little cunt already full of cum, already dripping from when I fucked you into the mattress this morning."

Well, holy shit. My mouth drops open, and my pussy tightens around him instantly. Growly, dirty-talking Colt is my weakness, and this man just guaranteed that I'm going to be his perfect slut for the rest of the day.

Let him do whatever he wants. I'll eagerly allow him free use if it guarantees more of *this*.

His hard cock presses into my lower back through our layers of clothes. I want him inside me. I want him thrusting deep, railing me hard and dirty out here in the middle of the barn, pumping me full of cum again, because yes, he fucked my brains out already this morning.

Colt lets out a feral noise, "Jesus. *Fuck*. I should put you on your knees and give that filthy mouth of yours something to do."

God. Did I say all that out loud?

"Please. I want you inside me." My fingers curl, nails scratching against the wood grain.

"Give me what I want first. Then I'm going to fuck you until you're so full I'm spilling out of you." His teeth dig into the side of my neck, and I feel it building. The tingling, roaring sensation winds up from my toes as he works me harder.

"I can feel you shaking." He twists his hand and presses his thumb over my clit, and I cry out with the added sensation. "I'm going to be inside you the rest of the day. My dirty girl, you just want to be filled over and over, don't you?"

"*Mmmmfuck.* Daddy. Yes." I'm aching, throbbing, and my climax starts to wind higher.

"Such a good girl for me. That's it." Colt's words coax me towards the edge, the wave threatening to crash at any second, and just as I'm about to explode, he stops moving.

My body jerks with the suddenness of how he's halted so abruptly. I'm panting, gasping.

"What the fuck was that?" His voice is a gruff whisper.

Blood pounds so hard and frantic in my ears. I can't hear a thing.

Only, the next moment I do. Like a gunshot going off.

A truck door slams, right outside the barn.

"Holy fuck," I croak and Colt rips his hand out of my leggings, his body suddenly rigid as he grabs me by the shoulders and drags me inside the stall.

His hand presses over my mouth as he covers my body with his, and we both listen for more noises from outside. My heart hammers at a frantic pace inside my chest. I can scent my arousal all over his hand. Oh my god, what is going on? My post-and-nearly-second-orgasm brain is woozy and foggy and is struggling to connect dots. Meanwhile, my pussy is busy sobbing, crying out at the unexpected loss of Colt's touch.

"Yo, Dad. Are you out here?"

Oh god.

OH GOD.

My eyes nearly fall out of my head. All the blood drains from my face. I stare straight down the barrel of Colt's hazel gaze and watch his eyes flick quickly between the open stall door, before coming back to meet mine, then they squeeze shut.

His mouth forms silent curses, and he takes a deep inhale through his nose. When those eyes open to look at me once again, there's a storm of emotion there.

"Dad?" Kayce hollers, louder this time. Boots scuff over gravel. Another slamming of a vehicle door.

"Oh my god," I whisper into his palm. Shock is starting to register. Kayce is here and I don't know what that means, but holy fuck. *Holy fuck.* He could have walked in here... he could have seen... it means he's back, and my time with Colt is over and...

The man standing over me swallows heavily. His stubbled throat bobs, then he does what he's so fucking good at doing. Being quietly capable, he takes this insanity by the horns with both strong hands.

Dragging his palm away, he grips my chin. The expression in his eyes burns into me, fiery and filled with an emotion I can't decipher. It's only a long second, but he holds me firm, staring at me while my heart kicks into overdrive.

This can't be happening.

Colt leans down, quickly brushing his lips over mine. "Stay in here. Do what you need to do with the horses. I'll find out what's going on."

Then he disappears.

That kiss was too brief.

I want him to come back.

No. I refuse to accept reality. That cannot possibly have been our final moment together. My heart lurches, and my stomach falls into the piles of shavings on the ground. And oh god, he's got my lace panties tucked in his pocket... what if they fall out, or they're not fully hidden?

My shaky hands fly up to my mouth. Fingertips brushing over

the place that is still tingling and wet from the brief moment his lips tenderly caressed mine just a second ago.

I don't know how long I stand there, with my shoulders slumped against the wooden paneling, while my ears strain for the sound of voices outside. Only, I can't hear a goddamn thing over the chaotic beat of my heart drumming in my ears, and the rushing of my blood, and I'm pretty sure my tongue has gone numb.

How am I supposed to do what Colt just said? What did he even say? I feel like I can't think of anything, except the fact that if Kayce is back, it means the road has been cleared and that five minutes ago was possibly the last time I'll ever feel Colt's warmth or mouth or touch.

It's monumentally unfair.

Even though every moment with Colt was technically stolen, it feels like the cruelest of punishments. We've been robbed of the last little fragments of pleasure and time together. Time that what we thought we still had has now evaporated as quickly as a water droplet falling onto a sizzling hot grill.

Sucking in a wobbly breath, I smooth my hands over the front of my leggings, making sure I don't look like I was begging to get bent over and railed by my ex-boyfriend's dad out here in the middle of the barn. Then, I push off the wall and cut an unsteady path toward the doors.

As I pass the horses, they puff out breaths and shake their heads and ears. They seem equally unsettled by this new intrusion into our private bubble. Or maybe I'm just projecting my own emotions onto them right now.

With every step closer to the outside world, masculine voices grow louder.

Passing the next stall, I spot a rake leaning up against the wall and quickly grab it. This feels like the kind of moment when it would work in my favor to have something in my hands. Another few paces and their conversation grows louder, I can definitely make out Kayce's voice and Colt's deeper, more gruff tone.

Fuck. This is it. My free hand quickly brushes over my hair, it's up in a high ponytail today and still seems to be in place. I don't remember Colt tugging on it or digging his fingers against my scalp like I love it when he does... oh my god... my body tenses at the renewed rush of realization that I might never have his hands on my body again.

Shit. My grip tightens around the handle and my steps falter a little. Suddenly, I'm trying to remember where my things have been left. My clothes. My Kindle. My toothbrush. Mentally cataloging each room, my mind immediately darts around the interior of Colt's house. How much evidence might be left lingering inside to give away the fact that we've fucked on nearly every surface and that I've spent every single night in Colton Wilder's bed for weeks now?

Will Kayce walk through those doors and immediately be able to detect the avalanche of secrets and lies we're both holding back from spilling forth?

Swallowing down a giant lump in my throat, I can't think of anything that might look immediately out of place. Even though it's been only the two of us here, at least we didn't tear each other's clothes off in the lounge or kitchen yesterday, and I can only guess if there's any of my things in Colt's bedroom that surely won't be the first place Kayce goes when he enters the house anyway.

Right now, I don't have time to continue my minor freak out about any of that, though, because I've reached the doors. It's like a magnet relentlessly pulls me towards the scene I'm about to find outside—the one where my ex-boyfriend and his father are standing around having a conversation in the yard like everything is completely normal.

Only, my wildest imagination could not have pictured what I actually come across as I exit the barn.

There are a thousand different scenarios I had run through of what it would be like when Kayce finally returned to the ranch.

In not one single one of those, did this picture play out.

Clutching the handle of the rake beneath white knuckles, I stop dead in my tracks.

There aren't just two men out here talking, there's a third person with them.

Colt has his arms folded across his chest, back turned to me. Kayce looks up with an expression I can't read fixed on his face. And when the familiar sight of the girl from the cafe with her poker-straight black hair, and bleached tips turns to take in my arrival, my eyes fall to her stomach.

Her very rounded stomach.

Her very pregnant stomach.

CHAPTER 30

T he past two days were supposed to be full of all things *Layla*.

I should have been soaking up her feather soft kisses and running my mouth over her thighs and devouring the way her eyelashes flutter against her cheeks when I press my lips to her forehead.

Instead, the road up the mountain was reopened ahead of fucking schedule, my son is back on the ranch for the first time in weeks, and he's brought his piece of ass from town with him— who he's managed to get pregnant, no less—and this feels like all my nightmares have coalesced.

Like blood clotting an open wound, the worst possible sequence of events have formed a thick, gooey mess everywhere I turn.

Now, we're all stuck under the same roof together, while Layla is still here, and my final chance to spend time with her has been ripped away. I don't really know what I expected those last moments to bring. But does that fucking matter? Either way, there's now a gaping hole of unknown where my opportunity to hold her and openly stare at her over my morning coffee should have been. Maybe there was a tiny piece of me that thought Kayce might not come back, and that we'd be granted another extension to this thing between us... but then what?

What did I goddamn think was going to happen after the inevitable moment that hammer fell? A looming point in time when Layla would head down the mountain, collect her car from the mechanic in Crimson Ridge, then disappear out of my life for good.

Something I do know, is that I've never been fucking busier. Which is absolutely because I have to stay away from Layla and not keep stealing glances at her, and try my damnedest to keep a lid on the roaring sensation inside my chest that threatens to boil over at any moment. That's all I can do. My only defense is to ensure my body and mind remain occupied with fencing and the cattle and riding out to the furthest reaches of this ranch. While every second I stare at Devil's Peak, a deeply charged longing and wistfulness echoes around my brain like a thunderstorm, wishing Layla was right alongside me.

Of course, I could invent a reason for us to take the horses and head off somewhere secluded together. Of course, I could. It wouldn't be difficult to come up with a job that required both of us, but now that Kayce is back, those kinds of things needing done out here would naturally fall to him. There would be one too many questions if I tried to include Layla in the picture instead, and I'm too fucked up by the unexpected intrusion of my own goddamn son returning to be able to think clearly.

Hence why I've disappeared, on my own. Again.

From what I can tell, the beautiful girl with silky curls and the greenest eyes I've ever had the fortune to wake up beside has been doing much the same. She's busied herself with the horses from dawn until dusk, and I don't fucking blame her.

It's taken every ounce of my self-control not to seek her out while she's been working. Another reason why I've taken to riding out to the furthest boundaries these past couple of days.

I don't trust myself not to touch her.

Any second I'm near, the temptation is too fucking powerful, a force drawing me to put my hands on her.

And not purely in a sexual way, either. My fingertips itch to stroke a tendril of hair behind her ear, to drag Layla against my chest and inhale her sweetness, to feel the tiny puff of air gust past her lips against my neck when she laughs at something stupid I've said that isn't funny, but she seems to find it amusing all the same.

While I've been out roaming in the open and wrangling barbed wire and fixing posts just to keep my hands busy, I keep replaying every interaction since we first met. The way she looked at me at the gas station that day made me feel like I was twenty years younger and I don't know what fucking came over me to talk with her and flirt a little, but it seemed like the most natural thing in the world.

Would I change a thing, knowing who she was?

The worst part of me—the selfish asshole who wants to do everything in his power to keep this girl—knows I wouldn't.

It's getting damn near dark as I get closer to the yard and the barn. Up ahead, the headlights of Kayce's truck flick off, and the idling motor cuts, which tells me he must have just gotten back from feeding out while I've been in my self-imposed exile at the southernmost boundary on the ranch.

"You always were fucking pedantic about those fences," Kayce calls out, dragging his frame from the truck cab and then slams the door behind him. Shaking his head in my direction, he leans up against the tailgate waiting for me to draw nearer. Who knows where his pregnant girlfriend—or whatever it is that she is to him —is hiding out in the house. He certainly hasn't made an effort to explain things between him and this girl, Chyannah, and I haven't been in a mood to ask or have a conversation lasting longer than about five minutes. For the time being it seems we're all ignoring the glaringly obvious pregnant elephant in the room.

Just fucking fantastic.

"Yeah, well, you want something done right you gotta do it yourself around here," I grunt, swinging down from the saddle.

He chuckles and scuffs a boot in the dirt.

"Hey, so it's only a week until Layla finishes her contract up here, right?"

On hearing her name, my neck heats, and every muscle in my shoulders stiffens like a board. At least Kayce is used to me scowling at him all the time, because that's the only expression I can muster upon hearing her name in his mouth.

"Something like that." Muttering, I fist the reins, folding the leather on itself.

Kayce toes the ground with his boot. "Look, I don't know if you know, but I'm pretty sure it's her birthday not long after she leaves here."

My knuckles have gone white. Of course I fucking know. Her birthday is the twelfth of March, and I've already given her a present, and I want these two intruders to fuck right off so that I can enjoy having her all to myself.

But instead of saying all that, my teeth grind. I run my hand over the horse's neck to ground me, and I grunt something that could pass as a response.

"Chy and me, we thought it'd be fun to take her down to Crimson Ridge tomorrow. Give her a proper night out, especially since she's been trapped up here for weeks. It's that spring festival they put on every year. There's gonna be tons of people in town for it. I bet that girl can't wait to get out and hang with others her own age." He crosses his arms and flashes a typical Kayce smirk, and not for the first time in the past forty-eight hours, I want to smack my own son in his mouth. "No offense, old man, but Layla must be more than ready to escape this mountain and get back to normality."

Jesus Christ. I'm glaring at the gravel and fucking grateful for the fading light, because there is a ball of emotion wrestling inside my chest. On one hand, I'm furious that Kayce thinks he has any right to even look at Layla, considering the fact he's got a pregnant chick sitting in my house on my ranch doing nothing but using the Wi-Fi, leaving candy wrappers everywhere and binge watching trash TV. On the other, he's just picked open a scabbed wound. The part of me that worries maybe Layla *does* feel like she's been trapped on this ranch.

What if she can't wait to escape here... to escape me?

I have to work hard to dislodge the lump occupying my throat.

"Have you actually asked Layla what she wants?" I huff out a reply. It's the best I can do while trying to keep my temper from flaring.

"Nah, but she'll be cool with it." He drums his fist on the back of the truck. "I think she's still working in the barn. Since you're headed over there anyway, can you let her know that's the plan for tomorrow? I'm fucking starving, there had better be some leftovers lying around I can heat up." Kayce barely gives me a second glance, jogging off toward the house while I'm left staring at the back of his head.

Just like that. He's going to most likely eat all the food, leave dirty fucking dishes everywhere, and wants to take Layla to a bar in town tomorrow.

I hate everything about this.

Blowing out a long breath, I steel myself to head into the barn. To the place where I honestly have no idea what I'm going to find once I'm inside. Is Layla going to be anything but pissed off with seeing my face after I've been an asshole and avoided her for two whole days?

How do I not drop to my knees and tell her I've laid feverishly awake both nights, about two seconds away from sneaking into her room and scooping her up to bring her into my bed, just so I can hold her.

When I get inside, the barn lights are still glowing and soft music drifts from somewhere down the far end near the tack room. Fuck. That constricting band tightens around my chest, knowing that any second now, I'm going to see her. I'm going to see her, and I can't reach out for her exactly like my soul craves to.

As the clip of hooves and scuff of my boots announces our arrival, I see movement, and that's when Layla comes into focus.

She's carrying a saddle and pauses, eyes locked on me, pink lips slightly parted.

Her hair falls over her shoulders in two long braids, but it's her eyes I'm immediately drawn to. Even from here it's obvious they're reddened and puffy and it twists a knife in my gut to know without a shadow of a doubt that my girl has been crying.

"Fuck. Layla." I'm moving before I can think. I want to call her baby, or angel, or anything to let her know that she means the goddamn world to me. But there's also a rope wrapped and knotted around my tongue, knowing that even though Kayce is inside and it's just the two of us right now, we can't risk anyone seeing or hearing something that is none of their fucking business... *just in case.*

"Colt." Her eyes widen and dart over my shoulder. Even though I know no one is behind me, that subtle glance makes me falter. "Don't. It's fine." She shakes her head and bites down on the inside of her cheek, continuing to put the saddle away.

"That's more than enough for one day." I keep my voice low. Beginning to sort out the horse beside me, but keeping an eye on whatever Layla is still fussing around with at the same time. I know she's avoiding going back to the house. It's what I'm fucking doing, too.

"Like I said, it's fine."

"Layla..."

"Colt."

I take a deep inhale, wishing like hell there was any kind of damn alternative other than this scenario panning out right now. "They want to take you down to town tomorrow night since it's going to be your birthday soon. Kayce asked me to let you know."

"Tomorrow?" She finally stops and looks at me. Eyes going round.

"Yup." I lift my cap up and dig my hands through my hair before wedging it back on my head with a touch more force than necessary. "I didn't know what to say when Kayce approached me about it outside. He wants to give you a night out to celebrate or some shit like that, and unless there's a good reason not to go..." I falter. Fuck, I don't really know what to say. Because at that very moment, I hear it. There's no good reason for her to decline their offer of going out without raising questions or suspicions. We must both reach the same conclusion at the same time as those unspoken words hang in the night air between us.

"Yeah. I get it." Her lips twist. "It's a nice gesture." God, I hate that her eyes are so red—that she's obviously been upset. I just want to pull her into a hug and cook her a meal and have her cuddled into me in front of the fire.

"You don't have to." I hold her eyes, trying to convey everything that I want to say, but can't.

"Nah. It's fine." She shrugs and walks over to pick up her phone, tapping the screen to turn the music off.

Layla looks like she's ready to leave, and I'm trying to find a reason to keep her here just a little longer. Something that is neutral ground, just a regular conversation between two people. Anything that surely could be a perfectly normal reason to stall this girl from leaving.

"The money thing..." I blurt out. That causes her green eyes to whip up to meet mine. "Just leave it be between me and Kayce. You don't need to bring it up with him." Shoving my hands in my pockets, I take a step in her direction but keep my hands firmly tucked away. No risk of reaching out to grab her if I stand like this. None. At. All.

She immediately flushes and looks flustered as all hell, and that was entirely the opposite of what I wanted to happen by bringing the topic up.

"No. Honestly..."

"Layla. Listen to me. My son is a shithead who screwed you out of money that was rightfully yours. As long as everything is squared away on your end, it's really between me and Kayce to resolve now anyway."

I study her reaction. She looks like she wants to argue. There's a ticker tape of emotions playing out across her features, like she can't decide whether to admit defeat or get into it with me.

Eventually, she folds. Her shoulders sink, and she drops her eyes. "Thank you." Her voice is whisper soft.

"Don't even think about it. You've got enough to handle, leave my asshole son to me."

Her chin dips in a nod, and she starts to move. Fuck, this feels so wrong. There's an endless horizon of things I want to be able to say and yet nothing rises for me. It's cold and bleak and the weight of that sits heavy in my chest.

As Layla draws closer, having to pass by me in the central aisle between the horse's stalls, I intentionally step in the way, partially blocking her path. Not touching her, but the small motion halts her progress. She still won't look at me, but I see the way her chest rises and falls a little faster.

With my hands still shoved in my pockets, I duck my head quickly to check there's no one near the entrance to the barn. "I fucking hate this. It's killing me to see you upset," I whisper.

She shakes her head, swallowing hard.

"Come stay in my bed tonight. Be with me, baby. I'm going fucking insane without you." My voice is low, and I can't help the way it cracks a little. Admitting out loud even just a fraction of what I actually want to say.

Cracking like my goddamn heart.

Layla sucks in a sharp breath, but still refuses to look at me.

"We can't." Her voice is so quiet I can hardly hear her above the rustling and the munching of the horses.

Of course, she's right. I'm a desperate goddamn fool, and while it's only been two days, here I am ready to risk every fucking thing just for her. Because it's the absolute truth—I'm insane for her, and I'm going crazy without her.

How the fuck I'm supposed to survive once she leaves is an approaching storm front I'm willingly ignoring for the meantime. I guess it'll just drown me where I stand once it finally hits, and I'm left shivering out in the elements, completely exposed, with my chest ripped open.

"Then tomorrow night, do me a favor..." My jaw works, and my eyes dart back to that doorway once again, confirming there isn't anyone standing there listening in. "Wear something pretty, angel. Not for me... although I'll be struggling not to fucking stare, no matter what you're wearing. But wear something for you."

Layla doesn't reply. She doesn't say a word. All I see is the tension in her face, and the next minute, she's gone.

The sound of her soft footsteps, and sight of my girl walking out those doors leaves my heart slashed in two.

CHAPTER 31

Layla

"Who would have thought Colton Wilder could be so funny?"

The pregnant bitch sitting in the booth across from me covers Colt's forearm with her neon green press-on nails for the fifth time since we've got here.

He slides his arm away, removing himself from her clutches... again.

This is a horror movie. I've ended up in hillbilly hell, where the succubus slurping on a ghastly-looking mocktail, carrying the spawn of my ex-boyfriend, is spending the entire evening trying to hit on his father.

I mean, not that I have much of a moral high horse to ride in on, considering my past with both men. But fuck this bitch. I've chomped my way through my burger, aggressively dunked my fries in sauce, and resisted the urge to stab *Chyannah* in the hand with my fork.

Kayce is nowhere to be seen, of course. He abandoned us to the delightful company of Chy, and her attempts at getting into Colt's pants even while nearly six months pregnant, and disappeared off to a group of his friends over by the bar. He said he'd be back twenty minutes ago, and yet here we are.

The Loaded Hog has filled up for the night with some kind of annual 'end of winter' festival that goes on, drawing people in from miles around. There's a tent and festoon lights covering the outdoor beer garden, with a live cover band. A mix of classics interspersed with modern hits are obviously giving the Crimson Ridge crowd what they're after, seeing as the place is packed out tonight. Inside, it's standing room only, heaving with patrons, while outdoors, the makeshift dance floor is also shoulder to shoulder.

I've had to survive the past hour and a half sitting beside Colt in this tiny booth while we've listened to Chy talk about herself the entire time. Kayce keeps getting up and down to get himself more drinks, and I'm ready to crawl out of my skin.

My fingertips are barely clinging to the edge of sanity. It's loud and crowded and far too chaotic after the serenity of the ranch, and I know Colt must be writhing on the inside the longer we spend here. When I dared sneak a glance at him earlier for half a second while Chy was rummaging in her purse for gum, I could see the tic in his jaw working overtime. Not to mention how tightly he's gripped his beer the entire duration we've sat in this booth.

Tonight has been a battle, fighting every urge to reach for him below the table. All I want to do is brush a reassuring finger against his thigh, to let him know I'm right here, to somehow help him understand I still feel such a powerful connection between us.

What it comes down to is that I want to have the right to touch him openly, so badly.

We all drove down the mountain together in his truck tonight. No way in hell was Kayce ever going to remain sober enough to drive, and even though we've got a pregnant woman amongst us who could technically be the designated driver for our entire merry little group, I wouldn't trust that woman behind the wheel. Not up Devil's Peak after dark.

So, Colt is our ride, and he's nursing his solitary beer. I've had a couple of drinks with my meal, but I'm at the point now where I'm feeling like I need something stronger, just to settle my nerves.

"There's my baby daddy," Chy calls out as Kayce reappears and slides back into the booth.

Ew. Gross.

I have to school my features not to give away how weird I find this girl. It's also entirely unclear whether she knows about my history with Kayce, because neither have mentioned anything in the brief amount of time we've endured each other's company since they arrived at the ranch.

I've done my best to avoid both of them since their unexpected arrival at the ranch—successfully so, up until tonight. Then, while we were all stuck together in the truck on the trip into Crimson Ridge, they only talked about their mutual group of friends we were going to be meeting up with at the bar. So there hasn't exactly been an appropriate moment to politely enquire about whether the pregnant dickhead my ex-boyfriend has on his arm is aware of my brief, and forgettable, dating history with him.

However, as much as I might regret dating Kayce, it was also the thing that brought me to Colt, and I'm entirely conflicted about that. Can I hate the circumstances that helped me find the person who I'm almost certain is the great love of my life? Even if I can never have him and never tell him?

Fucking hell. I definitely need shots. Right now.

"Anyone want a drink? I'm going to the bar." I announce.

"Fuck yeah, let's get the birthday girl wasted," Kayce whoops.

Colt makes a noise that sounds like a snarl. "Kayce. Don't be a fucking idiot," he snaps.

"Jesus, Dad. Just because you're past going out and having a good time." The man-child sitting across from me who is *absolutely* an idiot rolls his eyes. "Come on, Layla. The others are all at the bar anyway. I'll introduce you to some fun people."

Chy spots someone she obviously knows, because she starts making squealing noises and flapping her hands, and even though it's a monumental effort to squeeze out of the booth considering her stomach, she croons something and smooshes Kayce's face, practically licking him, before heading toward a group of girls who look almost identical to her.

All of them have weird bleached patches in their hair. Half of them are also pregnant. And they're out in a bar. Go figure.

"You coming, old man?" Kayce drops an arm over my shoulder when I stand up, glancing over at the man I want to rush back to, who remains seated in the booth.

Colt quickly fixes on the spot where his son's forearm rests around the back of my neck, and I duck my head. Not wanting to give a reason for Kayce to think any of his father's decisions revolve around me. They don't. *They shouldn't.*

But fuck, I want them to. So badly, it aches.

"You go. The Hayes boys are over there. I should catch up with them."

Following the direction he just gestured in with his beer bottle, I see a group of men, ones who look closer in age to Colt, tucked away in the far corner of the bar. They're seated on stools around a high top, in a part that is still incredibly busy but with the greatest distance from the music and the dancing as possible.

"Sweet, then let's fucking go, Layla." Before I can get my bearings, Kayce has taken me by the elbow and tugged me off into the crowd, and I lose sight of my cowboy almost immediately when the throng of people around the bar swallows me up. With a little stumble, I manage to throw one last glance over my shoulder, casting a look back at the booth where we were sitting moments before.

It's already empty.

"Shots for the birthday girl. Layla fucking Birch."

"Yeowwwwww."

"Down it, girl."

There's a chorus of noise from the group of strangers around me as I toss back something that looks cherry red and wipe my mouth with the back of my hand. It burns a trail of cinnamon mixed with hard liquor down my throat.

Kayce's group of buddies are all here for a big night out it would seem, and as much as I don't want to be dropping shots at the bar with strangers—there's only one man I wish to be next to, and he has vanished into thin air—the allure of numbing myself has taken over.

My life is a train wreck, so why not cut loose and get drunk like the other twenty-something-year-old girls filling this bar tonight?

Alcohol settles in my veins like a warm blanket. I think I'm on shot three? Another is pressed into my hand, and I giggle involuntarily.

"God, no. I can't." There's a nice-enough seeming guy and his girl who have been matching me round for round.

"Wanna dance instead?" The girlfriend with short brown hair tied in a half pony, and big hoop earrings, grabs my hand.

"Sure." I'm still laughing. Alcohol has gotten the better of me, after the weird tension of tonight, and the fact I can't even remember the last time I went out partying, all of which combines to make me a total lightweight.

I think this girl's name is Mary. Or maybe Mandy? Whatever, she seems cool, and I let her drag me off into the crowded tent outside. There are other friends of hers she side-hugs and shouts their names to introduce me over the noise of the band, but the bass and the speakers are right beside us, and we're in the thickest part of all the bodies moving in time with the song being played.

It's sweaty and packed, and it's tempting to get lost in the feeling of being more drunk than I realized, while also trying to enjoy forgetting about everything.

Trying to forget the hazel eyes and scruffy beard and boyish, unruly dark hair I want to sink my fingers into.

Jesus.

Of course, the mixture of shots, loud music, and being crushed in on all sides by bodies means that I'm horny as fuck and desperately want to go find Colt. I know he's still here, he's our ride home —no, not home, the ranch.

The ranch that is not my home, but that I want to be my home, that feels more like home to me than anywhere I've ever lived in my entire life.

Words swirl in my brain. The song peaks, and the crowd around me rolls into a crescendo, belting out the words to the final bars, with hands thrown in the air, and then I think I hear the lead singer say they're wrapping up their set. Suddenly, the lights dim, and the speakers start pumping with a heavier, deeper beat. The atmosphere changes in the blink of an eye into more of a nightclub feel, and Mandy—or Mindy—or Mary—grabs me by the waist, dragging me into a crush of her friends who sway to the seductive, thudding rhythm.

My body is already feeling turned on and churned up, and this sultry tune isn't helping the situation between my thighs. I close my eyes and let myself float along with this group of girls who I don't even know, but who are here to have a good time. If there's anything I need to do right now, it's just to willingly slip into that vacant state.

Have a good time.

Forget about everything outside this crowded dance floor.

Allow myself to feel every thud, every pulse, every pound of the bass emitting through the speakers.

As it all winds through my blood, with heavy scents of perfume and sour beer and sugary liquor hanging in the air, I feel the bump of a hard body against my back.

Ignoring it, I carry on swaying. I'm not interested in dancing with anyone here tonight. Well, with the exception of Colton Wilder. Each time I crack my eyelashes open, my eyes now heavy with the way those devilish pre-birthday celebration shots have diluted my bloodstream, I see some of the other girls in the group beginning to pair off with guys who are guiding them to dance, to press close. Hands wrapping around waists and fingers exploring muscled shoulders. Squeezing my eyes shut does nothing to erase the fact that I want that.

What I would give for the set of capable hands I know so well to slip around my waist from behind. For his strong torso to press up against my spine. For our hips to fit together, giving our bodies a chance to find that natural, instinctive rhythm we have.

Is Colt a dancer? I don't even know. He probably would never, but Jesus, the man fucks like he'd surely know how to grind against my body to the beat filling this dancefloor.

Lifting my hands up, I run them through my hair to lift my curls off my shoulders. Swaying and swinging my hips, soft material swishes around my knees.

I wore a dress tonight. My favorite that I own. It's white and has cute little puffed sleeves with a ruched midriff that makes my boobs look incredible. I run my hands down to where it hugs my waist perfectly. This dress is far more girlie summer-picnic-vibes than a night out in a bar in early spring, but fuck it, I feel incredible whenever I wear it.

Colt told me to wear something that makes me feel pretty, and goddamn this dress never lets me down.

I didn't wear it for *him* as such, but I can't deny thinking about him the entire time I was getting dressed tonight. And holy fuck, I just wish the cowboy in question could come and slide his hands over my waist and murmur hotly in my ear just how pretty he thinks I look in it right now.

Another bump up against me jolts my attention, this time coming from the other side. My eyes pop open, because, *rude*. I know it's crowded, and most people dancing right now are drunk, but it's going to get old real fast if I'm getting jostled around too badly.

"Have a drink with me." A man's voice is just over my shoulder. He's not talking to me, but it feels uncomfortably close and makes my neck prickle.

"What about your friend?" Another voice comes from the other side of where I'm swaying around. I realize they're talking to one of the girls from the group I've ended up dancing with tonight. She giggles, clearly wasted, and tugs on my elbow.

"Yeah, it's my friend Layla's birthday. We'll have a drink with you."

I want to immediately say no, but it's when I turn around that my brain draws a blank at the scene in front of me.

The young girl, whose name I didn't catch when it was being shouted earlier amongst the music, is tipping her head back and downing the drink she's been given. There's a tumbler being pressed into my hand, and whoever is responsible tries to guide it up to my mouth.

For whatever reason, I'm slow to react, but I know that I won't be letting that drink anywhere near me. The lights are so dim. Flashes and pulses of a strobe keep getting in my eyes, preventing me from seeing clearly. But that's when it hits me. The subtle waft of that cigarette smell, and I already know. Even though I can't see their faces, and I never did see the man who cornered me the night of the bonfire. Spiders crawl over my skin because I'm certain it's them.

And the girl beside me has just gulped down whatever was in that fucking drink one of them gave her.

I can't breathe. It's so crowded, and the dance floor is a crush on all sides. Bodies that are way taller than me suck the oxygen from my lungs. Not to mention these two men—who I'm certain are the same Piersons who have been fucking with the ranch— the ones who have been threatening Colt's livelihood and who, from all accounts, like to prey on unsuspecting girls, both tower over me to the point I can't really make out their faces in the shadows.

"Go on. Be good like your friend here, since it's your birthday and all." The drink is shoved toward my mouth forcefully, and I manage to slap it away. Most of it spills on the man holding it, and he curses.

"Fucking stupid bitch."

"Oh, I remember this one. You're Wilder's little plaything

aren't you?" The creep who got in my face that day up at the ranch, Henrik, leers at me.

"She was a rude little cock tease up at the bonfire, too. Now that's not very nice, throwing a tantrum like that. We're just talking."

My throat tightens. These men know exactly who I am, and if the fact they've been going after Colt on his property is anything to go by, I don't need to be a genius to figure out that they're unlikely to leave me alone. They might not know the truth of our connection, but they know I'm another way to mess with Colt, and potentially hurt him in the process.

"Looks like you still need *feeding right*, girlie."

"Fuck off." I try to turn toward the girl who has probably been drugged, but one of them grabs my arm.

What I would give for that gun Colt taught me how to shoot, so I could tell these assholes to back the hell away. Because something tells me with a sick, twisting feeling in my gut that this is exactly how easy it is for these two to prey on girls and get away with it time and time again.

It all makes sense now. Why he was so insistent about me knowing how to protect myself if I ever needed to up on that mountain. Why he was concerned about me being left on my own without a way to ensure something like this couldn't happen.

Except right now, I'm surrounded by people, and it's the perfect cover for their particular method of targeting girls.

It's too easy to hide amongst dark lights and loud music and drinks flowing freely.

The grip I'm held by is so hard that it stings. The other man tugs the girl, who is much younger than me, out of reach, cutting her off and starts to lead her away.

They split us up with gut-sickening efficiency.

"Get away from her," I shout, trying to reach for the girl who I don't know, but suddenly feel intensely protective over. I'm sobering up real quick. Fuck knows what they just gave her, and right now, I'm feeling more helpless than ever.

No matter how much I shout and try to struggle against the man holding me, the music is so loud it drowns me out. He blocks me with his body, subtly covering my mouth with a hand that stinks of nicotine, and propels me in the direction of the exit. One that will lead us away from the bar, leaving the crowd, disappearing into the night air.

"We're just gonna have a quiet drink together outside, girlie. So play nicely now. No need to cause a scene."

"Screw you. Let go of me." My words are muffled, silenced against his palm. I do my best to thrash and make it obvious to someone—anyone—that I don't want this. I'm not agreeing to this man's demands, or him grabbing me, or the way he's forcing me to leave this bar with him.

The exit comes closer.

It feels like I'm invisible.

Can no one see what's going on here?

This is how easily it can happen, isn't it? Lost in an expanse of people. Right out in the open. Then, when morning arrives, it's all blamed on the girl who *asked for it*.

Just as my stomach flops in a sickening roll of helplessness, it's as if the wall of bodies part all around us. The girl who I'd been trying to get to is shoved in my direction, and a tussle breaks out. Gruff voices argue loudly above the music.

A giant palm clamps down on the shoulder of whoever had their hands on me, and one of his arms is twisted up behind his back.

"Let's fucking go, Pierson."

As my brain tries to connect the dots of what is unfolding, I see the flash of metal cuffs and hear the crackle of a radio clipped at the man's belt. It's all over before I know it, as they're both led away, and the immediate crowd has stopped what they're doing to watch what looks like a sting arrest go down right in the midst of this crush of partygoers.

Even though the music is still blasting, obviously there's chaos happening over the other side of the bar with whatever just transpired. I can't see past the heads of the crowd surrounding us, but right now, I've got a girl beside me who has potentially been roofied, and I don't even know her name.

Spinning in place, I try to look for Mindy—Mandy—fuck, whoever the girl's friend was, and can't see her anywhere. In fact, no one we were here with before seems to be in sight. And the girl, the one who just drank something laced with who knows what, has disappeared.

Oh god. What the fuck is even going on right now?

Heavy palms land on my shoulders, and I jerk with fright, heart lurching into my throat.

As I spin around, all of that worry dissolves into nothingness. I'm met with a set of familiar hazel eyes I want to dive into, bathe in, drown in, and never need to come up for air as long as I live.

Colt towers over me with an expression I can't decipher, and when he bends his head to speak right at my ear, my core clenches at the gritty edge to his voice.

"Bathroom. Right fucking now."

CHAPTER 32

T he lock clicks on the door and Layla stands before me, hands tucked behind her lower back leaning against the wood, hitting me with the biggest green eyes.

She looks like a fucking goddess.

I'm going out of my mind. This is the moment, right here, when I've officially lost it.

We're locked in this tiny bathroom together and I don't know how long it's going to be before Kayce or his pregnant girlfriend comes looking for where we've both gone, but I couldn't breathe without getting Layla alone.

Seeing what just went down, watching those assholes dare get close to her again, that's when it all clicked for me.

I can't fix what my grandfather did, no matter how often I've tried to right the wrongs of the past. These two men are intent on being just as predatory and abusive to others. Hayes didn't need more than a second to realize what they were doing, right out in the open because they've grown cocky and consider themselves bulletproof. This time, they were their own downfall, and I certainly wasn't about to stop him from making that arrest.

Not this time. Not when it comes to my girl.

"You ok?" I close the short distance between us, needing to touch her. Needing to check that she's alright.

She nods, her hands fly up to fist the front of my shirt, and I drop my head into her neck.

"So much better now." She hums, arching, giving me greater access to that sensitive spot right above her wildly fluttering pulse.

Her voice is a little thick and raspy with the drinks she's had tonight. I've tried to keep count, but without drawing undue attention by staring at her the entire time, it was impossible to know for sure. As far as I can tell she's not out of her head, or too far gone to make decisions.

At least, I hope to god the fact Layla followed me here doesn't feel like a choice fueled by alcohol and lust when she wakes up in the morning. We might have been inseparable for weeks, but I couldn't handle thinking that she might regret the risk attached to a moment like this.

Though, I'm not sure I'm capable of letting her leave my arms right now.

Sucking in a deep inhale, she smells like the only good thing in my life. The thing I'm so close to losing forever.

"Did you see what happened out there?" Her voice sounds raspy and sexy, and that reminds me I've been too entranced, nuzzling her neck, inhaling her scent like a madman, and haven't actually responded out loud.

"I did. Those assholes are done." I hate that right now I've only got a rapidly evaporating number of minutes alone with her, yet Henrik and Alton Pierson are who we're talking about. "Sheriff Hayes will make sure something sticks to them this time."

"That girl." Layla's fingers slide up around my neck. "They gave her something."

"Hayes had one of his off-duty's grab her. He saw what they did." My lips brush a hot, wet, seeking trail over her neck, and Layla whimpers. Fuck, it lights my body up to be able to touch her even though it has only been a couple of days. "Please don't stress, they'll make sure she's taken care of and is safe."

"I'm sorry, Colt. Tonight has been so messed up."

Don't I fucking know it.

"I know. God, I know. But you've got nothing to apologize for. What can I do to make it better, angel? Tell me."

"Unless you can erase everything outside..." Her fingers toy with the hair at my nape and I already know I'm about to make a reckless fucking decision.

One hand comes up to the front of her neck, settling over the slender column of her throat, and she makes a needy little noise.

"As much as I wish it was possible, I can't get rid of anything on the other side of that door..." My fingers flex in the way I know she loves, giving a little bit of added pressure that draws out another whimper. Lips hovering over hers, I'm damn well lost, all I see and breathe is this stunning girl. "But I can help erase those racing thoughts filling your head. Do you want that, sweetheart?"

"We can't... it's too risky... not in here..." Layla's pink tongue darts out to wet her lips, and I groan. There's nothing that could keep me away from her right now.

I'm so fucking gone for this girl.

Fuck the whole world on the other side of that locked exit.

I crash our mouths together and hoist her against me. Devouring every little needy noise she makes and the way our bodies fit so fucking perfectly. Spinning us both, I drop her onto the counter beside the basin. There's not a lot of space to move, but there's no goddamn way I'm letting that stop me.

"You're going to have to behave and keep quiet." Biting her lower lip, I slide my palms to ruck her dress up over her thighs. I want to spend forever tasting her mouth, but right now, I'm starving for more than just her kisses. I need her shattering on my tongue, and I need to get inside her, and we're already being risky enough by spending this long in here.

Dropping down onto one knee in front of my girl, that position allows my palms to skate across her skin at eye level. From here I can soak up every shaky breath and quiver she emits above me.

"Do I need to stuff your mouth with something, or can you be a good girl and keep quiet for me?"

I know, without a doubt, she's turned on as all hell right now. There's not enough time for everything I want to do, so for the moment I gotta ignore my intensely painful hard-on pressing against my fly and get my mouth on her.

"Oh god. I want you so bad." Layla pants, looking down at me.

"I know, baby. It's been hell for me, too." I drag her hips forward to perch on the edge of the counter, then press her knees wide.

"We can't do this." She protests, but that morphs into a gasp when I roughly hook my fingers beneath her panties, pulling them to one side, and cover her pussy with my mouth.

I don't have the luxury of endless minutes to argue this out. The longer we talk, the less time I've got to make her fall apart, and I'm a man fucking possessed. Feasting on her sweet cunt, letting her hold me tight against her swollen clit as she makes desperate, strained noises above me.

It's taking everything in her not to be loud, I can tell.

She's so goddamn sexy and perfect and tastes like *mine*.

Just as her thighs start shaking and her fingers dig into my scalp—just as she's almost fucking there—a heavy pounding bangs on the door.

Layla jerks above me, but I keep going. Stiffening my tongue to massage her clit faster and harder.

"Layla? You in there?"

"Oh my god," she whispers, panic causing her to go rigid. She pulls my hair, trying to get me off her. For a split second the thought crosses my mind. We should stop. I should stop. But that door right there is locked and I'm struggling to find any last shred of reasoning to deter me from this course.

Her taste is already on my lips, and I'm intent on seeing my perfect goddamn girl fall to pieces for me. No. There's no fucking way, I'm already in too deep.

"Layla?" There's more banging. It's Kayce, who is drunk, on the other side of the door while I've got my tongue shoved in Layla's pussy and she's about ten seconds from soaking my face as she unravels like a dream come true.

"Uhh... yeah?" She finds her voice, sounding more than a little shaky, meeting my eyes as I look up at her from the only place I want to be. I keep going, sucking and licking her clit, and shake my head from side to side. Layla draws in a sharp inhale when I dig my fingers into her soft flesh and work her relentlessly.

With my eyes, I let her know exactly how this is going to play out.

I'm not fucking stopping.

"Are you all good in there?" My goddamn son is still on the other side of the door.

"I'm—" I can tell she's about to come. *Whimper.* "I'm ok." *Gasp.* "Be out soon." Her voice cracks and there's a hitch in her tone. She sinks her fingers into my hair, holding tighter, directing me exactly where she wants me.

Goddamn I love this girl.

"Ok. I'm gonna go try to find my dad. He's disappeared somewhere, but I guess we should leave, if you're ready to get outta here."

I see it in her face. The scrunch between her eyes. The way her cheeks flush and the second her jaw drops open. Her climax tugs her under, body tightening as her pretty lips hang open.

"Ok. Yes. *Yesss.*" She sucks in a breath and it hits. The force of her orgasm makes her thighs squeeze my head, and her body jerks as the waves roll through her.

I don't waste another second.

Christ. I have no idea if Kayce is still standing somewhere just outside, but holy shit, my dick is rock hard and leaking pre-cum. I have to have her right here and now, fuck the consequences.

If a shitty bathroom in the back of a bar when Layla's had one too many shots is all we get, then it'll have to do.

Dragging her limp body off the counter, I twist her around, draping her torso over the flat surface to face the mirror, devouring the way her tits threaten to spill out the top of this dress that was obviously designed to worship her body.

"God, you're a fucking vision, angel."

"I need you, Daddy. So bad." She watches me through hooded eyes in the mirror's reflection as I free myself from my jeans.

Fisting the hem of her dress, I drape it up over her lower back, exposing her ass. Tugging her panties to one side again, I've got my cock in one hand, and glide it through her slickness to coat the head and nearly fucking die at how hot and wet and velvety she always feels.

"Christ. I missed your perfect little cunt."

"I missed your cock." Her teeth catch her bottom lip, and I hold her mossy green eyes in the mirrored reflection as I press forward. It's heaven. Right here with her, under these shitty fluorescent lights, being wrapped in her gaze as I shove forward into her tight, silky heat. It's always perfect with her.

We mold and fit together without question, and it's so much more than just sex, but holy fuck, if it isn't always so soul-destroyingly incredible with this girl.

"*Ffuuuck.*" Her eyes roll back in her head as I push forward.

"You're so fucking wet." My teeth are gritted. "Always so fucking wet." The feel of her is too much. Fluttering and clenching around me already, like she's still coming from my tongue before, or maybe she's so worked up she's already on the edge of coming again.

We're both wrapped up in the heat and desperation of this moment. Layla has her bottom lip trapped between her teeth, looking at me in the mirror the whole time as I thrust, and the urgency to have my girl takes hold. It feels like forever since we last did this, the temptation to draw everything out beckons, but it's too easy to completely lose track of time when I'm with her.

"I'm so close..." Layla whimpers, and that strikes a match. I don't know what fucking takes hold of me, but maybe it's the fact I know that *this time* is most likely to be the last time I ever get to be with her.

"You want to come?"

She makes a pleading noise. Her cunt tightening around my length as I punch my hips against her ass.

"Then let me hear it. Nice and quiet for me." My eyes hold hers in the mirror as the filthy, wet sounds of our fucking echos off the tiles. "*Shhhh*. Be a good girl. You're doing so well. We don't want anyone to find out I'm fucking you in here."

"You feel so good." Her whisper floats out, horny and soft as silk.

"Quietly, baby. I want to hear you begging. I want to hear you saying my name." Goddamn the way she grips me tighter each time I tell her to be quiet.

"*Please*. I miss you."

"You want me to fill you up, angel?"

"I want that so bad. *Yes.*"

"Do you want to walk out of here knowing your pretty little pussy is leaking my cum? Want to feel me running down your legs?"

Layla bites her lip so hard I worry she's going to end up bruised. But holy shit. *Holy shit.* The way she flutters and tries to suck me deeper. I'm seeing stars, and the pressure and need to blow inside her velvety channel is already locked in at the base of my spine.

"Please. *Please, Colt.*"

Hearing my name in that sweet little breathy whisper is what drags us both toward the edge.

"That's it, you're doing so well. Taking me so beautifully. You're always so fucking perfect." Beneath me, the girl who holds my entire battered and barely functioning heart in her hands is falling apart as I quietly murmur praise and talk her through it.

"Colt... Colt... Oh god. I..."

"I know, angel." My jaw is clenched tighter than ever, and my fingers dig so goddamn hard into the swell of her hips. Maybe it'll be the last thing I can leave as a reminder of us. Every brutal thrust forward reminds me that it won't be enough, because even if she walks out of here full of my cum and with bruises where my fingers have been, those temporary things will be gone all too soon. "I just want to own every inch of you and mark you as mine. You've got me going insane for you, angel."

Layla whimpers, eyes turning that deep shade of green. I know she's about to fall apart, and I know it's right there.

"Colt—I—"

She's biting back what wants to come out.

I know it because I'm doing the same thing.

Shaking my head, I grunt. "I'm not going to say those words. We're not going to, baby. Not here. Not in a bathroom. They're right there on my tongue. You know they are, and they're all yours, but it won't be like this because I would hate myself forever."

With that, I surge forward, snaking one hand beneath her panties to find her clit, and I pinch down on the pouting bud beneath my calloused fingers.

Layla's mouth drops open in a silent cry as she clamps down around my cock. Her climax drags mine out of me at the same time, and I'm cursing beneath my breath as I pump into her. Cum spurts in thick ropes, and time stands still for that moment when it's just our two bodies tumbling through that haze of pleasure and bliss together.

God, I don't know how long we've been in here. My brain is blank and my cock doesn't seem to get the message that we have to end things. I've gotta get Layla cleaned up and sneak her out of here before it's obvious she's been in this bathroom for a very fucking long time.

"Stay there, baby." I ease out of her and grab a couple of paper towels, tidying up quickly and tucking myself away. Helping her stand up, I turn my girl around to face me.

Her eyes are glossy. Both with pleasure, and I suspect, a whole lot of emotion.

I go to lower myself down, to help clean her up, but she stops me before I can sink to my knees and shakes her head. "No. Leave it. I want to feel you there."

Goddamn. I let the air whoosh out of my lungs, the crumpled paper falls discarded to the floor. Cupping her face in my palms, I seek out her lips.

This time when our mouths connect, it's slow and sensual and feels like divine torture. There's so much emotion flowing between us. It's written there in each achingly soft glide of our tongues as they slide and twine, each tiny flex of her fingertips as she clings tightly onto my wrists.

When I draw back and rest our foreheads together, Layla makes a pained noise. "Why does this feel like goodbye?"

Fuck. I know we still have to drive back to the ranch together tonight, and she's not gone from my life just yet, but my girl is right. This feels like something so much more than a desperate need to dive into each other while locked away in a bar bathroom.

Clearing my throat, I rest my lips against her brow. "I shouldn't admit this, so please don't say anything back, Layla. But one look at you, and I'm lost inside you. I'm sinking deeper, but it's the opposite of drowning. For what it's worth, whatever this is, I want it so bad it fucking aches."

Layla's eyes scrunch closed.

My thumbs brush her cheeks. I can't seek out her eyes, otherwise there is no chance of finding it within myself to walk away. "I'm going to go out there and make sure everything is clear. Wait a few minutes and then you should be ok to come out, alright?"

She nods. Her throat works down a heavy swallow.

And that's all we'll get.

I have to leave her, even though it fucking kills me to do so.

As my fist closes around the door handle, I suck in a long breath, pausing... contemplating if there's a potential version of this moment where I get to walk out of here holding her hand and we go home together. Where it's *us* and not the awkward drive back up the mountain pretending there's nothing entwining our hearts.

But I know that's not the case.

Assholes like me don't get that.

Layla has got her whole life ahead of her.

So, I turn the lock and slip into the dimly lit, empty hallway outside.

Alone.

CHAPTER 33

Layla

I can hardly breathe.

Everywhere I go, either Kayce is there with his stupid, blinding smirk, or Chy is clacking her acrylics against her phone screen. Then came the icing on the ugliest cake in existence: she had her massive pregnancy tits hanging out over breakfast this morning as she continued to flirt openly with Colt.

It's all too much, and I feel like I'm one second away from screaming.

Being outside with the horses has been the shred of sanity that I've clung to. There's hardly a spot left in these stalls that hasn't been thoroughly attended.

I'm sure these horses have never had so much pampering, but this is my refuge. I'd take one of them out for a ride somewhere, but in all honesty, I haven't dared to, because I know that's what Colt has done today.

After Chy's breakfast time near nipple slips and constantly staring at Colt's ass, he took off as fast as he could.

Kayce was nowhere to be seen, sleeping off the booze, until after his father had long left for some far-flung corner of the ranch.

Which left me faced with the prospect of having to spend time with the crazy pregnant lady, or the opportunity to make my hasty exit. So, I grabbed my coffee and practically ran out the door as soon as it seemed a *non-suspicious* amount of time after Colt departed.

God, my cheeks immediately heat, recalling last night. What we did in secret in the bathroom. How it felt so fucking hot and natural to be with him, followed by the moment when he touched my face so tenderly afterward.

My heart squeezes, feeling the ghost of his lips against my forehead. The brush of the pads of his thumbs against the apple of my cheeks.

For what it's worth, whatever this is, I want it so bad it fucking aches.

I lay in bed last night with tears brimming over, replaying those words. Curled into a ball in my giant empty bed, in a room that doesn't feel like my room at all.

How is it possible to miss him so desperately, when we're under the same roof, and we had sex only hours before? My cowboy feels like he might as well be separated from me by oceans and continents, not a few soft footsteps down a quiet hallway.

Gnawing on my lip, I brush Ollie. She's looking so gorgeous and glossy and positively preens under my strokes over her coat. I've taken extra time with each of the horses today, dragging out every moment lost in thought—deeply lost in memories of Colt.

I'm also feeling a sense of dread as to what is to come once my time here is officially up and I have to leave. I've got to collect my car, which apparently is fixed and ready for me anytime I'm ready to pick it up. Then, I've got to move on to my next placement.

My attempts to find a new job have been half-hearted at best. But I've seen a couple of requests from stables and dude ranches not too much of a distance from here, then some others that are a good few hours away.

The temptation is strong to look for somewhere as far from this mountain as possible. Because I simply do not know how I'll be able to work and live and continue to exist, knowing I could easily climb in my car and return to Crimson Ridge.

Maybe I need to look for something closer to where my graduation ceremony will be? That's at least a full day's drive away, in Colorado, if not more.

So far, I haven't had the heart to open any of Sage's recent messages. I know she'll be poised and ready to rip into me when I finally do discover the energy to hit reply, but as of right now, I don't know what to say. Maybe I need to tell my best friend I'm coming back home, and try to find somewhere to complete my apprenticeship close by.

There aren't anywhere near as many options for vet placements, but at least I could hug my friend and sob uncontrollably into her shoulder and eat ice cream in my underwear while I form a Layla-shaped imprint on her couch.

Totally normal behavior.

She wouldn't suspect a thing.

How fucked up is it to know that you're already going through heartbreak, and the loss of the greatest love you've ever known, when he's still right fucking there? When you can still catch his scent as you walk down the hallway and find his favorite coffee mug in the cupboard.

Even worse is the fact that he pretty much admitted that he felt everything I'm feeling last night. He didn't exactly say *the words* but he told me he wanted to. Colt told me he wanted to say them, but that he wasn't going to. Not at that moment.

I think I fell even deeper in love with him as he uttered that gritty whisper.

He respects me enough, and cares about me enough, that he wasn't going to give me something so valuable while I was drunk and needy in a tiny bar bathroom.

"So this is where you hide out all day, huh?"

A voice that makes my fine hairs stand on end comes from just behind me.

For a brief second, I close my eyes and take in a measured, deep inhale through my nostrils. *Be civil.*

"Hey, Chy." Turning around, I flash her a plastered-on smile, then promptly duck underneath Ollie's neck, to stand on the other side and begin grooming the opposite flank.

The side that I've already groomed. But Chy doesn't know that, so here we are.

At least I've got a thousand pounds of horse separating the two of us.

"Sure seems to keep you busy, being out here." Chy is peering all around. She's at least put on a coat and covered up her tits, but I can't help feeling like she's out here seeking the older Wilder man.

God, it's so fucked up. Why can't Kayce smell the bullshit rolling off this woman? Oh, wait. Not my problem.

"Just doing my job." I keep that smile on my face, but it feels like I'm just gritting my teeth.

"And you and Kayce's dad... you've been up here this whole time... alone?"

Oh, she isn't daring to go this route, is she?

"Uhh, well, firstly, it's my job to be here on the ranch. Secondly, he's my boss, so of course, I've been working alongside him." My eyes stay fixed on the glide of the grooming brush over the glossy flank. The fingers of my free hand stroke Ollie's nose.

She must agree something about this girl smells off, because she stamps a hoof.

"But, it's been weeks and weeks that just you two have been up here."

"Can't exactly leave the mountain very easily when the road is blocked, can I?" I'm trying to keep my voice level while talking through a clenched jaw.

I don't like where this conversation is going, nor her accusatory tone. Especially not the fact she's sniffing around looking for evidence of something that is one hundred percent true, but is none of her goddamn business. Whatever transpired between me and Colt does not need to be dug up or uncovered by this meddlesome bitch.

She sighs and leans a shoulder up against the stall. And yeah, I don't miss the way she looks me up and down.

"I hope there's no hard feelings, all things considered."

My throat tightens. "About what?"

"Oh, just the whole thing with Kayce..." She runs her tongue over her teeth, dark eyes still beady and narrowed on me.

"I don't know if I follow." Not that I want to. I'd quite like for her to fuck right off.

"He didn't tell you?"

"Tell me what?"

"That we first started hooking up last autumn, on and off... then you know, he moved away for a bit with his rodeo shit... but by the summer, he realized what he was missing."

My teeth grind. *Great.* So not only was Kayce taking advantage of my kindness—when I gave him a place to stay, and let him into my bed—but he was in an on-again-off-again *thing* with this skanky bitch.

I've never been more relieved for the fact we always used a condom and that I got myself tested as soon as we split up.

God knows what fleas this girl is carrying around.

Ugh, a shudder runs through me.

Kayce is the fucking worst. How many other random girls exactly like this one has he had on his roster of beds to hop between.

"Well, congratulations that you guys are... uhhh... starting a family." I really wish she'd just leave. This whole conversation is making my stomach churn.

"I knew he'd come to his senses." She cocks her head to one side. Still staring at me with a shit-eating look on her face.

Good thing I couldn't fucking care less. She can have Kayce and his drinking and his uselessness. If anything, my heart aches for the fact Colt is going to invariably get tangled up in this disaster that his son has gotten himself into. After having gone through his own trauma with unexpectedly becoming a father, he's now got an awfully similar situation come to shack up right under his roof.

"Ok." I shrug.

"So, you haven't had anything *happen* to you up here, Layla?"

"Excuse me?" God. This bitch might be pregnant, but I'm not above throwing some horse shit at her if she doesn't get the hint and leave me the fuck alone.

"Did Colton Wilder ever tell you the truth about Devil's Peak Ranch?"

My nails thread into Ollie's mane as I try to control my temper. There is nothing I want more than to be able to snap my fingers and vanish from this spot. To escape whatever this is.

"I'm guessing not." She continues. "Did you know his grandaddy was a filthy molester? That he assaulted women and got away with it? Colton Wilder inherited a property that, by all rights, should have gone to others in this town. The only reason it didn't is because old man Wilder lied through his teeth, and back in the day, fifty-odd years ago, who would believe a young girl working on a ranch up a mountain? Who would believe the underage girl with a baby on the way?"

I stop and meet her intense stare from across the stall.

"Let me guess. Those *people* you're talking about are the Piersons?"

Everything suddenly begins to slot into place. The real reason Colt seemed so reluctant to point the finger at them, even though he had evidence they'd been up to no good around his property. Why he was so protective over me. From what he's told me about how much he hated his grandfather, I don't doubt the man was capable of something so awful.

"And guess who got them fucking arrested last night... all because they were dancing with *you*." Chy just about spits the words in my direction. Her overplucked eyebrows arch as she dares me to confess to the reason why Colt might be acting protective over me.

But I'm not having any of it. I have no idea if Colt was involved with what happened last night. It's all a blur, but either way, it wasn't me they roofied. The other girl with me on the dance floor is the one they got to before anyone could stop them.

Folding my arms, I stand my ground. "I don't know what you

think you heard or saw, but it was one of Kayce's friends—and by extension, I'm assuming one of your friends—who those guys gave a drink to. One that I can only guess had something slipped in it."

She waves me off with her lurid claws.

"You have no idea about anything here, sweetie. I suggest you think twice before you let a man like Colton Wilder anywhere near you."

"Listen, Chy. I don't particularly care what you think you know, or saw, but I'm going to politely ask you to let me get back to work. I've got a job to do, and as you can see, there's plenty needing to be done up here."

"Oh, I can imagine." She gives me a smirk. "Is that the kind of work that requires you to be on your knees, Layla?"

This fucking bitch.

"There you are, babe."

Just as I'm getting ready to drag a pregnant piece of scum out of this barn by her hair, Kayce's voice cuts through the tension.

Chy whirls round, all fake smiles, making cooing noises at the man coming toward us.

"What cha' doing out here in the cold?" He doesn't seem overly affectionate or touchy with her, I've noticed. Not that I'm interested in the slightest about their relationship, but it hasn't escaped my attention that Kayce doesn't exactly seem to be acting like a doting boyfriend or father-to-be.

Maybe that's because he hasn't had any role models growing up to show him an example of that.

Jesus. We're all just as fucked up as each other when it comes to shitty family dynamics around this place. One big ball of generational screw-ups.

Yet another reason why I have no intention of having children of my own. Ever. No thank you, that's just not a path that is ever going to be for me. I've lived through a life of having a mother who didn't exactly want a kid. It was the easiest decision of my own knowing that I wanted to stay child-free by choice.

I know there are plenty of women out there who can't understand that, but the ones I've come across in my life who get it, get it.

"I was just coming to find you." Chy is all saccharine smiles as she winds herself around Kayce. "Let's get out of Layla's way. She's apparently got some hard work to do that requires her being on her knees for *hours*." Throwing me a haughty look, she drags Kayce off out of the barn.

My ears are hot, and I have to swallow down a lump threatening to rise in my throat.

I just have to get through the next week, and then I'll be gone.

Away from that bitch.

Away from the ghosts haunting Devil's Peak.

Away from the bullshit of Kayce and his shitty life decisions.

And gut wrenchingly, I'll be long gone from Colt Wilder.

CHAPTER 34

Layla

"Layla?"

The voice that makes my heart flutter drifts through the entrance to the stall where I'm working.

Since the run-in with Chy earlier, I've stayed here in the barn and carried on doing as many little jobs as I can find. My mind has been on a constant loop of worry after her insinuations and thinly veiled threats earlier.

Now, the man himself is standing there looking at me, eyes soft, with one hand tucked in the pocket of his jeans, Winnie's reins in the other. He's finally come back from wherever he's been hiding out, being busy all day on the ranch.

God, I just want to rush into his arms.

"It's late. You haven't eaten." It's a statement. The way this man knows that, reading me with a single glance, sends my emotions haywire.

I duck my head, not wanting him to see that I'm entirely *not ok* right now.

"I'm fine." A massive lie. But what else am I supposed to say?

"Is this about last night?" He starts working on Winnie's tack, but keeps his voice to a low murmur.

"No." Yes. Maybe. It's about everything and nothing and

mostly about the fact that I can't bear that I'm unable to be with him.

"I'm sorry—" He starts, but I cut him off. This is only going to make everything a million times shittier if I feel like he didn't want things to go the way they did between us last night.

"Please. Don't apologize." I suck in a shaky inhale. "But tell me the truth, did you get those guys arrested at the bar?"

Colt stops what he's doing, visibly stiffening. "They deserved it, and much more. You know that."

"But was it because of you... or because of me?" Fuck, I don't know what I'm asking him. That bitch has gotten to me. She's been in my head all day after her attempts at fucking with my mind earlier on. And all I've had is my own thoughts to swirl around in by myself.

"What brought this on?"

"Nothing... just, Chy was out here earlier. She said something about them and a connection with your grandfather... and look, it's best to ignore me, I'm just over-tired, I think." I try to shrug off whatever it was I was attempting to say. Because I don't even know right now.

"Layla." He comes right up close, and a part of me wants to step back, to put distance between us, but the more desperate, in love with him, part of me allows him to be near. "That girl is trying to start shit. She's a piece of work, and you know it." His voice is gruff and hard, but not because of me. I know that from the tenderness in his gaze as he holds my eyes.

There's a tic in his jaw as he looks me over.

"Are you ok?" He whispers, and for a moment, his palm lifts to cup my cheek.

So much longing flows through me, that I give in. I lean into his touch and close my eyes for a moment. The heat from his palm seeps into me and his masculine scent curls a delicious path through my bloodstream and I'm so close to throwing myself into his arms.

But I can't. We can't.

My eyelashes flutter open, and I turn my head into his touch for just a second longer, allowing my lips to meet his warm caress.

"I'd better go."

And I step back, dragging myself away once more. I'm going to be gone any day now, and I really need to remember that this man is not mine. We can't do this, so being strong and walking away is about all I can do right now.

IT'S LATE. The glowing digital clock on the stove says midnight.

I'd been lying in bed tossing around and unable to sleep, and eventually decided to make my way to the kitchen and grab myself a glass of water.

Except, as I flip the faucet off and turn around, there's someone on the other side of the island who I really, really do not want to see right now.

Chy cocks her head to one side and then leans her elbows forward onto the countertop. Her pregnant stomach is barely covered by the tank she's got on.

"Can't sleep, Layla?"

"Needed a glass of water." I shrug and hold up the glass in question.

There's a glint in her eyes as she thinks for a moment, then says words that send my blood running cold. "You know, you really should be more careful about cuddling up to your boss out in the open where anyone can see. How do you think Kayce would feel knowing you and his dad are out in that barn getting extra cozy?"

This time my expression must be a dead giveaway because she looks triumphant. Like she's finally secured the winning goal that she's been taking shots at all day in the hope of scoring.

"What do you want, Chy?" I grit my teeth.

"I want Kayce."

"Good. You've got him. He's already yours." I go to push past her and escape back to my room, but she steps in my path.

"No, you see, it's not as simple as that. I need to make sure that Kayce doesn't think his sweet little ex-girlfriend looks like a good idea to go back to." She flicks her eyes up and down my body, giving me a sneer. "So it's quite fitting really, that you're just a slut who's been fucking his father. Imagine how those rumors will multiply around Crimson Ridge if whispers were to start flying that Colton Wilder purposely lied to his own son and fucked his girlfriend behind his back. Because I can promise you, I'll have everyone believing that you and Kayce were still together, still madly in love, when dear old Dad started sticking his dick in his precious *Layla*. It'll be Colt's word against the gossip chain around town, and I'll tell you now, this ranch will be out of business quick as a flash if they hear how he's screwed over his own son... the upcoming rodeo darling, Kayce Wilder."

My mouth is hanging open. This girl is a fucking calculating piece of work. She's not only ready to take down Colt, his business, his ranch and soul's home, but she's ready to destroy Kayce's career while she's at it.

Chy looks me over. "Turns out the apple didn't land far from the tree, did it? Colton Wilder is a little *too much* like his grandaddy after all."

My fists clench. This girl is vile.

"What exactly are you after?"

"Be gone in the morning."

My heart thuds extra hard. I don't know what I was expecting, maybe money, but it certainly wasn't that.

"How could I possibly trust that you would keep your word?"

"With you out of the picture, Layla? Oh, I'd have no problem keeping your not-so-little secret. Anything I might, or might not have seen, would be forgotten real fast."

As much as I want to rip chunks of hair off this girl's head, I love Colt too fiercely. There is nothing I wouldn't do to protect that man.

"That's it? That's all you want from me?"

She nods and gives me a tight smile. "Yup." She pops the P and steps aside. "Happy packing, Layla."

DAWN CRAWLS a lazy path of pinks and purples across the horizon as I quietly shut the front door behind me. The scents of spring and chilled air hit my nose as I hoist my bag in one hand and carefully make my way down the steps leading away from the front porch.

Last night broke me. I couldn't bear the thought of Colt's life here, or the ranch, being threatened. It doesn't make sense for me to stay any longer, not when it might blow up everything Colt has worked so hard his entire life for.

Not when I'm due to leave within the week, anyway.

It doesn't change the fact that I'm a mess of emotions. I'm going to have to borrow Kayce's truck to get down to Crimson Ridge and leave it at the mechanics in order to collect my car when they open. I figure Colt can sort out giving him a ride down the mountain to fetch it—I left a note to that effect on the kitchen island apologizing for taking the vehicle without any warning.

I made up an excuse about an emergency with Evaline as to the reason for my sudden departure before anyone in the house was awake.

Although my heart is racing, knowing fully well that Colt usually gets up around this time. So every second longer I take getting my ass into this truck and off this mountain, increases the risk of having to face him and say a proper goodbye.

As much as I desperately want that, I also don't know if my heart can take it.

I've dumped my bag in the back seat and opened the driver's door, tossing my purse on the passenger side when I feel him.

My fingers curl into the metal frame.

"You got somewhere to be?" Colt's voice is thick with sleep, or maybe with lack of sleep. If his nights have been anything like mine lately, it'll be the latter.

I keep hold of the door, lifting my eyes to meet his where he leans a hip against the front of the truck. Dressed in his jeans and flannel shirt rolled to his elbows, even though it's cold out, and looking every inch the love of my life.

"I can't stay." My eyes hold his. Fuck. My bottom lip is wobbling already.

His brow furrows. Confusion passes over his features, but he doesn't say anything.

"Chy saw us." I swallow and it's about all I can manage to get out. "She promised not to say anything to Kayce, as long as I leave."

That brings a hard line to his jaw. The creases around his eyes deepen, and his shoulders visibly stiffen inside his shirt.

"We knew I was always going to be leaving. It's easier this way." My attention travels up to the house. Even though I know there's not much chance either of them will be up at this time of the morning, I'm especially paranoid after Chy's threats last night.

Colt watches me, looking like he's chewing over words to say. Then he simply nods.

My chest feels like someone has ransacked it. Stuffing my heart inside a torture device.

Is this going to be it? Is that all this moment will ever be for us?

I don't think I can face anymore pain, of saying goodbye when I can't say the kind of goodbye we both deserve. When in fact, I don't want to say goodbye at all. I want to stay right here and live out my days with this wonderful, captivating, rugged man.

So I dip my chin to try and hide the quiver of my bottom lip and stinging tears pricking behind my eyes, and slide into the driver's seat.

But before I can shut the door behind me, Colt grabs the frame. He fills the space, standing still, not touching or reaching for me, but he's right there all the same. His knuckles are white where he holds onto the metal as if he could crush it with one hand.

My eyes snap up to his, finding an expression on his face that is entirely wild and filled with a collision of emotion behind those hazel eyes I'll never stop seeing when I close my own.

"Layla..." He clears his throat, pauses, then when Colt speaks, his voice is quiet and rough. "Find that sweet spot, angel. Take your aim and hit that target. You can be anything you want. I have no doubt you'll succeed. That good heart of yours is tougher than you think. If you can survive an old bastard like me, you can reach the stars and have them falling at your feet, too."

With those words, the ones that break my foolish heart, my cowboy turns, and is gone.

CHAPTER 35

Layla

T flop down on my too-soft bed. Every limb cries out in agony from how hard I've been working lately. Soreness extends all over from how relentlessly I've thrown myself into each and every opportunity presenting itself to remain busy. I've spent the past fifteen minutes scalding myself under my hell-water shower in an effort to get rid of the smell of cow shit, or try to loosen the tension between my shoulders.

Yet my heart is officially the sorest muscle of them all.

Five months haven't dulled the ache that sits like a solid mass inside my rib cage, reminding me every single damn day just how much I miss the rugged cowboy I left behind when I drove my Honda out of Crimson Ridge without looking back.

Colt occupies my waking thoughts more often than I care to admit. Then, at night, he fills my dreams. I wake up thinking he's there with the mattress dipping beside me beneath his weight. I wake up turned on and moaning into my pillow because I've had the most vivid dreams of his hands and his tongue and his cock sliding into me. I wake up hearing his raspy voice whispering in my ear that I'm the best thing that ever happened to him.

Truth be told, I'm a fucking mess. Layla Birch is back in the season of life called surviving, and I'm barely managing that on a good day. Only, this time my survival mode is less *Ramen and going to bed with a grumbling tummy,* and more *my tears have soaked through my pillow because I'm an emotional fucking wreck.*

I mean, I've been blessed with job offers for all my work placements. Not only that, but every single location I've worked in during the past five months has paid handsomely for an apprenticeship, and they've paid overtime. Turns out having Devil's Peak Ranch on my resume has opened up a whole world of connections, where I've had stables and ranches and all sorts of businesses emailing me asking if I'd be interested in working with them.

The cherry on top of that pretty pie: I haven't had to pick up a single bar shift since I left Crimson Ridge. The income from my placements these past few months has been more than enough to meet all payments for Evaline's care.

I've worked exceptionally hard to get to where I am, now being only one week out from graduation. There's no denying that my resume speaks for itself, the difference now being that I've finally been able to have a reputable ranch stand behind me and give me a vote of confidence in my skills.

If I think about it too hard, I get all choked up. Each new opportunity that comes my way has Colt's handiwork all over it, but the man himself has been a ghost since I left the mountain.

Did I expect anything different? Did I think my cowboy was going to ride in and sweep me off my feet? Of course not. We knew what our situation was right from the very beginning and I guess it was some sort of strange gift from the universe that I was given just enough time to properly fall in love with him.

There wasn't any scenario where I drove away, and we kept in touch. He's barely in contact with the outside world. Doesn't have a cellphone that I know of. Doesn't use social media. What were we going to do, become pen pals over email?

Christ. I dig the heels of my palms into my eye sockets.

I have to be fucking strong and do this for myself. I can't be a silly girl with foolish daydreams who has no vision for her own future.

The only person I can depend on is me. I refuse to go through life reliant on someone else. As much as that fantasy—of life with Colt and the ranch—is appealing, it's also just that.

A fantasy.

My phone pings with an incoming message. Now that I'm in civilization once more, Sage is back to texting me endlessly. Not that I particularly mind. It gives me something to take my mind off wondering what Colt is doing approximately five thousand times a day.

SAGE:

Got yourself a hot af graduation outfit yet?

I'm thinking something that says professional...

But willing to suck dick to get a promotion.

God. You are a pest.

So is that a yes to the slutty but *very enthusiastic* employee look?

No.

And no, I haven't picked a dress or outfit yet.

Excuse me, but it's only one week 'til grad.

FFS.

You better not be in such a miserable state while I'm there.

I'm not miserable.

Oh sorry.

Just carry on, Eeyore.

Continue to persist with this charade.

That cowboy broke your heart, didn't he?

I wish you weren't so damn psychic.

Well, detecting how well looked after your pussy is... consider that my superpower.

Not all superheroes wear capes, you know.

No. You just parade around in devil horns and matte lipstick.

And I look FABULOUS while doing so.

At least I can take you out while I'm there.

Please tell me this graduation will have some hot vets who are skillful with their hands?

Jesus. I feel like I should hand out a warning before you arrive.

Put a cat collar with one of those bells on you so they can hear you coming.

Kinky.

So that's settled, I've got my agenda:

1. Get you graduated.

2. Go out for drunky-dinner.

3. Find you some uncomplicated, no-strings-attached dick to fill that cowboy-shaped hole in your heart.

... and your pussy.

I DON'T WANT anyone else, is what I want to text my best friend, while staring at the jet-black hat sitting on my nightstand. The one that I lie in bed with, sitting the brim over my chest as I soak up the scents of Colt still lingering in the fibers. All the while, wanting to spill everything to Sage. Would it be the end of the world if I admitted what went on between the two of us up on Devil's Peak?

Probably once I've had a single sip of champagne on grad day, I'll end up spilling everything anyway.

I guess that's a problem for future Layla.

> I gotta be up early tomorrow.

> Helping out at the local rodeo qualifiers.

Oooooh, you see?!

The universe is already providing.

Imagine the buffet on offer... all sweaty and smelling like horses (which I know is your kryptonite) and they'll be wearing those chap thingys you go feral for.

> *Eye roll emoji*

> Chap thingys?

You wouldn't last five seconds living in the country, babe.

Look. I'm a resourceful bitch.

I can do horsey-shit.

Watch me wrangle a cowboy. Like. A. Motherfuckin'. Pro.

> More like you'll be their helpless little roped calf within seconds.

Respectfully, I would quite like to be in the position of one of those baby cows.

I've seen videos online.

Just saying.

I'd happily thank a hot cowboy for the opportunity.

Oh god.

You really are something else.

I'm going to bed.

Sweet dreams, bish.

Love you. Can't wait to see your freckles.

Love you too, Sergeant.

BEFORE I SET my phone aside, I do the one thing I know I really shouldn't do.

I open the Devil's Peak Ranch Instagram page.

Call it an addiction, call it pathetic, whatever... I can't help myself from tapping on the account name perennially at the top of my search results.

The familiar sight of the iron lettering set against the cedar wood planks above the barn doors fills the profile photo. Scattered across the page are shots of the Peak, pine trees dripping with golden hour sunlight, and images of all the horses who I can't help but smile over when I zoom in on their sweet faces. As I do so, I can even hear them stamp and snort in their own unique patterns.

Unsurprisingly, the ranch social media page hasn't been updated all summer.

In fact, the last post was added a year ago, and looks like it must have been Kayce who posted it based on the fact it's taken from an elevated angle in the saddle, looking down on the arched neck and pointed ear tips of Peaches.

Blowing out a breath, my thumb hovers over the tab I definitely do not need to click into.

The place where I know there will be *regular* updates waiting for me to stalk. Not my proudest moment, but I've become more than a little obsessed with checking the tagged photos of the ranch. It's usually cute group photos of the visitors who have booked summer trail rides. There are a couple of familiar spots around the ranch that I recognize—even though the scenery is no longer shrouded in a thick coat of snow—and that hook inside my stomach tugs as I gaze wistfully through the assortment of recently tagged photos.

The ranch has been busy this summer, judging by the volume of images being added. There are usually a handful of new still shots and videos each day.

But I'm not interested in all the strangers smiling and apparently having the time of their life.

Each time I open this tab, there is only one figure I'm scanning for, and yet I never see him. His presence is there, however, even if it is an invisible one. Almost certainly, Colt is the person responsible for taking the photos I'm scrolling through, which makes me bite my lip with a tiny smile, imagining how scowly he must be at the prospect of having to handle phones and cameras on behalf of these people coming to the ranch for their dose of the *outdoors*.

I imagine his calloused fingers jabbing at smartphone screens, and the thought seems so ridiculous. Colt is exceedingly capable at so many things, but technology and cell phones just seem totally alien to try and picture in his big hands.

Tonight though, there is a cluster of freshly uploaded tags, and my heart lurches as I take in the photos with eyes bouncing quickly across the array of thumbnails.

There's a group of gorgeous, blonde, leggy girls who look like they're similar to my age, and most certainly could all be models. Each of their photos shows them laughing and pulling peace signs at the camera with their tongues sticking out. They've all had their photo taken with their horse, which immediately makes me grow possessive at the sight of them planting kisses on their graceful, long necks.

Not only that, but I can see from the progression of the images, this group have been one of the trail rides to spend a night at the cabin.

Colt's sweet spot.

Our cabin.

Fuck, tears prick the backs of my eyes, and my throat closes over.

I hadn't contemplated what seeing young women at the ranch would do to me. So far, it has mostly been families, older retired couples, or honeymooners.

But this—seeing half a dozen lithe, tanned, stunning creatures flooding the ranch's Instagram with their posts—is torture.

I'm a woman possessed. Scrolling and zooming in to examine every detail.

And that's when I gasp.

Colt.

I see him. Well, I see his profile and unruly hair in one of the photos, and tears begin to well up. God, he looks so good. Beard a little longer than I remember. Tanned forearms. Wearing one of his blueish-green flannel shirts rolled at the elbows, he's carrying a saddle as he crosses the background behind the two blonde bombshells who are laughing in the center of frame.

If my heart had ached before with missing him, catching this tiniest of glimpses is far worse than I could have ever anticipated.

He looks so fucking gorgeous, and now all I can think of is the fact these women have been staying up the mountain with him. They've been to the cabin where I watched him climb a ladder while hammering nails. Where we tangled together in the hot spring. The place where I left my heart bundled in those soft blankets in front of the fire.

It's impossible to look away. Even though I sniffle back hot tears, I can't stop myself from going down the rabbit hole. I'm clicking into their accounts one by one, discovering more photos that document the entirety of this group's time spent at Devil's Peak Ranch.

Then, the worst part of all. There's a picture of all the girls—it must be taken in the evening—and they're in the hot spring together, each wearing the tiniest of bikinis. The kicker...the real punch to my gut is the caption, which says, *'Thank you for showing us all such a good time, Colt,'* followed by a string of heart-eye emojis.

That's the point I crumble. Right then is the moment it becomes all too much for me, and I swipe out of the app with shaky fingers.

I feel nauseous. Colt was up there with this group of centerfold models.

The worst part of all, is that he has absolutely no reason *not* to be with someone else. He's not mine. Not my property. Not my cowboy.

Tears roll down my cheeks as I bring up the website for the ranch. Exactly as with the social media account, it hasn't been updated in forever. The only new details to be seen are the availability and booking rates for the current summer season.

Sprawling across the top of the screen is a gorgeous panoramic photo taken on a summer's evening, showcasing the ranch drenched in honeyed golden light, with a vista of horses grazing and a scattering of wildflowers. The same sight which greeted me that fateful day when I crested the final ridge and drove onto Devil's Peak Ranch for the very first time, looking for Kayce.

It's the exact view I stared at all winter from the kitchen window, only when I used to look at it, the place was covered in a snowy blanket. When I used to make coffee for the two of us as dawn crept over the mountain.

With the heel of my palm, I swipe the wetness off my cheek. Why am I bringing this webpage up? What am I even doing? Missing Colt like I didn't know was even possible, and desperate to somehow get in contact with him, that's what is going on. But what can a girl in my position hope to achieve by looking through the meager scatterings of information provided for the ranch?

There's a business email address listed. An automated booking calendar.

No, Layla. There is nothing for you here.

After all this time, Colton Wilder is not interested in receiving a feeble little email from me, just because I'm heartbroken and have convinced myself that he's been busy fucking his way through a bevy of ranch tourists for the past five months.

What I do have, is a job to get ready for tomorrow. Graduation in a week's time. The prospect of looking for a permanent position somewhere once I'm qualified.

That is my life. That is my reality.

And I need to snap the fuck out of this pathetic spiral of being addicted to Colt.

So, instead of doing the one thing I so desperately want to do, I lock the screen on my phone and roll onto my side.

My fingers reach out to brush over Colt's hat, sitting beside my pillow in the spot that allows me to cling onto the tiniest fragment of my cowboy. If it's there, I can at least pretend he's watching over me at night. Waking up and seeing it feels comforting somehow. Or maybe it's just masochistic behavior, I don't know and don't really care anymore.

Squeezing my eyes closed, I stroke the brim.

"You don't owe us anything, Miss."

I blink furiously at the mechanic standing beside my car. It felt like the longest wait ever sitting outside in Kayce's truck until the moment the workshop lights flickered on and they opened for the day. Then, when I walked in, hoping they wouldn't question my puffy reddened eyes, they took one look at me and handed the keys over.

"But... the parts... the work you've had to do?" I stammer.

"All settled up already."

"That's not possible." Rummaging in my purse, I grab my wallet. Surely this guy has got my account mixed up with someone else's shitty little car they've been repairing.

"Nope, she's all squared away." He sips his coffee and gives the hood an affectionate thump with his fist. "Good as new. She'll get you wherever you're off to bright and early this morning."

"There's been a mistake. The car is registered to Layla Birch." I

continue to pull out my debit card. At least I know the state of my bank account is far healthier than when I first arrived here in Crimson Ridge. Whatever these repairs cost, they might drain every last dollar of savings I've accumulated while working at the ranch, but since I've had weeks without needing to pay for living expenses, I've got a bit of a cushion now—for the first time in forever—that I'm sure will cover the bill.

The mechanic shakes his head again. "That she is, Miss. I know you might not have had a chance to grab a coffee yet this morning, considering how early it is, but I promise the full account is all settled."

I'm gaping like a trout.

"Colton had it all paid for a fair few weeks ago. Said it was ready for you to collect any time you were in town next." He opens my driver's door for me and ushers for me to get inside. "He did mention that you might try to pay for it, but wanted to remind you about something to do with your overtime clause and paying off vehicle repairs out of the extra hours worked up at the ranch."

I run my fingertips across the flat of the brim once more, recalling the morning after I left Devil's Peak Ranch and arrived to collect my car.

The way my capable cowboy had taken care of things, long before anything developed between us. Because that is just the type of man he is.

Allowing the tears to roll freely, I tuck my knees against my chest, once again softly crying myself to sleep.

CHAPTER 36

Layla

"You did awesome out there, Cassie."

I grin at the young barrel rider who is pink-cheeked and a little breathless as she hops down off her horse, having just completed her event with a personal best. She's a little bashful, but peeks out from beneath her lashes, a hopeful look in her expression.

"Do you reckon?"

"I don't reckon, *I know*." Giving her gorgeous horse a pat, I smile wider. "The crowd ate up every second, did you hear all that noise? Loudest cheers of the day so far."

She twists her lips, fighting the smile that wants to break free. "You're too good to me, Layla. Best hype woman I could ask for."

"Well, who else am I going to butter up to run and get me coffee and a donut when I'm rushed off my feet all day?"

"I got you, girl. Anytime. Flick me a text later on, and I'll hook you up with all the sugary goods." Cassie gives me a little wave and heads off toward her trailer.

I lean against the railing, watching over the next riders who are preparing to compete.

The energy has been high, bubbling with excitement all day. These regional rodeo qualifier events are always a lot of fun to work at because they're filled with so much hope. The participants and competitors are often supported by a big crowd of friends and family, and the days have a festival vibe to them.

Homemade signs clutched by proud grandmas. Hats waved in the air by doting dads watching their pride and joy out in the arena. Whistles from best friends who are hollering loudly for their buddies as they do their thing.

Of course, there is always a pang of longing that hits me square in the chest when I think about my own *lack* of family. It's inevitable in an environment like this, but in all honesty, I'm always so busy that I rarely think long on it at all.

Besides, I've got Sage arriving in less than a week. Graduation. There is a lot to look forward to...

"Layla fucking Birch?"

My head whips up at the sound of my name being called from somewhere amongst the crowd. No one here knows me, other than the competitors I've met a handful of times across some of the events, and the couple of other vet placement apprentices rostered on here today.

"What the fuck are you doing here?"

Oh my god. Kayce Wilder strides towards me with a broad grin plastered on his tanned face. As my wide eyes take him in, I see he's dressed in chaps and the kind of shirt that tells me he's competing.

I'm opening and closing my mouth. Eyes instantly darting just over his shoulder because if Kayce is here, is there any fragment of a chance that his father might be here also?

But I hardly get a chance to scan the milling crowd, because Kayce jogs up to me fast and intently, scooping me up in one of his big bear hugs while he spins me around.

"Ka—Kayce..." I stutter out his name as he sets me back down on my feet. "Are you here riding? I didn't know you would be at an event all the way out here."

It's at least a fifteen-hour drive from Crimson Ridge. On a good day. Not that I've stared at the map on my phone each night, calculating exactly how long it would take for me to get back there.

He leans an elbow up against the arena railing, lifting the cream-colored hat off his head and dragging a hand through his hair, before settling it back in place.

"Yeah, I've had to make up a whole lot of events. Running ragged all over half the country it feels like." Kayce beams at me. Something in his energy seems so much more settled than the last time I saw this man.

"How's it been going for you?" I chew my lip. Everything in me is fighting with the urge to peer over his shoulder, because I'm so desperately hoping Colt might be here with him. Realistically, I know that's impossible, mind you.

Colt wouldn't leave the ranch to come with Kayce to a rodeo event.

Besides, I can't exactly blurt out the hundred questions I want to ask about his dad without being a dead giveaway that he's occupying ninety-nine percent of my brain space.

"...fucking good to be back in the saddle, man."

Oh, god. Kayce has been talking the whole time. Hands gesturing. Broad smile flashing pearly whites.

More than one set of eyes are turning to stare at him. He's every inch the cowboy poster child, especially seeing him dressed in his competition gear. While it doesn't do anything for me, objectively, I can see that Kayce is a sponsor's dream in terms of looks and charisma, if only he can get his shit together long enough to put all that talent to the forefront and quit fucking around.

Shit. All of a sudden, the image of a pregnant Chy standing in the kitchen at midnight—her threatening me to leave or else she'd out me and Colt and potentially set Kayce's career on fire—flashes into my mind. He must be a father by now. The baby would have been born at least a couple of months ago.

"Layla, I feel like such a dick about it."

I haven't been paying any attention to what he's been saying.

"Sorry?" Swallowing, I try to focus on the man in front of me. My ex-boyfriend. The son of the man I'm intensely heartbroken over.

"The money. That fucking loan. I'm honestly so sorry, and I was in such a shitty place when all that went down... I never made a proper effort to apologize." Kayce rubs a hand over the back of his neck, and for the first time ever, I see him look genuinely remorseful about one of his screw-ups. "Fuck. You must hate my guts for doing that to you. I never meant for you to find out, figured I'd have paid it off before you ever knew I'd put it in your name."

His brow creases beneath the shadow of his hat brim.

"Umm... yeah... well, it all got sorted out with your dad then?" My tongue feels like it is too big for my mouth. I should be angry at him, I really should, but I'm just too fucking tired.

"Yeah, it's all squared away, but, for the longest time I couldn't figure out what the fuck the old man was going on about. He got me to work off the money I owed, after chewing me to pieces for screwing *you* out of money. In my entire life, I've never seen him go off like that before." He chuckles and shakes his head. "Of course, I had no idea what he meant at first, then after I'd listened to him rip me a new one for an hour about opening joint bank accounts and being financially irresponsible, the penny dropped that you must have spun him some bullshit story."

"Look, I didn't want you guys to have more grievances between you." My eyes drop and I scuff my boot in the dirt. "I only said that because I didn't want to give you more of a reason to have issues."

Never mind the fact that I went and made it a thousand times worse by letting myself fall in love.

"I'm being serious when I say, I truly am sorry. That was a black fucking time in my life, when I took advantage of you, and I made some terrible decisions from a dark place. You were always a million miles too good for a waster like me."

That brings a little smile to my face and I point at him. "Your words, not mine, Wilder. Anyways, how's being a dad treating you?" Is it weird he hasn't mentioned his kid yet? It's definitely weird. Mind you, this is Kayce Wilder after all.

Kayce barks out a laugh and nearly doubles over.

My brows knit together. What the fuck?

"Jesus. I completely forgot you wouldn't know about all of that."

"About what?" I scowl at him. It doesn't exactly seem like the kind of thing to laugh about. Not considering the way that bitch threatened me and was out to sink her claws into both Wilder men.

"Man... it feels like a fever dream, but it turns out I wasn't the father." He gives me a wry smile.

My eyebrows shoot up into my hairline. "Oh?"

"Yeah." Kayce cracks his knuckles, elbow leaned nonchalantly on the railing beside us like he hasn't got a goddamn care in the world. "Turned out the baby belonged to my dad."

There's a high-pitched ringing in my ears.

Every ounce of blood drains from my face.

What the fuck. What the fuck. What the fuck.

My knees feel wobbly.

"Holy shit, Layla. I'm just joking." Kayce starts belly laughing as he grasps my shoulder with one heavy palm.

I blink at him for a second and then promptly lose my shit. Punching his arm so hard, I hope to god it goes dead and he can't hold on properly for his next ride. Swearing at him like a sailor. All while he's cackling at me being a damn idiot. Eyes glistening with tears of laughter, he rubs the spot on his shoulder where I've wailed on him.

"You fuck face." I spit out. "Why would you say something like that?"

The man in front of me gives me a wink, wiping the corners of his eyes with the back of his hand. "Oh, that was too fucking good. How else was I going to get it out of you? I knew it."

"Knew what?" My stomach lurches.

"I knew there was something going on between the two of you."

ELLIOTT ROSE

I'm back to speechless mode. My brain splinters, and my jaw falls to land somewhere on the dusty ground beneath our boots.

"Hey, for what it's worth. Can I just say, you don't exactly look happy, but at least you look a good deal better than my old man does." Kayce shakes his head, smirking at me. "I don't need—or *want* to know—any of the details, but whatever happened between you guys, I'm cool with it."

"Kayce... I..." Fucking hell. Is he saying what I think he's saying?

"Layla, we both know I didn't treat you well. I'm learning how to not be a selfish shithead. You are much, much better off without me. My dad, while he and I might have our crap we're working through, he's a good fucking guy. What I do know is that he's miserable right now, and has been since the day you took off."

"We didn't want to hurt you." My heart thuds with an erratic rhythm. "Nothing was supposed to happen. Just so you know." This seems too surreal to fathom.

"Hey, I know that whatever we had together was hella fun at the time, but we were always going to probably be better as friends. Whatever you had going on with my old man obviously meant a lot more."

"How...?" I look at him, confused. He couldn't possibly know anything because I know Colt would never have let a single detail slip. That man is a locked vault of emotion at the best of times.

"I might have myself a pretty face, but I'm not blind. Judging by your reaction just now, and how shit he's looked ever since the day you left." Kayce shrugs his shoulders and spreads his palms. "Kinda obvious, really."

All the saliva has dried in my mouth. It's like the Sahara Desert in the back of my throat.

Shaking my head with confusion, I stare at him. "What happened with Chy?" The wheels are spinning in my mind.

That makes him grimace. "God. What a clusterfuck. Dad was the one who helped me clean myself up at first. He's been damn amazing, like a rock for me, even though I didn't deserve any of it. Helped me get sober. Then, about a couple of weeks after you left,

390

he was the one who sat me down and told me I needed to get a paternity test done."

"You hadn't had one done right at the start?" Eyes going wide, I whisper screech at him, looking around to make sure we haven't got a captivated audience for this conversation.

He shudders and scrubs a hand over his mouth. "I know, alright. *I fucking know.* Don't worry, Dad tore me a new one about all that, too. But the guy was so fucking solid for me. Was gonna be right there by my side through every step, no matter what, if it turned out to be mine. Helped me get my head on straight and made sure we went through the whole process."

Fuck. My heart squeezes. My capable goddamn cowboy was probably reliving every single torturous memory of his own experience with unexpectedly becoming a father, yet he was still prepared to be there for Kayce the whole way.

"So imagine my fucking surprise when it came back that I wasn't the father after all."

"What a bitch."

"Yeah. Gets even worse, mind you." He scrunches his face, wincing in anticipation of how whatever he's about to say next will go down. "Did I ever mention that she's related to the Pierson brothers—my cousins."

"You fucked your cousin?"

"Ew. No. They're all related through a grandfather or marriage or something, but not Chy and me. Anyway, turns out she had this big plan to claim the ranch by pretending the baby was mine. The three of them had cooked it up together."

"That's so fucked." I grimace.

"Yeah, man. After everything my dad had done to try and help them, too. I'm glad those pieces of shit finally got arrested for possession. It's nothing compared to the way worse stuff they've gotten away with, but at least something could finally be done to get them locked up."

"Your dad?" Colt had told me there was history there, but this sounds ominous.

"Shows what a decent fucking guy he is. It's actually a big part of what helped me start seeing him with new eyes once he explained things to me." Kayce lets out a low whistle. "That man spent years offering those assholes shares and partnership opportunities in the ranch. Spent a really long fucking time trying to make up for what my great-grandfather did. Knowing that the girl was left with a baby and nothing after what that prick did to her while she was just a kid herself. My dad always knew that their family line should have been entitled to some part of the ranch, even if the bastard hung himself without acknowledging anything in his will."

Kayce shakes his head.

"Dad went out of his way to give them equal ownership, rights to the land, everything. But they wanted *all or nothing*, and thank fuck he refused to just hand them the ranch and walk away like they threatened him to."

Holy shit.

"My old man has carried around all that guilt for so long. But I guess something changed. Now those fucks are in jail at least."

It's hard to take it all in. Although, I'm not surprised those two men ended up locked away. Sheriff Hayes alluded to the case against them being pretty much open and shut when he contacted me for a statement not long after I left Crimson Ridge.

I blow out a low breath. "Shit. Kayce. I don't know what to say. I'm sorry?"

He waves me off. "Don't be. I'm counting it as one of those weird fucking blessings in life. One that helped give me enough of a scare to realize what a colossal screw-up I'd been and how many terrible life choices I'd made in such a short period of time."

The announcer's voice blares over the loudspeaker system, the crowd cheers for whoever has just competed, and the sun bakes down on both of us with that typically fierce late summer intensity.

"So. Colton Wilder, eh?" Those blue eyes sparkle with mischief.

I groan, covering my face with my hands. "You must hate me."

Kayce continues to grin when I peek at him through my fingers.

"Nah, Layla. I'm being one hundred percent honest with you when I say it's cool. I'm all good. You're one of those... what do they call people like you?" He cocks his head to one side, then snaps his fingers. "Old fucking soul people... that's what you are... one of those old souls. Totally makes sense you should have someone who matches that for you."

"Can I just say for the record, this is not how I expected today to go. At all." I swear to god, this is about as far from what I ever thought a day working at the rodeo would bring my way.

A text comes through to Kayce's phone, and he digs it out of his pocket.

"Everything good?" I ask, watching him read it quickly.

"Yeah, I gotta run. But fuck, it was awesome to see you."

"Same for you, Kayce."

He pulls me in for a hug and this time I wrap my arms around him in return. Not entirely sure what any of this means, but feeling somehow like it was meant to be that I ran into Kayce Wilder today of all days.

"So, you working out here now, or what?" He gestures his chin around the arena.

"Yes, and no. I graduate next week. After that, I get to start looking for proper big girl jobs." I give him a mock salute and throw my shoulders back as he steps away.

Kayce's smile beams wide. "That's fucking epic. Congratulations."

"Thanks, Kayce. Good luck with your ride." My lips roll together. I so desperately want to stop him from leaving, to ask about his dad, to find out a little more about how Colt is doing. If he's not been great since I left—and while my heart does a little flutter to think that maybe he's been as tormented as I have been —it still feels too raw. It shouldn't be up to Kayce to have to be some sort of awkward go-between messenger for the two of us.

"You should call him." He turns on his heel, preparing to head off into the crowd once more, then raises his eyebrows while looking back over his shoulder, breaking into my thoughts.

That drags a laugh out of me, and I share a wry smile in return. "Like that's even possible. Remember... you told me yourself. No cell service. Shitty Wi-Fi." Rolling my eyes, I prop my hands on my hips.

"Cute. But you know what I mean."

"I'll think about it."

"Well, at least you know where the old man will be." He gives me a crooked grin, and touches the brim of his hat before jogging away.

"It isn't like that asshole is ever going to leave his mountain."

CHAPTER 37

Layla

"God, you are smoking hot. Ten out of ten, would bang."
Sage leans across the center console and wolf whistles at me as I slide out of the driver's side.

"Can you not?" I tuck the hem of my dress under my ass to make sure I'm not flashing everyone at graduation my underwear. "I will leave you in the car with the windows cracked, I swear."

"Just saying. Offer still stands. You... Me... if we're thirty-eight and still single..."

I lift my eyes to the puffy clouds scattering the blue sky, rolling my wrist at her to hurry up and get out so I can lock the car. "We're going to be late if you keep staring at my tits."

"They're truly magnificent." Sage hops out, slams her door, and then looks wistfully down, readjusting hers while standing on the other side of the hood. She's not exactly small in the breast department herself, but I've always had a lot more cushioning going on with mine. No matter our age, my girls have always been more ample. Much to Sage's chagrin.

"Come on. Bring your tiny titties, and let's go do this."

Sage gasps and clutches her invisible pearls, tossing her high pony over one shoulder.

We crunch across the gravel of the parking area, framed by

grandiose iron gates and archway of the stables hosting today's ceremony. It's one of those *old money* horse breeding facilities and the grounds look like something straight out of a magazine. Immaculate hedgerows, lush hundred-year-old oak trees, fancy checkered patterns mown into the sprawling lawn.

But all I can think as we stroll past the fancy brickwork and a gleaming fountain set in the middle of the courtyard, is that this place doesn't have a fraction of the appeal of Devil's Peak Ranch. There are Bentleys and Audis lined up outside the manager's offices, where I'm sure they strut around in designer cashmere and sip macchiatos.

Give me rugged mountain terrain and piles of firewood needing to be split any day. Give me hazel eyes, a scruffy beard tickling my neck, and the earthy aroma of black coffee.

Nope. Not the time, or the place for me to allow myself to start thinking about Colton Wilder.

Today is all about my graduation. About spending time with my best friend, who has flown halfway across the country to support me. This marks the first day of my future, wherever that might take me.

With a little push from Sage, I've even started to look at jobs in Ireland and Scotland. Maybe even Australia. At first, I protested that I couldn't leave the country... couldn't leave Evaline. But then she pointed out it would make no difference if I was two or twenty thousand miles away.

And as tragic as that reality is, of course, the smug little minx was right.

"Jesus. Do these people wipe their horse's asses with dollar bills, or what?" Sage hisses. "It's bougie as fuck."

"Right? Isn't it so *extra*?" A smile meets my lips. "But they sponsor the vet program every year and therefore host a gradua-tion ceremony worthy of the Hamptons... so pipe your judgmental ass down until we get outta here, ok, Sergeant?"

Sage gives me a two-fingered salute at her eyebrow. "Not a peep. Oh, wait..." She clutches my arm. "Bougie photo op alert.

These fuckers might be rich, but that view is to die for. Let me get a shot of you with those hills in the background."

I pout, my eyes drifting to the rows of white folding chairs filling up with fellow graduates and their guests who are milling around.

"Do we have to?" I'm not exactly in the mood for taking photos, but at least the outfit I chose for today feels like *me*. Sage helped me find a forest green silky slip dress that makes my eyes stand out, and presented me with a brand new pair of the prettiest fucking boots I've ever seen as a gift for graduating. They're the softest goddamn things, tan-colored with gold stitching and a little heel.

She's got a matching pair in charcoal... because, of course, she does. Ever the black cat in my life.

"Ok. Just quick. Then you gotta go find your seat."

Sage orders me around, living up to her childhood nickname. Insisting on a few different tilts of my chin to *find the light*. When we're finally done, she's grinning at my phone.

"Firstly, you gotta post that one real quick... Secondly, do we have time to go have a quickie in an empty horse stall? Because you, my friend, are doing things for me." She flutters manicured hands in my direction and shimmies.

My cheeks heat at the mention of quickies and horse stables, and of course, that makes my body vividly remember the man who could hoist me against a wooden wall inside the barn and have me moaning within seconds.

Snatching the phone out of her grasp, I quickly swipe through the half-a-dozen photos and choose a few to post. "Happy?"

"Extremely. Now go get your gown, and if you hear uncontrollable sobbing, or wailing, please know it has nothing to do with me."

Sage pecks a kiss on my cheek and shoves me toward the tent located off to one side of the stage where others are milling around to collect graduation gowns and caps from. There are a few faces I recognize among the others who are here to cross that stage today, but none that I'm friendly with. So I do that awkward smiling thing and get myself ready. Before I know it, we're all seated in alphabetical order, and there is some lady in a matching cream blazer and pencil skirt, dripping with gold jewelry, standing behind the lectern, addressing the crowd.

The next hour all passes in a blur. I fidget in my seat and don't really pay attention to anything being said by the important-looking woman up on stage.

There's a prickling awareness as time drifts on, that I can't shake—as if I'm being watched. It's a ridiculous notion because Sage is the only person here for me at this ceremony. The rest of the crowd are friends and family of the hundred or so other graduates getting ready to do their walk across the dais.

Any insane ideas I've got in my head about a certain cowboy being here for me today, are just that. Insane ideas. My overactive imagination has gotten all riled up after running into Kayce last week, and now I'm being silly in even thinking that he might have mentioned anything to Colt.

I mean, I can only assume he spoke to his dad about it. Or maybe not. Kayce is out on the road competing, so he probably hasn't been in contact with the ranch at all while he's been doing his rodeo thing.

Not to mention all the everyday obstacles in the way of contacting Devil's Peak Ranch, and its owner, on a good day.

People from the row in front of me start to get up out of their seats one by one, and I blow out an unsteady breath. *Smile. Smile. Smile.* This is everything I've worked for. All those long days and nights pouring drinks at shitty bars and times when I was certain my life was going to collapse.

I'm here.

I've achieved this incredible thing.

Me. Layla Birch. I did that.

Since I'm in the B section for the roll call of surnames, pretty quickly it's my time to follow the girl seated to my left. I hear my name being called out, and everything condenses down into a tiny little tunnel of awareness as my feet carry me across to where the woman with perfect teeth and flawless makeup and soft fingers murmurs something, shakes my hand, and presents my certificate.

The ripple of applause continues as I smile and pose for the official, cliché hand-shake photo. That's the moment, the split-second I allow my eyes to furtively scan across the crowd. I immediately see Sage giving me a one-woman standing ovation, and I can't fucking help the quick flickering look I give the rest of the crowd.

My stupid heart deflates, because, for the tiniest moment, I don't know... *I hoped.*

I hoped he would be here.

As much as I tried to pretend that glimmer wasn't there, it was. That foolish, romantic heart of mine, combined with the way the back of my neck tingled for the duration of the ceremony...

But, no. Of course, the sea of faces staring back at me is composed entirely of strangers.

Hurriedly collecting my certificate, I'm off the stage in a blink and return to my seat, while the remainder of the ceremony passes in more of a whirlwind.

I nibble on my bottom lip. Maybe I'll send him an email after all, to let him know I've graduated and show him a copy of my certificate. He was my *boss*, and helped me get to this very place.

God, he was so much more than any one thing to me. My cowboy, for a brief moment in time. Possibly even my lover? I feel like I can only consider what we had to be so much more than a singular, defining word.

An email. A few lines to say hello. That would be totally normal and not like a stalker, right? Just a quick, friendly message, thanking him for the work placement and recommendation on my resume.

However, despite those sentiments, my heart is a bird with a tender little broken wing. What would I even say? Colt hasn't attempted to contact me at all, not even when it was my actual birthday, although the man gave me his hat as a gift and insisted I took it with me when I left Crimson Ridge. Which in all honesty, if our circumstances were different, that's the cowboy equivalent of going down on one knee. So, while Kayce might have given us his blessing—and all the relief that comes with knowing he wouldn't hate Colt forever if something more was to happen between us—I can't deny that it leaves me feeling unsettled all the same.

At no time during the past five months has Colton Wilder made any move to communicate with me, and the tears that accompany my head hitting the pillow every night are threatening to make a dramatic entrance.

Blinking quickly, I fight it all back down. There is no way I'm ruining this makeup.

Although, if tears do escape, at least I won't be the only one here today with running mascara. I can pretend they're *happy* graduation tears.

"Now, can I ask that all graduates return to the stage, and we'll take one last photo before you may all go celebrate with your nearest and dearest." The woman leans into the microphone and joins the rapturous applause as the final person completes their walk.

We are all arranged into tiers, a photographer waves her arms around, making sure she can see all of our faces, and I wrestle my expression into a semblance of a smile. Shutters click. People cheer.

"Thank you, and happy graduation!" The rich lady dressed in cream and gold shouts while there are some quick hugs between myself and the strangers around me on stage, excitement finally spilling over.

It takes a moment to make my way over to the steps leading off the platform, and as I grab the handrail, my eyes lift to the large oak tree just off to one side of the area where the ceremony has been held.

Broad shoulders I would recognize anywhere.

Hazel eyes.

Roguish hair.

A black shirt with cuffs rolled up and dark jeans.

My fingers grip the railing so tight my knuckles pale. I feel like if I don't hold on for dear life, there is every chance I might fall face-first down these steps.

Colt stands under the shade of the leafy branches, leaning one shoulder against the broad trunk, watching me descend from the stage. One hand is tucked in his front pocket, and in the other, he's got something wrapped in brown paper.

Oh my god.

I'm floating, unsteady on my feet. My racing pulse and utter disbelief carry me across the grass. While I don't want to immediately start crying at the sight of him, not wanting to look like I've been a complete and utter disaster without him, I can't fucking help it. There is no way to fight back the surge of emotion rolling to the surface like waves thundering against a shoreline. By the time I close the distance between us, reaching the dappled shade and cool patch of grass, there are already hot tears rolling down my face.

"Hey, baby." The rich, rumbling tone of his voice winds straight into my bloodstream. A smile creases the lines around his eyes, and he scoops me against his chest in a tight hug. My graduation cap tips off my head, falling onto the ground, and I don't give a single fuck. His warm, secure palm cradles the back of my neck, while the other hand presses into my spine. My cowboy is here, and I'm a mess. Blurry vision. Silent sobs. The longer he holds me, the more that faint scent of leather mixed with cedar coats me, fills me, nourishes me back to life.

It's like all the vividness of the world rushes back in, and for the first time in five agonizingly long months, I feel like oxygen has returned to expand my lungs.

"Angel, you look beautiful," he says against my hair. Not letting me go. Keeping me tucked into his chest and the sound of his voice reverberates through every inch of my body. "Sorry I was late."

I sniffle and pull back enough that I can crane my neck to look at him. His palm cups my cheek, and a thumb strokes my tears away. "How did you know..."

"Took me a minute to get here after you posted that photo."

Blinking fast, my stare flits between his eyes and his mouth. Surely those were not the words he just uttered. How could this man have seen my photo? He doesn't own a phone. Stubbornly avoids social media.

"You don't mind that I turned up uninvited?" He's still holding me tight and I'm clinging to the material of his shirt like he's going to evaporate in a cloud of smoke if I dare loosen my grip, but there's a line that forms between his brows. He lets his thumb glide back and forth, tracing my cheekbone, where dampness lingers as evidence of all my crying.

I shake my head. "These? These are happy tears." The happiest.

"Thought it best to hang over here. Didn't want to risk that you'd be puffy eyed for your photos... then while I was hauling ass to get here in time, I started to worry that maybe you'd see me and you *wouldn't* cry, and then if that was the case I'd feel like a right asshole for crashing your graduation."

My lips roll together. God, this man.

"Colt—"

"Wait, let me get this out, Layla..." He brings his thumb to rest over my lips, interrupting me. "I've driven all night rehearsing what to say. Do you know how many times over these past months I sat in my truck and nearly drove to find you? You're right here, deep in my bones, angel. I can't even tell you, having to physically stop myself from coming to hunt you down, it was hell. These months have been the worst fucking time of my life.

"I've been sitting in the truck all morning staring at this goddamn phone I've tried to learn how to use—and I suck at this shit by the way—figuring out how to even fucking find you, knowing that you were here and that it was your graduation. That it was going to kill me if I couldn't see you achieve this amazing thing in person. Yet, all the time, feeling like I don't deserve to be part of any of it, but that I'm hoping to fucking god you'll let me.

That you'll let me follow you around this earth, wherever you want to go from here on out, because it doesn't matter how much I love the land and the ranch, I love *you* more. More than I ever thought was possible for an asshole like me. You own my black fucking heart, and I couldn't go another day without telling you how deeply I'm in love with you."

My heart sits in the back of my throat as my cowboy pours his out to me.

"I love you, Layla. This thing struggling to beat inside my chest when you're not near, is yours. Whether you want it or not, and I don't blame you if you never want to see me again... but I had to give you the time and space to achieve this incredible thing you've worked so hard for... and I had to come and tell you, had to see your beautiful green gaze fall on me at least one final time, and tell you that every night, these emerald eyes are all I see... all I will ever see will be you."

He pulls the hand that has been settled against my spine around to slide between us. Wrapped inside the brown paper, tied with rough twine that I instantly recognize as from the barn, are an assortment of wildflowers from the paddocks of the ranch. I can smell the faint traces of hay and pollen and they're the most gorgeous thing I've ever seen. They feel like home, dwarfed in the big, calloused palm of this man who I am entirely consumed by.

He feels like home.

"Colt?" I sniffle, tracing the edge of the paper and gently touching one of the soft petals, before returning his stare.

"Mmm?" His palm slides beneath my loose curls to cup the back of my neck. Fingertips playing against my skin.

"Kiss me, please."

"Thank fuck." He breathes, ducking his head to crush our lips together.

He tastes of mint and love, and all the parts of him I've missed so deeply. The wetness of his lips finds mine, and the tingling scrape of his beard against my skin is everything.

It's soft like rain, tender, while also being just the perfect amount of rough. The epitome of Colt and the type of man he is.

He doesn't press further. Although the blood singing beneath my skin wants nothing more than to throw my arms around his neck and climb him right here, there will hopefully be much more time for that *later*. God. I hope so. I hope this means he's here and he's not going anywhere.

With a groan, he pulls back slightly and rests our foreheads together.

"Tell me I'm not dreaming right now?" he murmurs. Voice husky.

"Umm... hate to interrupt." Sage's voice drifts through, bursting our little bubble. When I tilt my head to look her way, a little sheepishly, she's got a grin a mile wide and a glass of champagne in each hand.

"Hi... uhhh..." My throat bobs a quick swallow, and I reluctantly turn away from where I've managed to plaster myself against Colt's front.

Sage's dark eyes are bouncing all over the place, taking in the bunch of flowers, the sight of the cowboy behind me, and fix with lightning precision on the place where his palm covers my hip. I feel every fingertip outlined as the weight and heat of his hold seeps through the material of my dress, tugging me against his torso.

Thank god he doesn't seem in the mood to let go of me, because I don't think I'm capable of standing straight on my own right now.

"Crimson Ridge cowboy, I presume?" My best friend takes a sip from one of the glasses.

"This is my best friend, Sage." I fluster.

"Colton Wilder. Pleasure to meet you, Sage." I can feel the man behind me make a motion to dip his head in a nod. His strong fingers press harder into my hip, signaling that he has absolutely no intention of letting go of me, even if it must be taking everything in him to override his usual inclination to offer a handshake.

But then, Sage raises her glass in return with a dazzling smile—her own version of a greeting right now, seeing as both of hers are full.

Colt's well ingrained cowboy manners are let off the hook for now.

Except, my best friend narrows her eyes on mine as she cocks her head to one side. That grin turns wicked, and she lasers in on me with a look I can interpret without any words needing to be exchanged.

I scrunch my face up. *I know. I know.*

"Wilder... funny how that name sounds incredibly familiar." Sage is absolutely never going to let me live this down. No doubt this moment will be held over my head forever, but my best friend is officially the gift I don't deserve because she lifts one shoulder and looks back over at the crowd gathered by the hospitality tent. "Nice to meet you Colton... we've got a dinner reservation at six, so I'm going to go ahead and add you to our table... and while you two... uhh... catch up, I'll be over there stuffing my face with mini quiches made with five types of gourmet cheese imported straight from France."

"We'll be over to join you soon." I roll my lips together and then mouth a silent, *thank you.*

"I'm taking this, by the way." Sage spins on her heel and waves the second glass of champagne that was meant for me but has now been commandeered.

Leaning back against Colt's chest, I hear his quiet laughter. "Looks like I've got some explaining to do over dinner."

"Sage is amazing, but I'm sorry, she will absolutely grill you like a steak on a flame."

"Worth every moment." Colt nudges me to turn back around, and I gladly do so. "Although, I don't want to interrupt what the two of you had planned this evening."

"Nope. Stop right there." I reach up and touch his beard. "I want you to come join us."

"You sure?"

I bite my bottom lip, hiding the world's biggest smile. "Want to hear something, cowboy? I want nothing more than to eat your stew and lug firewood around and sneak bits of carrot to the horses. But I could do those things anywhere. The only reason I want any of that is because *you* are there. None of it matters if you're not part of it, if you're not part of my life."

He studies me, brushing my hair back off my forehead with the touch I've been craving for months now. It's a monumental effort not to whimper when his fingers glide over my skin.

Colt's eyes are flecked with gold in the dappled sunlight coming through the leaves above us. "All my water glasses and coffee mugs live on the bottom shelf now. Every morning, I pour myself a black coffee in a cup that still feels like it has your fingers imprinted on it."

"Your hat lives on my nightstand."

That brings a twitch to his lips, and butterflies erupt in my stomach at the smile hiding there.

"You're my miracle. The *good* that an asshole like me was never meant to know... I told you I couldn't think of a word to describe what it felt like having you arrive in my life... and all I can think is that you're my wildflowers after the winter, you're the first crackle in the fireplace when it heats up, you're the sun chasing away storm clouds. Baby, you're my goddamn miracle."

My fingers curl in the front of his shirt. "Keep that up, and I might never stop crying."

He chuckles. The sound settles in my veins like honey. "God, I love you, angel."

"I'm so in love with you, cowboy. You don't even know."

EPILOGUE

Layla

"So, what you're saying is, you learned how to use a cell phone, had a crash course in Instagram, and then stalked my social media until you tracked me down?"

I roll my lips together and let my eyes drift all over my cowboy filling the driver's seat. Colt has one hand draped over the wheel, the other interlinked with my fingers, or maybe it's me who has him locked in my grasp. Either way, I can't help myself from leaning in his direction across the center console.

Have I stopped touching this man since he turned up out of the blue at my graduation ceremony yesterday? I don't think so.

There are a million ways I need to shower Sage with appreciation and make things up to her, because my best friend took everything in her stride. Suitably interrogating Colt over dinner last night, being utterly charming, then offering to drive my car back to Crimson Ridge. All so that me and Colt could travel together in his truck.

I could have kissed her on the mouth.

"It's not as big of a deal as you're making it out to be." The man in question grumbles, and I practically bounce in my seat like an excited puppy.

"I still can't believe Kayce taught you."

Colt shakes his head, letting out another gruff half-protest.

I've forced him to tell me the story several times, not skipping over any details.

Turns out, after running into each other at the rodeo, Kayce took it upon himself to play Cupid. He arrived back at the ranch with a brand new cellphone and made Colt sit at the kitchen counter for two days straight learning how to navigate not only a smartphone but social media, too.

Once they'd argued their way through the crash course in technology, he forced Colt off the mountain and told him he needed to *go get the girl.*

Unlikely as it might seem, considering our history, Kayce was the one who ordered his dad around—telling him it was the least he could do to try and make up for all the shit he caused for both of us in the past year.

Inwardly, I haven't been able to stop grinning at the fact this rugged man did what he did, coming to find me and bringing me home.

Because this man, whether he's at Devil's Peak Ranch or not, is the only place I've felt a sense of home. Colton Wilder is my safe place to land. My person.

I can only hope to be the same for him.

"Well, I can get rid of the damn thing now, anyway." He shoots me a scowl.

"Why?" My eyebrows arch up.

"I found you. What do I need it for now? I'm not letting you go, baby."

My heart does a pitter-patter, swooning all the way into his hands at that admission.

"What if I wanted you to keep it?"

Colt lifts my fingers up to his mouth, keeping his eyes on the road he grazes them with his lips. The light touch of wetness mixed with the scratch of his beard sends a shudder through me.

Along with a pulse in my clit, recalling how his mouth covered every inch of my body through the night. Mapping and studying every inch of my figure, like he was committing it all to memory again after so long apart.

God, I really am just a heart-eyed, horny mess for this cowboy.

"There's no cell coverage at home, we've got the radios, I don't need to carry that thing around." He nips my forefinger.

My pulse thuds a little harder.

"I think you might want to keep it..." This man has got me all hot and bothered, and we've only been driving for a few hours.

"Can't think of a reason why. It'll just get busted sliding around in my truck. Or sit in a drawer. I'm never gonna use it," he mutters.

Oh, I think I might find a compelling reason, or two.

"So, you're telling me that you *don't* want me sending you dirty photos or videos?" Trapping my bottom lip between my teeth, I preen with anticipation when he grips my fingers tighter in response to my words.

"How's that supposed to work when I won't have any reception?"

It takes a monumental effort to hide the smile that threatens to take over. The tone in his voice just changed completely, and I can see him adjusting in the seat.

Seems like Colton Wilder might be a little interested after all.

"Do you like the sound of that, Daddy?" I tease, tilting my head and fluttering my eyelashes as he sneaks a look my way out the corner of his eye.

A low noise comes out of him.

"Think of it like a special treat whenever you're in cell range, or connected to the Wi-Fi... there might just be a photo... or a video, waiting for your eyes only to enjoy."

Colt shifts his weight again.

God, I love knowing that he's turned on.

"I much prefer the real thing, baby." The gritty tone of his voice makes my pussy flutter. "You might have to show me some examples first."

Well, I can't argue with that.

My thighs squeeze together. It's been so long missing him and wanting him, my body aches to be connected again.

Glancing quickly out the window at our surroundings, I see that we're currently driving through remote forested hillscapes, some kind of national park.

"What's got you biting that lip so hard, hmm?" Colt reads me like a goddamn book. "Wanna tell me what you're thinking about?"

Blush stains my cheeks and I can already feel the familiar pooling heat building low in my core. No matter how much time we spent wrapped up in each other last night, my body is absolutely on board with *more*.

Colt shifts his hand, untangling our fingers and bringing it down to land on the stretch of bare thigh exposed by my dress.

"Let me tell you what I'm thinking about, angel." Colt grips my thigh. Hard.

My blood starts to race.

"I'm thinking that I love how these summer temperatures feel."

His hot palm sears my soft, sensitive flesh.

"I'm over here thinking about going for a leisurely drive to nowhere in particular when it's weather like this."

Gliding his palm higher, he nudges the edge of the cotton material, keeping his eyes on the road as mine bounce between where he's touching me and the veins on his hand resting on the steering wheel.

"I'm thinking about you wearing one of these little sundresses, with no panties on."

A gasp escapes me as he roams along my skin, pushing my dress up further as he goes.

"Me with my hand between your thighs."

I can't help whimpering, while he does exactly that. Fondling me over the top of the soaked lace covering my pussy.

"How does that sound, angel?"

His touch is hungry, inviting, a temptation for me to spill the details of exactly what I want this man to do to me out here in the middle of our road trip as we make our way back to Crimson Ridge.

We're in no hurry.

We've got all the time in the world.

Holy fuck, I want him inside me.

"Please?" I exhale shakily as he rubs over the fabric right above my clit.

"You need me to take care of something for you?"

"Yes, Daddy."

Colt blows out a breath, dragging his fingers to the edge of my panties and toying with them. Torturing me by not sliding beneath or towing them aside like I want him to.

"Here I am trying to find reasons not to pounce on you again... then you give me those green eyes, and I'm defenseless."

Good, because I most definitely want to be pounced on. Repeatedly, if possible, during this road trip.

"I missed seeing the view from your backseat."

A rough, deep noise fills the space between us.

My fingers move to unbuckle my seatbelt, but Colt clicks his tongue. "No. Don't even think about getting out of that seat. You're gonna stay right there, and you're gonna let me play with you through these drenched panties. You'll wait like a good girl until I find somewhere we can pull off the road."

My whine turns into a moan as Colt resumes leisurely circling and pressing through the fabric.

To look at him, you really would think we were on a lazy drive to nowhere, his gaze stays firmly focused on the straight road ahead. Except, as my pulse flutters frantically in my clit and my throat, my eyes track down to his lap, and the bulge in his jeans gives away just how much he's desperate for this as well.

The next few minutes pass in an agony. I'm panting, going out of my head, by the time he steers us off the road.

It looks like some sort of forested area with signage for public walking tracks, and to my immense relief the place is deserted.

"Slide these panties off, angel." Colt instructs as he guides the truck to a stop facing into a bank of trees. He's carefully angled us so that even if another vehicle pulls in, they aren't going to be able to see anything.

Of course, I scramble to do as he says, before he's even applied the handbrake.

"The middle of summer, and you're still out here begging to be fucked in the backseat with all our clothes on." The corner of his lips twitch as he leans over and unbuckles my belt for me.

I nearly die when I catch sight of the boyish, mischievous look in his hazel eyes.

"Maybe that's our thing." I dart out my tongue to run across my bottom lip.

Colt hums a noise that I'm hoping is an agreement.

God, please let this be our thing because, holy fuck, that's hot.

"Hmm, this time, I definitely *do* want you in my lap so I can enjoy these perfect tits that I've missed while you squeeze my cock like a fucking dream."

He gives me a heated look, slides out his door, then shifts into the back. Spreading his knees wide, I'm already climbing through the gap before he's had a chance to settle into place.

I do my best spider monkey impression and hurl myself at him. Straddling his lap, while my fingers thread into his curls and our mouths sink together. I officially cannot get enough of my cowboy, of his beard against my skin, of his calloused palms roaming over my body, of the heat pouring off him.

"You gonna get yourself off just riding my thigh, angel?" Colt runs his mouth along my jaw, trailing down the side of my neck. "Or you gonna undo my belt and let me fill you again."

Another wanton noise leaves my throat.

"Oh god, I need you inside me."

Colt shifts his hips, allowing my fingers to make quick work of freeing his erection. The clank of his buckle, the quiet glide of leather, the metallic rasp of his zipper, it all builds my body into a dizzying spiral of need.

Pushing his briefs down allows his thick cock to spring free, and I can't get enough of knowing that we can be together without having to think about time or anything except being in this moment.

Now, we get to simply enjoy each other, and it's more than I could have ever hoped for.

Closing my fist around his length, his cock pulses beneath my fingers. Thickening further, which only heightens how desperate I am.

"*Mmmfuck*, baby. Rub that drenched pussy all over my dick. You're so fucking wet... my good girl, always dripping for me."

God, I love the filthy mouth this man treats me to.

We're both fixated on the spot where I tap the head of him against my clit, then rub through my slickness, coating his length.

His fingers sink into the fleshy part of my hips, and he lifts me up so that I can fit him to my entrance.

"Oh god." I moan as my weight sinks down his shaft, the perfect stretch of his head crowning my center, followed by the way being filled by him at this angle makes my eyes roll back in my head.

"Angel." The dark groan from Colt is so achingly sexy. "Feel how slippery you are, already full of my cum."

My pussy clamps down on him in response, because that image, of the fact he's already spilled inside me a number of times since last night, including once already this morning, is so filthy I can hardly breathe.

"Christ. Relax for me, baby. Let me get all the way inside your sweet little cunt."

"I love it when you talk to me like that." My breath hitches, fingers digging tighter into his hair as Colt pulls me down his length and thrusts up into me at the same time.

We both groan with pleasure as he bottoms out.

"Tell me I'm not dreaming all this." Colt's rasp is accompanied by sucking down over my fluttering pulse point.

"You're right here with me, cowboy." I moan, starting to shift my hips. "Fuck, you feel so good."

"Pull your dress down for me, angel. Show me those perfect fucking tits while you fuck yourself on my cock."

Colt keeps his tight hold on my hips, rocking into me, making me whine with pleasure. With him buried so deep, he hits that magic spot I swear would have me willingly crawling for this man at any time of day or night.

My fingers hook my thin straps, tugging them down my shoulders, letting the top half of my dress fall away. The material bunches at my waist where the hem is rucked up.

"Goddamn, no bra and full of my cum? You sure I'm not dreaming?" He murmurs hotly, before taking one of my breasts into his mouth and sucking down.

I love being a whole lot of slutty, just for him.

"Oh, fuck... oh my god, *Colt*."

He keeps going. Torturing both of my tits as I start to lose it in his lap.

"Jesus. Keep squeezing like that, I'm gonna pump you so full, you'll be making a mess, dripping all over my front seat for the rest of our trip. You like it when my cum runs down your pretty little thighs, don't you? My dirty girl who loves getting railed in my truck."

That wicked mouth drags over my sensitive nipples, tugging so hard I moan loudly, rippling around his thickness as the wave of my climax hovers at the crest.

"I'm so close." Another whimper is all I can manage as Colt takes over, fucking up into me and roaming his hot, wet mouth over my tits.

"Rub your clit." He grunts.

My hand dives between my thighs and that's the match that lights the flame.

It only takes a few circles before I fall apart, jerking and moaning, while Colt lets out a rough, desperate sound and drives up into me. His cock swells and unloads and I'm so out of my head with pleasure I feel like I'm reduced to soaring bonfire sparks.

Words pour out of me. I tell him how much I love him, over and over. How I never want him to let me go. Quickly followed by me begging him for more, because my desire apparently knows no bounds.

Colt cradles my body, guiding me backward, until I'm lying with my spine against the door. He withdraws, sucking in a hiss as he does so; all the while, his adoring gaze covers my body.

"This heart, it belongs to you, Layla Birch." My cowboy wedges himself between my thighs.

"I'm never letting you go." That sinfully skilled tongue runs up my inner thigh. "I'm never leaving your side." His hot palms spread me as wide as possible, and just before he sinks his mouth down over my pussy, he fixes me with a molten, hazel stare. "Now let me clean you up, baby. Make sure you're properly filled just the way you like to be."

Colt pushes his tongue into me, tasting both of us there, roaming all over my hypersensitive flesh. He fucks his cum back into me, and my eyes drift back in my head with how fucking good it feels.

But this man knows my body inside out, and somehow manages to wind me into another climax in record time.

By the time he's finished ruining me, treasuring me, my thighs are shaking and I'm boneless.

I'm dragged up and into his lap, panting. Colt cups my face, guiding our mouths together as I float my way back down from wherever he spun me off out of my head to. I taste both of us on his tongue and my heart could burst with how relieved I am to be back in his strong arms.

As we make out, slowly, languidly, I feel his fingers hook my straps. My drumming pulse gradually settles as he takes his time to caress my skin, threading my arms through, and setting everything back in place.

"Angel, you better believe you belong to me, but I belong to you." He murmurs quietly, lips hovering against mine. "I love you so fucking much."

"I love you, cowboy."

My fingertips trace his jaw, his beard, then slide into his dark hair.

"Take me home."

THANK YOU FOR READING

I absolutely fell head over heels for these two, and I hope you enjoyed Colt and Layla's love story. I just wasn't ready to let them go. Want to stick around and see a little more? Grab the extended epilogue from Daddy Colt's POV:

https://www.elliottroseauthor.com/bonuses

Loving the Crimson Ridge world and don't want to leave? Me either... Make sure to come and join my reader group - this is where all the announcements and first peeks will be happening on any future bonus content:

https://www.facebook.com/groups/thecauldronelliottrose

Ready for a sneak peek at the first chapter of Book Two in the Crimson Ridge series, with our naughty boy Storm?

KEEP READING...

—

INSTAGRAM | TIKTOK | FACEBOOK

BRAVING THE STORM
CHAPTER ONE PREVIEW

F ucking snow.

Living in this part of the mountains is pretty goddamn awesome if you hate people, but it means putting up with being entombed in a grave of white powder and ice for what feels like half the year.

Tires crunch. Gravel sprays. Heavy metal pulses through the speakers. My truck rounds the final bend, and the A-frame peak of my roof comes into view.

How long has it been since I was last here? With one hand on the wheel, my other reaches up to rub the back of my neck as I try to think.

A little too long.

Although, that transient shit has been my entire life before settling in this place. Plus, I don't mind helping a guy like Colton Wilder out.

He's about the only person in Crimson Ridge who doesn't listen to gossip or rumor.

But fuck me, after weeks of taking care of his ranch for him while he's been away, and helping his son out as he prepares for his next rodeo event...I am more than ready to collapse in my own bed.

Pulling up outside the cabin, everything is dark. Conifers stand like proud, ominous sentinels around this place. Keeping watch over the only location I've ever felt like I can truly rest. Even if there's no guarantee that will always be the case for a guy like me.

The sky above is clouded over, concealing any stars or moonlight from efforts to peer down on Crimson Ridge tonight. Drifts of snow are clumped around here and there, glowing that eerie shade of white even through the darkness, and I already know I'll need to do a thorough check around the property after not being here to see to things. But that can all wait for the morning.

Right now, I just want a hot fucking shower, and a stiff drink.

I grab my duffel from the passenger end of the bench seat, slinging it over my shoulder, and heave myself out of my truck. It's only a few strides to cross the gravel and make it up the couple of steps to my front porch. As I shove the key in the lock and step inside, the warm scent of cedarwood floats up to greet me.

Fuck. Can I even be bothered with lighting the fire? Suppose I should, before I throw myself in the shower at least. The old girl needs time to get some heat into her bones, right now it's as frigid as a nun's cunt in here.

When I go to kick each boot off, my hearing pricks. The hairs on the back of my neck raise, and my skin prickles. Something moves deep inside the house, and I'm immediately on edge.

Not something... *someone.*

The distinct sound of shuffling, moving, is human. Not an animal who managed to find their way inside seeking shelter from the tail end of winter.

Setting my bag down softly, so as not to make a sound, I know exactly where my hunting knife is, but that's back in the glove compartment of my truck. I also know where my rifle is stashed in my bedroom, but that's down the hall in the direction of the noise.

Not that I need either of those things to defend myself against some fucking idiot thinking they can break into my place. People don't scare me. I've got a body built off the back of willingly tangling with nearly two thousand pound, angry as fuck creatures.

When you've sat on the back of a bull that wants nothing more than to toss you and stomp your ribs into the dirt, that shit fundamentally changes your perspective on life.

With a shrug to get rid of my jacket and free up my arms, I roll my shoulders inside my shirt and flex my knuckles. Tattoos and the flash of silver from my rings peer back at me in the darkness. Fitting really, whoever this is can wear a face full of my ink and take an imprint in the shape of my metal bands as a gift when they run their sorry asses back down the mountain.

It'll be some hillbilly dipshit who married their cousin creeping up here. Thinking they can poke around my property and find the stacks of gold they all think I'm sitting on after a pro career. Acting like I'm rich or some shit. It won't be anyone who lives out in these parts. While I might not be friendly with every single person who lives on this mountain, no one from the Peak is dumb enough to pull a stunt like this.

The short hall leading down to the bedroom is almost pitch black, but I see where whoever this is straight away. Soft light and shadows move on the other side of the open bathroom door, and I slow my progress when I realize there's music softly drifting from within.

Music?

That makes me pause. I've crept this far on silent steps, and now my mind is turning the situation over, trying to make sense of whatever is going on.

I hear a feminine sound, a hum, and my eyes squeeze shut. Dragging a hand through my hair, I tilt my head back.

Goddamn, it wouldn't be the first time a fucking buckle bunny has let themselves in up here.

Even though I'm mildly hacked off that whoever this is has turned up unannounced and uninvited, my dick stirs. The thought of a quick fuck, before I kick them out and send them packing back down to Crimson Ridge, sounds pretty damn appealing.

Being stuck up at the ranch and buried in the snow on top of Devil's Peak for the winter has had my balls on ice. Literally.

The blackened, twisted part of me wants to make this a game. This cunt thinks they can slip into my house and make themselves at home? Well, this is my arena, my rules.

Silently, I inch toward the open entry, and keep myself hidden in the heavy shadow as I make my plan to find out who the fuck is in my house and exactly what sweet flavor of pussy is going to be on the menu tonight.

As I watch on with hungry eyes and a rapidly hardening cock through the doorway, the girl inside has her back turned. She only has the small lamp above the mirror switched on to see by. It's dimly lit in here, like the rest of the house, everything shrouded in shades of black and gray.

With her back still turned to me, she hums along with whatever folky, girly shit plays through the speakers on her phone.

Then she starts to get naked.

Entirely unaware that I'm here, and fuck...it's the hottest thing.

This girl isn't doing a strip tease to try and seduce a pro bull rider. She's not a girl on a pole shoving her fake tits in my face. She's not a buckle bunny offering to get on her knees in a filthy back alley at three a.m. to suck my cock 'til I blow all over her face.

No. This is someone who is sexy and curvy and slowly removes each item of clothing because it's at her own leisure. Like she's enjoying all this for no one but herself.

Jesus. My cock is begging to get in there and make a reacquaintance with whoever the fuck this girl is. I've fucked my way through life, never doing repeat hookups—even during a regrettable goddamn catastrophe of a time better left forgotten—but I certainly don't remember *her*.

If I'm really honest with myself, there's no way I would.

I don't remember them.

I don't remember their faces or their names and I certainly never kept their numbers they tried to sneak into my phone contacts when they thought I wasn't looking.

Her arms tug the cropped sweater she's wearing over her head, revealing a pair of high waisted leggings. Fuck. No bra. Just an expanse of smooth, olive skin and a flare at her hips. There's the tiniest roll over the top of her waistband and that softness makes my mouth water.

Having a handful of pliant flesh to squeeze and dig my fingers into, leaving a bruise or five in the shape of my grip, is my favorite type of fuck.

The long dark curls hanging midway down her back swish over her skin as she moves. Dragging my gaze down... down to an ass that is absolutely begging to be palmed and spanked and pounded into while I fill this girl's cunt from behind.

My breathing grows more ragged as I lurk in the shadowed hallway, continuing to devour the sight of the feast preparing herself for me. Because there's only one reason this girl is in my house, and if she's here in search of my dick then I'm going to enjoy every second of playing with my meal.

She strips off the rest of her clothes. Sliding those skin-tight leggings down, panties gone at the same time, revealing even more to me. Humming along to the music, this girl is entirely lost in what she's doing. Oblivious to her surroundings.

I'm fully hard and have to quietly, carefully readjust myself. The head of my dick has already started leaking at how fucking hot this girl is. Her arm lifts and I can't help but notice a small tattoo, fine line text curving around the outer side of her breast. Tits that even from here, from a barely there glance side-on, I can see are heavy and full and just made to be tortured.

As she bends over, to fully tug those sinful, fitted leggings off, that's what breaks me. I catch a glimpse of her from behind. Soft and dusky rose-colored pussy lips peek out at me.

Just at the moment she's fully naked, still halfway bent over, I strike.

My long stride closes the gap between us in a second. Wrapping one hand around her throat to lock her against my front, my other hand fumbles with my button and fly. As I do so my knuckles graze against the bare skin at the top of her ass, brushing her lower back. Maybe I'll paint that part of her later with my cum.

ELLIOTT ROSE

"Darlin'... that's no way to go about begging for my cock. Kinda rude to be letting yourself in without asking." I growl, lips pressed against her ear. "But you're lucky tonight. I'm feeling generous. So much so, after watching that little performance, I might even let you come."

She's rigid as a board beneath me. I feel her throat work frantically, pulse fluttering in the side of her neck beneath my tattooed fingers. This girl is short compared to me, barely reaching my chest. Her head tucks perfectly against my torso, and my filthy thoughts are already running wild at the prospect.

"Now, I'm gonna bend you over that sink so I can fuck you into next week... then you're gonna get the hell off my property."

She yelps as I relent a little pressure on her throat, easing back off her windpipe ever so slightly. As I do, her hands fly up to pry my fingers away, but I'm not in the mood for anything that isn't my version of this game. I spin us towards the vanity so that we're both facing the mirror.

Catching sight of her front-on for the first time, I have to stifle a feral noise.

Fuck, she's got amazing tits. Hard nipples stare back at me in the reflection and the soft glow of the lamp light, and I decide right then and there, I already know there's going to be a second round to this game. I'm not going to pass up an opportunity to come all over them. Mark her the fuck up and slide my dick between them... then I'll let her go.

I mean, she is naked and waiting for me in my house, after all.

She really should count herself lucky I'm interested in fucking her more than once to begin with.

As I position her body exactly where I want her, keeping tight hold over her neck, my other hand shoves my briefs down. Freeing my aching cock and I give it a couple of firm strokes, swiping the pre-cum off the tip. Goddamn, her cunt is right there and the heat flowing between our bodies makes my head spin with anticipation.

Her hands fly out to brace against the counter as I tighten my hold on her throat, using the leverage to bend her forward. The action makes those perfect tits hang a little lower, full and soft.

But it's her eyes.

Eyes that stare back at me, wide like a doe's in the mirror.

Dark eyes that seem somehow familiar. More than familiar.

I was sure I didn't recognize this girl, but now I'm ransacking my mind, trying to place her.

"What the fuck?" She croaks, sounding panicked and strained. Her voice finally breaks free as she braces herself against the sink with one hand and tries to claw my fingers away from her neck with the other.

"Uncle Stôrmand?"

I go still.

Jesus.

Fuck. *Fuck my life.*

My hand is on my rigid, leaking cock, and I'm staring at my niece's nipples.

COMING NOVEMBER 2024
Adopted Uncle x Gruff Tattooed Cowboy

https://mybook.to/bravingthestorm

ACKNOWLEDGEMENTS

Crimson Ridge, Devil's Peak Ranch, Colt and Layla's love story, it all arrived in a whirlwind during the middle of the night when I was very much supposed to be on deadline for another book. Now, here we are. Their story is out in the world, and I'm so excited to share more swoony cowboys and forbidden love stories in this series with you all.

To my wonderful Mr. Rose, who supports my disappearing off and being lost to the Words—I love you with all my heart.

Lazz, you are my champion, listener, alpha reader, support Queen extraordinaire... the Elliott Rose - verse would cease to function without you and your magic. ILY.

Sandra, you absolutely slayed the game with this cover. Your gift for creating something PERFECT never ceases to amaze me. I swoon so hard for how incredible you make my books look on the shelf. *More please*!

Heather, I'm forever grateful for your hype, your notes, your love of these worlds and characters. THANK YOU.

Amy, I can't even begin to find the words for how much I appreciate your time, energy, suggestions, and excitement as I was writing this story. You helped me get across this finish line with this book more than you will ever know.

ACKNOWLEDGEMENTS

To my incredible supporters on Ream, thank you for taking a chance on an indie author and hanging out in my world month to month! Elle … you Goddess, you… from my smutty little heart I send the biggest hugs. You have no idea how much it all means, and I adore the lot of you!

Of course, bringing a book like this to life takes a village behind the scenes. To my alpha, beta, and early readers, you are absolute magic and thank you for pouring so much love over our foursome. Thank you for being accomplices in my mischief, the chaos of chapter drops, and my endless questions.

My Street Team, you are EVERYTHING. My ARC team, I send all the gruff dirty talking cowboys your way. To everyone who has shared about this book, hyped, *gently* insisted on a bestie reading it, you are just so damn wonderful.

To every single person who has helped promote one of my books, I am besotted with you, and swoon with heart eyes every time I get to see your creativity and excitement for an Elliott Rose character or story.

From the bottom of my heart, and from Daddy Colt and our girl Layla… we send you all our love.

xo

LEAVE A REVIEW

If you enjoyed this book, please consider taking a quick moment to leave a review. Even a couple of words are incredibly helpful and provide the sparkly fuel us Indie Romance Authors thrive on.

(*Well, that and coffee*)

ALSO BY ELLIOTT ROSE

Port Macabre Standalones

Why Choose + Dark Romance

Where the Villains get the girl, and each other.

Vengeful Gods - MMMF

Noire Moon - MMFM Prologue Novella - September 2024

Macabre Gods - MMFM - October 2024

—

Crimson Ridge

Chasing The Wild

Braving The Storm - November 2024

Taboo - Adopted Uncle - Cowboy Romance

—

Nocturnal Hearts

Dark Paranormal-Fantasy Romance, Interconnected Standalones

Sweet Inferno

(Rivals to Lovers x Novella)

In Darkness Waits Desire

(Grumpy x Sunshine)

The Queen's Temptation

(Forbidden x Shadow Daddy Bodyguard)

Vicious Cravings

(MMF x Enemies to Lovers)

Brutal Birthright

(Academy Setting, Teacher x Student)

ABOUT THE AUTHOR

Elliott Rose is an indie author of romance on the deliciously dark side. She lives in a teeny tiny beachside community in the south of Aotearoa, New Zealand with her partner and three rescue dogs. Find her with a witchy brew in hand, a notebook overflowing with book ideas, or wandering along the beach.

- Join her reader group *The Cauldron* for exclusive giveaways, BTS details, first looks at character art/inspo, and intimate chats about new and ongoing projects.
- Join her Newsletter for all the goodies and major news direct to your email inbox.